D0467578

THE PLAYGROUND OF THE GODS

Other books by Cathy Cash-Spellman

NONFICTION

Notes to My Daughters

FICTION

So Many Partings

An Excess of Love

Paint the Wind

Bless the Child

THE PLAYGROUND OF THE GODS

CATHY CASH-SPELLMAN

A Time Warner Company

A Brandon Tartikoff Book

Warner Books, Inc., 1271 Avenue of the Americas, New York, NY 10020

 A Time Warner Company

Printed in the United States of America
First Printing: January 1996
10 9 8 7 6 5 4 3 2 1

Library of Congress Cataloging-in-Publication Data

Cash-Spellman, Cathy.
The playground of the Gods / Cathy Cash-Spellman.
p. cm.
ISBN 0-446-51701-1 (hardcover)
1. Man-woman relationships—Fiction. 2. Islands—Fiction.
I. Title.
PS3569.P445P58 1996 95-32020
CIP

Book design by H. Roberts

This book is for

Conny Cash
Beloved Sister and Friend

For encouragement, insight,
laughter, and love, there's
no one like you in the world

and for

Dakota Cash-Spellman
Beloved Child of My Heart

You fill my life with joy and
love, adventure, wisdom, and
trust in the future

ACKNOWLEDGMENTS

This book owes many debts of gratitude . . . debts of knowledge, goodwill, and spirit. I send my heartfelt thanks to the following people for their kindness to me and to my work.

Brandon Tartikoff, whose original idea and enthusiastic support given at all the right catalytic moments on this odyssey, made magic happen.

Maureen Mahon Egen, who not only edited with inspired insight and sensitivity, but truly *believed* and heartened in the clinches . . . with thanks for giving me back my faith.

Larry Kirshbaum, whose encouragement, optimism, and laughter were more appreciated than I could ever say.

Robert Gottlieb, who was foursquare in my corner when it really counted, with sage advice, knowledge, support, and strength.

Rick Hegenberger, who so generously shared his enormous expertise on aviation as well as his spirited sense of high adventure with me, in order to get my characters airborne in a way that was both spectacular and correct. I couldn't have gotten this one off the ground without you, Rick.

Elyse Gross, whose dedication and incredible command of the word processing of this manuscript not only kept me going in the eye of the hurricane, but kept all the complex pieces of this puzzle exactly where they were supposed to be, against all odds.

Debra Goldstein, reader extraordinaire, for her kindness, intuition, and enthusiasm.

K. T. Maclay, whose consultation on Mexican proverbs and language wasn't nearly as much fun as her consultation on dirty jokes, although both were astute and greatly appreciated.

Christopher Donald, whose remarkable mountain climbing and rescue expertise was singularly important and gratefully received.

Juliet Rynear, whose encyclopedic knowledge of poker would do credit to a riverboat gambler; who made it possible for Thoros's friends to have a lot of fun with their games.

Clare Hayden, whose linguistic skill and enthusiastic goodwill helped put correct words in the mouths of Thoros, Nelida, and Emilio.

Catherine Peterson, whose knowledge of sports statistics contributed to keeping Tiffany and Jack happily talking to each other.

Tina and Bill Flaherty, whose terrific insights about both the men's psyches and the battle of the sexes were inspiring, enlightening, and great good fun.

Shelton Leigh Palmer, for both friendship and promotional creativity far beyond the call of duty.

Valerie and Joel Brodsky, for their wonderful ability to make my photos always look better than I do.

For my family, who live my book-related adventures (and all else) on a day-to-day basis with more generosity of heart than anyone could ever believe:

Conny Cash, my beloved sister and friend, who knows all, gives all, understands all . . . whose loving help, confidence, support, and wise counsel make my books and my world far better than they could otherwise be.

Dakota Cash-Spellman, beloved child, and joyous traveling companion on the road of life. I love you, sweetheart. More than fifty million thousand and the sun, moon, stars.

Harry Cash, dearest father and friend, who inspired and encouraged me every day of his life, with all the love and grace that were the hallmarks of his being. I miss you, Papa. So very much.

Roe Callahan, my architectural guru, who designed, built, *and* demolished Mora Utu in the interest of my unfolding story, with knowledge, skill, endless patience, and considerable grace and wit. I couldn't have constructed these adventures without you, Roe.

Natalie and Ched Vuckovic, who always pitch in with kindness, love, and verve, to add joy and special friendship to Dakota's life and mine.

PROLOGUE

The azure sea slapped rhythmically at the launch, which bobbed, restless and three-quarters filled, in the shallows off-shore. Thirty-three tawny-skinned natives sat pensively in the vessel that was to remove them forever from the home of their ancestors. They had reluctantly made this choice to venture into a modern world where their children would learn not of Nature and the Gods, but of airplanes, computers, and cell-phones, the Power objects of a new age far beyond their understanding. But they were leaving a great deal behind.

The island paradise of Mora Utu gleamed iridescently in the blazing tropical heat, its long stretch of sun-drenched sand a sensual ribbon of white against the brilliant sea. Eighteen miles wide and nearly thirty long, it lazed upon the South Pacific's surface like a mountainous crescent moon, embracing a lagoon of the sort that usually lived only in pirate books and dreams.

Like a heat mirage, an aged native man shimmered out of the dense vegetation beyond the beach, and began to make his way slowly toward the water and the waiting launch. He carried an elaborately plumed staff, more fitted for Ceremony than for walking, and his ancient shoulders were mantled by a generous bird-feather cloak that fluttered behind him, although the air was still.

Halfway to the beach he stopped and turned to contemplate the far-off mountains one final time. Then he raised his arm, forefinger outstretched in elegant authority, and inscribed a series of deliberate circles in the air, encompassing the entire island in his ritual gesture.

The native onlookers murmured as if expecting some immediate response from Nature, but the old man had again resumed his unperturbed progress toward the boat, and the island remained serene. Reaching the shoreline, he waded out to the launch in confident, even strides, and allowed himself to be handed up deferentially into the boat. The reverent natives bowed their heads at his arrival, and he seated himself in the stern, head held high, face to the open ocean. No trace of emotion rippled his ancient countenance as the small craft left the world of his people behind forever.

He had no need to look back, for he had set his seal. Payment would be exacted, and the law would be served.

Only fools thought they could pay the price of buying Paradise.

Part I

MORA UTU

The Gods play games with men as balls.

Titus Maccius Platus

ONE

Sixty-three-year-old Thoros Gagarian exuded power. Women liked that; men either envied or admired it, which was much the same thing. The fortune that had made this excessive power possible was entirely his own doing.

Six feet four with the long-boned, agile strength of his mountain ancestors, Gagarian had their wiliness, too. It was apparent in the feral eyes that took in everything, and in the barely visible mouth that turned up just a little at the corners, the hallmark of a horse trader who's used to trading well. *Rug merchant*, an enemy had called him once, derisively, and Thoros had smiled the wily, knowing smile. "Thank you," he'd replied. "My father would be proud to know the gift has been passed on."

Thoros snapped shut the drawer of the burled satinwood desk that would have dwarfed an office of ordinary size, and leaned back expansively in the old leather chair that had grown, over the years, to fit his body like a well-worn baseball mitt.

It was poker night; his favorite night of the month. Long ago, this had been a weekly pleasure, but life's demands had scattered the key players, so that now the six old friends assembled only one evening each month. But, the change in timing to accommodate the demands of their varied schedules was the only deviation Thoros permitted in the game. This circle of friends was important in a way that was unclear even to him—five men of power, money, and accomplishment, who demanded nothing of one another but camaraderie, high-stakes poker, and the security of absolute silence about whatever passed among them. He would have felt poorer without them, bereft in a visceral way.

Thoros looked around the elegantly paneled room in which he spent so much of his life, with quiet satisfaction. He was feeling expansive tonight, and replete, as he took inventory of his world. Being a billionaire provided for all creature comforts and gave him his pick of beautiful, cultured women many years his junior. His only heir, Marcos, had turned out to be a mensch with the balls for the business, and he had damned good friends. Life was better than what Thoros had dreamed in his tenement, immigrant childhood. Better by far.

The office door opened, and Marcos Gagarian strode into his father's domain, as if cued by the older man's thoughts.

"Excellent work on the Paramount deal," Thoros complimented, looking up from the desk at his darkly Levantine son, who bore the profile of his mother's Greek ancestry. Marcos grinned acceptance, but didn't pursue the topic. He was proud of his work on the deal, but not inexperienced enough to feel smug.

Marcos was somewhat in awe of this street-smart visionary who was his father; Thoros seemed to him larger than life-sized, and a formidable act to try to follow, although it had never occurred to him not to do so. Marcos knew the evolution of Thoros's accomplishments as well as if he'd traveled the grueling road himself. How he'd made his first big fortune in aviation, his second in hotels, his third in Vegas, and after that, it hadn't mattered what Thoros Gagarian set his Midas touch to; money followed money, as inexorably as the sun rose and set. Marcos knew on some cellular level that his father possessed the gift of a mighty imagination, always envisioning how *big* things could be, always intuiting the fiduciary tricks and shortcuts that would make it all become reality.

Marcos Gagarian had made his father's history a lifelong study, as if it were his doctoral dissertation. Others had speculated that envy spurred him to make his own mark in his father's domain, but that wasn't true. Marcos both loved and admired Thoros, and hoped that someday he would measure up to the extraordinary standard that had been set in the Gagarian household. And in truth, he had both the genes and the intellect for the task.

"Got a minute before the big game, Dad?" he asked as he walked toward the chair that flanked the big desk. An easy deference characterized his manner toward Thoros; it was just shy of friendship—respectful and aware of the propriety of maintaining distance from so exceptional a man.

Thoros smiled indulgently. "I can spare ten or so, if that'll do for you," he said. "I'm a little late as it is." His voice was deep, authoritative, but softened somewhat for Marcos.

Thoros liked his stalwart, rugged son well enough. The boy had guts and the instincts of a falcon on the hunt where the business was concerned. Which, as far as he could see, was the only thing other than respect that a man's son owed him.

"It's this Aquilar negotiation," the younger man began. "I thought I'd bounce an idea off you."

Gagarian made no reply, but sat back in his chair to listen. It was not in him to make life easy on his son. Fair, maybe; but never easy.

"They're smart and they're tough, Dad. But I think there's an Achilles' heel."

Gagarian waited.

"They think I'm the errand boy," Marcos continued, "and at the last minute, you'll swoop in, and then they'll get down to the short strokes."

Gagarian's slate-gray eyebrow raised itself, awaiting clarification. "Does that bruise your ego?" he asked in a tone that allowed no margin.

Marcos looked startled by that thought.

"No way," he replied earnestly. "It just seems to me, maybe we can use that mindset against them pretty effectively. If we let them think they're playing the second string, maybe we can do an end run and cream them, before they know they've been hit."

The eyebrow descended. It was good to see that the rug-merchant gene had successfully made it to the next generation. He nodded approval. Thoros had never understood men who gave no quarter in business to employees, but indulged their sons. The damned fools got what they deserved when they did that. Expect the world of whoever works for you; ruthlessly root out those who don't measure up, reward those who do. That was the Gagarian philosophy, and it worked. If Marcos hadn't measured up, Thoros would have loved his son no less, but the boy wouldn't have gotten anywhere near the business.

"Old man Aquilar has a weakling and two bullies for sons," Thoros replied, thoughtfully. "His reasoning may be clouded by that. What do you propose?"

"Let him think he's got me by the short hairs. Draw the talks out long enough to leverage the stock. I've already got a handle on the weak links in the outstanding shares. I think a little pressure could hand us the whole pie without giving up any crumbs."

Thoros nodded. It was a sound plan—one that needed no further discussion at the moment.

He rose and put his favorite pen in his breast pocket, the gesture that always closed the office day. Marcos stood, on cue.

Relieved that his father hadn't said no, "Give my regards to the Godfathers," the younger man grinned. As long as he could remember, the five poker players had been his father's friends. Long before they had grown rich and renowned, these men had been fixtures at the Gagarian house on poker night.

The two men left the quietly opulent office and moved into the deserted corridor of desks that during business hours housed the essential workforce of an empire. Thoros was taller than his son, and Marcos was wider, stockier, but both moved with a genetic similarity, a steady, forceful stride in which a millennium of warfare in tough mountainous terrain had put stealth and power and surefootedness into the gene pool and the race memory. Even in repose they looked somewhat dangerous.

They headed toward the elevator door and home.

TWO

Nelida sniffed the air with a disdainful frown and rolled her eyes to heaven. Cigar smoke wreathed the green felt table that dominated the center of the room used exclusively for poker. She pursed her generous lips and carried the heavy tray of drinks to the table, a chore she had done for most of the thirty years she and her husband had worked for Thoros Gagarian. In the beginning, the budgets and the men's bellies had been leaner, she thought with an internalized smirk, but the smoke had always been the same.

Jack Doherty glanced up at her and smiled. "You're one good-looking woman, Nelida," he said with a conspiratorial grin. "Have I told you that lately?" He was a good-natured man, she knew from past experience, the sort who genuinely liked women. He had a face that could have been carved in a mountain, craggy and lived in, but she liked what was behind the face.

"You are so kind, señor," she replied with a flirtatious smile, "and so correct."

General laughter greeted the interchange. There was something indefinably sensual about this Mexican woman, despite her indeterminate age. And she carried herself as women of great beauty do at nineteen or ninety, with absolute confidence in her ability to attract.

Tony Capuletti reached out automatically to pat her ass, but she sidestepped him with a deft swirl of her ruffled peasant skirt. "Señor," she said gravely. "There is an hombre in the backyard who sleeps beneath a grass quilt because he touched this body without permission. I would not wish for you to join him."

"What'd she say?" Tony asked, with an uncertain laugh. He had a dark Mediterranean complexion and a jaw as bull-like as his personality. More salt than pepper marked the full head of hair he prided himself on.

"Fuck *you*, what else?" Alex Barclay-Fontaine replied smoothly, prompting more merriment. Alex's Oxford intonation made even expletives sound refined. He also looked the part of a gentleman, although his sandy, somewhat wavy hair and ice-blue eyes, fired by a wry intellect, made him look younger than he was.

The Mexican woman flounced out of the room, agile as a flamenco dancer, the laughter of the men trailing behind her.

"Quite a little spitfire, for a servant," Tony Capuletti snorted, with a face-saving smirk. He was less polished than the others, but he was a good man to have at your back; the kind who came through in the clinches and never tallied up favors given over those received.

"Calling her a servant would probably merit a grass quilt faster than touching her body," Thoros replied, amusement in his deep voice. He'd always suspected that there was more to Nelida than met the eye, but had never been sure just what. More than once over the years, he'd tried to bed her, but she'd eluded him with such finesse that it had charmed more than annoyed him.

Alex looked up from his cards, a wicked smile edging his lips. "Only the rich have *servants*, old boy," he said, intending to smooth the waters, "the *filthy* rich have retainers. How long have Nelida and Emilio been with you, Thoros? I seem to have known them as long as I've known you."

"Since God was a boy," Gagarian replied, good-humoredly. "Thirty years—maybe more. Whenever it was I got smart enough to realize a couple would be less expensive than a wife, and demand fewer lies."

Every man at the table knew there was only one area of life in which Thoros Gagarian had not triumphed completely, and that was marriage. He wasn't a shallow man emotionally, in fact, his passions ran deeper and wider than most, but somehow he'd never found a woman who was equal to his gargantuan nature and appetites, nor one who could hold his restless attention very long.

Thoros had married the first time at twenty-one; when that foundered, he'd chalked the disintegration up to youth and marrying above his class. But, when his second marriage ended similarly, he'd resigned himself to being systemically incapable of upholding the kind of commitment that women absurdly seemed to require in marriage. Thoros considered himself first and foremost a realist; in business he rarely held a company for more than seven years before growing restless, so why should a relationship be any different?

Not that this emotional shortfall posed a serious problem to him; he had learned over the years to happily make do with the many, when one could not provide. As life flaws went, he found his own a manly and acceptable one; certainly it was no reason not to be at peace with himself and his world. His friends, had they bothered to waste so much thought on it, would have agreed with his assessment.

"Anybody here planning to play cards in the near future?" Tony cut in, tiring of the interruptions.

"What's the ante?" Doherty asked, taking a serious swig of beer from the mug at his side. Jack Doherty came from the South

Side of Chicago; there were rough edges under the civilized veneer he'd acquired along with his money. But there was strength and a generous nature evident in his face that tended to endear him to both men and women.

"Roughly the price of the first house I ever built," replied H. Douglas Rand, who sat to Jack's left. He was tall and slender, with round architect's glasses on a patrician nose. The once-russet hair was slicked straight, although it was slightly longer in back than strict WASP barbering demanded.

"Not anymore, buddy boy," Tony snorted. "I hear nobody even calls you on the phone if they don't expect to spend ten mill."

Rand smiled. He'd worked hard and long to become the prime architect for the rich and relaxed.

"What're we playing, gentlemen?" Jase Shindler interposed, his tough, square face as pleasant as it ever got to be, when he was being himself. His alert, self-satisfied eyes radiated a canny confidence. "Is this Hold-'em night again?"

"Not on your life," Alex, the dealer, responded. "I'd like to take your money the simple, old-fashioned way. Five-card draw." His was a shark's smile, a feeder's smile. Alex could charm the petals from a rose, his mother had said of him in childhood. "Or the tuppence from a beggar's cup," his father had added, knowing him somewhat better.

"You've got as much chance of taking Poland as you have of taking my money," Shindler replied amiably, starting the betting at five thousand. He was the most successful publisher in New York; the one on the magazine covers and newspaper gossip pages, the one who graced the best tables, and name-dropped the greats and near-greats he knew, with every course.

"Raise a thousand," Barclay-Fontaine said, as he tossed his chips casually into the pot and turned toward Rand. "Speaking of ten-million-dollar architectural phone calls," he said, "how's our host's version of Xanadu coming along? Is he still buying up Old Masters to decorate the walls?"

"Indeed, I am," Thoros interjected. "They fetch a better price than old mistresses."

Rand smiled expansively at the statement and at the turn the conversation was taking.

"Reraise," he said, after looking judiciously at his cards. He had an odd face, too long and narrow for its breadth, too delicate somehow in its sculptured planes to seem entirely male. Yet, with its fussy glasses and imperial expression, it was just aristocratic enough to seem somewhat handsome. That its aristocracy was bogus and studied wasn't readily apparent to the world.

"I'm afraid ten million barely paid for the airstrip and the plane accommodations on Mora Utu," he said, turning back toward Barclay-Fontaine. "The rest of Paradise cost somewhat more. To say nothing of the small fortune Thoros had to pay the natives for their island in the first place. And, it's nearly completed, to answer your question, Alex."

Thoros Gagarian's complex face lit up with pleasure. "You know what they say, ten million here, ten million there . . . pretty soon it adds up to real money." He had hoped the conversation would touch on Mora Utu, so he could spring his invitation in just the right way. Thoros had a gift for grand gestures—it was one of his more winsome strengths that he enjoyed sharing his comforts with friends.

He tossed his chips onto the pile offhandedly, and sat forward in his chair—the silver-black mustache gave a look of Byzantine piracy to his face.

"Mora Utu is nearly complete," Thoros said, pride of possession in the statement. "Rand tells me there are a few more finishing touches before the work trailers leave forever. . . ." He smiled in Rand's direction, and Rand nodded acknowledgment, equally pleased with the conversation.

"So to celebrate the completion of what I'm assured is the

most luxurious and provocative private preserve on earth, I'd like to propose 'Boys' Week Out.' I want you all to come with me to test-drive my new toy."

"It beats the hell out of coming to my place for pasta," Tony quipped with a hearty laugh.

The response to the invitation was enthusiastic and unanimous.

"There are a few provisos, however," Thoros continued, with the look of gleeful guile they all knew well. "Every man brings a Trophy along. One fabulous woman—"

"Not a wife, I take it?" Shindler interjected, and everyone laughed. He, Rand, and Tony were the only ones in the group who were currently married.

"Certainly not. Someone suitably lovely to grace both the island and whoever's bed she happens to land in."

The table exploded with laughter.

"So she doesn't necessarily dance with the bloke what brung her?" Alex asked, the cultured British diction relishing the slang.

"Precisely. No wives. No significant others. No commitments, however brief they might be."

"Like the office grab bag," Doherty put in. "Only long distance."

"Don't be so crude, dear boy," Rand said with a sly smile, his mind racing to figure out whom he could bring to fill this particular bill. "Think of it more as a respite from the *Sturm und Drang* of life's little drudgeries."

"Marriage certainly falls into that category," Capuletti responded for everyone. He had a fast mouth, often crude, and generally funny.

"I'd say it's the least we can do for an old friend, Thoros," Doherty answered for the table. "Somebody has to check your new place over to see if all the bugs are out."

Shindler took his pocket planner out in a practiced gesture.

He'd have to give a little thought later to what to tell Ellie. He felt a slight pang of conscience at the dishonesty that would be required here, but things hadn't been going well at home lately, and after so many years of marriage, it was crazy to be overscrupulous anyway. There'd been plenty of other women over the years, one-night stands and affairs of varying lengths, but they were usually accidental and not quite as premeditated as this. He liked to think of them as little fender benders in the road of life rather than major accidents.

"So when do we go?" he asked.

"I say we hold next month's poker game on the island," Thoros replied. "Will that give you enough time to get everything up and running, Rand?"

H. Douglas Rand nodded judiciously. "The compound structures are complete. The Great House, the guest satellites, the runway, the outbuildings are all ready for a test run. Needless to say, Mora Utu isn't staffed yet—"

"Nelida and Emilio will come with us," Thoros cut in. "The kind of week I envision requires a certain amount of discretion, shall we say? and the fewer prying eyes the better. I feel certain that men of your mettle won't mind roughing it a bit."

He turned his attention back to the cards in his hand, then looked up again. "And perhaps, to keep this little adventure confidential, it would be best not to let your people know your exact destination. I propose a ten-day hiatus . . . say Thursday through the following Sunday. We'll all meet in Oahu for the flight to Mora Utu . . . Why not let the world think that's as far as we're going?"

THREE

Thoros picked up the phone and dialed.

The cultured European female voice on the other end was low and throaty. Such self-assurance in a single hello, he thought, remembering her with pleasure.

"Justine?" he queried, knowing it was she. "Thoros Gagarian."

"Thoros?" The reply seemed modestly delighted at the news. "How nice to hear from you." She resisted adding, *after four months.* That would have sounded miffed, which she wasn't, really, and she wouldn't have admitted it if she were.

"Are you still flying?" he asked, leaning back in his chair, warming to the task at hand.

"Indeed," she answered, the voice smooth, sensual, in control. "Sometimes even in an aircraft."

He chuckled. "I'd like you to join me and a few friends on a week-long excursion to Paradise."

"Most men are satisfied with a few moments in Paradise, Thoros. How like you to expect a week."

"I have this island, you see. In the South Pacific . . . it's called Mora Utu. I've had it fitted out for pleasure. H. Douglas Rand designed in every comfort he could conceive."

"Rand? That odd, lanky man with the funny glasses, who's the new Michael Graves? He's awfully good, they say. Awfully expensive, too, so I suppose he *must* be good." She laughed, a musical but somewhat world-weary sound.

"Rand and I have known each other since we were boys," Thoros went on, "even before he was expensive. At any rate, it seems I have this pleasure palace and no one to take my pleasure with . . ." He let the thought trail.

"Why the flying question?" she countered. "Do you want me to be the one who ferries you about?"

"I thought you might try out my other favorite toy for me."

"Your G-IV? I saw a photo of you with it in the aviation press."

"Are you type-rated and current?" he asked.

"I'm rated. But you know it takes two to land those buggers. Are *you* rated, or is there another pilot aboard?"

"Only us. And yes, I'll fly co-pilot. Any objections?"

"None at the moment . . . When is the trek to begin?"

"April seventh. Will you come?" Thoros was amused by her judicious reluctance. *The duration of passion is proportionate with the original resistance of the woman,* Balzac had said.

"I don't know, yet," she answered. "Who else is invited?"

Thoros rattled off the men's names.

"Quite a list," she mused. "And mostly married. I don't think I'll have much in common with their wives, do you?"

"There'll be no wives," he said definitively, and Justine laughed, this time heartily.

"Men are such scoundrels," she said with indulgence. "Are there to be bimbos then? I don't suppose I'll have much in common with them either."

"Who gives a damn what the other women are, Justine. You can always ignore them and lavish your attentions on me."

"I wouldn't dream of doing any such thing, darling. The quickest way to bore a man is to lavish attention on him."

"Then just come for the sun and amenities, my dear. And to play with my plane."

"How could any girl resist such a silver-tongued invitation?" she asked, a smile in her voice. Justine felt she knew a great deal about men. They were indulgent little boys, whose self-centeredness tended to escalate with their bank accounts. Bedroom and boardroom were their long suits, of course, but they did have other splendid points, too. She'd never really felt that sex with women measured up, and men were infinitely more fun to be around than women. As daughter of the French Ambassador, she'd had ample opportunity to examine all sorts of them—different nationalities, sizes, shapes, proclivities; different social stations. And she wasn't above picking up a handsome street-boy if the mood struck her.

"I'll fly your plane to Paradise," Justine said finally. "I've always liked moving beyond the boundaries of earth."

Thoros replaced the phone in its cradle, content.

Justine Cousteau was beautiful, sophisticated, and sexually quite inventive, he remembered. Rebellious and arrogant, too, of course; the legacy of too much privilege and an imperious nature. But she had a swift brain, and an almost male attitude toward life that was refreshing.

Justine, on her end, was thoughtful for a moment after hanging up, wondering why she'd said yes, and why it excited her so. Thoros was an interesting specimen, of course, and anything H. Douglas Rand designed was sure to be exquisite. It would provide good fodder for the cocktail circuit to have been the first to see Thoros Gagarian's private playground.

And he was not a lox in bed, as she recalled. Definitely interesting, in fact. Surprisingly intent on her pleasure, even though their one encounter had been something of a fluke, and not on either of their agendas. And then there was the G-IV to have fun with. It pleased her vanity to be able to fly with the big boys. They were always so surprised by her competency. She had a genuine talent for aircraft; had she been born poor, she probably would have used it to earn her keep. But Justine had been born with a silver pacifier, and earning her keep had never been an issue. Nonetheless, she flew every hour she got the chance, and as her father and a great many of her friends kept aircraft, that was very often.

There were other issues to consider, of course. Like the fact that he hadn't called after their first encounter, and that he did intrigue her more than the ordinary. Perhaps it would be a lark to find out what Thoros Gagarian was really all about.

Jase Shindler had his secretary place the call to Hailey Devereaux in Beverly Hills. She'd be the perfect showpiece for the trip. A starlet on the ascendant, lithe, big-breasted and blond, with legs up to there, and enough sex drive to have propelled her out of the anonymous mass of Hollywood hopefuls and into the gossip columns and the kind of supporting roles that got you noticed by the power people.

"Hailey, darling," he opened. "Jase, here. I've got a lovely surprise for you."

"Jase? Jase Shindler?" she cooed. "I'll bet it's not as good as *my* surprise, darling. I'm getting married on Sunday! To Arnie Edwards of Open Warfare." She sounded breathless with glee, like a four-year-old on speed.

"Open Warfare? The rock group? How terrific." Jase hoped he sounded considerably more enthusiastic than he felt. An Arnie Edwards marriage couldn't last longer than the lipstick she wore to the reception, so there was no point in burning this bridge. Hailey'd be back in circulation before the sun crossed the yardarm.

"Damn!" he spat, as he put down the phone with disgust. He shouldn't have waited until the last minute to make these plans, but it had taken a while to determine which woman on his list had all the requisites. Drop-dead gorgeous, hot, young, and publicity worthy, just in case there were photo ops at the airport in Hawaii. He could always tell Ellie that she was with one of the other men, or that he was wooing her for a book. He'd learned long ago the value of being available to photographers wherever you found them.

It was the last requisite on his list that had caused the glitch, of course. The Trophy couldn't be a brain surgeon, but she had to be able to hold a coherent conversation; a week could get to be a very long haul if your companion had a single-digit I.Q. It was just rotten timing that Hailey was marrying that asshole; she was smarter than she looked, borderline witty, and perfect on all counts.

Shindler impatiently pushed back his chair from the desk and looked around the office to be certain all important papers had been put away. He glanced out the door as he turned off the lights.

The giant publishing office spread out before him was silent and empty, a far cry from its bustle by day. He locked the door behind him, and headed briskly toward the elevator. When Liz Cavanaugh emerged from her cubicle without looking right or left, she nearly knocked him down.

The papers she'd been carrying cascaded to the floor; the pencil that had been clenched in her teeth made her murmured apology hard to comprehend.

"Must be a pretty hot manuscript to make you move that fast," Shindler said, stooping to help her collect the scattered pages. He would have been angry, except that she was damned good-looking. The long legs and trim ass looked first-rate as she bent to collect the fallen manuscript pages, and the ample tits visible beneath her blouse as she bent down looked promising.

"Actually," she replied with a small laugh, "it might have fallen from the sheer weight of boredom. So you don't need to feel guilty." She tried to quell her rising nervousness. Jase Shindler was a legend in publishing, and she'd been fantasizing about him ever since she'd landed her job at his company.

"I make it a point never to feel guilt," he countered. This one had possibilities. "Do I know you?"

She grinned. The face was pretty, not beautiful, but it was animated by intelligence and wit, and there was a midwestern robust lifeforce that was appealing.

"I'm probably too low on the food chain here, for an august presence like yourself to know me. *Yet,* that is," she replied, relaxing a little; he really seemed nice. "But you should. I'm awfully talented."

"And hardworking," he answered with a chuckle. "Late nights, carrying manuscripts. And modest."

They both laughed and she stuck out her hand to be shaken.

"Liz," she said. "Liz Cavanaugh. Assistant editor, minion and slave—in thrall to Frank Schultz."

He nodded. "So old Frank's out drinking Michael Crichton under the table and you're here grinding out the work, eh?" He was having fun with the conversation, and with watching her substantial boobs wiggle under the soft silk blouse every time she laughed. He thought he'd make her laugh again. *It must be jam 'cause jelly don't shake like that.* He'd heard that line somewhere, and it hadn't seemed quite apt till now.

"Well now, Liz Cavanaugh," he said, putting the papers he'd gathered down on her desk emphatically. "An august presence like myself detests dining alone, so I insist that you come with me to Michael's."

She looked up, hesitant, or merely surprised, and her heart started thumping again, disconcertingly. *Stop that!* she admonished herself. *Just because he's the most important man in publishing and you've got a slight crush on him is no excuse to act like an idiot.*

"Come on," he encouraged, steering her deftly toward the door. "It'll put you up a dozen notches on the food chain."

Liz grabbed her jacket and handbag, and followed him, wonderingly, to the elevator.

"This is exactly like chapter thirty-eight in *Gentlemen Prefer Blondes,* where Lorelei gets whisked away in a chance encounter."

"I beg your pardon?"

She shook her head, laughing softly.

"It's this weird gift I have. Every word I've ever read is permanently stored on the hard disk of my brain. It's called total recall. Some sort of recessive gene, I think. It comes in handy for editing."

"I imagine it would," he replied, calculating. *This one will do for Thoros's island,* he thought with some relief. *She's pretty enough, a surprisingly lush body, an amusing conversationalist . . .*

"I don't suppose you recall all of Robinson Crusoe verbatim," he began as the elevator doors were closing on them. "I've been thinking about a little trip to an island in the South Pacific. . . ."

Tony Capuletti was trying to keep his breathing under control enough to talk. Fucking StairMaster! *I'd like to get the son of a bitch who invented this frigging piece of shit.*

Tiffany Johnson, PR director for the nationwide chain of gyms, stood at his side, trying not to smile at his macho efforts. She'd done an hour and a half of weights this morning and would do a half hour of aerobics before she packed it in tonight. She could work the StairMaster till its gears gave out without getting winded.

Tiffany was five foot eight, a former cheerleader for the Chicago Bears, and the black version of the all-American girl. She was athletic enough to have a 3rd Dan black belt in Goju

Ryu karate, and beautiful enough to turn most heads. Not that she was black, really. More a warm honey color that suggested a few other genetic strains had contributed to the bloodline somewhere along the way to Tiffany.

Capuletti'd had his eye on her for several weeks now; she looked delicious, ripe for the picking. She was definitely his woman of choice for Thoros's island party—even the fact that she was black would make everyone else sit up and take notice. Everybody knew what black chicks were like in bed—wild, primitive, insatiable. And that body in a bikini would make him the envy of all his poker buddies.

"Five brothers, huh," he said in reply to her family description in progress.

Her large dark eyes sparkled with good-humored vitality. "You bet. There is *nothing* I don't know about men. From the cradle up."

Tony's weatherbeaten face wrinkled into a smile. "Yeah? Like what?"

"Like they're big lovable babies," she said with happy indulgence. It was obvious, from what she'd already said, that she adored her brothers. "And they've got much simpler needs than we do—sex, fun, money, success . . . that's the whole enchilada for them. And kids. Sometimes. I mean every once in a while you find a guy who really digs his kids. Like my brother Obie—he's the best dad you'd ever meet. Anyway, they just don't have the same complicated needs we do, far as I can see." She didn't bother to recount exactly how much she'd seen. How she'd been fending off the male of the species since little Tobey Wilson had tried to pull down her underpants when she was eight. "I only want to play doctor," he'd said. *Only want.* Only want. Tiffany had no doubt at all about what men only wanted.

Not that she minded, all that much. There was nothing she loved better than a hot lover and a cold beer, but she did wish there could be more to it than that. Every girl dreamed of happily ever after, even if she knew damned well it was a fairy tale.

"Listen, kid," Tony was saying. "How'd you like to go to Paradise with me for a week?"

Tiffany made a sound that would have been giggling if she hadn't been so polite. "I'm sure every minute with you is Paradise, darlin'," she said with a disarming smile. "But I don't know what girl could take a whole week's worth."

Capuletti laughed. This one was a corker. He could tell exactly what she'd be like in the sack. Athletic, spunky, a whole lot of fun.

"I'm serious," he said. "I got this friend. He's one of the richest guys in the world, and he has this South Sea island he owns where he's just built some kind of Paradise Acres. I'm going for a week. You could come with me."

Tiffany looked intrigued. "And how exactly do I pay my guest bill? Let me guess . . . six nights and seven days of sex, sex, sex. Am I right?"

Tony looked aggrieved. "Only if you want it, sweetie. No pressure. Just a lot of fun in the sun. Besides, what've you got to look forward to here? A lot of guys with short arms when the check comes, who've only got one thing on their minds, right? So what's to lose?"

That was another good thing about men, Tiffany thought. They gave you the chance for terrific adventures. She wanted to see, touch, taste, feel everything life had to offer, and men were always the key to that.

"Who else is going?" Tiffany hedged, giving herself time to think. Tony wasn't the world's most attractive guy, with his gruff speech and macho bullshit. But on the other hand, this did sound like an opportunity.

"Five pals of mine," Tony answered, knowing how to hook his fish, now. "All big mahoufs. Thoros Gagarian, Alex Barclay-Fontaine . . ."

"You're kidding!" she squealed, genuinely impressed. "He was on TV last night. Meeting with the President about some Middle Eastern thing."

"Yeah, yeah. He's always got his kisser in front of some camera. Then there's Jack Doherty."

"No!" Tiffany bubbled excitedly. "I don't believe this! He owns the Chicago Bears. I was a cheerleader for *his* team."

"So you know him?"

"God, no! I mean, I met him at parties and stuff, when I was cheerleading. But I never got to *know* him."

"Well, now's your chance, babe. We'll be gone ten days. H. Douglas Rand built the place and it's supposed to be a real pleasure palace."

"You mean like the Playboy mansion?"

"Better, babe. More upper-class. I told you these guys are a class act. So, are you in or what?"

Tiffany's animated eyes clouded over for an instant. What to wear? And she couldn't tell her mom and dad. Maybe not even her brothers could know about *this* trip. But the possibilities . . .

"I'm in," she said with genuine delight. "How many bikinis do I pack?

H. Douglas Rand bent his long, lanky frame over the drawing board in Francesca Corbo's office and examined the unrolled blueprints of Mora Utu.

It was years since he'd had to labor over a drawing board. Years since he'd had to do anything much of an architectural nature, other than wine and dine prospective clients and then claim credit for the designs that emanated from the talent on his staff. Intuiting client needs and wants was his métier. Pandering to their fortunes, and their fantasies . . . offering to create for them the buildings of their dreams. Home, office, compound, or palace, he had built them all for the richest and most influential people on earth. A heady thing for a poor boy from London's lower class . . . a boy with ambitions as big as The Ritz and twice as grand.

"Chesi," he said in greeting, as a dark-haired young woman entered her office and was startled to find the owner of the firm staring at her work.

"Mr. Rand," she replied, uncertainly. "I didn't realize we had an appointment." Chesi had a reserved manner, despite her Mediterranean origins.

"We didn't, my dear," he responded, a certain intimacy in his tone. He had a good voice, she thought. Deep. Melodious. Maybe the most attractive thing about him, really. He'd always seemed to her a sexual enigma, as if the decision of male or female hadn't quite been made yet. Maybe it was the elegance, the sophistication, that disconcerted her. In the rarefied circles in which Rand traveled, it was important to be chic. Savile Row suits, Hermès ties, Bijan accessories . . . did he ever wear the same cufflinks twice? Maybe that accounted for the sexual uneasiness she'd always felt around him, but he just never seemed quite male, despite the fact that he was married to some frosty blueblooded woman who was always being photographed by *Town and Country* or *Architectural Digest.* At least not male like the men in her family. Strong, tough, Old-World Italians, even in the New World. Her father, her brothers. Maybe it wasn't fair to compare H. Douglas Rand, in his impeccable elegance, to a family of hardworking immigrants. She shook her head to clear it. *"Pay attention, Francesca!"* her mother would always admonish, sounding sterner than she really was. *"Get that head out of the clouds."* But it hadn't been the clouds where her head resided. It was in tall buildings, and small ones. In hotels and castles and any structure in which man challenged the gods by building shelter and then embellishing it.

She forced her attention back to her boss.

"Mora Utu, Chesi," he was saying. "Can you give me an update?" It was months since he'd been on the island.

Francesca smiled, relieved. There wasn't anything she didn't know about this subject. Mora Utu was her baby and occasional second home. As Project Coordinator, she had met every challenge, pored over every schematic, nursed every crisis, intuited every need, for the better part of two years, from inception to very near the finish line.

"She's just about up and running, Mr. Rand," she replied earnestly. "So far, all the systems check out just fine. A few bugs in the electrical, maybe. A little desalinization problem last week that had to be dealt with. I was actually planning another inspection tour in a week or two. If everything measures up to my expectations, Mr. Gagarian can take possession on the first of May."

Rand moved his angular frame to her desk and half leaned, half perched on the corner, with his arms folded over his chest. He seemed to be appraising her. She wondered why; he'd never paid more than perfunctory attention before. Maybe it was the importance of this particular project. Thoros Gagarian was his close personal friend, according to office scuttlebutt.

"As it happens, Chesi," Rand began, "I'm planning a trip to Mora Utu as well. Mr. Gagarian wants to take a few of his closest friends and their guests to try the place out. A sort of dry run, before the press and the rest of the world become privy to its existence. He'd like to do that this month."

Chesi looked startled. "The work trailers are still all over the place, Mr. Rand," she began, "and it isn't staffed yet—"

"I understand perfectly," he interrupted, warm oil in his voice, "but that's what he *wants*. Thoros has a Mexican couple who can run the show for a week, and he'll fly in anything that's needed." He cleared his throat.

This was a delicate sell. He had to let her know that it was a business command performance, without scaring her off with the more personal elements of the week. There was absolutely no choice but to bring her along; Chesi was the only one alive who had the specific knowledge of Mora Utu he'd need to maintain the facade of having designed the place. It was lucky she was good-looking enough not to be out of place. She had those large, dark liquid eyes that were both intelligent and mysterious, as if what you saw on the surface was only a hint of something Vesuvian that lay beneath. The body was good, too. Maybe better than good. Yes, she would do.

"Mr. Gagarian has invited a few of his most trusted friends to join him, the first week in April. I will, of course, be going, and I thought perhaps you'd like to come with me."

"I'm a little confused, Mr. Rand," Chesi said, obviously embarrassed. "Are you asking me to be your date? Or is this strictly business?"

He frowned inwardly; all Project Coordinators had the need to examine everything on the head of a pin. To nail down specifics. It was what made them good at their jobs. It was a trait he loathed in women.

"A bit of both, I suppose," he answered, forcibly softening his eyes so as not to betray the annoyance he felt. "Professionally, you need to be there to make certain all's running smoothly, but I see no harm in our having a bit of fun along with the other guests, do you? After all, Chesi, it's one of the most splendid pleasure preserves on earth, in no small measure due to your fine efforts."

Only somewhat mollified by this reply and still confused over what he was really asking, Chesi said nothing, and Rand pursued his advantage. "Shall we say the week of the seventh? Two weekends plus a week, is what Thoros fancies. I assume that's good for you? I know you wouldn't want to disappoint me on so important a project, Chesi."

He was out the door before she had a chance to reply. Which was fine, since she hadn't a clue what to say.

Marika tossed back her blond head and laughed the throaty, sensual sound from any number of her TV commercials. Her exquisite body moved fluidly within the wisps of spaghetti-strapped red crepe that served as a cocktail dress. On her wrist was the Bulgari bracelet from one of the men who liked to show her a good time; at her throat was the Harry Winston diamond heart from another.

Jack Doherty turned his head in the direction of the laughter and lost his train of thought in the conversation he'd been holding. She was perfect. Just what he'd been seeking for the island.

He excused himself and headed toward the owner of the laugh.

"I'm Jack Doherty," he said with an affable confidence, moving in on the man already speaking to Marika.

"And I am Marika," she replied, appraising him as deftly as he had appraised her. He looked rich. That was good. He looked exceedingly comfortable, like he might own the place. That was even better. And there was no doubt at all about the fact that he was interested. She smiled her very best smile and held his proffered hand just a little longer than necessary. The man who'd been speaking to her melted back into the milling group of cocktail party people, knowing he'd been overmatched.

"What brings you here?" Jack asked.

"My friend John Brooks said the host put on the absolutely greatest parties," she replied with a dazzling smile. Her accent was distinctly Swedish, lilting and charmingly confused on certain consonants.

He chuckled. "I didn't know John was such a good PR guy for my hospitality."

"So this beautiful home is yours?" There seemed more syllables in *beautiful* than usual.

He nodded assent. "So much so that I know a spot where we could ditch this noisy crowd and talk a little easier."

Without waiting for permission, Jack took Marika's elbow firmly and steered her toward the closed double doors beyond the revelers. She moved like butter, he thought as he propelled her. And that voice . . . Maybe there were few mysteries left that the dress didn't reveal, but what the hell, he'd never been a subtle guy.

He opened the doors to his library and headed her toward the burgundy chesterfield by the bay window, with his best winning smile as firmly in place as the stirring in his jockey shorts that accompanied it.

Unless she turned out to be an idiot or an ax murderer, she wasn't getting out of here until he'd charmed her into being his Trophy for the island gig. None of his cronies would produce a better prize than this one.

Marika settled her endless legs into a suitably provocative pose and prepared to concentrate very hard on whatever Jack Doherty was saying. She'd perfected the technique long ago, of looking into a man's eyes and appearing to be enrapt by whatever he had to say, no matter how boring. It helped, of course, to make sure your breasts were pushed out just enough, nipples visibly bumpy through your dress, then all you had to do, really, was hang on every word, laugh well and appropriately, name-drop a little, so they understood the magnitude of the competition, and you pretty much had them where you wanted them. It was hard to respect men when they were so easily manipulated, but fortunately that was unimportant. It was easy enough to respect what they had, what they controlled, what they could provide.

What required skillful use of intuition was that you just never knew which one of them would be *the* one to provide the big break. She'd known since she was twelve that sex was what she could trade for stardom. That was fine. It was her gift, her natural resource. But you had to be exquisitely careful about choosing the right bedmates. She'd seen gorgeous girls get shopworn, fast; shopworn, and a drug on the market. She had no intention of letting that happen to Marika.

She was going to be a star, not just another pretty face on the cover of *Vogue.* A bona fide, A-number-one movie star with a zillion-dollar home in Beverly Hills and a zillion-dollar husband to go with it. Maybe it would take more than one husband to make the climb, but men were definitely the ladder.

Men like this one.

Marika smiled dazzlingly again, hoping it wasn't out of context with whatever he'd just said that she'd lost track of. Not that men really cared if you kept track, as long as you were admiring.

Just to be certain, she brushed her left breast "accidentally" against his hand that lay on the sofa back. *That* always covered any gaffs in conversation. It had something to do with a week on an island in the South Seas, something about rich, famous men. Marika's instincts went on full alert.

Alex Barclay-Fontaine was a good deal better-looking than Henry Kissinger, and his Public School accent made him pleasanter to listen to. He did a great many of the same things as Henry, who was his longtime friend and colleague, but he did them with a far-reaching flamboyance that the media loved and exploited whenever it got the chance. Confidant of kings and presidents, Alex did the Boston to Washington trek as often as other men hopped the 6:02 to Greenwich. Harvard was where he taught a rarefied genre of economics, but the world was his constituency.

An elegant man with the arrogance of both breeding and privilege apparent in every gesture, Alex possessed a humorous intelligence that was intensely charming. There was a roguish seductiveness about him that captivated people. Alex was used to overpowering everyone with his laser-beam brain, just as he was used to getting his own way, but, over the years, he'd found that women required the development of a special technique he was quite pleased with having invented.

Alex loved to spar with smart women, and he loved to put

them down. He'd discovered that, curiously, the more he denigrated them, the harder they tried to please him, so he'd evolved a system of subtle, clever thrust and parries, always looking for an Achilles' heel and then exploiting it. Eventually, the women would realize what he was up to and depart, but in the meantime, he derived great enjoyment from the cat-and-mouse skirmishes, and the unbridled sex the game always generated.

Alex had always preferred brilliant women as bedmates. "Great sex is really an elitist activity," he'd been quoted as saying by *Vanity Fair.* "All pleasure is predicated on one's capacity for imagination . . . ergo, the smarter the woman, the greater the imagination, the better the sex." This well-publicized statement had made him the most sought-after bedfellow of the moment, and had provided him with a hell of a lot of fun.

Which was only part of the reason why Christie Gibbs had been pursuing him so relentlessly for an interview on ABC. The other was that an interview with him had the potential to rocket her career forward exponentially. She needed a sizzling name with whom she could generate some controversy. The sex angle, combined with his stature in setting economic priorities for the current White House, was the perfect ticket. Alex had thus far avoided her efforts deftly, so it had come as a surprise when he'd taken this afternoon's phone call, without the usual secretarial Cerberus guarding his gate.

Christie clutched the phone in one hand, pushed her abundant honey-blond hair out of the way with it, and grabbed the pad and pen that were nearly appendages. An interview with Alex Barclay-Fontaine would elevate her out of the wannabes and into anchorwoman territory. *Whatever it takes,* she admonished herself as she forced her excited breathing to a bearable rhythm and willed her voice to sound nonchalant. She was a lot smarter and tougher than her baby-faced-blonde image, which looked so great on TV, suggested. Maybe a good offense was the best opening gambit.

"I can't believe you're taking this call, Mr. Barclay-Fontaine. What happened? Did the sunlight hit me in a certain way, or did that Santeria high priestess I consulted really know what she was doing?"

Alex chuckled good-naturedly. This one was smart and feisty, just the way he liked them. Which was why he'd kept her dangling so long, despite the Meg Ryanesque face and the lithe young body he'd noticed at several press functions.

"I'm flattered you'd go to such lengths for me, dear girl," he replied smoothly. "Fancy selling your soul for an hour of my time."

"Don't be too flattered," Christie rejoined cheerily. "It wasn't my soul she wanted. Fifty bucks and an introduction to my manicurist did the trick."

He smiled again; she could hear the amusement in his voice.

"I've decided to give you that interview you've been clamoring for, Christie . . . and do call me Alex, won't you . . . the one about the economic package I've proposed for the President."

Christie's heart beat faster. "I'd be thrilled if you'd do that, of course, Alex," she countered. "But in fairness, I should tell you I'm really hoping to pursue your *Vanity Fair* quote about sex being an elitist activity. You must know you've got every woman in New York speculating on her own sexual I.Q. . . . and since you're the only man on earth who's ever made economics sexy, that's the tack I'd like to take with this piece."

Just what I was hoping you'd say, dear girl, he thought happily. "What an intriguing and unexpected notion, Christie."

Yeah, I'll bet! she thought.

"It gives me a grand idea, actually. I've got just the place in mind for you to do your research on sexual economics. Do you know Thoros Gagarian, by chance?"

"I've met him. But I can't say I *know* him. What's he got to do with it?"

"He has an island in the South Pacific that is, perhaps, the ultimate expression of capitalist excess. No expense spared, no luxury unimagined, no fantasy unfulfilled." He let the bait dangle.

"And . . ."

"And I'd like you to go there with me . . . We could flesh out your piece in Paradise. Thoros has invited some intimates to join him for a week. Jack Doherty will be there, and H. Douglas Rand, who designed the place, and Jase Shindler. . . ."

Christie's mind was in overdrive. Was this a sexual come-on, an interview, both? Did it matter? It was an *opportunity.*

"Are you propositioning me, Alex?" she asked, giving herself time to think.

"Only if you want it to be that, dear girl. I am never pushy. I merely thought it would be a fine chance to see neo-Keynesian capitalism at its very best."

Alex was enjoying himself. Christie would do just fine. She was beautiful and smart, the first two requisites; she was not so famous as to be burdensome, and just hungry enough to take the bait. Perfect in every way.

He changed tactics. "Christie, my dear," he said, earnestly, in his best negotiating tone. "I'd like you to be my guest for the week. Really I would. You'll get your interview, a week in Shangri La with some of the most interesting men on the planet—great future interviewees, by the way. You'll take your pleasures as you choose, and only if you choose. And the worst that happens, I'll turn out to be a bore, and you'll come home with the best tan in television."

Christie Gibbs was already planning what she would tell her producer.

Thursday, April 7

You believe easily, that which you hope for, earnestly.

TERENCE

FOUR

Thoros glanced sideways at the woman in the left seat of the cockpit and smiled inwardly. She didn't know he was alive for the moment, so intent was she on the task at hand.

Justine wasn't a small woman, but she was dwarfed by the man-sized controls and the vast array of equipment around her in the cockpit. EFIS tubes, auto throttles, DAFCS, EICAS, and old-fashioned manual trim wheels, the tools of the trade for keeping the beautiful G-IV airborne. Capable of cruising more than 4,000 nautical miles at 45,000 feet and 460 knots, it was the best of its breed of bizjets. That alone made it worth having. And it was the perfect way to ferry his guests from Oahu to Mora Utu without having to refuel.

Thoros found Justine's concentration strangely sexy. Alert, controlled, there was intensity apparent in her aspect, but no stress, no fear. There was also none of the flip, easy banter that had characterized their earlier encounters.

He watched her bank the sleek aircraft to the southwest,

engage the DAFCS system and settle it comfortably into its cruising altitude, then visibly relax. He was enjoying himself already.

Thoros had always loved to fly. From the first single-engine barnstormer at some forgotten country fair when he was thirteen years old, flying had called to him, had been his dream and his release from poverty, reality, childhood, and limitations. Flying lifted and freed him, and he had recognized its power to transform his life from that first encounter.

It had never been a surprise to him that he'd made his first fortune in aviation; buying obsolete aircraft after the war and reconditioning them for industry, creating his own airline and his own international empire, on the wings of what his airline could carry and accomplish. Anything that provokes passion has the potential for fortune-making; he knew that in every Armenian cell of his body—always had known that.

Over the years, Thoros had met many men who shared his passion for flying. Never, before Justine, had he found a woman whose obsession matched his own.

The group had assembled in Hawaii, flying in from their various destinations to meet at the private jetport. Discretion was of the utmost importance, Thoros's longtime secretary, Margaret, had stressed to the women when disseminating the commercial plane tickets that had brought them all to the Big Island. The press mustn't get wind of this outing. *Nor the wives,* Margaret had thought wryly as she said the words. Despite the fact that she'd willingly have thrown herself on the railroad tracks for Thoros had he asked it of her, she'd been around him long enough to have few illusions about the propriety of his sex life. She'd even been a participant, briefly . . . but that had been long, long ago.

Tiffany glanced around the passenger cabin of the G-IV trying not to look as awestruck as she felt. The plane was unbelievably luxurious.

Soft, caramel leather sofas and chairs seated all fourteen passengers comfortably, with room to spare. The two Mexicans, who were acting as steward and stewardess, had produced food from the galley that looked and tasted as if it had come from a fancy New York restaurant.

Tiffany watched the other women, knowing instinctively the calculation with which they were sizing one another up. The competition was formidable by anybody's standards. She wished her brothers were here to see the kind of company she was keeping. Tiffany almost giggled at the thought of her five brothers let loose aboard this incredible plane, with these amazing people. Especially that Swedish model—who looked like sex waiting to happen.

Marika felt Tiffany's appraising gaze and looked at her with a cat's smile. Marika was assessing the playing field, too; she was unquestionably the most beautiful woman there, but that didn't mean the others were dogs. The Frenchwoman in the cockpit with Gagarian was gorgeous *and* chic. The one with the publisher had a drop-dead body, and even the quiet architect had an exotic Mediterranean sexiness that she seemed utterly unaware of.

And then there was Christie Gibbs from ABC to contend with, Marika thought, as she continued her mental inventory of the competition. She could be useful, but it wouldn't pay not to be wary of her, too. Christie was street-smart—you could sense it in the way she took in every detail with her eyes, and in her relentless questioning. Even when she wasn't doing it overtly, it was easy to see how she probed and poked at every single person she encountered.

Satisfied with the mental appraisal of her competition, Marika turned her attention back to the men. Jack might be the one who'd brought her to this party, but he didn't have to be the one who took her home. Not if there were bigger game in the stadium, and if this wasn't a crowd of heavy hitters, she'd never encountered one.

FIVE

Mora Utu lay like an amphibious emerald on the turquoise belly of the South Pacific. Thirty-five hundred nautical miles from Hawaii, twenty-two hundred from Samoa, twelve hundred from New Guinea, it combined the loftiest characteristics of each of these islands in its languid topography.

A riot of tropical flora made the landscape lush as Eden. Picture-perfect mountains reached eight thousand feet into clouds that were peaceful, except for volcanic activity every few hundred years or so. The volcanoes in turn had provided black lava beaches, as counterpoint to the breathtaking white strands from which occasional black lava deposits rose like Henry Moore sculptures, silhouetted against the brilliant blue sea.

Mora Utu's airstrip, fifty-eight hundred feet long, ran parallel to the ocean. It was eerie to see so high-tech a facility carved out of primal nature, like finding a computer terminal in a lotus grove. Eerie too, was the fact that there were no ground personnel to man the place.

"Where are all the airport people?" Tiffany blurted as they disembarked.

Tony chuckled. "This isn't an airport, sweetie. This is an airstrip in a private preserve. There are no ground personnel here. Only an automatic weather station."

Chagrined at her own naïveté, Tiffany shrugged at Liz, who smiled back in empathy. This was heady stuff for all of them; even among the rich, there were degrees of having.

The warm-moist tropical air smelled appetizingly of frangipani and pineapple. The tropical sun was high in its early afternoon orbit as the passengers disembarked, stretched their legs, and headed toward the two parked vehicles that looked like tropical tourist jitneys, topped by yellow and white awning-striped canopies.

The small, dark Mexican man, Emilio, ushered several of them into one of the vehicles, and promptly got behind the wheel. He and Nelida had been here before and knew the property well enough. Thoros motioned to Justine and the remaining passengers to enter the second vehicle, which, he indicated, he would drive. Justine noticed the proprietary smile he lavished on the surroundings, like a proud parent trying hard not to brag about his son.

"This is breathtaking," she said enthusiastically, as he put the jitney in gear, and glanced behind him for stragglers. "Your island, Thoros . . . it looks as if the Gods might envy you."

He laughed softly, pleased by her observation. "Playground of the Gods," he answered. "That's what it means, you know. Mora Utu."

"What will you buy next, old boy," Alex teased his host. "I hear Marbella's available, or perhaps Australia?"

Pride was obvious in Thoros's responsive smile, but who could blame him? Christie thought, as she settled her wrinkled silk safari jacket around her, and reached for the small camera she was never without.

"How far to the compound?" she asked, craning her neck to see beyond the immense palm trees that ringed the beach, momentarily blotting out all but the high peaks beyond.

"Not far at all," Thoros answered, shifting the jitney into gear, and pulling out. "I wanted to stay very near the sea, so we are quite close to the mean high-water mark. I'll take you on tour of the place, later, of course. After we've settled in for a few hours, I thought we'd meet in the main house for drinks at five."

He signaled Emilio with a wave of his hand and a quick burst of some staccato Spanish dialect; the tiny caravan started up the beach toward the cloud-ringed mountains beyond.

SIX

The brilliant white of the Mora Utu compound shimmered miragelike in the sun's intense afternoon glare. Exotic pink, turquoise, purple, and chrome-yellow accents gave the huge structure a gemlike quality.

The Great House itself was at the center of an immense free-form crablike configuration, in which twelve smaller two-story houses—each with its own private pool and veranda—radiated out from the central structure like satellites tethered to a mother ship. All these interconnected dwellings embraced a courtyard that contained a vast, tiered pool and fountains.

"Are those orchid trees?" Liz blurted, startled by the profusion of exotic flowers that were evident everywhere the eye could alight—in pots, on the sides of banyan trees, in baskets hanging from all manner of branches. "I mean, I know there's no such thing, but that's really what they look like."

"Seventy varieties of orchid have been planted here," Thoros answered, easily. "Are you familiar with Xaxims? They're organic pots handcarved from the fibrous core of a specific palm tree grown only in Brazil. The fiber in the pot walls provides perfect humidity, oxygenation, and temperature control so the plants can thrive anywhere. And, of course, they don't look like pots at all, so the plants appear to be growing out of whatever environment they're placed in or on."

Liz just nodded; she'd landed in Oz.

Even the most jaded of the travelers were startled by the magnitude of the structure, and the perfection of its setting. Thoros dropped off the group en masse at the edge of the path leading toward the central pool, and Nelida showed each to a satellite guesthouse, where their luggage was delivered by Emilio within minutes. They would meet at five in the Great House for drinks.

"The guy who said money isn't everything hadn't seen this place," Tiffany quipped to Liz, her next-door neighbor, after a cursory examination of what would be her home for the next week. "Have you checked it out yet? There's a tub the size of Cincinnati and a bidet, and a wall full of gadgets I don't even know the names of, much less what they do."

Liz laughed. "Not even the rich live like this, Tiffany. I mean, the Sultan of Brunei maybe, but not the merely filthy rich . . ."

"Come on in and have a drink with me," Tiffany prompted, feeling giddy with the excitement of all that was happening. "The bar at the Polo Lounge isn't this well stocked."

A spacious seating group dominated the ground floor of the guesthouse; an entertainment center covered one wall, the bar, another. The furnishings were an impeccable mixture of native oceanic artwork and fine European antiques.

"My cottage is totally different from yours," Liz said wonderingly, looking around. "So we know for sure this isn't a Holiday Inn."

Tiffany grinned. "Yeah. Like a lot of Holiday Inns have Matisses on the wall."

The two women had hit it off on the plane and had asked for accommodations near each other. It would be fun to have somebody to talk to about all that was happening . . . somebody other than the men.

"I must have the Jasper Johns suite," Liz countered. "Supersleek modern furnishings and art—Motherwell to Mapelthorpe. Have you gone upstairs yet?"

Tiffany laughed. "Just for a second . . . I didn't think my heart could handle any more excitement. Let's give it a longer look."

The two women climbed the stairs like conspiratorial schoolgirls peering into the headmistress's quarters.

Liz stood at the head of the staircase, awestruck by the view that materialized beyond the king-sized bed. A wall of glass flooded the huge, airy room in yellow-gold tropical sunlight. The mountains, shrouded in a silvery-lavender glow beneath a halo of cumulus clouds, were set like a distant backdrop to the lavish room.

"This is absolutely gorgeous," Tiffany breathed, "but you'd sure feel like you were fucking in a fish bowl if you ever had sex here."

"Not necessarily," Liz answered, searching out a switch on the wall, like the one she'd found in her own house. She pushed the button and elaborate silk blinds were lowered from a hidden reserve in the ceiling.

Justine had seen far too much of privileged lifestyles to be easily impressed, but this place was extraordinary by any standards, short of the Hapsburgs. She'd been on Malcolm Forbes's island, and on several owned by Rothschilds, but nothing she'd ever seen compared to what Rand had designed here, and Gagarian had paid for.

Justine had decided to stay with Thoros in the main house rather than remain alone in the guest wing, as the other women had done. She'd made that choice a prerequisite for accepting Thoros's invitation, without explaining why. None of the other men interested her in the least as bedfellows for the week, and she was certain the women were to be a sort of pool for the men's club.

She had no desire to be part of any girlish chitchat, when reality set in, nor to listen to their laments, when they realized the price of their week's vacation. What she did want very much, now that she'd seen Mora Utu, was to explore this remarkable creation and the man who had commissioned it.

Justine found the male gender consummately interesting and attractive, in a tantalizingly enigmatic way. In her assessment, sex and power were the alpha and omega of men's psyches, but they ran the world, so one had to adjust and to admire them for their accomplishments. Besides which, she *liked* them enormously—and they both liked her and lusted after her, which was gratifying and enjoyable.

"Government, the Military, and the Church, my dear," her father, the Ambassador, had told her early in life, "these are the only three bastions of genuine power left in the world, other than sex, of course. See that you learn to deal with them all appropriately." Many had instructed her about the sexual component of life, so Justine had come to grips with all these realities early on. She'd always known that eventually an alliance appropriate to her station would be made for her—by herself or by her family—but it would probably not be for love, which made her rebellious, and not anytime soon, which relieved the tension a little.

"Women who marry for money and position," her mother had always maintained, "get exactly what they want, my dear. Women who marry for love never do." Justine had seen little since then to refute her mother's logic, although she'd hated the cynicism that had prompted the statement, and wished with a certain wistfulness that there could be some middle ground for love of the kind that the poets proclaimed and that those more idealistic than she, believed in.

Maybe that was why Thoros intrigued her so . . . he was dimensional beyond the ordinary, and apparently far more baffling than she'd thought in their first encounter. Mora Utu was unquestionably the brainchild of a visionary of some sort, not just a very rich and self-indulgent man. A visionary with a romantic streak.

Justine sipped the wine Nelida had poured for her, and wandered from room to room exploring the main house, while she waited for Thoros to emerge from the shower. She'd decided to let him finish, then begin her own ablutions; no need to let him think she was an easy mark, just because she'd opted to share his lodging. Men never appreciated what they didn't have to work for, and a woman could play hard-to-get as easily in a king-sized bed as on the other side of the hall.

She wore a nearly see-through linen shift over naked skin. Being freed to the late afternoon tropical breeze that fluttered through the curtained louvers felt joyous, and she knew exactly how seductive she looked with nipples and buttocks an easily visible topography beneath the delicate white fabric.

She would set the ground rules for the game when Thoros was finished showering. She would be sexy and seductive, while keeping him guessing how long it would take to get her into bed and what he would have to do in order to achieve that goal.

Justine had already observed Thoros with a practiced astuteness, intuiting his fantasies, calculating the ways in which other women probably came on to him. She would do nothing he expected. Her skills in bed were beyond the ordinary; she knew that and dismissed it as irrelevant. The *real* challenge had to do with her skills *before* they reached the bed. The seduction . . . the dance of intellects that made it all worthwhile.

Justine had already decided what her tactics were to be in this encounter. She would challenge him intellectually, letting her body make the point of what was to come. She would be cool, calm, more than a little mysterious, and she would keep him guessing, never letting him get the upper hand . . . even if she might let him fantasize that he had it from time to time. Then she'd bed him at her pleasure, not his.

She sang a French schoolgirl's song softly as she watched the sparkling water through the louvers. She knew so well how this game was played. But, sometimes, like this moment, for whatever inexplicable reason, she wished there could be some surprises.

SEVEN

Christie strolled with Marika at a leisurely pace up the elegant loggia that connected the satellites to the "mother crab's" body. That's how the reporter thought of Rand's design—a central female crab body, with two huge claws reaching out toward the sea. The predatory image pleased her—a pirate's paradise bought with the spoils of corporate pillage. It would be the opening gambit of her piece on Mora Utu, if all went as she hoped this week, and she got the story out of it that she wanted.

The two women had been housed in guest satellites next to each other, and had met on their way to the five o'clock rendezvous. Marika, Christie noted with amusement, walked with a studied sexuality, her model's hip-thrust posture making her seem doubly available. Christie grinned a little, walking slightly behind her, thinking that with this assembled cast of characters *something* newsworthy was bound to happen before the week was out.

They left the loggia and entered the Great House, for the first time. Christie's eyes were involuntarily drawn to the intricate mosaic ceiling a full fifty feet above them; she felt as if she'd entered a cathedral. Where in God's name had Thoros found craftsmen to do *that* kind of work in this century? Europe? Asia? He must have imported artisans from the four corners of the earth to achieve this level of extravagant detailing. She glanced around the foyer that was the hub of the house, making mental notes; the marble floor and circular stair that ringed the huge columnar space gave it the august majesty of a sultan's palace or a museum.

"*Winged Victory*'s probably on the second floor," she quipped, looking around with fascination. To the right, off the foyer, was the dining room; she did a quick mental inventory of chairs and stopped counting at thirty. An ancient bust of Caesar Augustus occupied one marble pedestal, a tall, slender Giacometti another.

"This way, Christie," Marika was calling to her, beckoning to the opposite side of the foyer. "They're gathered over here."

Christie glanced to her left, through the intricately carved double doorway to the spacious living room beyond. "This place is like the Vatican," she murmured under her breath. "Everything is sized for kings."

"Or queens." Marika laughed happily, putting her best seduction-smile firmly in place as she entered the window-walled room that looked out toward the sea.

Sofas the size of '58 Buicks flanked a Diego Rivera glass and iron table, vast as a skating pond, that occupied the room's center. Chairs and ottomans and loveseats dotted the floor like a flotilla of ships at sea, all in some unspoken architectural alignment that permitted both an immense seating group at the center, and ancillary groups in several other areas throughout the room. It was an ingenious array that provided for occasions of state, yet afforded intimacy, and a tropical sense of spatial largesse.

Marika and Christie were the last of the group to join the

gathering. They saw Thoros standing near the room's center, gesturing expansively, while the rest were milling in cocktail party mode around him. Everyone had changed from mainland clothes to afternoon silks and cottons; the relaxed atmosphere suggested they'd doffed their New York and L.A. attitudes, along with their wool and gabardine. There was laughter and electricity in the air—an undercurrent of excited anticipation.

"I know you'd all like to see more of the facilities at Mora Utu," Thoros began expansively. "I would myself. So I've asked Rand to tell us a little about what he's designed here, and then to conduct us on an orientation tour tomorrow. From what I've seen so far, he has exceeded even *my* fantasies, which I assure you, is not an easy task."

H. Douglas Rand rose on cue, and posed his long frame decorously against the mantel. Francesca realized she'd felt a momentary clutching of the stomach at Gagarian's words: "*What he's designed . . .*" It wasn't Rand's design—it was a design of John Mackey, who worked for Rand. John's innovative genius was in every detail of Mora Utu . . . as was her own, for that matter. It wasn't *just* her passion for perfection of detail that was reflected here, so that every system worked brilliantly, in an elegant, harmonious dance of technologies—but there were a hell of a lot of her *ideas* implemented here as well. As Project Coordinator for Mora Utu, she'd supervised every nuance of its architectural creation, solving problems on the spot as they appeared; designing, redesigning, rethinking concepts, making them *work* against the odds. There was only so much that could happen on a drawing board—the rest happened on-site, as the building took shape organically, and began to impose its own will on you and demand that you rise to the occasion of its needs.

Francesca chided herself mentally not to feel so proprietary; Rand *owned* the company, he had every right to take credit for its achievements. She forced herself to listen less critically to whatever it was he was saying.

"Part of the reason for Mora Utu's exquisite beauty is the fact that this is a volcanic island," he expounded. "We had to take that into account, of course, in all our visions. . . . Even though Mauna Matua has not erupted in over a thousand years, the smaller volcanoes have done so every few hundred years or so—which is what provides those remarkable natural sculptures you may have glimpsed on the beaches. And, in case you're at all worried about weather, I should mention we've typhoon-proofed the house as well, although I'm happy to report there hasn't been a really devastating tropical storm here since 1857."

Typhoon-proofed! Francesca thought, frowning. *There's no such thing as a typhoon-proof dwelling—not above the ground, anyway.* They had taken precautions, of course. Like special wind bracing for stability and stress-resistant materials spec'd wherever feasible. But it certainly wasn't nature-proof; no building ever was. Any architect who'd ever seen the results of fire, flood, hurricane, or earthquake could hardly afford to feel smug about Mother Nature. Francesca's analytical mind always balked at generalities or overstatements.

"I understand Mora Utu means Playground of the Gods," Jack Doherty put in. "Just who were these Gods, and exactly what were they playing?"

Thoros smiled as he replied. "The indigenous natives were the last of the Moreyiba tribe, very primitive, very given to superstitions and religious excess. They probably practiced blood sacrifice, I'm afraid, a while back, and maybe cannibalism, or so I'm told. Remember, by South Pacific standards, we're not all that far from New Guinea, where, no matter what the tourist board would have you believe, cannibals still practice their blood rituals to this day. Which is probably why nobody ever found a trace of young Rockefeller."

"You mean there are cannibals on the island with us, now?" Christie asked, instantly alert.

"No, no, my dear, not a one. I bought the last remaining natives along with the island, and . . ."

"You *bought* the natives!" Tiffany blurted, unable to restrain herself.

Uncomfortable looks all around made it obvious that everyone in the room had forgotten she was black, until that moment.

Thoros cleared his throat, a gesture he used to restore order at meetings. "There were only a handful, really, my dear. They accepted my offer quite readily after some negotiation . . . The young ones realized their old way of life was doomed, and they were grateful to relocate."

"Isn't that what they said about the guys in the hold of the slave ships, too?" Liz snapped. *"Jus' cain't wait to get out of Ghana, Massa . . . love them leg irons."*

Uneasy laughter rippled around the room, and Thoros started to speak again but Tiffany interrupted. "Didn't the old ones want to stay?" she pursued. "I mean, where could they go?"

Liz responded before Thoros could. "Yeah, there are so few jobs for headhunters since the recession."

He raised a slightly disapproving eyebrow. This one was fast on her feet. Better watch her.

"The old ones considered this sacred ground," Francesca volunteered, to smooth over the disruption. She'd spent a great deal of time researching this island and knew far more about its history than Thoros did; overdoing her homework was nearly an obsession with her, a way to guard against unnecessary slip-ups. "They believe their Gods live on Mauna Laupelia, that high peak you see from everywhere on the island. They believe that Mora Utu is the most beautiful spot on earth, and the Gods' favorite place for R and R—hence the Playground of the Gods sobriquet. Gods like to frolic like everybody else, I guess."

"Thank you, Chesi," Thoros took over. "She's quite right, of course. The good news is that the natives, young and old, now have eleven million dollars with which to populate a new island."

"Yeah," Jack Doherty said with a grin. "It's probably Ibiza."

"And the Gods?" Liz asked sweetly. "Did they relocate, too?"

Thoros relaxed and smiled back at her. "There was no need for that, my dear. I told them they could stay and play with *us*."

Francesca barely caught Nelida's hand gesture out of the corner of her eye; some kind of sign against trouble, she thought, intrigued. Like her own Italian grandmother might have made against the Evil Eye.

She herself had no patience with superstitious nonsense. The best way to ward off evil was to leave nothing to chance—to cross every *t* and dot every *i*, twice. It amazed her that most people blamed Fate for their own stupidities. Not that it ever paid to fly in the face of God. *He always wins, Francesca,* her mother would have said. *And what could it hurt to be respectful?*

Dinner would be served on the beach to kick off the week's festivities. Dinner jackets for the men, women to be as dressy or undressy as they chose. Everyone was to reassemble at eight o'clock.

EIGHT

Liz knocked on Christie's door, feeling unusually confident about the way she looked. After three abortive choices, she'd settled on the sexiest dress she owned, a white crepe shift that accentuated all her best parts. She had a good body, some even said a great one—a gift from some long-buried courtesan ancestor, she liked to think. Near-perfect breasts, flat belly, muscles in all the right places. She worked out like everybody else, when she could spare the time, but that wasn't what did the trick. Good genes did.

It always amused her to see the shock on men's faces when they got the drift that underneath the business suits, the tortoiseshell glasses, and the long light brown hair she usually wore in a status-pull during the day so it wasn't fussy—there was *the bod.*

She wasn't sure why she'd decided that this particular dress looked so right tonight, except maybe her aggressive nature had been aroused by the heady competition. Liz liked to win. And while Marika had an edge on all of them, she sure as hell didn't hold all the cards.

Christie opened the door. "I'm glad you're dressy, too," she grinned. "Who the hell knows what's appropriate for a formal dinner party on a beach!" The aqua silk two-piece cocktail dress she wore set off her blond hair, now unfurled and curly. The dress had a flippy little skirt that made her legs look long and svelte, and spaghetti straps that showed plenty of bare shoulder, despite the trailing scarf thrown carelessly over.

"I feel like I'm in the Miss America contest, don't you?" she said as they headed toward the main house and the beach beyond. "Tiffany gets Miss Congeniality, Francesca gets Miss Aloof, Marika gets Miss Tits and Ass . . ."

"And Justine? What's her story, do you think?"

"Can't tell yet. Haven't seen enough of her to zero in. Miss Bitchy, Rich, and Spoiled, probably." Christie, Liz noted, had the face of a pre-Raphaelite cherub and the tongue of Fran Liebowitz.

They reached the end of the loggia and saw the magnificent expanse of beach straight ahead of them; it was already set with tables and chairs planted randomly in the sand. They could see that the two round tables had been incongruously set with fine linen, crystal, and porcelain. To the left of them, an immense driftwood fire blazed in an elaborately constructed wooden pyramid.

"Whoa, Nelly!" Liz whistled, startled by the scene. "Looks like *Fahrenheit 451* out there, doesn't it?"

"Who said three billion dollars can't buy happiness?" Christie responded, as they ambled toward the assemblage of people standing cocktail party fashion on the beach.

"Nobody I know," Liz laughed as she kicked off her shoes, to match the rest of the barefoot gathering. "Why on earth was I dumb enough to wear pantyhose?"

The champagne in everyone's glass was replenished so readily all evening that goodwill bubbled up in its wake. *It's impossible not to feel merry and sated, in the face of such self-indulgent surroundings and such agreeable company,* Liz thought, as she struck up an animated conversation with Alex Barclay-Fontaine, who seemed quite a bit more interested in her than Jase Shindler was.

Nelida and Emilio somehow managed to serve the beach-side dinner as deftly as if they'd been in a formal dining room with a pantryful of help, and Justine played the role of Thoros's hostess with the grace and aplomb of an empress. She was surprised to discover that she was having fun.

The original couplings had shifted nicely, Thoros thought, watching with a practiced eye, pleased with himself for having orchestrated such a complex human symphony. He was not surprised by most of the choices.

Tony Capuletti had staked out Marika from the instant her taut bare midriff arrived on the beach. He had a bulldog-like persistence when he wanted something, and he obviously wanted her badly enough to jostle a few friends out of line to get at her.

Marika knew unerringly when she had a man where she wanted him, and so far, Tony was the only one here she could be sure of, which puzzled and disconcerted her—usually all men fawned over her. Jack had struck up a conversation with Tiffany about football that had nipped Marika's flirtation with him in the bud, and so far, everyone else seemed content with his own dinner partner. Marika decided to keep Tony on hold until she figured out which of these men she really needed to land; she'd said no to sex with him all day just to keep him dangling.

Tiffany tilted back her head and laughed, a warm, genuine sound. "How on earth did you get lucky enough to own a football franchise?" she asked eagerly. Jack could see in her forthright eyes that she really cared about his answer. A thousand women had asked the same question, but only because of the money—Tiffany seemed interested in the sports that had driven him to the money.

"My dad died when I was a kid," he replied in non sequitur.

"My mom had a real rough time with five boys to feed and clothe. She took in laundry, scrubbed floors, you name it. She was a great lady."

Tiffany's brows knitted in puzzled interest. "I don't understand how that got you to football."

Jack smiled. "I worked every after-school job in the world to help her out. Gophered in a meatpacking plant, swept floors at the local candy store, loaded trucks . . ." His voice wandered off into history. "Anyway, baseball, football, and prize fights were the dreams that kept me going. I ate, breathed, slept sports. I lived with my radio attached to my ear and hung out at the gym where the fighters worked out, any spare minute I could scrounge. I knew every statistic . . ."

"Me too!" she said excitedly. "Sports facts. Statistics. I'm a whiz. Really. Try me."

Jack leaned back and thought a minute. "Okay. You're on," he said, skeptically. "Who was the guy who knocked Dempsey through the ropes at the Polo Grounds?"

Tiffany grinned.

"Come on," she said. "Everybody knows that was the Wild Bull of the Pampas, Luis Angel Firpo. Dempsey landed on some guy's typewriter at ringside. Give me one for the big kids."

Jack chuckled. This was one of his favorite games, one he played better than anybody. "Okay," he said with relish. "Let's try another sport. What guy, who was famous for something else, was in the Chicago Cardinal backfield the day Ernie Nevers played his forty-point game?"

"Jim Thorpe," she said smugly. "Nevers made six touchdowns by rushing that day—the record still stands. Thorpe, who was an Indian, was one of the guys who raised the American flag on Suribachi. Now, *you* try one. We're at the Polo Grounds. Ninth inning. Two men on base. Who hits the three-run homer that goes down in the history books, and what color hat is his girlfriend wearing on the cover of *Life* magazine when they do the story?"

"Bobby Thomson," Jack answered, grinning. "They called it the Shot Heard Round the World. I'm color-blind so I can't be sure, but I'll go with yellow."

The two collapsed with laughter, Alex seated next to them on the right, reached to his left and took hold of Liz's hand.

"These two apparently don't need our company, my girl," he said conspiratorially. "It's a pity you're obviously not the kind who's courageous enough to ruin her hair with a midnight dip in the ocean. If you were . . ."

Liz was about to reply when Thoros stood up and *ting*ed his glass with a spoon, for silence.

"Looking around me at all this beauty—not only of nature, but of the women who have agreed to grace our week's pleasures with their presence—I am reminded of how very fortunate a man I am. Blessed in my good friends, in my good fortune, and in my new home. I'm honored to have you all here with me to share my domain. The Gods and I welcome you to our playground."

"You always did keep company with big shots, Thoros," Tony interrupted. "Now it's Gods, yet."

"I would expect nothing less from a man of your stature, Thoros," Alex interjected smoothly. He raised his glass. "To our host on Olympus. And his generosity in sharing it with us poor mortals."

"Hear, hear!" everyone affirmed the toast and Thoros smiled benevolently, his sharp, dark eyes surveying the gathering. He looked very handsome in the fire glow, and very much king of all he surveyed.

"Indulge me, my good friends, old and new. I feel such an abundance of feminine beauty as is gathered here tonight should be applauded in an individual way. So, I want each man present to raise his glass to the woman seated on his right, and say a few words of welcome and delight.

"Jase," he prompted, looking at Shindler first. "You're the great wordsmith. Let's start with you."

Shindler nodded, completely comfortable on the spot and in the spotlight. Toasts were one of his many specialties. He stood up, bowed elegantly as a dancing master toward Chesi, and raised his glass toward her with a theatrical flourish.

"To Francesca Corbo," he said, relishing the ethnicity of the name. "Who hides the passions of her Mediterranean ancestors beneath the decorous trappings of a first-rate brain. I suspect you understand far more of Paradise than its architecture, my dear. May you find your own wild nature hidden in this Xanadu you helped create."

Everyone hooted and applauded at such off-the-cuff eloquence, each man wondering what to say to outdo him.

Chesi looked equally embarrassed and surprised. She lowered her eyes to the table as the others murmured audible approbation. Finally, realizing that she should respond in some way, she looked up solemnly and said simply, "Thank you"—which occasioned considerably more merriment.

Jase raised his glass to her once again, smiled, then sat down.

"Your turn, Rand," Thoros pressed.

H. Douglas Rand turned his intense smile on Christie Gibbs. "To your incisive, inquiring mind, my dear," he said, annoyed that he hadn't prepared something better ahead of time. How like Thoros to put them all in such an awkward position. "To your sensuous voice, and your robust yet fragile beauty. My design for Paradise couldn't ask for a more worthy reveler."

Jack's turn was next. He was quite obviously taken with Tiffany and he was good at one-upmanship, so all the other men sat back expectantly.

Jack thought for a minute, then raised his glass in a gentlemanly salute. "To Tiffany," he said. "Maybe the only woman on earth who loves the '55 Dodgers like I do."

That's good, thought Tiffany. *No bullshit. He likes me.* She smiled warmly, blew him a kiss, then turned her attention to the upcoming speaker.

Tony was already on his feet, although none too steadily. He held up his glass, spilling some as he did so.

"To Marika," he said. "*Bellissima, bellissima* Marika. A woman so beautiful, even the stars must feel envy." He sat down, satisfied and happy; who knew better than a Sicilian how to tell a woman she was desirable?

"How about you, Gagarian?" Shindler prompted, his mood expansive. "You've put us all on the hot spot. What've you got to say for yourself?"

Thoros smiled broadly as he rose from his seat, glass in hand.

"Antsyaleet, vore guh hoosam kez mortsnel dall," he said directly to Justine, in a low intimate voice. *"Abakayeet, vore guh hoosam yeraznerov letsnell; yev nergayeet, vor nuhbadaguhs eh serove voghoghell."*

"Wait a minute!" Tony called out. "Cut out that Armenian bull crap; we want to know what you told her."

"It was an old Armenian proverb, my friend—very hard to translate adequately. I have toasted the lady's past, which I hope to make her forget, and her future, which I hope to fill with dreams. . . ."

"What about her present?"

"That, my friend, I have left up to the lady." Justine's eyes locked with Thoros's and she smiled ever so slightly.

The rest of the evening was filled with so much goodwill, good food, and abundant laughter, that even the more reticent among the guests had to let down their guard. Some returned to their houses for swimsuits, some just stripped to the layer of clothing closest to skin, and headed for the ocean.

Music merged with the insistent sounds of the sea. Emilio played his twelve-stringed guitar, and Nelida sang long Spanish-songs of love, unrequited and otherwise, in the embering glow of the great bonfire at the edge of the brooding ocean. By eleven-thirty, most of Thoros's guests had drifted from the beach, in couples or alone. It had been a courtly and sensual evening, the kind that happen seldom enough in life to make them memorable.

Chesi emerged from the inky, moonlit water, and wrapped the terry robe she'd found in her bathroom closet around herself. She was a superb swimmer and had spent her summers lifeguarding at the Jersey shore from the time she was thirteen. She cast one last look at the nearly empty beach; the scene was quiet now and surreal. She wondered why she had such an eerie feeling that some price was about to be exacted. Maybe it was just her old Catholic guilt that said you had to suffer for your pleasures. Or maybe it was the tension of all the sexual innuendo that had escalated with the drinking, but something was making her uneasy.

It had been a relief to leave the crowd on the beach and swim alone, even though she knew better than to think it was a safe thing to do. It was obvious that everyone was supposed to choose a bedmate, and quickly. She felt relieved that Rand hadn't come on to her; perhaps he wouldn't push it too far, knowing they had to work together after this week was over. But you never knew with men; even the ones who were decent at the office could act like assholes when they got you alone somewhere.

Chesi wasn't a prude, she liked sex as much as the next woman, but she didn't like feeling it was expected in payment for the week's lodging. She'd just have to play it by ear for a while.

Rand had already asked her enough technical questions about the compound to reinforce her conviction that he needed her for crib notes. Most likely every question his pals asked would force him to come to her for the answer; that fact in itself could probably keep any sexual shenanigans off the week's agenda.

Who cares! she thought finally, as she climbed the crystalline beach toward her temporary home. The evening had been lavish, the players were a heady, interesting mix, and besides, architects hardly ever got to inhabit the fabulous places they designed, so this was gravy.

She hummed a little Sicilian melody her grandmother used to sing, as she walked. It was a glorious night, in a glorious place, and she had decided to enjoy herself. Being an architect was such a grind, in grad school and after. Never time for parties like other disciplines had, never time for anything but calculus and drawing boards, her slide rule and calculator like extra fingers. Not that the dream wasn't worth it . . . but sometimes it was hard not to wonder what it would be like to be free to be frivolous, at least a little . . . or to have time for some kind of life beyond architecture. So, just for a little while, perhaps she would play along with this silly fantasy, in a place that even the Gods thought beautiful.

Justine had left the beach several minutes before, and Thoros stood alone beside the half-cleared dining table as he tied a dry towel around his wet swimsuit, and prepared to join her at the house. He felt replete and thoroughly pleased with himself. Jase Shindler ambled by, also alone. He was carrying a woman's shoe, obviously left behind by someone, Thoros wasn't sure who.

"I see you've tucked Justine away with you, Thoros, you sly dog. I thought your rules of the game stated no one could sleep with the woman he brought."

Thoros's eyes crinkled at the corners, as he smiled. "My prerogative as host," he said simply. "I changed the rules." Both men laughed and parted company at the entrance to the house.

Thoros had been giving considerable thought all evening to

the best technique for bedding Justine; he anticipated a complex and interesting seduction. Or perhaps *chess game* would be a better word for what would go on between them. He was looking forward to it very much, indeed. He had an immense sexual appetite, but he'd always known how to control it, not let it control him. He'd seen too many men make jackasses out of themselves because they let their cocks do their thinking. But controlled or not, the appetite was there. Maybe not as urgently now as when he was young, but no less intense.

Justine lay across the huge antique bed that dominated the vast bedroom. The flesh-colored teddy she wore was trimmed with ecru lace, and clung to the superb young body beneath, like a satin skin. She had been undecided, until a few moments before, whether she would let Thoros make love to her this first night. But the beach party had been provocative, sensual, and the tropical languor had seeped into her bones in a primal way that had made her feel the liquid, silken wanting that keeps the world in motion.

She wondered if it would be different for them tonight; lessened from their first encounter, which had been almost by chance. Both stranded unexpectedly for one snowy night in Gstaad, introduced by friends, then left to their own devices, the snow too heavy to meander far. In a way, that would be easier, less complicated; she was just coming off a love affair that had left her wary. On the other hand, she enjoyed the cat-and-mouse quality of early romance; men were always at their best in early courtship mode, striving so hard to be winsome, willing to kill themselves in the effort of sexual conquest. And Thoros was an interesting man. Too old for long-term liaison, too surfeited with women for any illusions to remain, but interesting, nonetheless.

Justine felt dizzy with sensual expectation, now that she'd decided to let the games begin tonight. She wished Thoros would hurry with whatever had delayed him, and when the minutes ticked by without his arrival she decided that there was little reason to wait. She reached down to touch the places that had begun to throb with expectation and spread her thighs to expose the damp core of herself to her own exploration.

She paid no attention to the shadow that fell across her face when Thoros came in and stood at the foot of the bed staring down at her.

"Don't steal from me, Justine," he said, his voice low and intense. "It's my place to pleasure you."

"You were late," she replied simply. There was a challenge he read in her eyes that asked what he could offer her that would be better.

Justine watched his face as he shed his towel and swimsuit, dropping them unceremoniously onto a damask chair—the casual deliberation of it excited her, making her realize how profoundly she wanted to make love at that moment. It was a strong male face, part kindness, part cruelty in the eyes that were full of sexual knowing.

"Turn over," he said, and she complied. He ran his hands over her body in a proprietary way, carefully, as if intuiting it, strong fingers tracing shoulders, back, buttocks, legs, searching for understanding of what lay beneath the surface. He spread her thighs with infinite tenderness, then pushed himself inside her suddenly, surprisingly, without another gesture.

Justine gasped at the quick intrusion, feeling strangely exhilarated by the suddenness. She arched to meet his thrust, but he didn't move at all as she'd expected him to. Expecting her surprise, Thoros leaned his mouth close to her ear and whispered, "Lie very still, Justine. I'm going to make love to you."

"No!" she said sharply, pulling herself free of his flesh, leaving him surprised, now. There was a kind of confused annoyance in the knitted brows, and in his eyes, disappointment.

Justine smiled reassurance and putting both hands on his chest, pushed him back down onto the silken coverlet.

"I want to play," she said as she moved in beside him, one hand still on his chest and the other on his erect penis, her fingers caressing the most sensitive skin of all, proprietary, light as butterflies, as she spoke. Her eyes took in the terrain of him, skillfully, calculating, deciding where to go next.

Thoros resisted the urge to fight her for control, watching her eyes take in the whole of him. His erection felt more engorged with every circle of her hand, and he realized, surprised, that he had to struggle to keep from coming, like a boy. It aroused him that she'd turned the tables so effortlessly, had drawn the battle lines of pleasure so swiftly, about who would be in control of the night. But he was not a boy, to be bested so easily. Thoros reached beneath her body as she knelt and forced his fingers to intrude into the hot wet center of her, his thumb still on the outside of her mons, bracing the movement within. He had her attention now, he knew. Could feel it in the tightening around his moving fingers, evening the odds.

Laughing, she bent her mouth to his penis, opening her swollen self to his touch, knowing they were brilliantly matched in this, the oldest game of all.

Friday, April 8

What we anticipate seldom occurs,
what we least expected generally happens.

Benjamin Disraeli

NINE

Thoros looked rested and anticipatory. There was an air of exuberance in the group he surveyed, just finishing their breakfast on the sun-streaked terrace. The morning after their first evening in Mora Utu had dawned perfect and languid; soft island breezes wafted scents of exotic blossoms, and small, colorful birds swooped over the pool, as if sent by the props department to complete the tableaux.

"Today is dedicated to pleasure and exploration," Thoros said expansively, as he stood up to gain everyone's attention. There was an easy grace about him this morning the women hadn't seen before, as if the taut springs had loosened a notch. "This morning, I propose to take you on tour of the compound itself first, then explore the beaches, and finally, head out toward the foothills of Mauna Lopelia, the sacred mountain." He paused, his canny eyes surveying the group's body language and seating choices; obviously, last evening's festivities had facilitated some choice-making. Several couples had formed and, by and large, everyone looked comfortable and compatible.

"After lunch, everyone can feel free to go his own way, of course. Justine and I plan to go sailing; if anyone wants to crew we'd be delighted. . . ."

Rand turned to Christie. "Do you sail?" he asked eagerly. "Shall we go with them?" She nodded yes to both questions; he'd already consented to an interview when they got back to New York.

"Christie and I will crew for you," he called over to Thoros, who smiled acknowledgment.

"Chesi and I were thinking of maybe snorkeling out toward that small barrier reef," Jase said casually. "We're both pretty experienced in the water."

Thoros nodded. "Excellent—just see Emilio for whatever equipment you'll need."

"I don't suppose you're up for a hike in the jungle, by any chance?" Alex asked Liz, sotto voce. "Inasmuch as you're not European, I expect it would be too much to ask."

Liz laughed; she was in such a delicious mood this morning that his manipulative badinage seemed more amusing than annoying. "My middle-American legs love hiking," she answered sweetly. "Must be from traipsing around all those cornfields as a child."

"Tony? Marika?" Thoros prompted. "What's your pleasure?"

"We'll go on the tour with you this morning, Thoros," Tony answered for both. "But I think we'll hang around here this afternoon. Maybe hit the beach." Marika didn't dissent.

"Let's stay here, too, Jack," Tiffany whispered quickly. "I'd rather catch some sun and conversation than play anything." Jack smiled his response. He couldn't think of anything he'd rather do than spend some time alone with her.

"That's it then," Thoros answered, pleased at the prospects of the island day. "Let's meet back here in ten minutes and be on our way."

* * *

The two jitneys bounced along the not-quite-finished paths, their fringe swaying vigorously. Thoros drove the lead car, Emilio the other, stopping every few minutes to point out interesting sites to the visitors.

"The tennis courts have been surfaced, if anyone cares to get some exercise," Thoros said, waving his hand in the direction of the newly constructed courts. The fences surrounding them had been planted with heavy enough foliage, so it was difficult to see in, but it appeared there were plenty of courts in the complex.

"The golf course won't really be complete until next season, unfortunately. It was designed by Arnie Palmer, to incorporate simulations of a few of my favorite holes from round about the world—like the sixteenth at the Greenbriar and the third and ninth at St. Andrews. I'm told it usually takes the better part of a year to manicure greens into proper shape, but because we're in the tropics, the growth is accelerated somewhat on Mora Utu. So, the course is playable now, even if it's not yet perfect." He motioned to Emilio to move on.

They stopped near a one-story, many-windowed building on the right side of the path. "That white stucco building over there is our gym . . . weight room, Nautilus, punching bags, sauna, et cetera. There's also an indoor track for runners, and one of those newfangled rock-climbing simulators."

"With a mountain range and lava cliffs, you need a simulator?" Marika piped up, obviously indignant.

"Are you a climber?" Thoros asked, surprised.

"Ya. I climb," she said emphatically. "I love to climb."

"We'll have to go climbing together while we're here, then," Thoros responded, intrigued. "*Not* on the simulator." It was a strenuous sport, and one he very much enjoyed. He'd always believed that his competency in climbing was a gift from his mountain-bred forebears.

The small caravan took off again, this time heading in the

direction of the water. They pulled to a halt just shy of the sand dunes, and Thoros waved a large hand toward the sun-dazzled ribbon of white sand and turquoise sea.

"My boat is in Cannes at the moment, but I intend to have the crew run it down here quite often during the coming year, as a sort of ferry for guests, when I'm not in need of it myself. So, I do hope some of you will return here when you can get away."

"Some ferry," Jack whispered to Tiffany. "It's about a foot and a half smaller than the *Queen Mary.*" She giggled appreciatively, wondering what it would be like to own a yacht.

"Right now, however," Thoros continued, "for those of you who enjoy water activities, we can offer quite a selection of possibilities. The Cigarette boat is in residence, if any of you get a kick out of speed—the sloop we're going out on today is an easy-handling craft for any serious sailors among you . . . and there are other smaller craft just for fun. Sunfish, rowboats, dinghies for the fishermen, a speedboat for the water skiers, and so on.

"One word of warning to the swimmers, though. We're putting in barrier nets wherever feasible, but this is the South Pacific after all, and there are sharks, so it's important to stay alert in the water and to swim in pairs."

Thoros turned the jitneys inland toward the lush mountain range that formed the island's core. Several minutes further into their journey, a large expanse of land under cultivation came into view on the left side of the road. As they drew close, they saw Nelida working on her hands and knees in what appeared to be the beginning of a vast garden. The two vehicles pulled to a full stop and Nelida waved cheerily to the visitors to disembark.

"Welcome!" she called out, wiping her hands on the gardener's apron she wore. Getting to her feet with surprising agility, she came toward them.

"A good deal of the fresh food for Mora Utu's tables will come from here, once Nelida has her little farm up and running," Thoros said. "She and Emilio have already spent time here getting it started, and she's talked me into importing several Mexican gardeners to give Mother Nature a hand."

"Look at that incredible herb garden!" Liz said excitedly, eyeing a patch of ground covered with varied green sprouts that seemed set apart from the rest of the little farm; it looked about fifteen feet square, crisscrossed by eighteen-inch footpaths.

"You've laid it out like a sixteenth-century monastery garden, haven't you, Nelida?" Francesca asked, intrigued by the orderly array. "There's a sacred geometry to the proportions, isn't there?"

"Very good!" Nelida said, agreeing to the praise. "Nelida does not cook with other people's herbs."

"Enough garden gossip, ladies," Thoros called out, bored by horticulture and impatient to move on. "We have quite a bit more ground to cover before we go our separate ways."

The women returned to the jitneys, enchanted by what they'd seen. They passed the croquet field, the stables, the storage sheds, and the construction crew's leftover work trailers, before clearing the limits of the compound and heading off toward the coastline again. They drove for nearly fifteen minutes before they neared the water.

"Epeirogenic uplifts created this island," Thoros explained as he drove. "Volcanic underwater explosions spewed gas and rock and lava skyward, millions of years ago, forming the great crescent-shaped atoll that is Mora Utu. Originally, only wind-whipped coasts with desolate rocks, and steaming craters full of volcanic ash or lava must have existed here." He pulled the vehicle to a halt, and motioned for everyone to get out for a better view. Emilio's vehicle pulled up just as the first group alighted.

The cobalt sea was far different here, from the side of the island closer to the compound; wilder, darker, more primitive beaches stretched burnished and black for miles. Thoros pointed out distant lava caves that honeycombed the coastline, and the soft sedimentary rock that had solidified into weirdly exotic shapes, which rose like Easter Island statues to dominate the shore.

"As you can see," Thoros shouted above the sound of the roaring water, "here we have black, gritty volcanic sand. While it looks beautiful and benign from a distance, up close there's something fierce about it, something alien."

"Like a Klingon summer resort," Christie offered, taking it all in.

"Exactly," he said. "We're not used to this."

"I am," Liz laughed. "I'm Irish. The Cliffs of Moher have this flavor, and some spots around Dingle. Not the beaches, of course. Just the wild, volcanic seascape. I love the exoticism of it . . . the wild, primitive power."

"Hear, hear!" Alex applauded, putting his arm around her shoulder casually. "You make this sound a great place for a rendezvous."

"I was thinking more of a typhoon," she said. "Can you imagine the primal beauty of this place in a storm?"

"Actually," Thoros said, "the natives paid a great deal of attention to guarding this place in time of storms. You see, those lava caves are sacred—they're the burial places of the ancestral bones. I understand they'd go to any self-sacrificial length to protect the caves in a big blow, and legend claims the priests had some way of surviving natural disasters there. Our geological surveyors couldn't figure out how. Fortunately, there haven't been any really major typhoons here in this century."

"What kind of creatures are there in this ocean?" Tiffany asked, fascinated by the difference between this and any other beach she'd seen. "It's all so different—I expect some kind of sea monster to crawl out."

"Sharks, dolphins, manta rays, orcas, barracuda, lobsters, turtles, you name it," he answered easily, smiling at her naïveté. "And a few surprises, too, like scorpion fish—and the tun snail that grows so huge, it's been known to slake its carnivorous appetite on humans. Although, not often."

"Hard to imagine a snail ever catching a human," she said with a shudder. "These guys must be a lot speedier than the snails I've known."

"Tuns prey on trapped creatures," he answered. "There are all manner of dangerous predators in a coral sea, like this one—giant clams that can snap shut on a hand or foot and keep you prisoner long enough for some other creature to turn you into lunch."

Tiffany grimaced. "Anything else you'd like to tell us before we go for a swim?"

"Only be sure to avoid the crocodiles," he answered with a twinkle. "But they're only a bother near the water holes on the golf course."

The group piled back into the jitneys and Thoros headed them away from the beach and inland toward the mountainous interior. As they crossed the wide marshland, flocks of birds rose in disorganized clouds or flight formations, startled by the unusual human intrusion.

"There are eighty different species of birds of paradise alone here, I'm told," Thoros called out to the group above the raucous cries of the brilliantly plumed flight formation. "And any number of parrot species, cockatoos, cockatiels, et cetera. Also, doves and ibis, inland a bit. Even a strange, flightless bird that's quite intriguing, called a . . ."

"Cassowary," Liz prompted.

Thoros laughed. "You really do have total recall, don't you? Alex told me, but I doubted him. A formidable gift if you use it well."

"I've always found it handy. It makes me a great date for a bird-watcher."

"And a few others, I'd wager," he replied, feeling generous. This was going to be a fine day in the finest place on earth.

The road became less defined as they traveled inland; the grade began to steepen slowly as they started the long ascent of foothills that led toward the distant peaks. The gnarled and scrubby vegetation that had marked the lowlands unfolded into lavish jungle. Jasmine, hibiscus, and frangipani made the air redolent with heady perfume—poinsettia, laurels, and rhododendron peeked out from under canopies of Pandorus palm and creeping bamboo.

"There are over three thousand varieties of orchids here on Mora Utu," Thoros told them, delightedly. "Between the savanna, the jungle belt, and the rain forest, you can probably find every species of plant and animal you've ever imagined."

"So, what's the bad news?" Tiffany called out from the second car. "What kind of dangers do we have to watch out for?"

Thoros pulled over to the side of the road and stopped, letting the engine idle. "Excellent question, Tiffany," he said, getting out and stretching the driving kinks from his long legs. "Not that any of us will be alone far enough outside the compound ever to be in any real jeopardy, but it always pays to know what your environment might have up its sleeve."

He had everyone's attention. "The dangers here are much the same ones you'd encounter in any tropical or equatorial place. Insects like scorpions, mites, fire ants abound—there are malarial mosquitoes too, so insect spray is essential, if you're wandering about in the bush. There are two other fever-bearing insects whose names escape me." He smiled a little. "But I'm sure Liz will name them for us any minute now.

"There are snakes, of course. Mostly harmless, but two poisonous varieties—a species of adder, and the black mamba. Pythons can be dangerous too, if they grow large enough to grapple with a human, and many do, here.

"There are also leeches, which, while not deadly, are rather revolting, so you'll do well to avoid the swamps. And there's quicksand to consider, along with the possibility of poisonous food or water. Needless to say, none of these dangers exist inside the compound.

"Oh, yes," he added to lighten the mood. "There are also eighteen species of hallucinogenic plants indigenous to this island. A veritable treasure trove for those who would prefer to spend their holiday *out* of the body, rather than in it."

Everyone laughed, as they were supposed to, and resettled themselves in their vehicles. Thoros turned with one last thought.

"We won't be able to cover more than a fraction of the island this morning, ladies and gentlemen, but I did want to give you a taste of its variety and potentials. In the interest of everyone's afternoon plans, I'd suggest we go only a little farther up the mountain—just high enough for a good view of the terrain below—and then we'll head back and disperse to our various pleasures. We'll be here for ten days, so there should be ample time for exploration as the week progresses."

Two hours later they were back at Mora Utu's gates, everyone captivated by the extraordinary beauty and grandeur of Thoros's domain, and more aware than they had been on arrival that it was a genuine jungle out there, not merely the Disney variety it had seemed when they disembarked from the G-IV.

Liz and Alex, who had decided to spend the afternoon hiking, had been walking for over an hour, so that the savanna beyond the compound had given way to rolling hills and then to rockier byways.

The tall urbane man who walked cheerfully at her side was a disarmingly pleasant surprise, Liz had to admit, almost against her will. Literate, cultured, and educated to a fare-thee-well, as her father would have said, he was also charming, quick-witted, and humorous; he'd made her laugh frequently on their trek, with his irreverent wit and funny anecdotes about famous politicos he seemed to know intimately. He was an excellent hiker, too, experienced and comfortable with distance.

"Have you heard the one about the Italian tourist who traveled to the most famous bullfighting village in Spain?" he asked.

"Not yet," Liz responded, enjoying herself enormously. It had come as a shock and a disappointment to her that Jase didn't intend to be her date for the week, despite his having invited her. She hated to admit that from the moment of the invitation, she'd fantasized liberally about what the week would hold with him. But Alex wasn't seeming such a bad replacement, at the moment.

Alex motioned toward a relatively open patch of grass that looked like an inviting place to stop, and they sat down, pleasantly tired.

"It seems this tourist made his way to the best restaurant in town and was just about to dine, when a great fanfare came from the kitchen and the waiter carried in the specialty of the house, and set it before a man seated at the next table. In the center of the plate were two immense balls."

"As in *balls*?" she asked, amused.

"Indeed. 'I want what he's having,' the little tourist said excitedly. 'Oh, no, señor,' answered the waiter. 'This dish is served to only *one* patron, and only once a year, on the day of the great bullfight. You must make a reservation one year in advance.'

"'Put me down for next year, then,' the tourist said, salivating. 'My name is Giuseppe.' And off he went. Next year he appeared, placed his order, and waited expectantly. Again came the fanfare, and the entourage from the kitchen. And the plate, on which, alas, were two tiny little balls.

" 'There's been a terrible mistake!' Giuseppe cried. 'This looks nothing like what I saw last year.'

" 'What can I tell you, señor?' said the lugubrious owner. 'Sometimes fortune goes with the matador, sometimes with the bull.' "

Liz laughed heartily and leaned back on one elbow; the sun

shining on her face flushed from the long walk made her look particularly pretty.

"You're really quite a beautiful woman, Elizabeth," Alex said admiringly. "Why on earth do you wear your hair in that unattractive ponytail?"

Liz's good humor faded instantly at the left-handed compliment. "Why do you always do that, Alex?" she asked, annoyed that he'd spoiled things so abruptly.

"Do what?"

"Snipe like that. You're always baiting or putting down. But only with the women, I've noticed."

Alex smiled. "Women rather like being challenged, I've noticed. Keeps them on their toes."

"Is that what you call it? A challenge? It's just a calculated manipulation. I'm surprised any woman would put up with it. I know they do, of course. I do read *Vanity Fair*."

"And everything else, it seems," he answered, unperturbed by her rebuke. "Will this editing business be enough for you, do you suppose? Growing old and squinty over dusty manuscripts. Or does the fact that you're here this week suggest you have an Achilles' heel and fantasize about being filthy rich and having high adventure?"

"Deft change of subject," she responded, keeping the scorecard straight. "And being this rich does appear to have a helluva lot more going for it than going hungry, from what I've seen so far."

"Hunger is an anomaly to rich people, you know," Alex said, smiling. "It is very difficult for them to make out why people who want dinner do not simply ring the bell for it."

"Bagehot," she said with a self-satisfied smirk.

"I beg your pardon?"

"Bagehot said that."

"Really? Fancy that. He was a damned insightful fellow then, wasn't he?"

"How about this one," she responded, warming to the repartee. "If the rich could hire other people to die for them, the poor could make a wonderful living."

This time Alex laughed aloud. "You are a most amusing person, Elizabeth."

"Despite the ponytail?"

"Aha! Gotcha with that barb, eh? You see, it works."

"Only to annoy—not to ingratiate."

He smiled, rather genuinely, she thought. "And, what precisely *would* ingratiate me with you, dear girl? I'd rather like to give that a whirl, I think."

Liz checked the fast riposte that had sprung to her lips, and took a breath; it was a fair question that deserved an answer.

"I'd like to know something *real* about you, Alex. Something that's not one of your manipulations, and not media hype. I mean, it's rather hard to imagine you as a child. Did you spring full blown from the brow of Zeus? Or were you found floating in a basket among the Nile reeds? And why did you choose to be an economist, and a broker of international alliances?"

"Ah, yes," he said. "Alliances. The union of two thieves who have their hands so deeply inserted in each other's pockets they cannot safely plunder a third."

Liz chuckled, but continued. "I'd like to know how you became a regular at 10 Downing Street and 1600 Pennsylvania Avenue . . . that kind of thing."

"Really, Elizabeth, I'd expected better of you. These are Christie questions."

Liz frowned. "You're doing it again, Alex. I find it really irritating, and to tell the truth I have no intention of rising to the bait." She stood up and brushed away the undergrowth that was clinging to her pants. "Let's walk some more," she said briskly. "Judging by the angle of the sun, we'll have to turn back soon."

Alex rose, too. "I had a twin who died at birth," he said unexpectedly. "I felt guilty about it in childhood—as if I'd outmaneuvered him in the womb and somehow wrought his destruction. Later, I rather fancied that I carried his spirit along with mine in some inexplicable symbiosis."

"A karmic fellow traveler?" she answered, softening a little. He was trying to make amends by sharing an intimacy.

He nodded judiciously. "I was always first-rate in school . . . top honors in every form, that sort of thing. A headmaster once offhandedly said to me, 'You've enough brains for two, Alex,' and I thought, *That's it, then. Jeremy's brain is in there too.*"

"Spooky and burdensome," she pronounced.

"Wasn't it, though." They walked a moment in silence.

"What about your parents?" she prompted, finally. "How did they handle your guilt about your twin?"

"I doubt they ever knew about it. Or would have felt it their place to interfere, if they had known, for that matter. We Brits don't fawn over our children as you Americans do. No, *no!* now don't get all huffy again—that was not a put-down, just an observation. Emotions simply aren't our long suit, they're too damned uncivilized. And in the class to which we belonged, children rarely see their parents until adulthood. Governesses, cooks, butlers, riding instructors, tutors, and any number of other assorted servants oversee one's children until they're packed off to boarding school."

"It sounds rather lonely."

"Not at all," he said with a smile. "Remember my karmic fellow traveler."

Liz smiled, too. "It sounds emotionally deprived, then. I can't help thinking of my three sisters' kids—it's a miracle they can breathe independently for all the hugging and nurturing they get. Growing up in the middle class in the Midwest provides a lot of stability to little people, I think."

"So why aren't you there providing well-hugged little midwesterners to the world?"

She laughed and shook her head vigorously. "It's a great

place to come *from*, not to stay *in*. I wanted a wider world, a bigger pond, fewer constraints, anonymity from my neighbors. . . ."

"And a place to use that quick brain of yours, I'd wager."

"That too."

"Cream rises, after all," he said with a smirk. "Intellect is the great determinant. If you're smarter than your peers, ambition will drive you to the arena where you can duke it out—rise to your full stature."

"*The Peter Principle*," she laughed. "Everyone rises to the level of his own incompetency."

They both laughed.

"I must tell you a secret, Elizabeth, since you've badgered these intimate memories out of me. As a child, I would sometimes see youngsters on the street or in a restaurant, who had these conspicuously demonstrative parents . . . ones who hugged them and fussed over them, dads who beamed as if their progeny sported halos. I thought them hideously unseemly, of course. But there was something attractive about them, too. I can remember wondering what it would be like to change places with them for a week."

"Like *The Prince and The Pauper*?"

"Precisely. To be fawned over and coddled and praised unrelentingly did have its seduction. Like eating all the chocolates in the world—you know you'll be dreadfully sick, but it might be worth the price."

Liz tilted her head to see him more clearly; he looked younger, more vulnerable in this revelation, and he was a very good-looking man.

"You're nicer when you're human, you know, Alex," she said.

"Ah, but my clients don't pay me to be either nice or human, Elizabeth. As a matter of fact, they'd probably be quite appalled to think I had the capacity for either condition."

"You don't seem like a man who worries much about clients. You're too much 'to the manner born' for that."

Alex grinned. "The same training that abnegates cheerier emotions abnegates fear, I expect. It's quite astute of you to know that." They walked in silence for a while as the path got steeper and more difficult to navigate.

"And what of you, my midwestern surprise package?" Alex asked, finally. "Now that I've bared my family skeletons, the least you can do is bare yours."

She took a deep breath and sighed audibly. "My father ran a small family-owned business that made farm machinery. I adored him. My mother was a tougher act."

Alex heard the confusion and sadness in the reply and admonished himself to proceed with caution. Generally, it didn't pay to know too much about a woman. Enough to set the proper barbs, enough to pull the strings, enough to appear interested, but not enough to trespass boundaries that could lead you into treacherous terrain. But he was having fun with this one, and felt curiously free of ordinary constraints today.

"Oh dear," he replied with mock dismay. "Women and their mothers. Fertile ground for armchair therapy, I'm afraid. What was her ghastly affliction?"

Liz said wistfully, "She was a rare bird, actually . . . but sad as November. She always seemed to be carrying some historic sorrow about with her, like a giant rock, Alex. It weighted her down, so I always thought of her as an injured eagle straining for the sky."

Alex lived by knowing truth when he heard it. Truth expressed poetically was always such a lovely surprise.

"She sounds intriguing and tragic. May I ask how things went awry between you?"

"I think her heart had been injured by a loveless childhood," she replied thoughtfully. "But her intellect was staggering—so she confused knowledge with love, and tried to bestow on us kids the only gift she had to give, which was knowledge. She was a presence to fill an armory, really . . . mind alert as a laser, passions unregenerate and mighty."

"So you admired her, apparently, but couldn't quite love her?"

Liz nodded confirmation of the insight. "She criticized those she loved with the relentlessness of an evangelist. I was flayed too often to ever feel loved, but I did appreciate her brilliance."

"And you were the prize intellect of the litter, I'd wager, so you got flayed oftener than the rest?" He watched her as she frowned in answer—this was becoming interesting. He mentally cautioned himself not to launch any barbs against this momentary vulnerability.

"I had a very strange childhood, Alex," she said earnestly. "My mother lavished on me the obsessiveness of her pent-up genius, I guess—and my total-recall gift was the perfect foil for her need to teach. So she taught me poetry and music, literature and philosophy—she presented history as if it were a vast continuing soap opera—I remember on my fifth birthday we pretended to fly to the fifteenth century to visit the Medicis, but she said it wouldn't be prudent to stay to lunch. She taught me the succession to the French and English monarchies by cataloging their mistresses."

He laughed, imagining this brilliant woman and child trapped in a cornfield.

"Life might have been different for her if she'd been born at the other end of the Women's Movement . . . or if she'd been male, of course. I always thought she was styled for Mount Rushmore, rather than housewifery. Fitted to lead great armies into battle, but perverse Fate made her a scholar in the scullery, instead."

"She sounds remarkable," he said genuinely. "Whatever happened to her?"

Liz paused a minute, deciding how to express her complex feelings in an answer, then plunged ahead.

"She had a sad ending, really," she said. "It was as if she carved *herself* in granite, finally, and pitched her battles with those she loved best. She died desperate and sad, I think, despite everybody's best efforts to make her happy. I always wished I could have liked her better."

Alex, who'd been walking slightly ahead, turned suddenly, so that Liz nearly collided with him. He scooped her into his arms and kissed her soundly, lifting her slightly off the ground in a bear hug as he did so.

Liz felt her heart quicken and kissed him back, surprised by the skill and tenderness of the kiss; by the exuberance of his manner and the crisp male strength of him as he held her. He was taller, broader than she'd thought, and there was no denying his charisma.

"*That* was for all the love we didn't get as children," he said with an understanding smile, as he let her go. She was surprised to find herself wanting more. "Wasn't it Chesterton who said, 'The family is a good institution because it is so uncongenial'? I'm glad to know you, Elizabeth Cavanaugh. I would never have imagined Jase Shindler would have the good judgment to invite someone like you. I'm beginning to think we may have quite a splendid week."

They continued their hike, conversation easy now, fluid. "Now, to answer your question," he said, "I think I decided to become involved with government because of something Ambrose Bierce said about peace being a period of cheating between two periods of fighting. I suppose I thought it seemed so cynical it must be true, and if true, it must mean the cheating all had to do with money, so my fascination with economics and history made it the perfect métier for me."

"Didn't Bierce write that wonderful little poem about history," Liz continued eagerly, "that describes it as, '*an account, mostly false, of events, mostly lies, brought about by kings, mostly knaves, and soldiers, mostly fools'?"*

"He did, indeed, my girl," Alex answered, enjoying himself and her. "And he was mostly right."

TEN

Jack and Tiffany lay on the wet sand in the shadow of the great volcanic rocks that made the character of the Mora Utu beach unique. They were having fun now that lunch was over and they were finally alone. Rand and Christie were off sailing with Thoros and Justine, Jase and Chesi were snorkeling off the reef, Alex and Liz had wandered off in hiking boots. Marika was still with Tony, somewhere in the compound, but she had already accosted each man in turn like a predator on the scent. It was apparent that she intended to seduce someone useful before this was over, if she had to sleep with every man on the island in succession. Not that any of the men were protesting, but they did seem to have their own priorities at the moment.

Tiffany smiled to herself as she dangled one long finger in the small tidal pool left in the sand by the receding wave. She looked at Jack, lying stretched out beside her, and wondered what his age was. Late fifties, somewhere, she guessed. But in pretty good shape for that; you could see he'd spent a lifetime working out. In fact, while she was practicing her katas on the beach this morning, she'd seen him running in the distance; the long easy stride of someone used to exercise, used to pacing himself in the battle of the body. She'd been relieved to see that Jack didn't seem concerned over Marika's defection. As a matter of fact, none of the men except Thoros seemed very proprietary about the woman he'd brought to the party, and couples were forming of their own volition.

Jack felt her watching him, and smiled up lazily. He hadn't felt this good in a long, long time. It had been a rough winter in business; not that he'd ever be poor again, that was for damned sure, but it had been a killer year in which every skill he'd mastered in the old days—the South Side of Chicago street-smarts and the infighting of the pro-boxing racket he'd grown up in—had been needed to win.

"I've got a tough one for you, Tiff," he said good-naturedly, half sitting, half leaning on an elbow. "There's a runner on third, with no outs in the fifth inning of a three–three game. The batter hits a two-hopper to first. The runner hightails it for home and the first baseman sends an easy out to the catcher. You with me, babe?"

She tucked her legs up in front of her and nodded confidently. "You haven't lost me so far."

"Okay. So, why is this lousy baseball, and when did it happen in a Dodger game?"

Tiffany frowned, rifling the baseball Filofax in her brain, then brightened. "A runner at third with no out should *never* try to score on a ground ball, unless he *knows* he can make it to safety. If there's a runner on second, the advance runner should try to make it home with no out or maybe one out, if the defense has a chance for a double play." She paused for breath. "Okay, that's the easy part. Now, for the rest." Her brow furrowed for a long moment, then she brightened.

"Okay—1984. Dodgers–Cubs. Marciano Duncan was the

rookie on third. He broke for home and shouldn't have . . . it was an easy out."

"So why shouldn't he have made a run for it?"

"Because the Dodgers' best hitters, Pedro Guerrero and Greg Block, were coming up next, and the guy at first base was playing up on the grass. Only a rookie would have made that kind of a dumb move."

Jack leaned back with a short laugh, and shook his head. "You are absolutely unbelievable!" he said. "I got coaches working for me couldn't have given me that tight an answer. How'd you learn all this stuff?"

Tiffany smiled her delight at his responsiveness to her knowledge. Her white teeth looked dazzling in her dusky face, now flushed with sun and good times.

"I had five brothers, Jack. I used to chase them around, trying to make them *want* to play with me. You better believe, I had to play what *they* played, but I wasn't as big or strong as they were, so I had to get me an edge—and I had this really great memory for plays. So, I studied them like crazy till I knew more than anybody about any sport you could name, and that made me a hot ticket. They used to show me off to their buddies. You can't imagine how much money they won on me, setting up guys who didn't know I knew things. . . ."

Jack reached over, unexpectedly, and pulled her down to him. He needed to kiss her; he hadn't planned to at this moment, but she looked so young and fresh and full of life, her breasts straining the fabric of the bikini, her belly sandy and glistening. But it was more than that that drew him to her, he knew. She was real and human, not working the room like Marika, or calculating everyone's news value like Christie. Tiffany was herself, take it or leave it, and he was enchanted by her, as he hadn't been by anyone in a hell of a long time.

There was salt in the kiss she returned, with surprise and

genuine pleasure. It was a playful kiss, not a wild seduction. A kiss that said don't worry, there'll be time for this.

There was to be a formal dinner tonight, Jack knew—tuxes and gowns and all the trappings of women's fantasies. He'd wait till then to make his big move. He couldn't risk offending her, or making it seem he thought she was easy. But tonight would definitely be the night.

ELEVEN

Liz sipped her coffee beside the small pool at the back of Chesi's guest pod; it was nearly six o'clock Friday night and soon they'd have to dress for dinner. They were both in beach robes, resting gratefully after the day's exertions, munching on fruit Nelida had brought for them, along with a steaming pot of espresso. The day had been geared to pleasure, with everyone pairing off as they chose and doing whatever they'd wanted all afternoon. It seemed the rhythm of the week would include free-form days with occasional group activities offered, then communal dinners each night, a happy enough arrangement.

Chesi tossed her dark wet hair side to side in the late day breeze like a shaggy dog after a dip.

"Do you get the feeling we have about ten minutes to pick a dance partner for the week, and it won't be the one we arrived with?"

Liz nodded, frowning a little. "Obviously," she said. "It's just like we're in *The Story of O.* We're here at the Château for sex, and if we don't pick quick we'll be trussed up and handed over to the first guy who rings the doorbell."

"How do you feel about that?"

Liz leaned back, holding the steaming mug up to her lips with both hands in a leisurely way. "Ambivalent, I guess. I'm embarrassed to admit it, but I came here with a slight crush on Jase—I mean, he always seemed so dashing and larger than life, seen from afar in the office and the trade papers. But he hasn't given me the time of day since we hit Mora Utu. In fact, looks to me like we're all up for grabs here." She paused for a sip. "Aside from that, I rather like being here on Shangri La South. It's exciting to play with these rich, powerful guys, and to see how the other half lives. On my editorial salary, I can't afford a *life* never mind a lifestyle, so it's great to wallow in all this luxury for ten minutes. But I don't quite know how to handle this office-grab-bag routine. What'll they do if we don't cozy up, throw us into the volcano?"

Chesi laughed grimly. "I didn't have much choice about coming this week, you know—I mean, this place is my baby. I've eaten, breathed, and slept Mora Utu for two years. I know every circuit breaker like the veins on my ankle, so I was excited about being on the 'inside,' you know? *Living* this place, instead of just *thinking* it. But it gives me the heebie-jeebies to even imagine sex with Rand—I mean, how could I ever face him over a conference table, and besides, he is *definitely* not my type."

"Who is?" Liz asked.

Chesi looked thoughtful. "I'm pretty analytical. Gagarian's definitely the pick of the pack, but he's taken. Doherty has the hots for Tiffany. Rand I don't want. Capuletti I wouldn't touch with a trowel. Barclay-Fontaine has dibs on you . . . so that leaves Shindler, who has an ego the size of Antarctica, but seems to be on my case in a pleasant enough way. So, if I'm going to sleep with *somebody*, I suppose he's the best bet, if it won't give that crush of yours fits. I could always close my eyes and think of England."

Liz laughed out loud. "It was Queen Victoria who said that, you know—she also wrote such sex-crazed diaries they burned them after she died. Anyway, my crush has been crushed. After today, I'm leaning toward Alex, so feel free to do as you will with Jase. Actually, I thought that smoldering Mediterranean line he laid on you the other night was hilarious. You looked like you'd swallowed a hop toad."

Chesi laughed, too. "On second thought, maybe I'll just let them throw me into the volcano."

Alex teased the shattering orgasm from Marika's superb body with knowing mouth on her swollen clitoris and two fingers moving rhythmically deep within her.

He'd been horny as hell when he returned from the hike with Liz, but not wanting to make a move on the young editor too soon, he'd found Marika's steamy availability a perfect substitute.

He felt the smooth wet center of her tighten on his fingers in a series of small shudders, as her lean body arced ecstatically, and finally lay still.

Alex gently edged his head away and moved his own large body deftly into place on top of hers. The first orgasm had been just to give her pleasure and test her responses; satisfied that he understood her rhythm, he would now seek a different kind of satisfaction.

The next orgasm would be shared between them.

Friday night's dinner was over by eleven. Thoros had planned an early evening, knowing this would be the first major seduction night that would set the tone for the rest of the week. The men had had twenty-four hours to make selections and plan strategy, the women still had time to appear reticent if they chose, to play hard-to-get for another night. But from what he could see, there were only two potential holdouts among the girls—neither Chesi nor Liz seemed the types to leap into a casual coupling. He'd had a word with Shindler and Barclay-Fontaine earlier in the day about how they were faring, and they'd seemed confident all would go well enough. Shindler said he was dangling a book about women in architecture as bait for Chesi and he thought she'd come around in due time, and Alex seemed genuinely taken with Liz's whiz-kid knowledge. Jack and Tiffany were an easy item, Rand and Christie were thick as thieves, and seemed to be having fun; Capuletti was a shoo-in tonight with Marika.

Thoros breathed a sigh of relief as he ticked off the mental inventory, then tuned back in to what Nelida was telling him about tomorrow's menu. The guests had all left the dining room, but Nelida had detained him with a question. He glanced impatiently beyond her, out the large bay window, where he could see Justine walking on the beach near the water's edge; she was waiting for him, trailing the long chiffon scarf she'd worn at dinner behind her in the sand. She looked like Botticelli's Venus rising from the waves. Thoros dismissed Nelida as hurriedly as he could and left the house high with anticipation of the pleasure in store before morning.

Last night's sexual one-upmanship had provided lovemaking as good as any he'd ever experienced . . . maybe even better. He hummed a little to himself as he kicked off his shoes and walked toward her barefoot in the moonlit dark. This holiday promised to be one of the finer weeks of his life, and his island was everything he'd ever hoped it would be. All it really took to have a perfect life, he thought contentedly, as he drew near the beautiful woman at the water's edge, was that you be very rich and plan very well.

Saturday, April 9

Life is what happens while
you're making other plans.

John Lennon

TWELVE

Saturday morning dawned as lovely as every other day on Mora Utu; the surf crashed brilliant foam onto sugary beaches and the glass-clear sky promised nothing but perfection. Jack opened his eyes and smiled in remembrance of the past few hours; he and Tiffany had spent the night together after the dinner party, talking, laughing, making love. He replayed their sexual explorations in his mind, languidly, savoring the pleasure of the memory as he watched her sleep. She'd been everything he'd hoped and more; giving, exuberant, experienced, but not jaded. Her long, softly strong body was as rewarding as humans ever get to be, satin skinned, full breasted, and slender. He watched her even, centered breathing. Tiffany lay on her side, but one full breast and one long leg had slipped out from under the sheet covering, and the early morning sun filtering through the louvers made an awning-stripe pattern on her nakedness. He wanted her again. Wanted to touch and feel and seek, but there was something so peaceful and profoundly content in the way she was sleeping that he didn't want to wake her.

Jack got up, wrapped a towel around his hips, and padded barefoot to the kitchen to make coffee. Then he'd shower. Or maybe just go back to bed and stay there for the day with her; there was nothing important on the Saturday agenda until dinnertime. He smiled as he opened the blinds to another perfect South Pacific morning. This was shaping up to be a very fine vacation.

Tony wasn't a great lover, but he would do, Marika thought with a sigh, as she lay trapped by the tangle of legs and the heavy weight of his large body lying half on top of hers. She had ooh'd and ah'd over his performance, of course, one had to do that to reassure a man; he was well endowed and horny as hell, although his lovemaking was as rough-edged and bull-like as he was. She tried to extricate herself without waking him—the last thing she wanted was for him to wake up and do it again.

Unable to move, Marika sighed again, and lay back on the pillow, thinking how lucky it was she'd managed to catch Alex alone before dinner, so her own needs had been satisfied. *He* was a superb sexual craftsman; the kind of man who prides himself on the pleasure of his partner. Marika wriggled a bit with the memory of his slow, sure hands and mouth—he'd driven her mad before he'd finally let himself come. And even then it hadn't ended; she'd climaxed so intensely that she still felt the memory of it in her secret places. Jase had been quite a different story, an overachiever in bed, just as everywhere else. His technique was honed, and his staying power excellent, but his ego was too greatly in control to really care about a woman's pleasure, except as a reflection of his own ability.

Marika did a mental inventory in the dim light as she settled into sleep again. She'd been on the island only a day and a half and already she had managed to be intimate with three of the men. The others would succumb to her, too, she just had to find the right moment, then she would have more control over the week ahead. Men always revealed themselves, their character, their needs, in their lovemaking, no matter how secretive they were about themselves in other areas of life. She wondered if women did that too, but thought it unlikely. Women were subtler, and they had the ability to fake, which men couldn't. What a blessing *that* was—to be able to end an unpleasant or unsatisfactory episode relatively painlessly without hurting a man's fragile feelings. It wasn't a big deal to pretend ecstasy you didn't feel, if it made them happy, and you got compensated in some other way, she thought with satisfaction.

Of course, it would be fantastic to really fall in love someday, to honestly feel the kinds of emotions you see in movies; but in the real world that was very iffy. All she could rely on was the way men reacted to her face and body *now*, in this finite time when God and Nature had made her nearly perfect. She had to make that pay off quickly, before time changed the odds. The urgency of it all suddenly assailed Marika, making her nervous and uneasy—tomorrow she would do her best to make inroads with the remaining three men.

Alex, Jase, and Rand picked up their clubs at the small clubhouse and headed the golf cart out toward the first tee. Thoros had opted out of their game, Tony and Jack seldom played, so they would be a threesome.

"Perfect day for golf," Jase said, as he pulled his driver from the bag and sized up the fairway that stretched green and manicured in front of him.

"They're all perfect here," Rand answered with an easy chuckle. He was a superb golfer, as was Jase. Alex was good when he was in practice, but could be inconsistent if his schedule hadn't included much time on golf courses; it wasn't a game he particularly liked.

Jase thwacked the ball, and it shot in a perfect arc, landing with a single bounce, 270 yards down the fairway, just at the edge of the green.

Rand whistled appreciatively at the superb shot, then sent his own ball after it, landing only a few feet shy of Jase's.

Alex frowned as he stepped up to the tee; he wasn't really in the mood for this today, but was doing it to be congenial. He sliced a long drive into the rough, and made a rueful clucking sound as he watched the ball fall to earth in the tropical undergrowth at the edge of the fairway.

"Looks like one of you will be stuck with the trophy, if I keep this up," he said, good-naturedly.

"Speaking of Trophies," Jase answered, as they started walking toward the green. Rand got into the cart, and moved the bags on ahead. "How's it going with Liz?"

Alex looked at him, amused, wondering why the question. "She's grand, as it happens," he replied. "Interesting mind, wry sense of humor . . ."

"Great tits," Jase helped with the inventory.

"Those, too," Alex grinned.

"And Chesi? Not much wrong with her equipment either, from what one can see."

Jase nodded. "First-class body, actually. But a little reticent."

"Thinking of moving on, old boy? I'm sure Marika would be only too happy to oblige."

"Never walk away from a challenge," Jase answered with a short laugh. "Besides, Tony'd probably put one of those horses' heads in my bed, if I interfered with his plans."

Alex found his ball and skipped it out of the rough, toward the green. Jase and Rand both parred the hole and he bogeyed, then they all climbed back into the cart and proceeded with their game. Today was earmarked for leisure; there was nothing formal planned until dinnertime.

* * *

Marika found the pitons, biners, and harness in the equipment room; she'd brought her own rock shoes with her from New York. She'd finally left Tony sleeping off their first night together; he'd had so much to drink, he'd probably sleep till noon, and she had no intention of spending the day with him in bed.

Everyone she wanted to find seemed to have made plans for their Saturday that didn't include her, so she'd decided to free solo, despite the fact that she hadn't climbed much lately. Marika loaded up what she'd need for the climb, picked up a chalk bag, pitons, biners, and aretes, so she could aid the pitch, if she got in over her head while soloing.

It wasn't really a good idea to climb alone, if you weren't in practice, Marika knew that, but she was experienced and this was the perfect way to take a breather from Tony. Beyond that, she needed the sense of competency it would provide, and the freedom; the incredible fluid dance that is the nature of climbing. One of the things she'd always liked best about the sport was the sense of selfhood it provided; the chance to pit your physical skills against nature's inexorability. Because she was beautiful, everyone thought she had all the confidence in the world, but it wasn't true. Insecurity was easier to hide than it was to conquer.

It took Marika over an hour to make her way to the rockface she'd spotted while on Thoros's tour. When she finally arrived at the spot, she gazed at the climb, assessing it critically. She needed to think out her climbing sequences and locate the possible rest stances. Checking her equipment one last time before embarking on the ascent, Marika looked around at the terrain. This was an exquisite place and she was with extraordinary men; something remarkable would happen before this week was out, if she just kept her wits about her. For today, she would escape Tony's amorous attentions for a few hours, and feel better about herself in the bargain. There'd be plenty of time later on to make another conquest.

That thought heartening her, Marika made a conscious effort to clear her mind; there was absolutely no room for mental distraction in climbing.

THIRTEEN

Emilio poured more wine into each glass around the dinner table; only Liz put her hand over hers. She felt pleasantly tipsy at the moment, but another glass would put her in the danger zone, and being out of control in this crowd wouldn't be smart. All the men had been drinking for hours, and some of them had consumed such a vast amount of alcohol she marveled that they could remain coherent. Tony was drinking vodka along with his dinner wine, and both Rand and Jase had put away a considerable number of Glenlivets. Of all the men, Thoros and Jack seemed either to have consumed the least alcohol or to hold their liquor best. She smiled inwardly at the thought that they'd be the only two lovers worth a damn tonight, grateful that she didn't intend to try out any of the others.

Despite their formal dress, dinner tonight had proved to be another rollicking good time. Rand told a funny story about Christie outswimming what she thought was a shark; Jase regaled them with a ribald tale about Princess Di's sex life, which prompted Liz to mention a book proposal she'd received called *The Twelfth Level of Orgasm.*

"Obviously a work of fiction," Jase quipped, and the group laughed heartily.

"Not according to the author, who claims there are thirty levels, and no Chinese woman would settle for less than nine."

"One wonders why they don't look happier on the streets of Beijing," Alex chuckled, touching Liz's leg conspiratorially under the table with his own. Even he seemed more in his cups than was seemly.

"The author says American women never get beyond the fifth level, because it takes a thousand thrusts to go higher." Laughter exploded all around.

"Is that cumulative over a lifetime?" Jase asked.

"Only for you, Shindler," Tony shouted over the merriment.

"How long would it take for a thousand thrusts?" Tony asked, warming to the subject. "You're good with a calculator, Rand . . . how many hours are we talking about here?"

Rand smiled. "I haven't got one in this tux, as it happens, Tony, but we should be able to work this out in our heads, shouldn't we? Assuming one thrust takes three or four seconds, that's fifteen a minute."

"Now we know why the Chinese carry abacuses," Christie offered, a little tipsy.

"Fifteen times sixty is nine hundred to the hour . . ."

"Maybe they notch their night tables like the old gunfighters," Tiffany giggled.

Tony called to Emilio for another vodka. "So we're really only talking an hour and ten minutes, here, right? Not even long enough to raise a sweat."

"Except that the national average for lovemaking, according to *Sex in America,* is just under four minutes," Liz pronounced with a knowing smirk.

"That ain't lovemaking, honey," Jack said. "That's wham-bam-thank-you-ma'am."

"A fuck's a fuck, whatever you call it," Tony said. Several of the women exchanged glances; things could go over the line verbally too easily with this much liquor in play. Maybe it was time to call it a night.

"Okay, okay, everybody, the party's getting rough," Jack said with a good-natured laugh to smooth over Tony's gaff. "Time to pack it in."

"Now that Liz has given us all a goal to strive for," Thoros added with a chuckle, "I'd say this very pleasant dinner is over and we should be left to our own devices for the balance of the night. And don't forget, we've got big plans for tomorrow, so everyone sleep well."

They all left the table in good spirits and various stages of inebriation, and drifted off in differing directions, just before midnight.

Tony and Marika retired to his guesthouse and she walked upstairs to the bedroom, while he fixed himself another vodka, before following her.

Tony entered the room and sat down on the bed, kicking off his shoes; he was feeling randy as hell, if a little disoriented from all the booze. He watched Marika step out of the beaded gown she'd worn to the dinner party; it fell to the floor as if weighted, and lay in a glittering pile around her feet. Her body was phenomenal, as his growing erection attested. He smiled to himself with a glow of internal satisfaction; he had beaten out the other contenders—all his highfalutin buddies who looked down on the garbage business that had earned him his millions. Tony knew they were his friends, knew they'd stick by him if he ever needed them, but he also knew they looked down on his money. Construction and sewage didn't measure up to diplomacy, architecture, publishing, or Vegas real estate on the glamour meter. But tonight that didn't matter at all. He'd beaten them out of the best Trophy on the island and now he was going to have some fun.

Tony intended to cover the distance to where Marika stood so he could claim his prize, but the combination of vodka and wine had taken a toll. He rose abruptly and unsteadily; the bed-side table tipped, as the lamp and the glass of Stoli he'd brought with him from the bar toppled to the floor. Cursing audibly, he tried to steady himself. *Shit.*

Tony straightened his stocky body up with difficulty, trying to arrest the room in its queasy orbit, then he staggered toward Marika, who was trying not to look as disappointed as she felt. She pulled a silk T-shirt on quickly over her bare skin just as Tony neared her. He reached for her wrist with one hand, and her shirt with the other.

"You don't need that, baby," he muttered, speech slurred by alcohol. "I want to see what I'm getting."

Marika pulled her arm away and tugged down her shirt, de-terminedly; she was annoyed that he'd had too much to drink, but she'd dealt with drunks before. There was no need to fight with him, she reminded herself; if she played it right, he'd be out for the count in another ten minutes and she wouldn't have to hurt his feelings. But it was a real pain that she'd bet on the wrong horse for tonight. How stupid to be the most beautiful woman there, and have landed this drunken lout.

"Be gentle with me, Tony," she purred, edging away from his potent breath. "Marika wants to have some fun with you tonight. Look," she said, pointing toward the bathroom, "this beautiful bathtub should be filled with champagne bubbles. Come bathe with me, and we'll play a little game. . . ."

"Fuck the bubbles," he said gruffly, grabbing her again, harder this time. Marika tried to extricate herself from his grasp, but he was intent on pulling her toward the starkly modern bed across the room.

Marika's uneasy smile was glued in place as she let herself be pulled along—she needed time to think how to escape. It wasn't the thought of sex with him that repelled her, but in his sodden condition tonight, it would be disagreeable sex, and she didn't want that at all. A girl could be hurt by a drunken man too easily, and it would take him forever to come, even if he could maintain an erection, which she doubted. She'd have to cool things down quickly, without offending him.

They reached the bed and Tony pulled her down beside him without ceremony.

"Tony," she said determinedly, as she tried to extricate herself from the sudden tangle of arms and legs. "I don't want to do it this way." She was surprised to find that he had her pinned; she was tall and lithe and had always felt she could protect herself.

"What way do you like it, baby?" he breathed heavily, covering her body smotheringly with his own. Tony's mouth was inches from her face, his heavy body a leaden weight on top of her slender form. "I'll give it to you any way you want it."

Marika tried to pry herself out from under him, but the lock he had on her wrists was powerful, and she felt him pushing his penis against her pelvis; it felt only semihard.

"Tony!" she said, more insistently this time. "Let me go, you're hurting me."

"So you like to play hard-to-get," he breathed into her ear. "I know how to play that game, too." He groped between their bodies for her crotch, and grasping the lace La Perla bikini panties she was wearing, he ripped them in half, hurting her as they tore.

"No!" she said. "Stop that! Get away from me!"

"You little bitch!" he spat, angry now as well as horny. "You're just a little cock-tease, aren't you? Out there strutting your stuff for the boys, laughing up your sleeve while their balls turn blue." His voice was guttural, hostile, and Marika began to panic. This was turning ugly—no one had ever made her feel so out of control before.

"Let me *up,* Tony, right *now!* You're hurting me," she demanded, fear edging her voice. "I can't do it like this!" She struggled against his oppressive bulk and managed with one great wrench to nearly free herself, but Tony reached for her throat with his large hand, pushing her head back onto the bed, stretching her chin upward painfully. His other hand dug into her naked crotch.

Now genuinely terrified, she shouted, "No! Get away from me! Leave me alone!" This was *not* okay. This was not even sex—it was getting to be something else. Mustering every ounce of animal strength she possessed, Marika pushed Tony back, and wrenched herself out from under his grip. She was strong and athletic, even if he did outweigh her by eighty pounds.

She'd nearly made it off the bed when she felt her neck snapped backward so hard that she saw stars, as Tony lunged after her, catching her long loose hair in his hard hands. She screamed, and the blow that interrupted the sound knocked her off the bed completely. Marika hit the floor hard enough to cause a momentary blackout.

Terror flooded her as she tried to scramble up to safety, but he was on top of her again, punching her, strangling her so she couldn't breathe. Blood pounded in her ears with such force that she thought her head would burst wide open. She grabbed for the leg of the table, *anything,* to make a sound, to find a weapon, anything to escape this lunatic.

But he was hard now, and exhilarated; hard with conquest and bloodlust and the need to make her beg. And she wasn't Marika anymore. She was every woman who'd ever mocked him or put him down—every woman who'd ever needed to be shown who was boss. He wanted to pinion her, to plunge his engorged penis right through her body until she begged for mercy. She was clawing at him now, with those cock-tease red nails of hers, the little bitch. And she didn't even look good anymore, tears streaking her mascara down her cheeks. Who the fuck did she think she was, anyway?

Marika managed to free her mouth from his smothering hand and screamed, one long, piercing shriek, before his fingers were around her throat and there wasn't any air to scream with.

"Scream again, cunt, and I'll kill you!" he hissed into her ear as he forced himself between her resistant thighs. He slapped her again and again and again, until her ears rang and her mind numbed.

Marika didn't struggle after that because she knew he meant it, she had seen the bloodlust in his eyes. She just sobbed quietly as he rutted, and even after he was through with her, she lay there where he'd thrown her, hurt and dazed and feeling inexplicably responsible.

Lights were flooding on all over the compound. Marika's shriek had awakened everyone. Jack rose from bed fast and yanked on his trousers as he headed for the door. Thoros was already in the courtyard when he got there.

"What the hell was that?" Jase called from the doorway of his guest pod. "Was that a scream, or an animal of some kind?"

"This was no animal, señor," Emilio said with finality. Jase saw that there was a gun in his hand.

"Knock on doors." Thoros barked the terse order. "Account for everyone."

Rand nodded. "I'll take the west wing. You hit the east, Jack. Tony's in three, Alex in eight. Where are the women?"

"Who the fuck knows," Jack said, moving toward the first guest satellite. "Just start knocking on doors. And don't get your head count screwed up. Tiffany's with me."

Thoros nodded as the other men fanned out. "You're certain it was not an animal, Emilio?" he snapped at the Mexican.

"Not the four-legged kind, señor," the small man replied.

Minutes passed as Thoros stood in the center of his island world, confounded by what was happening.

"I've got everyone accounted for, over on this side," Jase shouted from the far corner. Jack made a thumbs-up sign for his end of the satellites.

"Where are Alex and Tony?" Jase called.

"Tony's in his room, with Marika. Alex is on the beach with Liz," Jack called back.

After their hurried inventory, the men stood for a long moment wondering what to do next. Finally, Thoros spoke. "Everyone seems safe enough for the moment," he said evenly, but there was considerable tension in his voice. He was about to speak again, when Emilio stepped forward definitively.

"I will look further in the morning, señor," he said gravely, as he holstered the 9mm Beretta with practiced authority. "It would be best to look no further tonight." *He already knows what he'll find,* Thoros thought, watching him, *but he's not telling me yet. That means one of my friends is involved in this.* There was an uncanny sixth sense Emilio had possessed as long as Thoros had employed him. The woman, too. He had come to count on them both as his intuitive eyes and ears on any matter that affected his domestic affairs, and although he'd never named the psychic gift they possessed, even to himself, he knew it existed and relied on it.

Thoros tied his robe tighter around him and stared out briefly toward the sea. Nothing must mar this week, or this place—Mora Utu felt like home to him. "There is nothing more we can do tonight," he said finally. Jack, Jase, and Rand looked at one another questioningly, then nodded agreement.

They said good night and Thoros turned back toward the main house, concerned and uneasy. He saw Justine standing silhouetted at the window, looking down.

* * *

Tony closed the door of guest pod 3, after assuring Jack that everything was fine. As far as he knew, Marika was still lying on the floor in the bedroom—maybe she hadn't even heard the knock on the door. She'd seemed pretty far out of it when he left her.

Nervously, he watched the men in the courtyard disperse, and glanced down at the robe he'd thrown on hastily to cover the scratches on his chest. He felt sober now. Sober and sick. Whatever had happened had been *her* fault, but women were funny about sex—they never admitted they were the ones who'd asked for it. He didn't want to go anywhere near her right now.

Marika's head was pounding and she felt disconnected from her body, as if it didn't belong to her. She heard muffled voices below in the house, but they seemed faraway and unimportant.

She pulled herself up unsteadily, intending to go someplace, she wasn't at all sure where. Her legs felt gelatinous under her, but she made her way to the bathroom, nonetheless, and stood in front of the mirror, transfixed by the unfamiliar image. There were ugly bruises forming, and bloody scratches on her breasts and back. Her nipples were scraped red and swollen from Tony's mouth and whiskers. Her private parts felt torn, sore, injured; she touched herself gingerly and winced as the blood that was trickling down her leg came away on her fingers. Her face was streaked with makeup, her hair tangled and matted with sweat. Drugged by exhaustion and the aftermath of adrenaline, she felt sick and numb, as she stared at her naked reflection in the huge mirror. The ghostly pallor staring back in the clean white bathroom light frightened her.

Finally, unable to bear the ravaged, unfamiliar vision of herself, Marika turned on the water in the shower and, zombielike, entered the enclosure. She stood there immobile for a long while, letting the scalding water run over her from head to toe. Finally, she sank to her knees in a sort of modified fetal position, and half lay against the cold marble of the tub, listening to the rainlike sound of the water cascading over her. Letting it blot out everything . . .

Nelida and Emilio stood at the foot of the pool long after the men had returned to their respective guest pods.

"It begins," she said.

He nodded. "Nature will not permit alteration on such a scale."

"Nor disrespect," she added. "There will be a steep price."

"The sexes are part of nature," he said, as if thinking out loud. "It may be more than the jungle which rebels."

"We shall see," she said ominously. "I have no liking for tonight's events."

"These gringos fulfill their destiny. No more, no less."

"Do not speak bullshit to *me*, Emilio. I am a woman . . . one of my kind has been harmed here and I have no liking for this."

"*Estoy ya comprometido al Poder que rige mi destino,*" he said relentlessly. "*Y como no estoy aferrado a nada, no tendré nada que defender.*"

"Sí," she responded after a moment, repeating a mantra learned long ago from her first Naqual. "I am already given to the Power that rules my fate. And I cling to nothing so I will have nothing to defend."

Sunday, April 10

If they could put one man on the moon,
why can't they put them all?

UNKNOWN

FOURTEEN

There was a slight gray haze hanging over the island the following morning, as if the weather reflected everyone's unease at the events of the night before.

Thoros had arranged an all-day junket to the far side of the island as the day's entertainment; the guests had been invited to breakfast early, together in the Great House, rather than in their guest pods. Nelida and Emilio had prepared an elaborate buffet that was now spread out on the terrace overlooking the central pool; the ever-present yellow birds darted in and out of the surrounding foliage to pick eagerly at the feast.

"Thoros, old man," Alex began, as he lifted a slice of mango from the tray of fruit on the sideboard, and landed it neatly near the eggs on his plate. "I think you'd best have a word with your God-friends about this weather. I thought it never rained in Paradise."

Thoros looked up from his coffee. "Don't worry, Alex. Emilio assures me it won't rain, and he's never wrong about the weather."

Jase surveyed the mood of the gathering and decided to give the conversation an upward nudge. "Tell us exactly what you've planned for us today, Thoros. Are we going in those jitneys of yours or on horseback? I noticed there were several Thoroughbreds and two Appaloosas in the stables."

Thoros was about to reply when Marika appeared on the veranda, the last to join the assemblage. She murmured a subdued response to everyone's greeting, her demeanor curiously reserved and unlike her usual studied ebullience. She said nothing as she made her way down the buffet line, picking a few pieces of fruit and a small slice of raisin bread from the heavily laden trays. Something in her body language caught Liz's attention and she walked over to where Marika stood staring listlessly at the buffet table.

"My God, Marika!" she said at the sight of the bruises on her cheek and throat. "What happened to you?"

All eyes riveted on the latecomer.

"I fell," Marika said quietly. "It's nothing, really."

On instant alert, Christie moved in closer. "Nothing? Don't be crazy—that's a really bad bruise on your neck. You don't get that kind of bruise from a fall."

Marika turned to Christie, eyes full of pleading. "Please," she said urgently, "don't make a fuss. It's nothing, really. I just don't want to talk about it." Her accent seemed more pronounced than they'd ever heard it, her demeanor radically changed.

Christie instinctively glanced toward Tony, who was watching them with eyes slightly narrowed; he looked like he'd stopped breathing. *What have we here?* Her reporter's instinct cataloged details, click, click, click. Something was way out of whack. Something that had to do with whatever had awakened them last night.

Alex and Jase tried to keep the conversation moving, and a

few of the women pitched in, but it was obvious that everyone was edgy now.

"Let's meet back here in thirty minutes," Thoros said, trying to impose his will on the scene. "We'll take the jitneys and a picnic lunch—Emilio has loaded in snorkeling and fishing gear, so you'll want to bring along whatever you think you'll need to spend the day and perhaps the evening outside the compound."

The men dispersed quickly, but the women, as if at a predetermined signal among themselves, all remained behind.

Christie spoke first, after the last man had departed. "Okay, Marika, what's the real story here? You didn't fall down any flight of stairs."

Marika's eyes were sullen, angry when she looked up from her plate. "Can't you just leave it alone?" she demanded, voice on knife edge.

Liz moved in closer. "We all heard someone scream last night, Marika. Was it you?"

"I can't talk about it," she said determinedly, her Nordic face simultaneously defiant and vulnerable. "I don't want to spoil things."

Francesca moved closer to the group. "That's bullshit, Marika," she snapped. "If something or somebody hurt you, we have a right to know. You're not alone on this island, you know."

Tiffany stood up quickly and moved toward the coffeepot to get Marika a cup. "Wait a minute, everybody—let's not gang up on the girl. Maybe she's trying to deal with whatever happened in her own way, and she'd like us to give her some space."

"Did Tony rough you up?" Christie probed, ignoring Tiffany completely. "I assume it was Tony you were with after the party."

"It's none of your business," Marika said, standing up, ready to flee. "I can handle this!" She looked like a deer caught in the headlights.

"It *is* our business if one of these men is a sadistic son of a bitch who beats up on women," Christie pursued adamantly.

"What do *you* care?" Marika blazed, facing her. "None of you like me anyway. You're probably glad my face is swollen and ugly!" Her voice was pitched too high, and she seemed on the verge of hysteria; her arms were folded protectively over her chest. Liz and Tiffany exchanged glances.

"Listen, Marika," Liz said quickly. "None of us gives a rat's ass about your face, to be honest. We all know you're gorgeous, swollen or not. We also know something lousy probably happened to you last night and we're trying to find out what. And, I don't know about the rest of you women, but I don't intend to go traipsing around in the woods with this crowd if there's a macho creep among them who likes to use his fists on women."

Justine had been silent until now, listening, watching; she knew she'd just heard the death knell of their idyllic week in Mora Utu. And, perhaps, more than that.

"Marika," she said, her beautifully manicured accent caressing the name. "I assure you I respect your wish to keep private whatever has transpired. But I also believe you must understand everyone's concern. If Tony, or anyone else, is dangerous in any way, it would be best for us to know of this for our own safety—we are, after all, rather isolated here on Mora Utu." Her matter-of-fact tone had a quieting effect on Marika, who was now standing with her back to the others, staring at the pool.

"Beyond all that, we are concerned for *you,* as clearly someone has harmed you. Having said all that, if you still wish to maintain your privacy on this matter, I believe we should all respect your choice."

Marika remained silent for another moment, then turned her face to the group. Tears were streaming down her cheeks, but neither the tears nor her bruises detracted appreciably from her startling beauty. "He raped me," she said softly, to no one in particular. "He beat me and he raped me." Her voice was more vulnerable than they'd heard it before.

"Bastard!" Chesi spat for all of them, amid a chorus of angry murmurings.

"What happened?" Christie pressed. "He was pretty sloshed when he left the party." She resisted a strong urge to whip out her camera and start taking pictures.

Tiffany put down the coffee cup and reached out to take Marika's hand into her own, wanting to make some human gesture of comfort, not knowing what it should be.

Marika sat down, bone-straight in a chair, a child in Mother Superior's office. Her voice was a hoarse monotone as she told her story. At one point, she opened the front of her shirt carefully to expose the scratches and the wide welts on her breasts, her usual ease at displaying her body replaced by an awkward hesitancy. The women looked and listened in shocked silence until she'd finished.

"She seems more embarrassed than angry," Liz whispered to Christie, "like she thinks *she* screwed up."

Christie nodded. "Raped women do that. They always blame themselves. *I should have stopped it, should have made him stop, should have seen it coming, should have worn a larger shroud*—you know, all the mind-fucks. I had the police beat, when I was a rookie reporter on my hometown newspaper. It used to frost my petunias to hear those poor battered women blame themselves, when their husbands and boyfriends should have been hanged, drawn, and quartered for what they did to them."

"I don't know about you girls," Chesi said, "but I don't feel much in the mood for romping around the island with the Boys Club, like nothing's happened. I think I'll ask for a rain check."

Justine nodded. "Tiffany," she said imperiously, as if giving direction to a servant, "why don't you take Marika back to her room so she can freshen up a bit. I think perhaps we women should have a chat amongst ourselves how to handle this extraordinary occurrence."

Tiffany ignored both the tone and the order.

Marika's head came up sharply. "No!" she nearly shouted. "I don't want *anyone* to *handle* anything. I don't want this week spoiled by this awful man. I'll just stay away from him. . . ."

"Don't be crazy," Christie snapped. "If you stay away from him, somebody else gets him. He's out of here, or I am."

"I will talk to Thoros," Justine put in, calmly, confidently.

"I think we should *all* talk to Thoros," Liz interrupted. "And I think we should make it clear that Capuletti has to go immediately."

"No!" Marika cried out. "Don't you see? Everything will be ruined! This week is important to me. I don't want it to be my fault that everything's ruined."

"Don't be an ass," Christie said bluntly. "It's all over anyway after this. How are we all going to sit around making chitchat with a rapist? As to it being your fault, that's a lot of guilty horseshit. You said no, that should have been *that.* Rape isn't sex, it's violence."

"She's right of course," Justine added definitively. "He was an idiot, and he has forfeited any right to our company. The only gentlemanly thing will be for him to depart. Thoros will make him see that."

Liz stood up as if she'd made up her mind. "I'd like to appoint myself spokeswoman if nobody else wants the job. My period's due in a few days so I'm in just the right mood for this. If anybody gives me a hard time, I'll eat his liver."

"I'll go with you," Justine said authoritatively.

"Would you like a backup delegation?" Chesi asked.

Justine smiled, as if to say, What need could there be for that? "It will seem less dramatic if we don't go *en masse.* We don't want to polarize them, after all. I will simply tell Thoros that Tony must leave. He is a civilized man. I'm sure he'll handle this appropriately."

Liz and Justine headed toward where they'd seen Jack and Thoros in conversation, as Tiffany pointed Marika in the direction of her guesthouse. She did it out of kindness, not to follow any order from Justine.

Christie made a wry face at Chesi. "Five to one our 'civilized' host sides with the Boys Club."

Chesi pursed her lips before replying. "That's not a bet, that's a sure thing."

Thoros let the Babel of enraged men's voices spend itself a little before taking control of the meeting in his study. The furrows that crisscrossed his forehead looked deeper than usual; his mouth was a single chiseled line. He had delivered the women's demand that Tony leave, knowing exactly what it would provoke in his friends; as he waited out the respondent explosion, he felt furious at Tony's consummate stupidity, and equally furious at the women's outrageous demand that he be banished.

"She was asking for it," Tony was saying, all his bovine tenacity in the belligerent tone. "This is all bullshit."

"Bullshit or not, my friend," Thoros answered relentlessly, "you're going to have to deal with it."

"Why the fuck did you have to rape her?" Jase put in angrily. "She was more available than Heidi Fleiss's girls." This would make lousy publicity if it got out, and Jase didn't need that.

"Look," Jack cut in. "What's done is done. The real question is do we just pack it in for the week, or is there some way to salvage the *Titanic*?"

"Have you considered letting me try a little negotiation?" Alex asked confidently. "That is, after all, what I do for a living. Gorby and George, Yeltsin and Bill, Arafat and Begin . . . I should be able to handle a gaggle of pissed-off women with one brain lobe tied behind my back."

Jack laughed out loud. "Yeah, right. I'd take Russians and Palestinians any day in the week. They're talking rape here, guys . . . not a lousy choice of restaurant."

Rand was seated at Thoros's left, seemingly lost in thought, his elbows on his knees, one hand cradling his jaw. His ice-blue eyes were full of calculation, and his jaw tight when he spoke. "You can forget negotiation here. It won't work. But bribery might."

All eyes were on him as if E. F. Hutton had spoken.

"Like what?" Jack asked.

"I don't know, exactly. But some princely sum that will look too good to refuse. From what I've seen of the lovely Marika, she's up for sale. Why not buy her silence?"

Thoros raised an eyebrow, then nodded encouragement. "I *would* prefer that we try to salvage the ten days we've all put aside," he said, wondering if that was still possible. "I'd like to put this unfortunate incident behind us as quickly and sensitively as possible. Bribery might be a solution."

"I'm not paying that cunt-tease one fucking red cent," Tony exploded, looking aggrieved. "That bitch isn't extorting money from me—"

"Can it, Tony!" Jack cut in. "You fuck up, you pay up. She's not going to turn down fifty G's."

"Fifty G's!" Tony exploded. "You're out of your fucking mind. I wouldn't pay fifty grand to the Virgin Mary."

"Grow up!" Jase shouted over his bellowing. "This is a fucking disaster you've created, Capuletti. And it's our asses in a sling, as well as yours, if you don't ante up, or else come up with a better game plan. Do you have any idea what kind of damage those broads could do to us, if this story gets out? The newspapers eat this kind of shit up, and one of those girls is a frigging TV reporter, for Christ's sake. Not to mention what it could cost us in alimony if this gets back to the wives. So quit your bellyaching, and get your wallet out, before this turns into a first-class fiasco. . . ."

The sobering thought left silence in its wake. Thoros cleared his throat. "Unless any of you men has a better solution,

I think Rand's suggestion makes good sense. I'm not certain fifty thousand is the right figure, however. We can't turn this into a camel sale; the first offer has to be the last offer. I say we ante up a hundred thousand dollars—fifty from Tony, fifty from the rest of us. That should amply compensate the young lady for her bruises. I'll make everyone's silence the proviso, of course." He turned to Alex. "Perhaps you'd like to come with me on this rather delicate mission."

"What if they say no?" Jack asked, standing up.

Thoros smiled the horse trader's smile they all knew well.

"She won't say no."

FIFTEEN

Liz and Justine sat in the large garden listening to Thoros explain the men's position. It was just an unfortunate incident . . . shouldn't mar this lovely week . . . who's to say what really happened, behind closed doors . . . she was certainly aware of his sexual intent before going to his room . . .

"Excuse me," Liz broke in to the soliloquy. "You forgot one."

Thoros stopped, annoyed. "One what?"

"One cliché about rape," she replied amiably. "The one about 'she was asking for it.' That's a good one. Wouldn't want to leave that out."

Alex, who'd remained silent, interrupted quickly. "Let's not call it rape, my dear. That's the kind of emotionally explosive word that tends to unnerve people. After all, we don't *really* know what went on in that bedroom, do we?"

"But of course we do, *my dear,*" Liz shot back. "We know that a man abused a woman. That he physically overpowered her, and injured her, and had sex with her against her will. I'm reasonably certain that the bruises on Marika's throat and breasts are not self-inflicted. The word *rape* is certainly explosive, but surely you do see how applicable it is."

Thoros's eyebrows overlooked a scowl of epic proportion. "Let's put emotions aside here," he said, forcing his temper down. "Tony went too far—he says he was provoked; who's to say where the truth lies short of that. He's prepared to make it right—to do that he's given me a check for a hundred thousand dollars to hand to Marika to compensate her for her little problem last night. I feel that he's being more than generous and there's no need for him to leave."

The eyes of the two women locked for an instant across the intervening space before Liz rose to her feet angrily. "*Compensate* her for last night?" she said hotly. "Like a high-priced hooker gets compensated? Tell him to put it back in his pants!"

Justine touched her arm to stay her. "I believe we must let Marika decide for *herself* about this money, Liz—it isn't ours to reject," she amended quietly; some emotion that was hard to categorize underlay the words. She turned to Thoros. "But I'm afraid I do not find this man's offer generous—I find it offensive. I am *offended* by his actions, *and* by his idea of compensation. Furthermore, I do not choose to continue in his company. He is an uncivilized brute, Thoros. You cannot possibly imagine that we women can be comfortably in his presence after this, nor could we treat him as anything but a pariah."

"You can't be serious," Thoros responded harshly.

"Indeed, I am serious. But I am also civilized and therefore have no wish to interfere with anyone else's holiday, so I'll simply leave it at this: If Mr. Capuletti remains, I shall not."

"I'll second that," Liz added, "as will all the other women."

"Ladies, ladies," Alex cut in quickly. "This is really getting out of control. It was admittedly a nasty incident, one we all wish hadn't happened . . . but that's *all* it was. And it needn't affect everyone's life so dramatically. Tony's willing to make public amends. Why not let Marika decide for herself whether Tony's check sufficiently reflects his genuine regret over what happened."

Justine smiled, a very feline expression. "One can see how splendidly you must handle diplomatic negotiations, Alex. I remember hearing it said of you that you could cut someone's throat and he'd never notice, but I do think you are rather missing the point, here." She turned to go.

Thoros reached out and grasped her arm. "This is absurd, Justine," he said angrily. "You've got to calm down."

"*Calm down?*" she answered with considerable disdain, shrugging his hand away. "One wonders if *that* particular phrase has ever been used on a man." The two women walked away, their sandals slapping briskly against the garden stone.

"Damnation!" Thoros spat, his voice low and harsh. "It is impossible to negotiate with a woman. No matter what their intellect or their occupation, they think with their hearts and their cunts, never with their brains."

Anger radiated from Thoros like a forcefield. His week in Paradise, *his* Paradise, was jeopardized and he was furious.

"And what do you want to do about Capuletti?" Alex prompted.

"He is one of us, and he has been my friend for too many years to allow this stupidity to intervene. There isn't a man here who doesn't owe Tony *something*, you know that as well as I do. But he was a fucking imbecile to do what he did. He was a goddamned *fool* to put this particular fat into the fire."

Alex was about to reply, but Thoros had turned abruptly and departed, walking back to the main house, where the other men awaited word of the confrontation with the women.

Alex shook his head, and followed at a slower pace. This was just the kind of emotional kindling from which large conflagrations could spring. Violent acts beget more violence. Wasn't there something Baudelaire had said on that subject? He rifled the poetry card index in his brain as he walked, and made a mental note to ask Liz. She had the most extraordinary supply of literary knowledge at her fingertips; it made her quite an entertaining companion, really.

He hoped this wouldn't be war, but it certainly had all the classic earmarks. In fact, he thought as he fell in step with Thoros, the week might just have taken a turn for the very interesting.

"Fuck the lot of them," Shindler snorted derisively, when Thoros had recounted Justine and Liz's preliminary response to their offer of money. "There are more where they came from."

"Oh, really?" Alex replied. "Why don't we just fly in a busload for your delectation, Jase? I'm sure Justine would be happy to run a flying pimp service for you." Unlike the others, he had no illusions about the situation being easy to resolve.

"Wait a minute," Jack put in, hotly. "Let's not screw around here, guys. We need some damage control on this mess, pretty damned quick. If they hightail it out of here and squawk about rape, we're all in deep shit."

"Jack's right," Rand agreed; the last thing he needed in his PR paradise was a scandal. "Tony, I think it's in everybody's best interest if you go and apologize to this woman *personally.* You can give her the money or not, as you and she see fit, and we can calm this thing down before it escalates out of control."

"Apologize my ass!" Tony exploded. "I'd like to deck the little bitch."

"Which is how this all began, if you recall," Alex shouted. "You'd better get that temper of yours under control, *now,* my friend. And I *don't* think it's a good idea for you to go anywhere near *any* of the women, never mind Marika, with tempers running this high. First of all, let's wait for Marika's reply . . . *she* hasn't yet said no. After that, let Thoros and me handle it."

"Then *handle* it, for Christ's sake," Jase said angrily. "This is one fucking pain in the ass."

Rand smiled. "You mean you're not having fun yet, Jase?"

"I mean maybe Tony should *go*, rather than screw up the week for everybody. As a matter of fact, why don't they *both* go. Marika can spend her ill-gotten gains, and Tony can go construct a sewer somewhere and the rest of us can get back to the business of having a good time."

"You got a problem with my line of work, Shindler?" Tony growled. "It makes me a piss pot more money than your namby-pamby editor crap does."

"Gentlemen!" Thoros barked ferociously. "Sniping at each other will get us *nowhere.* Tony has been our friend since we were all boys. He made a mistake—we all do—and he's offered to make amends. Alex, you and I will calm these damned women down, whatever it takes, and by God, then we will proceed with our plans for the day."

Everyone on earth thought negotiating was an easy task that anyone could handle, Alex ruminated grimly, as he followed Thoros from the room. It would be fascinating to watch this debacle unfold; it might actually make a useful case study for his senior graduate students, with the names changed. A case study in what happens when you underestimate your opponent.

"A hundred thousand dollars!" Marika burst out when the story of the meeting with Thoros and Alex had been recounted by Justine. "That's incredible."

"It sure as hell is incredible," Chesi cut in vehemently. "These fine, cultured gentlemen are nothing but nicely disguised pigs!"

Christie cleared her throat. "Let's get real here, girls. This is one hell of a story we have coming to a boil. These guys are national news. A juicy sex-and-money scandal about the likes of these bozos would be bigger than Tailhook."

Justine wrinkled her nose in distaste. "Offensive as the

thought of that would be, it makes a superb negotiating point for us. I'm sorry I didn't think of it."

"I will *not* turn down a hundred thousand dollars," Marika said stubbornly, mixing up her *v*s and *w*s. "What's done is done and I can't undo it. Why should I not have this money?"

"Because you're putting a price on your body, that's *vy*," Liz replied, hotly. "It's tantamount to saying to that crummy son of a bitch, 'You can beat me and rape me and ignore my humanity as long as you pay me for the privilege.' " She turned to face the other women. "And while we're on the subject, it sure as hell puts a crimp in my enthusiasm for staying here for ten days with a bunch of creeps who think that's okay."

"Don't kid yourself, honey," Tiffany said. "*All* guys would think that's okay."

"A chilling thought, that," Chesi said with disgust. "But you're probably right."

"You're in a really weird position here, aren't you, Chesi?" Liz added, realization dawning. "You work for Rand—does that mean you're stuck here if he stays and we go?"

Francesca looked thoughtful for a silent moment, the frown making her face very serious. "If it comes to a showdown, I'm out of here with the rest of you. If I can avoid it coming down to that, it would probably be better for my career."

"Your career with Rand is history anyway," Christie said definitively. "Do you really think you can go back to the way things were after this whole botch? I don't think so."

"She has a point," Justine said. "Nothing will be as it was, now—we will all be walking on eggs until this man leaves. Even then . . ." She raised her eyebrows eloquently, then straightened visibly, as if she'd come to a conclusion.

"I propose we give them an ultimatum, which Liz and I will relay to the men. Capuletti goes immediately, or we all go. I'll fly us out of here tomorrow morning—I think the week's amusements are over in any case. This has all become far too awkward for pleasure."

"No!" Marika said petulantly. "You're all *crazy.* I want that money."

"Get *serious,* Marika," Christie said harshly. "What exactly are you planning to do? Take the money, keep Tony here, and then you go on the prowl for somebody else's date, or *everybody* else's date? If you take the money and we all stay as if nothing happened, it's like we *all* accepted the offer, and I, for one, think that sucks. So, I'm with Justine—let's blow this pop stand. And they sure as hell can't keep us from blabbing once we get home."

Justine and Liz waited at the appointed spot to deliver the women's final rejection of the men's offer.

Thoros's canny eyes took in their body language as he approached. There was anger in their demeanor, and bravado . . . also fear of some kind. That was useful, he thought, intuition in high gear; fear could be manipulated.

Justine spoke first. "Marika has decided not to take the money you've offered, Thoros," she said directly. "And I'm afraid we must tell you the decision of all the women is to leave here immediately, if Tony does not go."

"That's absolutely absurd, Justine!" Thoros responded in his most commanding tone, the one that cowed most underlings. He was genuinely shocked by the refusal. "You're reacting like a child. Tony is my guest, and I think he's made a damned fine offer here."

"He's a damned fine kind of guy by your standards, right, Thoros?" Liz put in dryly. "But by *our* standards, he's a rapist. So either he goes or we all go."

"This is *my* island," Thoros snapped, his voice tightly controlled. "And Tony is *my* guest here. How dare you presume to issue me ultimata? If you women weren't so pigheaded, you'd see that Tony's doing the right thing. That slut provoked him. . . ."

Justine's eyes narrowed, but Liz spoke first. "That's what we all are to you, isn't it, Thoros?" she said with considerable hostility. "Well, we *sluts* think this could make a fine story for the media. 'Sex Lives of the Rich and Famous . . .' "

"Don't threaten me, you little fool," Thoros warned low and angrily. "You don't know who you're dealing with. This is my island, and what happens here is private and privileged. If one word of this leaks out to the press . . ."

"You'll *what*?" Liz snapped. "Sic another one of your friends on us?"

Justine stepped between them. "Now who's threatening whom, Thoros?" she demanded. "This discussion is over. And so is your little holiday—we have no intention of remaining here beyond today. As to your threats . . . surely you know I have every bit as influential friends as you do, Thoros, a number of whom would revel in having an exclusive on this little tale of how you and your delightful friends frolic on your holidays. So get out of my way, and let me leave this island before I forget myself."

Justine pushed past the two men, with Liz at her heels. Thoros and Alex exchanged looks, Alex thanking his stars he'd kept his mouth shut. This mess was best left in Thoros's hands, so there'd be no recriminations later.

"I don't think we can let them go in the frame of mind they're in," Thoros said with great seriousness, after he'd recounted to the other men what had taken place at the meeting. "They're distorting the hell out of this, and it's escalating on a sliding scale of hormones. By the time these women get home, the story will have grown into a media monster."

"Short of tying them to a palm tree, I don't see how you can stop them," Jack said. "Justine can fly them all out of here, just like she flew them in."

"Let me ask a hypothetical question here," Rand said, seriously. "We could disable the plane, couldn't we? Just to give us enough time for everyone's head to clear."

Heads came up, all eyes on full alert.

"We *could* do that," Shindler replied, carefully, leaning forward. "Hell, Capuletti, Doherty, and I were all in the service, we know our way around planes. Thoros, you *own* the damn thing, you certainly know how to screw it up long enough for us to do some damage control with these bimbos."

Thoros nodded judiciously. "We *could* disable the radios and dismantle part of the electrical system, without a hell of a lot of trouble. That'd be easy enough to reconstruct later, so we could still use the plane."

"Are you guys *nuts*?" Jack asked, genuinely startled. "If you think they're pissed off now, what'll we have on our hands if we try to hold them prisoner?"

"We don't want to hold them prisoner, exactly, Jack," Rand amended. "Just give them time to cool down. They'll have made their statement, gotten it all off their chests as women love to do . . . and we'll have given it a chance to blow over. After a day or so of lying on the beach, they won't even remember what all the fuss was about."

Jack shook his head emphatically. "No *way!* You guys are absolutely crazy. Those girls aren't bimbos, they're damn well smart enough to tell us to go fuck ourselves in spades. If you're not careful, this thing could really blow up on us."

"I think Rand's right," Thoros said judiciously. "We need to buy some time to get back in the women's good graces. Let's put it to a vote. Any dissenters besides Jack?"

Reluctantly, heads were shaken no all around the room.

SIXTEEN

"There must be a book somewhere that teaches men all the same half-witted lines," Liz said with disgust, slamming down the lid of her suitcase.

"You mean like *calm down, stop acting childish, you're being too emotional,* and *are you expecting your period?*" Tiffany responded with a grim laugh. She hated leaving this place, just when things were going so well with Jack. And who knew if he'd even remember to call her, once they were back in New York and there were a million girls throwing themselves at him. But there really wasn't any choice at all since the rape.

Tiffany knew all about rape, firsthand. She was fifteen years old when her only sister had been raped and murdered. Sweet, beautiful Alana had never made it home from school that day that would live in Tiffany's heart forever, somewhere deep, where no one else could ever reach the hurt. An alley, a knife, a man who'd raped before, who would spend a total of eight months behind bars as payment for what he'd done; these were the memories called forth by the word. That's why she'd studied karate, so she'd never be powerless; advancing to 3rd Dan black belt rank before she began to feel safe.

Justine called to the two women from the doorway. "I'm headed for the plane, Liz, Tiffany. Please don't take too long getting there. Conditions are perfect for flying right now. I'd rather not tempt fate, and I don't want to get back to Oahu too late."

Tiffany picked up her two bags. "Yes, massa, right away, massa," she said to the retreating figure with an Uncle Tom grimace. Justine was already halfway down the walk and either didn't hear her or didn't care to acknowledge it, but Liz did.

"It's hard not to get your back up with her majesty's imperial attitude, isn't it?" she sympathized. "Justine is a tough act."

"Am I oversensitive, or does she always seem to be giving me orders like I'm the maid?"

Liz smiled knowingly. "To Justine, my dear, I'm afraid we're *all* the maid." The two hefted their suitcases and started walking toward the landing strip; the jitneys and both Mexicans were nowhere to be found.

"How will Thoros get his plane back?" Liz called out to Justine when they'd almost caught up with her.

"I'll leave it with his fleet captain," Justine answered, "and tell him to return to pick up the men. I don't imagine they'll stay the week without us, do you? Oh, and by the way, Liz, I'd like you to use that total recall of yours on the flight manual, once we're inside. It really takes two to land these aircraft, but if you familiarize yourself with the manual, I may be able to talk you through it."

"Oh, great," Liz said dryly. "I think I saw that scene in *Airport '79*."

On the runway, the G-IV lay sleek as a winged dolphin in the early morning sun, heat waves radiating off its shiny surface. Justine eyed the plane with practiced concern as she neared the runway; the doors were open, as if someone had disembarked only moments before. She dropped her bags on the concrete, and approached the plane at a run, suspicion propelling her; something didn't feel right.

Justine entered the cockpit and sat in the left seat, staring at the instrument console. She began the requisite prestart procedures. Agitatedly, she flipped the Aircraft Master switch to the On position, expecting the usually responsive beeps and whines of the EFIS and EICAS systems as they came on line, but there was only silence.

Frowning, Justine hit the Avionics Master switch and pressed the Push to Talk switch. Again, nothing. No electrical power. Dead.

"*Merde*!" she breathed, angry and frustrated at having been outwitted. "Sabotage," she said over her shoulder to Tiffany, who was standing directly behind her. "They've grounded us."

"What does *that* mean?" Liz asked, pushing forward.

"It means those bastards have disabled this aircraft's electrical systems." There was a fury building inside Justine that took her by surprise. This plane was *hers* as long as she was captain. It was the law of the skies, just as it had been of the seas for millennia. *No one* fucks with your craft while it's under your command. Not without paying a steep price.

"You mean we're prisoners here?" Marika asked with concern. Tiffany saw real fear in her face, and understood; once you've been utterly powerless, captivity takes on a whole new dimension.

"Prisoners?" latecomer Christie prompted, pushing her way forward. "They wouldn't have the balls!"

Liz cast a withering look her way and ignored the ridiculous statement. "What now?" she asked Justine.

The woman in the pilot's seat turned to face the others, now all squeezed in behind her in the cockpit. "I'm afraid they have disabled both the aircraft *and* the radio," she said quietly, but there was banked fury underlying her words. "They intend to keep us here, apparently. For how long, and for what purpose, I can't say."

"My God!" Marika whined. "I knew I should just have taken that money. Now look what you've done!"

"Shut up about the fucking money, will you?" Christie exploded. "You don't even know if that check would ever have cleared a bank. Tony might have written it without any intention of ever honoring it. Like, maybe you noticed he's not such an honorable guy."

"I think I'd rather sleep in the plane than carry those suitcases back to the house," Tiffany said, wearily.

"Actually," Chesi piped up, "that might not be such a bad idea, Tiffany. I mean, after this, do any of us really want to go back there with our tails between our legs, and make nice-nice with these creeps over dinner? We're out, bag and baggage, now—maybe we should *stay* out."

"You mean stage a *Lysistrata*?" Liz asked, intrigued by the notion.

Tiffany looked puzzled. "What's that?"

"The women of ancient Troy felt abused by their husbands," Liz explained, "so they staged a rebellion. No sex, no cooking, no cleanup—no wives."

"Did it work?"

"Is the Pope Catholic?"

"Rebellion sounds great to me in principle," Tiffany said, "but what do we do for room service?" She laughed, a little nervously. "I mean, are you really suggesting we stay *outside* the compound to stage this uprising and leave them in there, with all the good stuff? Are we stupid or what?"

"I'm suggesting *just* that," Chesi answered, moving to the front of the cockpit beside the co-pilot's seat, to face the rest.

"You see, *they* don't know how to run that compound, and we could sabotage its systems pretty easily from outside, if we wanted to. Then they'd be *in*, but without air-conditioning, or clean water, they might not *want* to be in."

Christie shook her head, disbelieving. "Don't be crazy. Rand's in there. He designed the whole place. He'll just fix whatever you break."

Chesi grinned. "Rand didn't design Mora Utu, Christie—a man named John Mackey did. And *I'm* the Project Coordinator—I know every nut, bolt, and wire on a first-name basis. Trust me, if the electricity fails in there, Rand will be lucky if he can find the light switch. I could make their lives miserable one system at a time, and he couldn't do a damned thing about it." She looked pleased at the prospect.

"But even if all that's true," Tiffany persisted, "we'll still be out here in the heat, with the mosquitoes and the creepy crawlies . . . and without any supplies. I think I'm gonna hate sleeping with snakes."

"For my money, we'd be sleeping with snakes whether we're in or out," Liz said, warming to the Lysistrata idea. "I, for one, would like to teach those arrogant sidewinders a lesson. Besides, now I'm really concerned about how far they're willing to take this thing, aren't you? I mean, what if we're in danger from them now that we're prisoners, like in *The Most Dangerous Game*? Next thing you know, they'll be giving us a five-minute start on the hounds."

Christie, undecided, turned to Chesi. "Could we steal what we need first? I mean, is there a way into the compound that we could loot through? Essentials. You know, medical supplies, food, blankets, tampons, whatever. That would even up the odds, at least."

Chesi was on solid ground now. "Absolutely. There are HVAC ducts big enough for us to get in and out with what we need before they ever know what hit them."

"HVAC?" Marika asked.

"Heating, ventilation, air-conditioning," Chesi replied absently, her mind now on overdrive. "I could hit the work trailers and load up on schematics and blueprints and whatever tools we'll need to do the job. If everybody agrees, of course."

"But I *don't* agree!" Marika snapped angrily. "I'm *afraid* out here without the men. I want to go back."

"You know, Marika, you're a real pain in the ass," Christie said, acid in her voice. "You're the reason we're out here in this fix in the first place."

Liz interjected quickly, "Look, I think going back in there could be a little dicey right now for all of us. Besides, if Chesi's right and we can even up the odds, I'll bet we could make them eat crow."

"The first odds we must alter," Justine said judiciously, "are those of this aircraft." She leaned down beneath the control panel, in search of something.

"What do you mean?"

"They think they've clipped our wings? Let's pull their tail feathers. Right now, Thoros thinks he can rewire this bird and leave on *his* own timetable. They've probably removed the engine igniters and the ignition boxes. If I take the fuel controllers, those bastards will never get out of here without coming to terms with us."

"You mean we could hold part of the plane hostage, too?"

"Exactly," Justine said, with a satisfied smirk. "Who knows how far they're willing to take this piracy. If they get nasty, we may need all the leverage we can muster. There's a tool kit under here somewhere; I'm no mechanic, but I do know the basic structure. . . ."

"*I'm* a mechanic," Tiffany offered, eagerly. "Really. My brother owns a filling station. I've been taking cars apart since I was twelve. And, I've got a real talent for engines—a feel, you know? A gift."

Justine laughed. "Bravo!" she said, holding up the toolbox triumphantly. "Let's show the boys what we're made of."

"Wait a minute!" Christie interrupted. "We haven't voted on this."

Justine looked at her as if she were a cretin. "Do we have a choice, really? If we allow them this piracy without a fight, we are totally in their power." She looked around, a queen sweeping the throne room full of servants. "Does anyone disagree with me?" she asked.

"Off with their heads!" Liz whispered to Tiffany, who grinned, then reached for the toolbox.

"Come on, sister," she said to Justine, amused that the high and mighty one now needed her services. "We got us some work to do."

"Wait a minute! Shouldn't we figure out where to stay before we do anything else?" Christie asked, pragmatically. "I mean, if we're not inside the compound, we have to be *somewhere*."

Liz broke in, "Alex and I went hiking yesterday . . . we really covered a lot of ground. I know a perfect spot for us, if I can remember how to get there . . . all these damned palm trees look alike, you know. It had running water, near a waterfall, so it's probably drinkable, and it's protected by jungle, but there's a clearing without all that undergrowth. . . ."

"How far away is it?" Christie asked, mournfully. "These suitcases Arnold Schwarzenegger couldn't carry."

Liz shook her head. "We'll never make it in one trip with these bags unless we can steal something with wheels."

"Maybe you should go scout out the possible campsite to see if it's suitable, Liz," Chesi said sensibly. "We can all carry in what we need, later, if it turns out to be the right place for us. Tiffany and Justine can do their thing with the plane first, while I get the blueprints, then we've all got the rest of the day to get organized before the men realize what we're up to. I just don't want Rand to get to the tools before I do."

"Why can't we just go back to the compound?" Marika whined, her accent more pronounced now.

Liz turned to her. "Look, Marika. They've disabled our escape route. For all intents and purposes, we're their prisoners on this island ten million miles from nowhere." She turned to the others for corroboration. "Did you guys tell anyone *exactly* where you were going? I didn't even *know* where the hell Mora Utu was—all I told anybody was that I was going to Hawaii with my boss. How do we know what lengths these guys will go to keep this thing quiet? We could be in real danger here, and nobody's even going to miss us for another nine days."

"You don't really think they'd harm us, do you?" Justine asked, incredulously. "After all, they're covering up rape, not murder."

"Did you really think they'd sabotage this plane?" Liz replied caustically.

Justine pursed her lips, but didn't refute the logic.

"We've all heard rumors about how rich, powerful men can make people disappear, if they need to," Chesi said, thoughtfully. "I just never quite believed it."

"They can't disappear *all* of us," Liz said. "There are too damned many of us."

Christie made a wry face. "Don't be so naive. There aren't too many of us for an accident of some kind to be believable. They could claim there was a plane crash, or a boating accident, or some crazy mishap, miles from nowhere—then they could get rid of us all in one fell swoop. They say those BCCI guys and their black ops did that kind of thing all the time for their big-business constituents."

"Really!" Justine said, with disdain. "Don't you think you're all being absurdly paranoid?"

"There's a psychiatrist I date sometimes," Liz put in. "He has this great sign in his office that says, '*Just because you're not paranoid, doesn't mean they're not watching you.*' "

Laughter lightened the tension a little.

"Look," Liz pressed. "I think we all know we can't go back

in there till Tony goes, and they start treating us like equals. We don't *really* know anything much about these jerks, except what we've read in the papers, right? So, I vote we take this one step at a time. Let's get a campsite, steal what we need to let them know we're really pissed—and after that the ball's in their court. I have a feeling we'll find out their intentions soon enough. Okay?"

After some murmuring, everyone agreed. "Then let's steal a couple of horses while we're at it," Chesi added. "We can use them for transportation and baggage carrying."

Marika looked up sharply. "I grew up on a farm outside of Stockholm," she said, the first bit of cooperation she'd shown. "I could get the horses for us."

Christie and Liz exchanged glances. Nobody trusted Marika to go anywhere near the men alone.

"I'll go with you, Marika," Justine put in quickly. "I grew up on horses too."

"But not on a *farm*, I'll bet," Christie said snidely.

Justine nearly curled her lip when she spoke. "What *matters* is not where I grew up, but that I'm an expert rider. Do you have a problem with that?"

"I have a problem with everything that's happened for the past twenty-four hours," Christie retorted. "And I don't give a rat's ass if your mother was a centaur, if it'll help get us out of here. But, before we go camping, or shinnying up any drainpipes to steal supplies, I suggest we just walk right back into that compound, and pick the cupboard bare. There's a helluva lot of stuff in those guest pods we can steal before they know their asses from half past two!" Without waiting for a reply, she turned and headed back toward the house.

Justine frowned after her. "She's right, of course, obnoxious though I find her. We might as well take what we can before they realize the war's on. And we should divide up for efficiency's sake. Liz, you take somebody with you to check out the campsite. Tiffany and I will go to work on the plane. The rest of you can go back in to collect gear and two horses. Chesi will probably need help to get the things she needs from the trailers, too."

"I think you should wait for me, Liz," Tiffany amended Justine's duty roster. "I've done a lot of survival training—you need me to help choose the campsite."

"Fine by me," Liz replied. "It'll take me some time to figure out where I'm going, anyway."

"We'll meet back here in three hours," Justine said, taking charge again. "That should give us each time to do what we must."

The women left their baggage on the runway and went off in differing directions.

Nelida and Emilio stood in the kitchen near the sink. Nelida's hands were deftly removing the rind from a mango and then paring the flesh into little moon-shaped slices.

"You have read the signs, my little pigeon?" Emilio asked softly. The men were in the next room and he did not intend for them to hear.

"There has been a transgression," she answered. "A debt has been incurred here."

He nodded, and picked up the fruit platter. "I will ask the mountain for guidance in this matter; she is old and knowledgeable," he said, as he moved toward the dining room.

"And cranky," Nelida added, as she watched him go, her dark eyes solemn.

It was about to escalate, and Emilio knew as well as she how impersonal were the Gods, and how inexorable. Whatever guidance they might receive would come from within themselves, for they, too, would be tested here. And in her whole long life, she had never known a God who gave any quarter.

* * *

Tiffany stood on a ladder under the opened access panel of the G-IV's right engine and stared into the intricate tangle of wires and machinery within the aluminum housing. She loved the smell of engines, and the sensible complexity of them. They excited her.

"Okay," she called to Justine, who was standing below her on the ladder, looking up. "What exactly am I after here?"

"The fuel controller is smaller than a toaster—it's located just about in the middle. . . . There, I see it! To your left and up, Tiffany. That black box connected to the fuel line."

Tiffany's eyes followed Justine's line of vision and connected with the small black casing.

"Got it! Give me a minute to figure out how it's installed, will you? Do I have to be careful of booby traps?"

"Not really. Just watch the fuel line. It shouldn't be too hard to dislodge the box, once you've disengaged those yellow and blue wires near your left hand."

All engines have a personality, Tiffany thought as she reached out with her intuition, respectfully—*what you have to do is connect with the soul of the machine, before you start to tinker.* Her brother Harlan would have laughed at her for expressing it that way, but he would have understood exactly what she meant. He'd been her mentor and teacher, and *nobody* understood the soul of an engine like Harlan did.

Tiffany unscrewed the fuel controller and carefully disengaged the red tubing and the yellow and blue wires that attached it to the rest of the engine. A wrench and a screwdriver were all she needed to accomplish the task.

"I've got her!" she shouted triumphantly. "Let me hand her down to you, so I can screw everything else back into place." She took two steps down the ladder and stretched her hand to pass the precious engine parts to Justine. They were small, but heavier than she'd expected.

"Nice work, Tiffany," the Frenchwoman commended.

"They'll have a collective coronary occlusion when they realize what we've done."

Tiffany finished her work, shoved the access panel back into place firmly. She wiped her hands on her pants and grinned.

"I could get to like plane engines," she said.

"Good," Justine replied. "Because somebody's going to have to get this G-IV airworthy after we're all finished tinkering with her. It's never as easy to repair as it is to sabotage, eh?"

"Not to worry, honey," Tiffany said with supreme confidence. "This engine and I just came to an understanding." They moved the ladder to the opposite side of the plane and Tiffany repeated her efforts there.

When she'd finished, Justine put the fuel controllers into the canvas backpack she'd brought for the purpose, and the two women moved swiftly off the runway. The first order of business when they got to camp would be to find a suitable hiding place for their stolen property, someplace safe from the elements and from prying eyes.

"We'll hide these together," Justine said. "In case anything happens to either of us, the other can retrieve it. But perhaps it would be best if the other women do not know its whereabouts, eh? We can't possibly reveal its location to Marika, and we can't tell everyone else and leave her out. So perhaps it should be our little secret."

Tiffany chewed on that thought as they waited for the other women to reassemble.

By late afternoon, the assortment of objects piled on the runway made an imposing, random heap. Blankets, pots, glasses, wine bottles, garbage bags, and myriad other items lay baking in the sun, as Liz and Tiffany emerged from the palm trees that ringed the airstrip, and hailed the group of waiting women.

Everyone had stripped down to tropical gear, whatever they owned that was coolest. Justine wore a large, floppy Panama hat,

Tiffany a baseball cap, backwards; everyone else had constructed some kind of baffle against the relentless sun, as they sat on their suitcases and waited.

"We've got the perfect place!" Tiffany called out excitedly, as she approached the others. "Liz was right about the waterfall—there's a stream and a pool and a good-sized clearing we can trim back pretty easily to get rid of insects . . . we're really lucky she spotted it yesterday."

"Sounds like my dream vacation," Christie groaned, disgruntled in the heat.

Liz threw down the pack she was carrying. "It's a really great space, Christie. You'll see—there's even shade that's actually *cool* near the water, and it's only a mile or two from the beach, so we can get there for fishing and crabbing."

"A mile or two?" Chesi echoed. "Maybe we just won't fish a lot." She remembered crabbing with her grandfather at the Jersey shore when she was a kid, but that had been right outside the back door.

Liz shook her head. "The tough part is figuring out how to get all this debris to the campsite. Most of the trip isn't too bad, but there's a steep stretch, and then a rope bridge. . . ."

"Oh, great!" Christie snapped. "Like in *The Man Who Would Be King*? The kind you fall off and get dashed to pieces on the rocks below, right? I've seen that movie."

"What shall we do about these mares? Can they make the journey?" Marika asked; she held the reins of both horses, as she scratched the nose of one absently. The Swedish beauty seemed totally at ease with the large animals.

"I'm afraid we can only use them as pack mules, far as the bridge," Liz answered. "We'll either have to keep them hobbled there, or send them back. But judging from the amount of gear you guys have collected already, we'd better start packing them up as soon as possible. We'll never make this trek after dark. Anybody think to bring rope?"

Chesi nodded. "The Dumpsters at the site were full of useful garbage. Nails, lumber, rope, you name it. The trailers, too. I've already swiped all the blueprints I need, and some tools. But there's plenty of good strong rope back there, if somebody will help me carry it."

It took the rest of the daylight hours to get what they'd collected to the campsite. Around dusk, Thoros and several of the other men came by to watch the women's efforts with amused curiosity, but no one approached them or questioned their plans.

SEVENTEEN

Nelida set the heavy tray of drinks on the sideboard and glanced at the men around the poker table, Sunday night. She smiled to herself at their self-satisfied laughter and easy conversation. That would all soon change.

The players tossed in their antes for five-card draw. Rand pitched the cards around the table, smooth and low, like the nuts player he was. Jase took a look at the possible flush in his hand and checked his bet, unable to open with the required pair of jacks or better. "I don't know about the rest of you men, but I think it's a helluva lot more restful without the women around here. Maybe we should just enjoy the quiet while we can." He turned his smile on Nelida. "You got some beers coming over this way?"

"Sí, señor," she said, deftly placing a frost-covered Pilsner in the coaster at his side. He nodded acknowledgment and turned his attention back to the cards in his hand, liking the look of them.

Alex opened with a five-hundred-dollar bet. He had two

pairs, sixes and fours, a strong opening hand. "I beg to differ with you, my friend, but while it's a helluva lot quieter, it's also a helluva lot more *celibate*, I'm sorry to say. I rather miss the women—and I was looking forward to our battle royal."

"What battle was that?" Thoros asked, with curiosity. He called the bet, hoping for a straight, or a pair up.

Alex's blue eyes crinkled with amusement. "Why, the battle to see which one of us grabbed the best Trophy, and could hold on to her against any assault from the rest of us, of course."

Thoros laughed loudly. "That is what it's all about, isn't it?" he agreed. "It really doesn't have to do with sex—just possessions and war games. Who takes the hill, who holds the hill . . ."

"And there were some great-looking hills in that crowd," Capuletti said with an obscene Italian gesture. The table exploded with laughter, and he called with a weak pair of sevens.

"How long do you think the hills are going to hold out?" Jase asked, chewing on a pretzel.

"Forty-eight hours, tops," Tony guessed. "Then we're gonna be stuck carrying back all that shit they took out of here. What do you think they're up to out there, anyway? Building the Bridge on the River Kwai?"

Jack looked up from the pair of threes in his hand. "I think they're mad as hell about the plane, and they're telling us to go fuck ourselves."

"Fucking *ourselves* does appear to be the only option at the moment," Alex said, ruefully.

"I suppose we need a parlay of some kind," Jase put in. "Let's hear them out, see if they've calmed down . . . give them a way back in. Like you do with kids when they box themselves into a corner."

Jack absently threw some chips into the pot, unfazed by his weak pair. "That's assuming they *want* back in. What if they don't?"

"We let them sweat out there with the pythons until we've

played enough poker," Thoros said, still angry at the turn things had taken. "Then we go home."

Considerably less comfortable in the jungle, six bone-weary women sat around a fire pit they'd managed to construct under Tiffany's able direction. She seemed to know what she was doing, and Marika had shown surprising outdoor competency, too, so somehow the task had gotten done, despite considerable grumbling and serious fatigue.

They hadn't been able to raid the main kitchen at the compound, so their first night's dinner consisted of cocktail snacks gathered from the bars in the guest pods; peanuts, pretzels, cheese, and pâté with crackers kept them from hunger, but didn't do much to lift their flagging spirits. Talking revolution was one thing, going hungry and sleeping on the ground was another.

Tiffany had made them boil their drinking water for ten minutes, even though it looked crystal clear; she'd also managed to make coffee with it, which those who weren't drinking the purloined wine were currently sipping.

"I can't believe I've been reduced to a point where I'd be grateful for Coffeemate," Christie mused disgustedly, as she stared morosely into the black coffee and struggled to find a new way to sit on the ground that wouldn't make her rump hurt worse than it already did.

"I know we're all too tired to breathe," Liz answered, over her cup, "but I think we'll feel better if we make some kind of plan of action about what comes next."

Murmurs of tired assent ran around the group.

Chesi stood up and stretched the sitting-kinks out of her legs. "I've been noodling a lot about our options, everybody," she began, "and I think if you'll hear me out, you may feel better about our possibilities."

"That's an easy bet," Christie grunted. "We couldn't feel worse."

Tiffany laughed. "Who told you *that* lie! You could be colder, hotter, snakebit or dead, girl. This isn't *half* bad." The others snickered uneasily; there was an unpleasant ring of truth to what she'd said.

Chesi cleared her throat to get their attention back. "I may not be able to solve all our woes, women, but I can at least give you a way to make the guys miserable if they don't come through with an apology and a plane ride out."

"Do our options include bug spray?" Christie asked, slapping at her arm.

"Here," Liz said, tossing a small spray bottle her way. "I hate bugs like the Devil hates Holy Water. . . . I've got enough of this stuff for Coxey's Army."

Chesi smiled and continued. "Now, let's say the good ol' boys are inside there snug and happy tonight, because they figure *they've* got all the amenities *and* the air-conditioning, and stupid us, we're screwed outside here in bug country. They've disabled the plane, and they don't know we've one-upped them on that score, so you can bet your ass they're sitting around the poker table right this minute, talking about how soon we'll be over our PMS and back in their beds. Right?"

Everyone murmured yes.

Chesi smiled her Don Corleone smile. "So, first we take out the air-conditioning, then the refrigeration, then their water-cleaning system. Let's see how smug they are when they're drinking salt water in the sweltering dark."

"Sounds just like where they belong," Christie said. "But the air-conditioning goes before the water?"

"You bet. It's like a warning shot over their bow. It won't cripple them, just show them we can sink their ship if they don't watch out. As I see it, if we sabotage their world in increments, it gives them a chance to deal. First, the A/C, then guerrilla raids on supplies, and finally we go for broke, if they're still not paying attention to us."

"Why not go for broke first?" Christie asked, getting interested in the possibilities.

Chesi shook her head, so her shiny ear-length brown hair bobbed in the firelight; she pushed it back absently. "You can't go for broke immediately, because it'll take me some time to disable the systems. The good news is there's no alarm here to deter me."

"Why not?" Liz asked.

"Thoros figured he's on an island and self-contained. Who's going to annoy him?"

"Ah, sweet overconfidence . . ." Liz said, smirking. "I like the idea that they're vulnerable in their comfy little fortress," she mused. "It's very Agatha Christie, like in *And Then There Were None*."

"So, how do we do it?" Tiffany asked, suddenly feeling sorry for Jack.

"What we need are the control panels that are, happily, outside the compound—they're always hidden in back areas so the only people who ever see them are engineers and people like me," Chesi explained.

"So they're accessible to us without their knowing?" Christie asked, more animated than she'd been all day, and less crabby.

"Very. There's this unobtrusive little building quite a ways back from the Great House, pretty much hidden by all kinds of vegetation, so probably none of you ever even noticed it. That's the nerve center for the whole compound."

"Nerve center for what?" Tiffany prompted.

"Basically, everything that runs on electricity. HVAC, lights, stoves, you name it. It houses these big generators, and their battery backups that look like a lot of car batteries lined up on the walls. I could take you all there tomorrow morning on a reconnaissance mission, if you like, so you can see how vulnerable it all is. Best of all," Chesi added, warming to her work, "the control house isn't where it was supposed to be. On the original site, we ran into granite that would have required additional blasting, so I moved the building site. Unless Rand really studied the plans carefully—and he probably didn't—he'll have to run all over hell and gone trying to find the damned thing."

"Okay, so take us through the drill, Chesi," Christie probed. "What do you do, and how soon do they find out you did it?" She pulled out the notepad and pen from her handbag and held them poised. There was a story in progress here; she'd better get her reporter act together.

"That's entirely up to us . . . we either cut the electrical system off all at once, or we start to limit the electricity, a little at a time. I'd vote for the latter, because it'll confuse the bejesus out of them, and at first, they might think it's just a bug in a new system." Chesi paused for breath. She looked around to see if everyone was following. All faces were alert and interested.

"I'd like to get a little diabolical here, and leave on all the ceiling lights, so we can see *them*, but disable all the wall outlets, so they can't use any appliances. Then I'd hit the stoves and cooking equipment, refrigerators, and so on, so they'll have to forage like we do. Then we hit the main transformer. . . . Boy, do I wish we had a gun, that'd make it real easy."

"Damn!" Justine exploded, jumping up. "Why didn't I think to look for the gun?"

All eyes were on her. "The G-IV!" she snapped. "There's no way Thoros wouldn't have equipped it with firearms." She was on her feet and moving.

"I'm going back there—if there is a gun, I don't want it falling into their hands."

"Going back for it, *now?*" Christie said, disbelieving. "Are you nuts? It's nighttime in that jungle, Justine. You'll never find your way to the airstrip in the dark."

"She's right, Justine," Liz agreed. "I'll go back with you at first light. There's no point courting disaster out there tonight. You'll fall in a hole and end up in the Bermuda Triangle."

Everyone slept fitfully through their first night out of the compound. Every sound brought someone to full consciousness, and even those who were not morning people saw the sun come up, and were grateful for it.

Liz and Justine got up before dawn, to make their way anxiously back to the landing field on horseback. They found a vacant lockbox in the cabin of the plane, and an empty box of Federal hollow-points in the waste bin. Someone had had the same idea as they, just a little bit earlier.

Monday, April 11

You might as well fall flat on your face,
as lean over too far backwards.

James Thurber

EIGHTEEN

Tiffany and Chesi wrestled the large tree branch into place, cursing like sailors. Thick, stabbing fronds tore at their faces as they pushed and pulled the ten-foot branch into the notch they'd prepared for it.

"Shit!" Chesi said, winded by the effort. "Doing this kind of thing on paper is a lot easier than building it from scratch. Maybe God didn't mean me for construction, only architecture." She stood back, then plopped herself down on a flat rock and surveyed their handiwork. It actually looked pretty good, which mollified her somewhat.

Tiffany swiped at a raw scratch on her upper arm, and stood back to get a perspective, too. "You'll be grateful tonight that we did this, I promise, Chesi. We have no way of knowing what kind of wildlife is out there ready to pounce, and the bugs are fierce."

Chesi nodded and managed a wan smile. Tiffany was so relentlessly good-natured, they all alternated between wanting to get on her cheerleading squad and wanting to deck her.

"I'll feel better with shelter of some kind, just on principle," Chesi agreed. "But this 'make do with what you've got' stuff is a real pain in the ass. I'd kill for a Home Depot."

Tiffany smiled indulgently. "The first time I ever did wilderness school I felt like that, too. Then, the second time, they got real tough with us—dropped us off alone in the woods and said they'd be back in three days. . . . Let me tell you, girl, I learned to be grateful for *everything* I could make do with. Like clean water when you're thirsty . . . or a few blades of cool grass when you're hot as blazes. A scraggly little shelter that keeps you safe feels better than the Taj Mahal. You'll see, desperation really puts things in perspective for you."

"Let's hope we don't get to find out too much about desperation, this week," Liz said grimly, getting to her feet again. "After *Lord of the Flies* and *Deliverance*, I thought I knew everything about wilderness survival. They just never told you about wood slivers under your fingernails and palm fronds in your eyeballs. I mean, getting buggered by morons is nothing by comparison."

Tiffany grinned. "You ain't seen nothin' yet, babe. This is only day two."

Christie and Marika were clearing vegetation from the campsite with brooms made of palm fronds. Ticks, spiders, and scorpions liked rotting undergrowth, Tiffany'd said, and they all feared snakes enough to be willing to work hard at clearing away anyplace a black mamba might find attractive.

Christie straightened up to stretch the crick out of her back, and wipe away the sweat that was dripping persistently into her eyes. "Liz says we need to make a circle around the fire with ashes," she recounted wearily. "It's supposed to keep the bugs out."

"In Sweden, we would put a hemp rope around the door to keep away the snakes," Marika offered. "If we have a long enough rope from the trailers, we could do that too?"

Marika had started to pitch in, as if being in charge of the horses had given her a berth on the team, but Christie didn't trust her or like her. She figured the same could be said for the others, but they were too polite to say so.

Justine surveyed her hands with disgust—dirty, torn nails, scraped knuckles; the fingerless riding gloves she'd scrounged from the stable had protected them a little, but not enough. The coconuts she and Liz had collected, along with the branches and firewood, had destroyed the last nail of her manicure.

"I would look forward to getting finished with this stupid coconut patrol," Liz groaned, "except that General Tiffany over there says we're supposed to dig a trench after this."

"You're joking! This is too much!" Justine exploded imperially. "Someone *else* can dig a trench, *not I.* This heat is too abominable for such labor. We'll be dead before we ever get to pee in it."

"I'm too dehydrated to pee," Liz said, swiping at the sweat on her face and flinging back her hair like a horse in fly season. "Besides, it's for drainage away from the shelter, not a latrine. God, I wish I'd read those Tom Browne survival books more carefully. I only remember half of everything important. Except how to make a still for extracting water from urine in a desert—that part really made an impression on me."

Justine rolled her eyes, unable to comment. She was sweating, achy, and dead on her feet. She straightened up with difficulty, then stretched her arms high above her head as if reaching for something. *She looks as lithe as a lioness doing that,* Liz thought, with a small pang of envy. There was privilege engraved on every bone of that self-centered body, but she'd obviously never worked hard at anything physical before. *Not that she's complaining too much—at least no more than the rest of us.*

"Justine," she said, suddenly deciding to share a confidence. "You probably know this breed of man better than any of us do. Just how much danger do you think we're really in from them? Would they kill us to protect themselves?"

Justine's brow furrowed slightly, considering the question. "I have certainly known men like these to resort to violent acts toward enemies who threatened them," she said judiciously, as if working out her answer as she voiced it. "You must understand, Liz, they are above the law, for the most part, in everything they do. And there is no heinous act that can't be concealed, if unlimited money changes hands. But I think we hardly fall into the category of mortal enemies for them. We're more of a petty annoyance, no? And, there are quite a few of us to dispose of comfortably."

Liz wrinkled her nose in distaste. "I think it sucks that we're even having to wonder about the likelihood of being murdered on vacation! Some week in Paradise . . ."

"Paradise has a tradition of being treacherous, eh?" Justine said with a wry smile. "But the game has just begun. We must play this one carefully, I think. Just to be certain."

"Do you feel we can trust Marika not to defect?" Liz pressed. "The rest of us seem pretty solidly on the same side."

"She has no convictions of her own," Justine replied. "Or at least not *our* convictions. But I think she will remain with the group. She's a follower by nature, not a leader."

"Do you really believe that? She's awfully used to center stage. Doesn't that alone set her apart from the common sway?"

Justine shook her head. "Her beauty is the only asset Marika relies on, not her brain. And now she knows that even her beauty can only manipulate them so far."

Liz nodded, unconvinced. "We should open negotiations tomorrow, don't you think? Getting off Xanadu South seems very attractive to me about now."

"Actually, I was expecting a delegation from the men before this—but perhaps they need to gloat a little longer."

"I've been thinking strategy, Justine. You know, I've always loved war books . . . it's a sort of specialty for me. Strategy, tactics, battle plans . . . I'm like Patton, certain I've been on all these battlefields before. Thermopylae, Moscow, the Argonne Forest, Corregidor . . ." She looked at Justine to see if she understood, but the Frenchwoman looked noncommittal.

"So, I've been strategizing. . . . I think they'll try to outwit us, soften us up with privation and the 'death of a thousand mosquito bites' for a few days. Then they'll wave a carrot under our noses, figuring we'll jump at the chance for a bubble bath."

Justine laughed, a musical foreign sound. Liz had grit, and intellect, she liked that—she was an amusing woman, the most interesting of the group, by far; if anyone there could be relied on it would be she. "Whatever they say or do, Liz, I believe we must stick to our guns. Let them know that all we desire is that the aircraft be fixed, and we all part company—if not friends . . . at least not mortal foes. Yes?"

Liz looked solemn. "They won't, you know."

"But why would they not? It would be so easy that way. And they'd be rid of us."

Liz shook her head. "They won't abandon Tony, and they won't just fix the plane and let us go. They'll try to sweet-talk us back into their beds, because then they'll figure they've neutralized us. It's an American guy thing."

Justine cocked her head to one side, and her sleek short bob swayed as she did so, making her look like a young Garbo. "You could be right. Then the question must be, *How do we neutralize them?*"

Before Liz could posit an answer, Chesi approached from the far side of the camp. "If you're game to come with me," she said to Liz, "I think it's time to start our sabotage sequence."

Liz looked up, happy to have a legitimate reason for escape. "I was praying I'd be saved from ditch duty," she said with a smirk. "Lead me to those circuit boards."

Chesi stood in the control-panel shed surveying the circuit boards judiciously. She had a wire cutter in her pocket, and a screwdriver clenched in her teeth, a blueprint in one hand and a hammer in the other. She mumbled something through the screwdriver, then spat it into her hand with a short laugh.

"I think I've figured out how to do this in just the right sequence," she said to Liz. "First, the A/C, then the wall outlets, then the food storage, then the stoves . . . and of course, the coup d'état, the ceiling lights. I'm saving the water for my pièce de résistance." She glanced at her watch. "But for today's effort at making their lives at least as miserable as ours, the air-conditioning and the refrigeration will never see sundown."

Liz grinned. "What can I do to help?"

"Just keep an eye on the door while I fiddle with these panels, will you? What I have in mind should only take a few minutes, but this is no time for prying eyes."

NINETEEN

Is it me, or is it stuffy as hell in here today?" Jase demanded, standing in the kitchen at eleven o'clock. "And by the way, while I'm complaining, why the fuck aren't there any phones on this island, Rand?" He was never at his best in the morning, and less so in the current circumstances.

"Because Mora Utu isn't *completed* yet," Rand bristled, as if talking to an unpleasant and backward child. Everyone's temper was getting edgy. "Phones are the last installation to go in."

"Relax!" Tony called from the other side of the room. "Thoros will get a message to his people, somehow. We can't really be cut off from the world—not in 1996."

"Really?" Jase said, disbelieving. "I left strict orders for nobody to annoy me for *ten days*. So did everybody else, I imagine. Looks to me like nobody's even going to start looking for us till then."

"So, the worst thing that happens is we play a lot of poker," Tony said. He was tired of all the bellyaching; it was easy enough to read the innuendo underneath all of it—everybody blamed him for spoiling their fun, when all they had to do was forget about the damned women and they could still enjoy themselves.

"You're right," Jase agreed, his tone slightly less belligerent. "We're here for a holiday, why not have one?"

Tony felt a little relieved. They'd all been friends a helluva long time, poor and rich, with power and without. They were an odd lot on the surface—it was hard to remember now how they'd all gotten together. The same hunger probably had brought them to the same trough. But it was Thoros who had been the marriage broker among them all; he who had made the selections, and after a time of testing, had brought each new arrival into the circle.

"Want to go fishing?" Tony said suddenly, throwing the idea out to the group. Rand shook his head no, still annoyed by the phone question. The mood had shifted after the women left; now you never knew where the next complaint would come from.

Jack shook his head, too. "Thoros is taking me on an island tour. As long as we'll be here for a few days, I'd like to know the island a little. I think he's hoping you'll come, too, Rand. You know Mora Utu better than he does." Rand nodded; a day outside the compound would be a respite from petty annoyance.

"I'll go fishing with you," Jase said, surprising Tony. "The water looks pretty good for fish today. Any idea about the tides?"

Thoros put down his coffee cup. "Check with Emilio; he's got remarkable knowledge about such things. He can show you to the boats and fishing gear as well."

The men dispersed to their chosen occupations for the day.

The sound of the oars dipping into the soft ocean swells was rhythmic and peaceful; the two fishermen had left the fancier craft behind and opted for a rowboat. The land smells had diminished as they pulled farther out toward the open ocean, and the sea smells—metallic, fishy, salty, clean, and primal—had cleared their nostrils and brains.

Jase was in a better mood than he'd been in since Saturday night. Rowing made his muscles feel alive again and he loved to fish; had grown up doing it on Lake Michigan and in the mountains of Montana, where his family had kept a ranch that was used on holidays. He wondered suddenly where Tony had learned to fish; he looked damned competent working on the bait and tackle, with the confidence of one who doesn't need instruction.

"Where'd you learn about fishing, Tony?" he asked, squinting into the sunlight that bounced brilliantly off the phosphorescent sea.

Tony smiled crookedly, memory surfacing. "My old man was a longshoreman," he said. "He worked the docks so long he knew every fisherman on the piers. Sometimes he'd work the fishing boats for extra dough when he wasn't too drunk to keep from falling overboard. I started working the commercial fisheries when I was eleven or so . . . just about the time he split with my mom, and disappeared." He looked out over the surrounding waters with a practiced eye. "This looks like as good a place as any to drop a line. Okay?"

Jase nodded. The solitude of fishing tended to make a man show something of himself. Not that talking was a requisite, far from it—but there was something about the sea that provoked honesty.

"How'd your mom handle all that?" he asked, securing the oars and reaching for his tackle.

"She was a boozer too," Tony said, distaste, anger, sorrow all evident in his voice, despite the decades; there was more there, too, that Jase couldn't identify readily. "He used to beat the shit out of her whenever he got drunk, so I guess she was glad to get rid of the bum when he finally took off. Not that she didn't deserve it—she was boffing every guy in town who'd hold still long enough." He laughed shortly, and cast his line out in a silvery arc, before it settled below the waves.

"That's rough," Jase acknowledged, casting his line, not quite as well or as far, on the other side of the boat. "I didn't like my mother much, either," he offered, watching carefully the direction of the line beneath the surface. It was important to intuit the depth of your line, not to misjudge. "She was a calculating, coldhearted blue blood from one of the best families in Detroit. I could understand why my father screwed around, once I was old enough to think about such things. '*Wouldn't want to get caught in her gearbox,*' I used to say to my pals. She was like a social machine—wind her up, she did the right charities, used the right forks, said the right words, wrote the right checks. Beyond that, there wasn't much to hold on to."

Tony nodded, and reeled in his line a little, then let it out again. He watched it ride the current for a while. "You know," he said, finally, "it's funny how I felt about my old lady. Love-hate, I guess the shrinks would call it. I really cared about her, felt sorry for her, even though I hated her for letting him do what he did. Later on, when all the guys knew she was a tramp, I got real embarrassed about her . . . more than angry, you know? Like some kind of rage. But, it was like I could only hate her part-time, no matter how many times she disappointed me. Christ! He was a mean son of a bitch when he was plastered."

A bird circled lazily in the sky above them, slowly riding the air currents, powerful wings looking almost in repose. Then suddenly, it dove. As its plummeting, sleek body broke the surface cleanly, desperate fish leaped from the depths and skittered over the water, in wild escape. The school of fish was too big for the bird, too fast and too many; it flopped about in frustrated circles, diving again and again in vain. The two men in the boat watched for a while in silence, grateful for the diversion from a conversation that had too much intimacy for comfort.

* * *

Jack, Rand, and Thoros reined in their horses at the top of a steep gorge that dropped sheer cliffs to a white-water river, crashing and bubbling, below. It wasn't a wide rift in the earth, perhaps no more than fifty yards across at its narrowest point, where a sturdy rope bridge hung suspended.

"Why don't we head north, toward the mountains, Thoros," Rand suggested. "There's a spectacular view of the entire island from the foothills of Mauna Lopelia."

Thoros nodded and the three men turned their horses in that direction. Rand and Thoros seemed perfectly at ease on horseback, Jack noted, not feeling the same, in the least. He knew how to ride, having forced himself to learn a while back when he was trying to acquire social graces to go with his new money, but it had been quickly apparent to him that riding would never be a sport he'd choose for fun. He followed the visual trajectory of Rand's pointing finger and winced—it looked like another forty minutes at best before they'd stop for lunch.

By the time they finally reined in to rest, the three horsemen had gradually climbed more than a thousand feet on the lowest slope of the long-dormant volcano. Rand stopped on a wide plateau and swept his arm out expansively over the incredible vista below. Sore as he was, Jack couldn't help but respond to the visual magic that stretched in every direction. No wonder Thoros loved this place; you'd have to be soul-dead not to be knocked out by its beauty. The three dismounted, hitched their horses, and took out the food and drink they'd brought along in their saddlebags. Jack was happy to be out of the saddle, and stretched his legs, grateful for the solid ground beneath.

The ride and the vista had loosened the knot of tension that had been strangling all of them, ever since Sunday morning's revelation. Thoros opened the small cooler Emilio had provided and pulled out three bottles of beer and an opener. The men sat on the warm earth, and ate in relative silence until the sandwiches and the first beer had been consumed. As they opened the second one, they began to relax and feel more garrulous; they stretched out comfortably beneath the afternoon sun that filtered through the foliage above, and started talking.

"How exactly did you find this island, Thoros?" Jack asked, taking a swig from the second bottle, and relaxing for the first time in a while. "You never did say."

Thoros's face changed, Jack noted, when he spoke of Mora Utu; he became less remote and more boyish, as if the sheer pleasure of ownership of such a place fulfilled some dream.

"I had an agent looking, of course, for years," he answered, "the same one who found Malcolm Forbes his place near Fiji. Every once in a while he'd come up with some possibility, and I'd fly down to check the place out. But none of them ever really called to me, or made me lust after them. Not that I really knew what I was looking for, mind you, and I certainly didn't need another house. . . ." He drifted off into memory, briefly.

"Then about five years back, I was in a bar in Singapore and I heard these two Chinese talking about a place called the Playground of the Gods that might or might not be for sale. The name spoke to me, and I knew I'd have to find out more. So I introduced myself, and that was it." He smiled, pleased with himself, and the outcome of the story. "From the moment I set foot on Mora Utu, I knew this was my Paradise, what I'd been searching for. It took me the better part of two years for the negotiation to go through—the natives weren't keen on giving it up—but there were so few of them left they really couldn't hold out forever."

Rand was propped on an elbow, surveying the landscape with a knowledgeable eye. "Did you ever wonder *why* you could dream all this, Thoros?" he asked suddenly. "I mean, you came up the hard way—like Jack and I did—you weren't *born* to the privilege of buying your own world, if you felt like it. Have you never wondered where the scope of your passions came from? How did you *know* you deserved to have it all?" It was an odd question, but it seemed an earnest one, so Thoros considered his reply before answering.

"I can remember as a boy, thinking, *somebody* gets to own it all," he replied, formulating the answer in his mind as he spoke. "*Somebody* gets to be king of the world, and it's not just those born to money and power, either—as a matter of fact, they're usually the ones *least* able to hold on to their fathers' kingdoms. That's it, I suppose," he said, brightening, as if he'd just figured it out for the first time. "I always thought I was supposed to have a kingdom, but somehow I'd been dropped off by fate in the wrong place—in a linoleum landscape that was utterly alien—so I had to fight my way back to where I was supposed to be." He laughed a little at himself, and his face softened from its usual piratical aspect. "The first time I ever flew in an aircraft, I knew that flight would be my way back to my kingdom."

The other men smiled too, because they understood perfectly. If you didn't have dreams, you got nowhere. If you didn't believe you deserved better than fate had handed you, you'd never have the balls for the exhausting climb.

Rand didn't look at the others as he spoke, but continued to stare out at the tropical perfection spread before them like a Cézanne landscape. "I don't know if I've ever told you about my own humble beginnings," he said musingly. "I've spent a lifetime reinventing them, so not many people know the truth." He stopped, as if deciding exactly how much of this truth to expose.

"I was born to a housemaid and a groom," he said, finally, "*belowstairs*, as they say in England. My mum and dad worked in the home of Sir Henry Dowding, the British industrialist and railroad titan. They were both from the South End, but they were employed in this great mansion with twenty in help . . . so when I opened my eyes to the world, I was in as splendid a house as any boy with an incipient predilection toward architecture could dream . . . but it wasn't mine."

He smiled ruefully, and looked the other two in the eyes for the first time, his expression complex. "But I was a superb sponge, so I learned to speak as His Lordship spoke, and to eat as the family ate *abovestairs*. I used to spend my time in the wine cellar with the butler learning to tell good years from bad . . . and the groom's son, of course, could ride like a cavalryman. . . ." His voice faded with reminiscence. "Then, when I was in my teens, my family emigrated to the U.S., and, fortunately for me and my ambitions, my British education was so far superior to what the American system offered, that I was able to win a scholarship to college, and later to the Yale School of Architecture. You see, I always felt I *belonged* back in that Georgian manse I'd been born in. And I had seen firsthand the psychology of dwelling places—the stamp that the four walls of your childhood places on your spirit. How grandeur expands the soul and poverty limits it."

Rand saw that he had their full attention. Thoros spoke first. "Strange," he said, musingly, "how little we men ever really know about the intimate details of each other's lives. I've known you half a lifetime, Rand, and I never knew any of this."

"Hunger and dreams are potent goads," Rand replied in non sequitur, "but at the bottom of it all, my friends, I think the decisive factor is that we *believe*, truly *believe* that we deserve more than other men. And that is why we get it. It's this conviction that causes us to succeed, I'm certain of it—because we remain displaced persons until we can create for ourselves what we need . . . the environment where we finally belong."

"So you think Thoros *needed* this island?" Jack said, intrigued by the certainty of the other man. "Life seems simpler to me, you know," he said with an easy smile. "You hate poverty, so you work hard and you make money . . . and then when you've seen what there is to have in the world, you go after your share. Simple as that."

Rand cocked his head and smiled. "But there you have it,

old boy. Precisely my point. A man like Thoros thinks his share should be *all there is*."

The day was so pleasant that Thoros felt renewed. Mora Utu was everything he'd hoped for; the land and the sea filled him with a sense of destiny and completion. By the time the three men returned from the mountains he was certain that the difficulties with the women could be handled—he'd never faced a negotiation that didn't have some equitable solution for all parties. He would put his head together with Alex tonight and come up with a means of smoothing the troubled waters, so everyone could enjoy their time together as he'd intended. He rode into the stable at the compound, tired and more content than he'd been for days.

Tony was hurrying toward them, shouting something.

"The air-conditioning's all screwed up, Thoros!" he called out. "It's hot as hell in the house and there's something wrong with the lights. We've been waiting hours for you guys to get back so we can figure out what the fuck is going on."

Thoros and Jack reined their horses to a halt, as Thoros turned to Rand for an explanation.

"Must be a glitch of some kind, Thoros," the architect said calmly. "These things happen in new buildings. I'll see to it." He dismounted and hurried to the house, hoping that what he'd told Thoros was not as far from the truth as he feared.

TWENTY

"You took my bug spray!" Christie shouted at Marika. The intense late afternoon heat and humidity had hung on into the evening, and all the work on building the shelter had everyone exhausted and on edge. Christie's usually perfectly groomed hair was lank and damp now, tied back in a lifeless ponytail, and there were bluish circles under her eyes from the difficulty she'd had in sleeping. She grabbed for Marika's large Hermès bag to retrieve her prized possession.

"Don't be *stupid!*" Marika shot back, hanging on to the bag with a death grip.

The other women stopped their chores and looked at one another, not knowing if they should interfere.

"Me, stupid? That's *great* coming from Miss Tits and Ass with the I.Q. of a sparrow. Give me my goddamned bug spray!" Christie tore at the giant leather sack, but Marika defended it with a violent shove that sent her opponent sprawling across the clearing.

"Stop this!" Justine shouted, moving between the two women. "You're both acting like idiots."

Liz bent to help Christie up, and purposely moved in front of her to keep her separated from Marika. "Come on, girls," she said, "we're all tired and on edge here—we just can't let it get out of control. Every one of us wants to punch somebody, but it won't do any good at all to act it out."

"She took my bug spray!" Christie insisted, close to tears, her usually collected demeanor gone.

"What is this *thing* you've got for bug spray, woman?" Tiffany said, moving forward with a small bottle in her hand. "Here, I'll share mine with you. It's miserable enough in this heat without being itchy, too, and we've stirred up every mosquito in the known world by making this camp."

Liz turned toward the others with an exasperated expression on her face. "Look, everybody, I've been thinking . . . just waiting here is really getting on everybody's nerves big-time. We need to get some mutual respect going."

"Fat chance!" Christie said with a sniff.

Liz frowned at her and kept going. "Maybe if we find out what talents we each bring to this party it would help. I mean, everybody here probably has special gifts and competencies—trouble is, we don't know each other well enough to know what we've got to offer. I just found out Tiffany has a black belt in something or other . . . maybe she could teach us self-defense. Marika knows horses, that's an important skill. What else have we got in our arsenal? I'd really like to lay it all out and see how it could help us. Let's face it, we don't know how long we'll be stuck with each other."

"Great idea!" Chesi said with genuine enthusiasm. "We wanted *them* to respect us . . . I guess it's the least we owe each other."

She looked around for support, then plunged ahead. "I'll start, if you want . . . just to get the ball rolling. My strength is my knowledge of the compound, the enemy's fortress. I'm your demolition team. I'm strong physically, too, and I like to work with my hands." She paused to think. "I also have one of the great green thumbs, and I make a mean lasagna, but I hope to God we're not here long enough for those skills to prove useful." She sat down and waited for someone else to take her place.

Marika rose. "I know horses and other animals," she said, somewhat defiantly. "I can birth them, and nurse them, and do nearly anything with them. I speak seven languages, five fluently. My body is very strong and sound—I've been hiking and rock climbing since I was a little girl, and hunting every kind of game. I am a superb shot with pistol, rifle, or shotgun, and competent with a crossbow." She thought for a moment, as if checking her memory banks for more, then sat down. It wasn't a bad list of skills, and the looks passed around the group seemed grudgingly impressed.

Tiffany stood up next, less ruffled by the hardships than were her companions. "I can help with the plane because of my experience with engines," she said eagerly. "And I'd be happy to teach you all about self-defense if you'd like me to. I've been an aerobics instructor, too, so if anybody wants to keep in shape over the next few days, I could organize a group or some games or something. Let's face it, we're working hard here, but we're not having any fun, and I think that's getting to everybody's disposition in a big way." She smiled an open, no-hidden-agendas smile, and sat down.

It was Liz's turn. "I have this weird gift of total recall, you know?" she began. "So I know a little bit about a lot of things—I guess I can be a sort of reference library. And I'm a war buff, so I'm pretty good on military strategy and tactics, which might be useful in negotiation."

"Who the hell said you're the negotiator?" Christie shot back with considerable hostility. "You and Her Highness over there just took it upon yourselves to be the mouthpieces back at the compound, and you did a pretty lousy job of it, or we wouldn't be out here."

"That's not fair," Chesi defended the others. "The men called the shots by disabling the plane and holding us prisoner—it wasn't the negotiators' fault."

Christie was on her feet now. "Look. I earn my living *talking*," she said. "And I'm pretty fucking good at it, so I *demand* to negotiate for myself next time. I'll be damned if I'm going to let you two get me killed."

Everyone started to talk at once.

"Nobody's getting killed, Christie," Justine said, with authority. "And as to negotiating—your emotions are much too raw to be able to negotiate wisely. Let someone with a cool head do it."

"Like *you*, Miss Arrogant Spoiled Brat?" Christie spat. "Just because you're used to getting your own way doesn't mean you'll get it here. And I'm fucking well tired of your imperial noblesse oblige."

She turned on the group. "Am I the only one here with the balls to tell her the truth of what we think of her?" Uncomfortable glances went around the circle.

"Some diplomat you'd make!" Chesi snarled, standing agitatedly. "Face it, Christie, none of us is perfect, you and me included. And nobody volunteered for this vacation from hell, but we'd damned well better make the most of it, or we're really screwed. I know those fuckers in there are figuring *A*, we can't hurt them, and *B*, we can't get along with each other well enough to make a team. And I'll be goddamned if I want to let them get away with being right! So Justine is spoiled, and I'm irascible, and you're a royal pain in the ass . . . so *what?* We're *all we've got* until we get off Gilligan's Island—so why don't you just get off your fucking soapbox and tell us what it is you bring to the party!"

Chesi's vehemence pulled Christie up short. She stared at

her for a long moment, mouth open, on the verge of response, then surprisingly, she changed her tack.

"You're right," she said, defeated. "I was out of line. And, we *are* all in the same boat, so I'll pull my oar with the rest of you. As to what I can throw into the pot . . ." She stopped to take inventory and to calm herself down.

"I'm feisty . . . I guess you got that picture. I'm relentless when I want something, like a bulldog with a bone. Most of my skills are more useful on a subway than in a jungle, but I'm smart and incisive about people—I can read a meeting and figure out what's really going on. And, I know a lot about war games . . . I'm an army brat—my father did two terms in Nam, plus Korea. I've got a brother who's a lieutenant colonel in the Air Force and there isn't any kind of military strategy I didn't absorb with my pablum. And it just so happens, Norm Schwarzkopf is a friend of mine. I wish to hell he were here."

"You're joking!" Justine put in. "Army brat, I can believe—you have the swagger for it. But the Persian Gulf War general as a confidant? That's too much. How would you ever meet such a man?"

"I stalked him," Christie replied, with defiant pride. "I wanted the kind of interview Barbara Walters would have sold her mother for, but I was too lowly at the station to pack the clout for an introduction through channels. So I stalked him."

"You're serious, aren't you?" Liz asked, intrigued. "How'd you ever get through that phalanx of protectors? I mean, I tried to get to him for a book, but I hit a wall of Cerberuses."

Christie grinned. She shifted into a less belligerent stance and said, "Actually, it was pretty funny—I mean I finally captured him with his pants down."

"Oh, no," Liz groaned. "Don't tell me my hero Norm is a lech?"

"No, *no!* That's not what his pants were down for. I mean, I researched him up one side and down the other, found out all his habits, who guarded him and how, when he was likely to be alone. . . . Well, it turned out the *only* time he wasn't followed around by a troop of underlings was when he was in the latrine. So I used my military connections to get where he was. Then I sneaked myself into the men's john before the base closed up one night, and staked it out till morning. He was so stunned to find me in the crapper with him, it gave me the minute I needed to blurt out my story, introduce myself as Harry Gibbs's daughter. . . . You see, my dad served with Norm in Nam—anyway, he said he liked my pluck and my ingenuity in outwitting his guards and finding a hole in his security net. *And,* he remembered that Gibby'd gotten the Silver Star at Da Nang, so we had a lot to talk about." She paused for breath. "And he gave me the best exclusive human-interest interview that came out of that whole stupid war."

"Way to go!" Liz said with real enthusiasm.

"Superb story!" Justine added, a hint of admiration in her tone. "It took extraordinary resourcefulness to pull that off. No wonder he rewarded you."

Christie accepted the accolades with a gracious smile. "Anyway, I do know a lot about war." She sat down.

Only Justine was left. She didn't stand up to speak but stayed where she was, knees up, arms wrapped loosely around them. "Christie wasn't entirely wrong about me, you know," she said. "I am arrogant and thoroughly self-indulged—I rather prefer that to *spoiled.* I detest physical labor, and believe it should be done by servants—and, I assure you, I will avoid it wherever possible." She smiled languidly, her self-confidence seemingly undamaged by current circumstance. "And to be brutally frank, I would probably not have chosen *any* of you as my new best friends. But that is neither here nor there . . . I am also a realist. *So.* What do I offer this impromptu Inquisition? My skill as a pilot, of course. My intellect, which is considerable. My knowledge of powerful men, the language they speak, the impulses that compel them. But, at the end of the day, I imagine my most useful asset is this: I expect to win—the rich always do."

Silence greeted this extraordinary assessment. Finally, Liz rose again to speak, when a stirring at the edge of the clearing caught everyone's attention. Nelida appeared at the perimeter of their camp; she was carrying a large sack over her shoulder, which she put down heavily on the ground as she surveyed the assemblage, before greeting them.

Watching her, Liz realized what a commanding presence the Mexican woman had. She exuded a sort of female power that was hard to quantify, and a confidence that made Justine's look paltry by comparison.

"I have decided to be with you in your rebellion," the older woman announced without elaboration.

"She's a spy for the men," Marika said quickly. "They have sent her to watch us."

"What the hell do you want to join us for?" Christie asked with considerable suspicion.

Nelida smiled. "In a war between *hombres y mujeres,* you have need for the wisdom of elders."

"We have need for a bazooka," Liz said with a short laugh, "but how do we know you're *not* a spy?"

"This you must learn from your own place of knowledge. What I tell you of this means nothing."

"What's in that big sack?" Tiffany's curiosity got the best of her.

"Food. Herbs. Cook pots. You will need strength for the battle ahead."

"What battle is that, Nelida?" Liz queried. "All we want is to get off this island."

"What you want has little to do with what will be," Nelida replied mysteriously. "Forces have been set in motion that are not easily contained."

"You sound like a soothsayer," Justine snapped, annoyed.

"Will we take a long trip over water, too? That's really what we have in mind."

Nelida ignored the cynical tone. "There will be a journey, yes," she said judiciously. "For some it will be longer than others." She turned her attention back to the pack she'd placed on the ground.

"What about your husband?" Tiffany asked, puzzled. "Where's he stand in all this?"

"He is a *brujo* . . . he remains with the men, as he must. He would not attempt to keep me from my work."

"Will you cook for us, then?" Marika asked, and Nelida looked up and smiled as if at a foolish child.

"I will cook. There is much you will need to learn and many ways to be nourished."

"Do you know what's poisonous?" Liz asked, beginning to consider Nelida's value. "There's food all around us, but we're not sure what we can eat safely."

"I will instruct you," Nelida answered, gravely, "it is not difficult to learn. Never eat red food in the jungle—there are exceptions, but for now you will be safer with no red. Eat nothing that makes your skin sore or itchy when you touch it. Toadstools and mushrooms are very dangerous unless you have much knowledge. . . . If you find a food with hair, remove it with your hand and wait to see if a rash is produced. Some things that grow will cause blisters on your skin—these, too, are to be avoided as food. If you are uncertain, show the food to me. I will catch a monkey and cage him . . . he will be the taster for uncertainties."

Liz and Tiffany looked at each other questioningly; Nelida could be a real asset if she wasn't a plant by the opposition. Chesi walked toward the older woman—there was something about her that was reminiscent of her own grandmother. Which was weird, really, since she certainly didn't look like her little Italian grandma. But there was something in those eyes that was familiar.

"Welcome to our world, Nelida," she said amiably. "Need some help with whatever it is you've got in there? It looks like Mary Poppins' satchel."

Nelida smiled acknowledgment of her acceptance, handing a small saucepan to Chesi. "*Que revuelva la olla aquel que tenga hambre,*" she said with a good-natured chuckle.

"What does that mean?" Chesi asked.

"He who has hunger, let him stir the pot," Nelida replied, and Chesi knew she meant something more than what she'd said, but wasn't sure what.

Tuesday, April 12

No one can make you feel inferior
without your consent.

Eleanor Roosevelt

TWENTY-ONE

Emilio placed the ornate tray on the sideboard and poured a cup of coffee from the great silver urn that dominated the space, just as Thoros entered the breakfast room.

"Where in thunder is Nelida this morning, Emilio? I've been calling her for over an hour. There were no clean clothes laid out and . . ."

"She has gone, señor."

"Gone? What in blazes are you talking about, Emilio? Where could she go?"

"To the women, señor. It is her obligation."

Jase and Alex reached the breakfast table just as Thoros exploded. "You can't be serious, man! What would she do that for? Has she gone loco? . . . Has everybody gone loco?" His face was ruddy with frustration.

"Who's gone loco, and who's gone where?" Alex asked, walking in on the heated exchange. Thoros turned on him angrily.

"Emilio claims Nelida has defected to the women."

"What the hell for?" Tony asked, entering the conversation, from the doorway.

"Excellent question, my friend," Thoros boomed, trying to calm himself. It wasn't like him to be even marginally out of control, but his nerve endings seemed very near the surface this morning. Without the orderliness Nelida provided, nothing ever went as planned.

"Answer the man, Emilio! What lunacy has sent Nelida to the women? Is she trying to talk sense into them?"

"No, señor," Emilio answered, unruffled by his employer's volatile outburst. "She has gone to advise them."

"To advise them?" Rand echoed. "About what?"

"To know their own hearts with correctness," Emilio answered enigmatically.

Alex moved closer, intrigued. "What does that mean exactly, Emilio? Why is this her concern?"

"It is a thing of women, señor," the little Mexican said simply, as he turned to go.

The men looked at one another, not knowing whether to laugh, or reprimand him for his insolence.

"But she works for *me*, Emilio," Thoros reiterated, genuinely confounded by this turn of events. "How can she just *leave*?"

"Obligation, señor. It is not a simple matter." Then he was gone.

Thoros shook his head at this extraordinary sea change—Nelida gone, Emilio altered in some way, no longer subservient, oddly independent.

It was inconceivable that this was happening. His island, his week, his well-ordered life, and now even his servants, coming unglued.

"What on earth do these women *want*, Alex?" he asked, sounding genuinely baffled.

Alex laughed heartily. "Freud asked the same question, old boy. And probably in the same tone of voice." He slapped Thoros on the shoulder in a comradely fashion and proceeded to forage for his breakfast.

Thoros had something else preying on his mind this morning; he hesitated for a moment, after the interchange with Emilio, deciding whom to take into his confidence about his latest unpleasant discovery. Then, deciding to follow his first instinct, he headed out toward the pool where Jack was sitting and hailed him.

Jack put down the papers he'd been going through, and stood up to greet him. "What's on your mind, Thoros? You look damned serious."

Thoros shook his head to indicate that this was a private conversation and should be held out of earshot of the rest. Wonderingly, Jack followed his friend to the beach.

Thoros stood for a moment without speaking, hands in his white duck pants pockets, staring out to sea. He seemed troubled, solemn. When he spoke, his voice was tense. "There was a .45 in the plane, Jack. It isn't there now. I don't suppose you've seen it?"

Jack looked hard at his host; the strain in the man's eyes made his state of mind an easy call. "No, Thoros . . . I haven't seen a gun. But, I remember Emilio had a gun the other night, didn't he?"

"Yes, but that was not the one from the plane."

Jack nodded. "Who else would have known it was aboard?"

Thoros kicked up some sand, absently, with the toe of his tennis shoe.

"Hard to say. Justine might have suspected its existence. Any one of us could have had access since we landed. I'm mad as hell at myself I didn't think to remove it sooner, but with everything going haywire . . ."

Jack looked hard at his friend's face, reading it. "You think Tony might have it? Is that the problem?"

"Tony's a good man, Jack. You know that. And a good

friend." He paused, deciding if he should say more. "This thing with Marika has brought out a side of him I hadn't seen. Not that he'd do anything stupid . . ."

"No. Of course not."

"But, I'd feel better if I knew."

"Have you asked him?"

"He said he hasn't seen the gun."

"Well, that's it, then."

Thoros picked up a small rock and held it in his hand for a moment, as if examining it for defects. Then he threw it out to sea in a high-arcing trajectory.

He didn't answer Jack, but nodded once, cryptically. Then he turned, and both men walked back to the house.

It was still early morning as Jase and Alex stood in the dense jungle undergrowth, intently watching the boar they planned to kill. Hunting wasn't new to either of them, although both would have preferred doing it with a rifle; but sport was sport and both were exhilarated at the prospect. They'd hoped for deer or some other species of large mammal, but none had shown itself. There was plenty of food back at the compound, but the opportunity to hunt wild game seemed to them a superb way to spend the day.

Jase felt the freedom of the moment like an adrenaline high. His world was a different battlefield from this sort now; jousting with agents and authors over lengthy lunches, fending off the green-eyeshaded munchkins to keep the balance sheet intact. But life hadn't always been just that for him. There'd been a time when the thick dark forests of Montana had provided plenty of chances to plumb the depths of his young manhood, in the company of other men. There was exhilaration to the hunt; a deep-down physical thrill of challenge that was primal and very male. Even the memory of it felt real and satisfying.

Jase carried a hefty spear and Alex a crossbow, a quiver of

arrows slung over the tall Englishman's left shoulder; both were excellent killing tools in the right hands and far more difficult to control skillfully than a rifle. Boars were unpredictable and strong as bulls, so both men were taking this task they'd set themselves very seriously; nearly any other kind of animal would have been an easier kill, but challenge was what sport was all about.

"I hunted boar, in Borneo just over a year ago," Alex had said as they tracked the animal, "but one of my bearers was badly gored on the second hunt. A downed male came back from the near-dead to charge one final time. . . ." Neither man had any illusions about the danger from their prey; both were on full alert. Jase had never hunted boar, but he'd bagged reindeer in Lapland, elk and moose in Montana, so he felt competent to the task.

The men were behind the animal's scent line now, but they could see from his wary movements that some other instinct had warned him all was not right. The feisty little hog stood still as granite, his head cocked sharply to the right, listening, sensing, straining to perceive the nature of his danger.

Jase raised his eyes and hand to signal readiness; Alex nodded, nocked an arrow to his bow, and drew back the string of the deadly-looking weapon with strength and precision.

Muscles tensed, absolute concentration in his expression, he let the arrow fly. Jase knew that if the boar wasn't downed by the first strike, the spear he carried would have to finish him off; and a mortally wounded boar would be a deadly opponent. He felt the adrenaline of the hunt surge through him, alerting every cell to full clarity, every resource of body/mind called to battle positions.

The speeding arrow found its target in a resounding crunch of rending bone, gut, and sinew. With a squeal of rage and pain, the boar dropped to his knees, his great tusked head groveling in the damp earth, twisting and turning in anguished frenzy. Jase and Alex held their collective breath, hoping the arrow had found its mark in a vital organ; heart or lung or spleen.

With a mighty effort, the animal lurched to his cloven feet and snorted, bloodlust in his fierce, desperate little eyes. He knew the position of his enemy now, and would take someone with him when he died. The steel arrow still protruding from his chest, the boar launched himself in Jase's direction.

Every human instinct the man possessed cried out to flee, but instead, he grounded himself treelike, willing his mind and body to stillness, positioning his spear for the kill as he'd been taught by his father's half-breed ranch foreman years before, and had practiced countless times since. Blood surged, ears pounded, focus narrowed to exclude everything but the onrushing beast and the fact that death would have one of them shortly in its grip.

The boar hurtled out of the undergrowth, shattering the morning with his shriek of vengeance. Timing . . . timing . . . Jase forced himself to wait, the animal nearly on top of him. He caught the boar full in the belly with his spear, and the impact crashed both bodies backward through branches, vines, and bushes, violently. Blood gushed hot and sticky over his hands, still clinging to the spear shaft; the foul stench of the beast enveloped him like toxic waste. To drop the spear meant death from goring as the lethal tusks struggled to find their soft-tissue target. Jase's inability to move or protect himself sent shock waves of primal fear through his body. The boar still had plenty of fight left in him, and Jase was pinned, helpless beneath the animal's weight.

Alex was behind the hog now, hunting knife in hand; he sliced the jugular in one deep, vicious motion, no easy task with so formidable a creature. A great shudder escaped the tormented pig; then, finally, he was still.

Winded, bloodied, and nearly flattened by the weight of the boar, Jase struggled to free himself of the stinking carcass.

"Superb archery," he gasped, his breathing coming in short rasps. "That sucker had a helluva lot of heart."

Alex nodded acceptance of the compliment.

"You're covered with gore," he said, helping Jase to his feet. "Let's get him gutted, then we can go for a swim to clean you up. A thousand years ago, they would have said a brave enemy's blood brings you good fortune."

"Then I'm really in for one fucking good time," Jase smirked, swiping at the gory mess with a handful of leaves. On impulse, he put out his bloodied hand for Alex to shake; the other man stared at it for a moment, then accepted the offered hand, and both men began to laugh inexplicably, a great surge of pride in what they'd done bonding them suddenly in some undefined way that a lifetime of poker hadn't.

It occurred to Jase that even a few days away from the mitigating influence of civilization had changed them all. Humanity was not so far removed from the beasts of the jungle, he thought soberly. *We do what we must to survive. Education, culture, money, exposure be damned. When the chips are down, we survive at any cost. At least, the fittest do.*

TWENTY-TWO

Nelida sang softly as she stirred the large pot of something that smelled tantalizing; it was a strange song in a haunting minor key, and oddly sensual. Chesi sat down on the ground beside the older woman, and emptied the bundle of sticks she'd been gathering onto the ground near the blazing fire pit. She was a morning person by nature and had been up since before dawn.

"You have done as you must?" Nelida asked the girl, as if she already knew the answer.

Chesi shook her head and smiled. "I've gathered plenty of kindling, but I don't think it's dry enough to use yet. Everything on this island is damp."

"I do not speak of firewood, child," Nelida admonished, "but of your work."

Chesi looked quizzical; she hadn't told Nelida of her decimation of the compound's electrical system the day before. How odd that the Mexican woman should know of it, unless of course she'd heard the others talking. For some reason Chesi found it pleasant to be called *child* by this woman, who sometimes seemed to her middle-aged and sometimes ancient as an archetype. The way she felt drawn to Nelida on some primal level she couldn't quite fathom, was at odds with her sensible, analytical nature.

"If you mean my sabotage mission," she answered, "I've begun by screwing up their electrical system . . . enough to confuse and anger them. I figure I'll take out the rest today or tomorrow, if they don't capitulate."

Nelida smiled mysteriously. *Her dark eyes hide so much,* Chesi thought, wondering if her own did the same. It was disconcerting to look into those shining, bottomless pools—she found herself wanting to keep staring, searching, but that was rude and silly anyway. She looked away, slightly embarrassed by her own thoughts.

"This is good," Nelida responded with satisfaction. "This is as it should be."

"Why, Nelida? Why *good*, and why are you on our side, not Gagarian's? I don't understand."

Nelida laughed, resonantly, like a Soleri bell-tree in the wind, sound beneath sound beneath sound. "I am with you because I am a *woman*. It is *good* because you will learn now of your own wild nature and I will advise you."

Chesi laughed, too. "*My* wild nature? Nobody ever accused me of having a wild nature. Except maybe my mother."

"Then they are all fools. Except your mother."

Chesi tilted her head to one side to see if she was being laughed at. It didn't seem so.

"So you're here because you are a woman, and Gagarian is a man. How does your husband feel about that?"

"Emilio would not attempt to keep me from my work. He has knowledge . . . for a man. They cannot feel or see as we do, of course." She laughed again.

"How so?"

"*La Que Sabe Todo,* the One Who Knows All, created woman

from a wrinkle on the sole of her divine foot, child. The skin of the sole feels *everything*, knows everything. Men do not have this gift."

"What a great idea!" Chesi said delightedly. "Except maybe it explains why we get stepped on a lot."

Nelida reached over and tapped Chesi's sneakers. "Then perhaps you must remove your blindfold," she said, in a kindly voice, and without another word, rose and went about her business.

An hour after breakfast, Tiffany surveyed the women lined up before her with a critical eye. All young, all in good-looking shape, but that didn't mean good aerobic shape. These days everybody pumped iron part-time for body sculpting, but that didn't make you physically fit. And self-defense was a whole other ball game. But, she'd promised to teach them to defend themselves in case of trouble, and this was as good a time to start as any.

"Look, women," she began. "You've asked me to teach you self-defense, so you have to start by understanding one important fact: The biggest handicap we women have against us in a fight is our *heads*, not our fists." She waited a moment for that to sink in. "Little boys grow up scrapping and tussling with each other—they learn to use their fists and elbows and knees, while we're still burping Betsy-Wetsy. Aggression is part of their natures, too—socking somebody in the jaw comes so naturally with testosterone that boys have to keep reminding themselves not to do it, so they can be vaguely civilized." Everyone tittered.

"We're built different. We're biologically programmed for nurturing, and we've been told by *everybody* since we were eggs and sperm to be *good little girls* and *never hit anyone*."

"I don't think I'd have any compunction about defending myself against a rapist or a murderer," Chesi put in, with conviction. "And everybody knows about mothers protecting their young—so the instinct must be there in us, somewhere."

Tiffany nodded vigorously. "Absolutely. And some women are more natural warriors than others—you really find that out in the ring. But for most women there's some built-in mind-fuck that stops you from performing at the crucial moment."

"Like what?"

"Like we *expect* to be overpowered by *any* man—and that victim mind gives an assailant a real edge. And, we don't really want to hurt anybody—*that* makes us hesitate right when we should kick ass. Sometimes, the only thing that can keep you alive, is your willingness to hurt or disable your opponent."

"So how do we learn to overcome all that programming?" Christie asked, really interested now.

"First you have to *believe* you can win—training can help with that. Second, you must learn enough skills to make you *feel* like you're competent. If you know you can put some bozo's lights out, you're more likely to do it. Third, you have to learn to visualize an imaginary attack scene, in your head—practice the attack scenario over and over, psychically—so when the time comes for aggression, you've already made the decision to go for broke.

"Look at it this way—you aren't going out there looking for a chance to kill somebody. The only way you'd ever be using this knowledge is if some guy means you grievous bodily harm. If that's the case, odds are he'll be bigger and stronger than you, and he'll have made the decision to hurt or rape you . . . so you better be willing to give it all you've got, or you're dead meat."

"I am Christian Scientist," Marika blurted, unexpectedly. "I could not kill anyone."

"Oh my God! Will wonders never cease," Christie said sotto voce, to Liz, who was closest.

"I didn't think our army was big enough to have a conscientious objector," Liz whispered back with a short laugh.

Tiffany took Marika's comment in stride. "I don't know any religion that says you shouldn't defend yourself against evil, girl. But you follow your own conscience here. I'll teach everybody what I know—what you do with it is entirely up to you."

She looked around, assessing the intent of the group. "Okay, so let's assume your opponent is face-to-face with you—he's bigger, stronger, and meaner, so what exactly can you do to save yourself? You'd be surprised how much—and how fast you'll learn it." She motioned Liz up from the group to help demonstrate.

"If your hands are loose, a hard palm-heel strike to the bridge of his nose can cripple or even kill a man by driving the sinus bone into his brain." She showed the technique; it looked pretty easy.

"A man's Adam's apple is incredibly sensitive, too—a palm or fist strike to the throat can keep a guy from breathing—and if he can't breathe, he can't hold on to you. Eyes are great targets, too—your thumbs can push in his eyeballs, no matter what size you are. Or you can haul off and box his ears, and believe me, if you do that hard enough, any man will ease his grip enough so you can run for cover."

She motioned Liz to a new spot. "Now, let's say he's got you bending down, like this," she said, maneuvering herself into a crouched position, with Liz poised as her assailant. "You just make a fist with your right hand, grasp it hard with your left, and shove your right elbow into his gut, or chest, or throat, with all your might." She demonstrated the technique, to a big show of appreciation from the watchers. This, too, looked eminently doable for a woman.

"And whatever you do," Tiffany added emphatically, "you *focus*. Like the Karate Kid, or your yoga teacher, or your favorite tennis pro, or your weight coach tells you, *focus* does the job. Your mind's undivided *intent* increases your power exponentially. If you focus on your punch or your kick or your elbow strike, you can really do some serious damage. And, by the way, don't look into your assailant's eyes unless you can look fiercer than he does. Martial artists, boxers, pro athletes, all psych each other out with their eye *chi*—so unless you're up to it, don't chance being overmatched. Just keep your eyes on your target to help your intent stay focused.

"Oh, I almost forgot . . . lips are real sensitive, too. If a guy's got you in a bear hug, squeezing the life out of you, all you have to do is grab his lips with both hands, and yank full-force in two directions at once, while you dig your nails in—and trust me, you'll get his attention."

"What about punching?" Liz asked, thoroughly fascinated. This sounded like anybody could do it.

"Punching's fine if you remember to punch *through* the opponent, not *at* him. Practice making a fist like this. . . ." She held up her hand and exaggerated the clenching of her fingers into the palm, then wrapping her thumb carefully around them into a tight drum. "Keep your wrist straight, so the full force of the long bones of your forearm drives the impact home—otherwise your punch will be flabby, and you might break your wrist. Now you just focus on a spot *behind* where you're aiming, and *push* the punch straight in. Or up. Or around." She showed a straight punch, an upper cut, a right cross in turn, then smiled.

"Now for the good news, girls," she said. "Women don't have the upper-body oomph men do, but our pelvises were built to rule the world! Your legs are potentially far more lethal than your fists, and when I get done showing you how to use your legs in a fight, believe you me, you can kick the stuffing out of anybody."

Before an hour was up, every woman was feeling a surge of confidence. They could *do* this . . . and that knowledge in itself was a powerful boost for the spirits. And they were having fun. Tiffany made the learning half lesson, half sport—by the time she was finished they were sore and weary, but eager for more.

Tiffany held up her hands and laughed her giggly effervescent laugh that had such lilt to it. She was the only one not winded by what they'd done for the past sixty minutes. "Enough for today, women," she shouted over the noise of their efforts. "Enough, enough! Tomorrow we'll start on our aerobic-fitness program to get you into shape for this kind of thing."

There were groans all around, which made her laugh again. "Look. You've all seen enough here today, to know that the first rule of the fight game is this: You're only as good as your wind. If you can't cut it aerobically, you're going down. If your opponent can outlast you, he doesn't have to be smarter or stronger—he just has to be on his feet when you're out of breath and on the ground. Got it?"

Heads bobbed affirmatively all around.

"You looked good, every one of you," she said encouragingly. "I hope you never need this knowledge, but if you do, the other guy better watch out." The group dispersed, but Tiffany called to Liz to wait a minute.

"You've got the gift, sister," she said seriously. "You could see that, couldn't you? Your instincts, your timing . . . you're a natural."

Liz nodded. "It's some kind of warrior memory. There must be past lives, because I have this weird gift for anything that smacks of battle. I swear I've been a general, a footsoldier, and everything in between, and it's all lurking just under this civilized female exterior." She looked ruefully at her current condition and laughed. "*Formerly* civilized exterior, I should say."

Tiffany smiled. "We all look pretty grim by now, don't we?"

"Except for Justine," Liz amended, "who looks like she just stepped off the cover of *Vanity Fair*."

Tiffany agreed. "Must be those high-priced genes of hers."

"It is hard not to be envious of Her Ladyship, isn't it?" Liz mused. "Beauty, brains, money, power, all the privilege in the world."

"Yeah," Tiffany said. "And her high-and-mighty attitude doesn't make it any easier. I don't like to be envious of anybody, it's such an unworthy emotion. But, boy oh boy, in Justine's case it's real, real hard to be my better self. I gotta tell you I was hoping to see she was a wuss today. But she isn't. She's got the stuff, you know?"

Liz nodded. "I saw it too. Probably had boxing lessons in the cradle."

"Yeah," Tiffany agreed. "Or maybe fucked the Olympic boxing team."

They both laughed as they went back to work.

"What the hell is wrong with the electrical system, Rand?" Thoros demanded at lunchtime, his temper pushing hard at the constraints he'd imposed on it. "Nothing is working right anymore and it's hot as Hades in here."

Rand answered in his best dealing-with-an-irascible-client voice. "The electrical system seems to have hit a little snag, Thoros. Nothing serious, I'm sure. Remember this place wasn't due to open for another three weeks . . . there are always a few last-minute bugs on every job site." Rand had been searching since yesterday for the control panels, thus far, unsuccessfully.

Only marginally placated, Thoros responded, "Well, then, just get the damned thing fixed, will you? We have enough aggravation at the moment without sweltering. And while you're at it, figure out what's wrong with the electrical outlet in my bathroom. I plugged in my electric shaver this morning and nothing happened."

"The lights are out in my house, too," Jack chimed in. "I felt like Stevie Wonder trying to get dressed this morning."

Thoros was not amused by Jack's attempt at levity. He glared at Rand, who simply nodded sagely.

"I'll have to find the control room and see to all this," he said as he turned to leave the room. What the fuck was Chesi up to? This had to be her doing. And where in the hell was that control room? He distinctly remembered where it was *supposed* to be, but it wasn't there now.

"*Find* the control room?" Alex said tautly, from behind a magazine, after Rand had closed the door. "I thought he designed the bloody place—doesn't he *know* where the control room is?"

"Do you think the girls could be screwing things up somehow, to harass us?" Jase asked. "Maybe they're trying to get our attention, so we'll negotiate?"

Alex looked thoughtful. "I think it's damned likely, actually. We should have kept communication open with the women from the beginning, Thoros. Our silence can only provoke them."

"Rand can fix whatever little kinks are causing these problems, Alex," Thoros cut in, halting speculation. "He would have told us if this were sabotage. Let's not waste any more time talking about it when we have an expert on the job."

"I'm sorry, old man," Alex persisted firmly, "but I think you're dead wrong not to reopen dialogue with the women immediately." The other men's eyes came up from their various tasks; it was uncharacteristic of Alex to provoke a direct confrontation. A laid-back probity was more his normal modus operandi.

Thoros's eyebrows knitted slightly and his lips tightened as if holding in an explosive response.

"What makes you say so?" he asked, his voice controlled.

Alex moved forward, hands in his pockets, body language striving for casual, nonconfrontive camaraderie.

"I believe they've got your king in check, Thoros. No one's going to win here," Alex said seriously. "Why not call it a draw and simply end the game now? There's really no great harm done, and if we act like gentlemen and admit they've played cleverly, odds are they'll probably decide to keep their mouths shut about all this. Give Marika her check," he looked pointedly at Tony, "and make sure it clears. Apologize to the rest, in our best gentlemanly manner, and let's put this painful episode behind us."

Thoros frowned.

Jack stood with his thumbs hooked on the waistband of his swim trunks. He'd shed all other clothing when the air-conditioning went down. "I agree with Alex," he said, his voice low and serious. "It's gone far enough. I intend to see Tiffany again, and I'd like to get back to work. If you men have a problem with eating crow, I'll do it. To tell you the truth, I think we've acted like assholes, so I won't have too much trouble saying so out loud."

"Let's bring this to a decent conclusion, Thoros," Alex prompted. "Apologize for our boorishness . . . tell them we sabotaged the plane because we couldn't bear to have them leave us . . . whatever it takes. This sort of thing is what I do for a living, Thoros—I do have a certain instinct where negotiations are concerned, and every instinct I possess is telling me we're tempting Fate by letting this go one whit further."

"No!" Thoros said emphatically. "They've ruined our holiday and wasted our time. They've spoiled something that could have been beautiful and memorable, and I've no intention of crawling to them with apologies of any sort. They should damned well come back and apologize to *me*."

Thoros turned abruptly and headed for the door, leaving Alex looking perturbed and thoughtful. Jase ambled over to him and spoke in a voice below earshot of the others.

"We could try it on our own, you know, Alex," he said. "It wouldn't take long on horseback to find their camp. As long as we bring them back into line, Thoros won't care that we took it upon ourselves."

Alex considered the suggestion. "Perhaps you're right. I

have a hunch we'll be courting disaster if we don't defuse this situation quickly."

Jase nodded and the two men left the house and headed for the stables.

"Thoros is taking this harder than I would have expected," Jase said, as they walked.

Alex nodded. "The ruination of his plan for the week seems to have made him quite melancholy. A trifle embarrassed, too, I'd wager. It's all scrambling out as anger, of course. We blokes aren't all that good at sorting our emotions or expressing them, are we?"

Jase laughed shortly. "I've published umpteen self-help books on that subject, and I'll be damned if I think we're even *supposed* to do either one." They rounded the corner and entered the cool dark stable.

"To tell you the truth," Jase added, with a small, rueful smile, "I've always had an easier time connecting with animals than with people. I was pretty much a loner when I was a kid—never really felt I fit in. But animals . . . they take you for exactly who you are. No bullshit, no hype. Just you. I made out better with them."

Alex raised his eyes to Jase's, startled and searching guardedly. "A surprising revelation from one whose prowess at deft conversation has put him on all the hostesses' A-lists."

"A learned response, that's all," Jase answered, lifting the heavy saddle and bridle from their resting places. "I taught myself to charm the birds from the bushes because it served my purpose, not because it came naturally to me."

Alex followed suit, collecting the tack he needed from the wall pegs. "I'll take that bay gelding, if you don't have your heart set on him," he said, walking in the direction of the far stall.

"I had my eye on that big black stallion, actually," Jase answered easily.

Alex raised an admiring eyebrow and laughed. "He's all

yours, my friend. He looks seventeen hands, and too mean, by half."

"That's what attracted me." Jase grinned, entering the stallion's stall. "Come 'ere, big fella," he said gently, as the horse eyed him with wary contempt and bared his teeth in an expressive snort. Proprietarily, Jase laid an experienced hand on the great black withers. "Take it easy, boy, we're gonna like each other," he cajoled, as he tossed the saddle blanket over the tall, aristocratic animal's back, then moved toward his head, bit in hand, with an easy, respectful confidence.

Alex marked the skill with which Jase handled the obstreperous stallion. It had seemed unnecessary bravado to choose so high-strung an animal, and take him into unknown and possibly treacherous terrain. But it was easy to see that Jase was the kind of natural horseman who could bend the worst-spirited animal to his bidding.

The two horses left the stable at an easy walk; then their riders turned toward the heavier foliage at the jungle rim and encouraged the horses to canter. They rode in silence for some time, into the steamy interior landscape, before Alex initiated conversation.

"You've been on horses all your life, I take it?" he said amiably.

Jase nodded. "That was the best part of my childhood," he replied. "Which is probably why I like riding so much—it makes me feel young again. I even proposed to my wife on horseback."

"Fancy that," Alex grinned. "Not quite as much fun as fucking on horseback, but portentous nonetheless."

Jase laughed. "I tried to get her to do that too, actually. Ellie's a terrific rider . . . been on the circuit and all, as befit her social station," he said, a wry note in his voice. "She was aghast, as I recall."

"Perhaps they didn't do that sort of thing on the circuit,

eh?" Alex laughed. "Hell of a lot of fun though. Not too late to give it a go, you know."

"Not with Ellie," Jase said, his voice sounding more wistful, even to him, than he'd meant it to. "Wives don't do that sort of thing. Only mistresses."

"Can't say from experience, I'm afraid," Alex answered. "I've managed to avoid the former rather skillfully. Although, as I get older, I'm beginning to wonder if I haven't missed something or other. Family, perhaps. Sons to carry on the name. That sort of thing, you know?"

Jase opened his mouth to reply when the huge stallion suddenly reared wildly, as an earsplitting shriek of pain or fear escaped its lungs. Caught totally off guard, Jase fought for control of the maddened, lunging animal, not knowing what had spooked him.

"Snake!" Alex cried out, struggling hard to steady his own mount.

Jase fought valiantly to stay in the saddle a moment longer, trying to regain control, then he felt the great horse collapse under him like a felled tree. Unable to extricate himself fast enough, he too went down, his left foot caught in the stirrup, as the two-thousand-pound animal hit the tangled jungle ground.

"Don't move!" Alex shouted, dismounting fast. "That fucker's somewhere in the brush with you."

Jase's eyes darted in the direction of Alex's horrified gaze and saw the coiled black viper swaying two feet from his face. A wash of nausea swept through him, nearly making him vomit; he gritted his teeth hard, desperate for self-control. The snake had struck down the stallion in seconds; it was obviously lethal.

The dying horse shuddered once, violently, raising its hooves in pathetic protest, and the unexpected movement propelled the snake into action. Trapped and helpless, Jase saw it pull back to strike; he closed his eyes in absolute certainty of his own death. But the strike never came. Instead, he felt, not saw,

Alex pluck the coiled body off the ground with a long, forked stick and fling it skyward. He heard the deadly creature land with a thud in the heavy undergrowth ten feet away.

"Good Christ!" Alex gasped as he dropped the branch and gripped Jase hard under the shoulders. "That was a mamba. Let's get you the bloody hell out of here, fast." Positioning himself on the ground behind Jase's body, he braced his feet against the horse's weight to shift the animal just enough so that he could try to pry Jase free.

With great struggle and considerable cursing, the two strong men finally managed to yank Jase out from under his dying mount. Numb and badly cramped, Jase's leg collapsed under him as he tried to stand.

"Son of a bitch!" he exploded, hopping up and down, trying to get the circulation moving again. "That was close."

"You've simply got to stop getting stuck under animals," Alex blurted, with a small, unexpected grin. "My nerves can't handle it."

"I owe you big-time," Jase said, meaning it. "Twice in one day is too fucking much!"

Alex nodded. "And the week's not over yet, is it?"

The two men stood for a long moment, trying to regain their equilibrium enough to move on. Jase bent to caress the horse's neck, and patted his nose to comfort him; foam dripped from the stallion's slack mouth, and his wide staring eyes were glassy. "We need Emilio's gun to put this poor brute down," he said. "What a fucking waste to lose him like this."

"He'll be dead before we'd return with a weapon," Alex responded. "The black mamba is one of the deadliest snakes on earth. I don't think there's an antivenom."

Jase looked up; unable to think of an appropriate response, he merely nodded, the lump in his throat enormous.

"Maybe we'd better go back," he finally managed to say, hoarsely. "I don't feel much like facing those women right now."

"Good idea," Alex replied soberly. "This day does seem a bit star-crossed for negotiation. My horse can carry us both."

"No," Jase answered, not looking back. "I need to walk."

Neither man spoke again until they were back at the compound; both were far more shaken by their brush with death than they had the means to express. The suddenness of the danger had shocked and chastened them. One moment all was well—the next, one of them might have been dead. Mora Utu was suddenly less benevolent than it had seemed, and the future far less certain.

TWENTY-THREE

Chesi put down the blueprint, her final decision made. She'd changed her mind about waiting any longer to take out the rest of the compound after talking tactics with Liz and Christie. They were both very savvy about strategy, and they'd convinced her that every hour now meant Rand might figure out her plan and interfere. And the men had made no move toward a parlay, despite yesterday's tinkering with the air-conditioning.

The Master Switch was just above her eye level on the west wall—with that disabled, all power to the compound would be cut off, but they'd still have the water-desalination system left as their sabotage ace in the hole. She'd keep that till last, in case they needed more leverage.

She stared at the switch for a long moment doing a mental inventory before the irrevocable act. If she pulled this switch, the overhead lights she'd kept blazing night and day would be extinguished, and all systems for food storage and cooking, as well as all backups, would be vanquished. She took a deep breath, her Sicilian forebears stirring in her blood, then she reached for the metal handle, gripped it tightly, and pulled it down with a sharp jerk. All whirring noises within earshot ceased. Unsatisfied, Chesi took a Phillips-head screwdriver and removed the plate that held the big handle. She slipped the handle itself from its moorings and stuffed it into the string mesh bag slung over her shoulder.

Part of her hated to wreak such damage on a place she'd put such blood, sweat, and tears into—another part felt a thrill of satisfaction at having pulled it off. If anything provided them the leverage to get off the island, it would be her ingenuity.

She turned her back on the destruction and closed the door behind her.

Jack and Tony were together in the sweltering kitchen of the Great House, in search of an afternoon snack.

"This heat is a royal pain in the ass," Tony said with unfeigned disgust. Sweat stained the armpits of his polo shirt, which clung to his chest and back like wallpaper. "Let's just put that frigging plane back together and get the fuck out of here. I've had it with this place."

"What do you propose we do about the women? Just leave them and send someone back later?" Jack answered shortly. The heat was getting to all of them; in less than a day, without the air-conditioning, the compound had become a hermetically sealed sarcophagus.

"They can rot out there for all I care," Tony said, staring disgustedly into a mayonnaise jar full of heat-spoiled slops. He picked up the mustard with a disgruntled snort and slapped some onto the sandwich he'd concocted. "And where's that little wetback who's supposed to be feeding us?"

"Emilio's upstairs, working on a stopped-up toilet. He's like a one-armed paperhanger without Nelida anyway, with everything going wrong."

"And what the fuck is Rand doing with his thumb up his

ass?" Tony added. "I thought he was supposed to be able to fix anything around here. So far he ain't fixed shit!"

"Where's Thoros?" Jack asked, as if he'd suddenly realized his host was missing.

Tony grunted something through a mouthful of food. "He's out on the airstrip repairing the plane. We're out of here either late today or first thing tomorrow, women or no women."

"No, we're not!" an angry voice bellowed from the doorway. All focus turned toward the man whose shape filled the kitchen doorway.

"Those infernal bitches have taken the fuel controllers," Thoros spat. "There's no way to fly that aircraft without them."

"Son of a bitch!" Jack said, sounding vaguely amused. "Ten points to them for resourcefulness."

"Ten points my ass," Tony said. "Now you'll have to get your regular pilot down here with another plane."

Thoros shook his head. "It's not that simple, I'm afraid. Our communications options are extremely limited while the G-IV's on the ground."

"Besides, even if we could radio for help," Jack put in, "we'd have to explain what happened. There's no way the story wouldn't get out to the press. We'd be better off figuring out a way to cajole the girls into cooperating in return for a ride out of here. That's probably all they want, by now, anyway."

Thoros looked about to implode with fury. "I'd like to strangle those damned women one at a time," he spat grimly.

"Emilio says he can send a message to his wife, to set up a meeting," Tony put in quickly.

"How's he going to contact her?" Jack interjected. "Have they got a cell-phone out there with them in the woods?"

"How do I know how these Mexicans communicate with each other?" Thoros snapped. "It may be smoke signals for all I care, they are Yaqui Indians after all."

"Yaqui Indians . . ." Jack mused. "What do I know about

Yaqui Indians . . . something . . . Hey, wait a minute! Wasn't that old guy that Carlos Casteneda was always chewing peyote with a Yaqui sorcerer or something? You don't suppose Emilio's using magic on us?" Jack's humor was lost on Thoros's black mood.

"I don't give a damn if he is, as long as he can find those idiot women and get this infinite stupidity over and done with." He stalked out the door, leaving Jack and Tony to follow.

"Seems to me a little magic wouldn't be the worst thing . . . ," Jack said with a wry smile.

Tony laughed, shortly. "Yeah, well, I'll bet the bugs, snakes, and heat will have done most of the job for us by the time we get there."

A screech of machinery followed by what sounded like a small explosion shook the kitchen.

Emilio was at the door. "The main generator, señor. The señoritas have blown the main generator."

TWENTY-FOUR

Thoros and Rand were out scouring the island for the control room. On the patio, Jack stuffed the papers back into his briefcase more emphatically than need be, and got up from the deck chair where he'd been trying to concentrate. A warm glass of beer stood idle on the table beside him, but he didn't reach for it. He felt restless and edgy. They were all edgy since the generator had blown.

A shadow fell across him, as Alex walked by; seeing Jack, the tall Englishman stopped to pull over a chair.

"Penny for your thoughts, friend," he said as he sat down heavily. He'd felt nervous as a cat since the snake incident and needed to talk to someone.

"They're not worth that much," Jack answered, looking over. Alex could sometimes be a priggish pain in the ass, but he'd been pretty solid since this all began.

The newcomer nodded. "I've seen it happen this way more often than not, you know. A small local conflict escalates into a world war, one stupid misstep at a time. You push me, I hit you,

you hit me harder, I blow up your house. . . . Nobody knows how it happened exactly, and nobody knows how to stop the juggernaut. Fortunately, this isn't global."

Jack picked up his beer, sipped it tentatively, frowned at its flat warmth, and put it down. "I've been thinking a lot about Tony. You know, Alex—remembering a few things over the years . . . the laughs we've had, the times he's done me a favor, or offered to, the strings he's pulled, that kind of thing. You could always count on him in the clinches—a tough guy with a big heart. Now, he just looks like a horse's ass with a dick for brains. I'm pissed off at him and I feel sorry and embarrassed for him at the same time."

"I couldn't have said it better myself, Jack. Women can make fools of the best of us, I'm afraid."

"Do you think you can still pull this off with negotiation?" Jack asked seriously. "Or will we have to use force to get the plane fixed?"

Alex shrugged. "If we can muzzle Tony while we talk, and keep Thoros's somewhat righteous anger in check, I think we can still pull it off. The women must want this to end as much as we do."

Emilio appeared out of nowhere; he had a habit of stealth that could be unnerving. . . .

"Do not be so certain of this, señor," he said, with some authority. Each of the men looked at him, startled by his interjecting himself, unbidden, into their conversation. He'd been acting odd since Nelida had left, but never before had he offered an opinion without being asked.

"Why do you say that?" Jack responded.

"It is a thing of empowerment, señor," the little Mexican replied. "They arrived here as girls. They become women now."

Jack and Alex exchanged looks.

"How do you figure that?" Jack asked, interested.

"They take on power when they declare their independence, señor. They honor their womanhood," Emilio said calmly. "The women are *able* . . . do not mistake this."

"Able?" Jase echoed sarcastically, joining in the conversation, and pulling up a chair beside the others. "How *able* can a group of twenty-something bimbos be, Emilio? You sound like you think they're as dangerous as that snake we ran over."

"Sí, señor! They are *peligrosas*. They are angry at your disrespect. One angry woman is a danger . . . six angry women are *muy peligrosas*."

"That's a lot of crap, Emilio," Jase said with disdain. "A consummate pain in the ass, yes. Dangerous, no. We have the compound, the plane, and years of experience in dealing with recalcitrant underlings. . . . We have all the money and all the power and all the brains—what exactly can they do to be dangerous?"

Emilio chuckled from the belly.

"What the hell is so funny?" Jase snapped, annoyed at being laughed at.

"You have the compound, señor, which they have turned into an oven. You have *dinero* that can buy nothing here. You speak of brains, but they have outsmarted you. You speak of *poder*, but on this island power may be different from what you expect. You are old, they are young—in itself, this is power."

"You're pretty damned sure of yourself, Emilio," Alex answered, snappishly, his nerves still taut from the earlier danger. "How is it you think you know so much more about them than we do?"

The little man met his eyes, his expression totally lacking in subservience. "I am a warrior, señor," he answered. "I respect other warriors when they come. It is best to give them honor, then let the battle decide the victor."

"You're a *handyman*, Emilio," Jase countered bluntly, "not a warrior. And if there's any battling to be done, I assure you there's no doubt whatsoever about who will win. And, this is a ridiculous conversation. Haven't you got something you should be fixing around here since nothing seems to be working?" It was apparent that Emilio was dismissed.

The Mexican chuckled again good-humoredly. He said a long sentence in Spanish, then walked away.

"What'd the old fart say?" Jase asked, disdainfully.

"The old fart was giving you the benefit of an old Spanish proverb," Alex replied. "It means, '*He who underestimates his opponent digs his own grave.*' He's a cheeky little bastard, isn't he, but rather amusing."

"Ever notice those eyes of his?" Jack asked, as he watched Emilio's retreat. "He has the eyes of an assassin."

"What are *you* drinking?" Jase asked, with a smirk.

"No, I'm serious. I've seen men before with eyes like Emilio's. On the surface he's earthy, likable, but you look into those eyes and there's cunning and calculation that isn't ordinary at all. I've seen that kind in the neighborhood, in the mob, in the ring, sometimes even in the cops. I don't know exactly *what* he is . . . but I guarantee you it's not just a handyman."

Jase shook his head. "You've been out in the sun too long, Jack. Somebody's going to have to put that little wetback in his place."

Jase walked away, but Jack and Alex remained on the patio.

"You're right, of course, about Emilio," Alex said. "He's at least a bodyguard. I saw him shoot once—years ago, there was a rattler that appeared out of nowhere on the path in front of us. He had the gun out in a blur and the snake was dead before I'd really focused on what was happening. I remember having the odd thought that if he'd been out there without the gun he would have done the deed with his bare hands. I've always rather stayed out of his way since then."

Jack shook his head. "This whole mess has us all spooked. To tell you the truth, I'll be happy to get off this damned island. There's something weird about the place . . . like a fruit that looks perfect, then you bite in and there's a worm inside. Far as I can see, nothing has gone right since we got here."

Alex looked quizzically at Jack. He was the last man he'd expect to wax mystical. But now that he'd said it, there *was* something brooding about this place . . . a discontented energy that felt barely contained, ready to erupt. . . .

H. Douglas Rand stood in the doorway of the control house and looked in shock at the decimation of the electrical systems of Mora Utu. *Shit!* She was smart and thorough. He cursed himself for ever having brought Chesi here.

Thoros Gagarian pushed past Rand unceremoniously so he, too, could see the control room.

"What in God's name have they done, Rand?" he thundered. "What have those infernal bitches done to my home?"

"Pretty much everything possible," Rand answered, too disgusted for subtlety. Not even his best client bullshit could smooth this over.

Thoros looked about the room, trying to wrap his mind around the magnitude of what the women had wrought. For one fleeting moment, despite the fury raging in his gut, he almost had to admire their balls.

Two things were certain. He would retrieve the plane parts and leave Mora Utu, immediately. And he would make them pay.

"Tell Emilio to set up a meeting with the women, first thing tomorrow," he said emphatically to Rand. Then he turned and left the scene of the sabotage.

TWENTY-FIVE

"Tonight, my friends," Nelida said portentously, "we will speak of the wildness you must rekindle in yourselves if you choose to live as *mujeres de Poder*, women of Power."

Everyone around the women's campfire was fatigued, but the valorous tenor of the older woman's voice revived them and made them pay attention; she seemed to have something important to pass on.

"The first lesson of Power," she began, her dark eyes snaring each pair of eyes in turn around the fire, "is that we are alone. We are born alone, we will die alone. All else is an illusion. We spend most of our lives looking for someone with whom to share the awesome responsibility of living—the decisions, the heartaches, the blame for our mistakes. Sometimes we even think we have found such a person . . . for a time. But, in the end, we face eternity and judgment alone. The warrior learns this lesson earlier than others, but it is the hardest one expected of a woman. Our *nature* causes us to dream of being part of a larger whole." She waited for that to sink in before continuing.

"You have drawn the line in the sand here. You have declared your intent to these men and said, *We are women of Power—we must be reckoned with.* Soon you will begin to feel the aloneness of your intent."

"But we're not alone, Nelida," Justine interjected. "We are a united front."

Nelida chuckled. "Every soldier who has ever gone to battle was part of a larger force. But every soldier who has ever died, died alone.

"The simple truth is that life is *un partido peligroso,* a dangerous game. And it is always fatal. When the clock strikes twelve, God will win. Of this you may be certain. But in the hours allotted to you . . . ah, in those hours you may have learned enough to make the game worthwhile."

Her mesmeric eyes traveled the group a second time.

"Do not think that the aloneness you must endure precludes the amassing of allies, for allies are not only *permitted*, they are *required* on a journey of the spirit. Before you leave this island, you will have found who among you are true allies. Just as you were each born to a single mother, but if you are blessed by the Goddess, you will have *Todas las Madres,* the many mothers in your lifetime—for your need for advisement will never be outgrown. When you are ninety, if you meet a woman of ninety-nine, she will have something of great importance to teach you."

She surveyed her audience with a practiced eye.

"Very shortly, you must learn to be dangerous!" she said with great vehemence. "You need *will* and courage and purpose, for you are wild creatures—no less than men are, but you must learn that the lessons expected of them are different from yours. You carry different seeds than they to fertilize the world; you carry the deep-knowing and the love-giving. The night-dreaming, soul-healing, body-comforting nurturance and intuition which make the world bearable. *All,* in fact, that is *unmeasurable* and therefore easily dismissed in a limited world that values only the 'seen' and the measurable. It is as if you carry sight in a world so blind it no longer knows that sight is useful! So you must *teach them to see,* but first of all, *you* must learn to *value* properly that sight which is your birthright. Otherwise, if you merely copy their ways, you will become like the mockingbird imitating the crow—you will be either a crippled crow or a counterfeit mockingbird!" They laughed nervously, and she paused.

"If what you're saying is true, Nelida," Liz ventured, "God has one lousy, meanspirited sense of humor—to make men and women so different from each other that we can never fulfill each other's needs."

"No, child," Nelida said, more gently. "This is not correct! Men and women *need* each other greatly. But they need themselves *first.* Just as they need to learn each other's *true value* as individuals of Power. We do not need to become the *same* as they—there would be no electricity to fuel the planet if negative and positive became one.

"Which, my daughters, brings me to the last lesson of Power."

"Which is?" Justine prompted, fascinated by this woman, but not at all certain what to make of her. "If the first lesson is that we are alone, what is the last lesson?"

Nelida smiled, an enormity of compassion in her face. "The final lesson of Power," she said softly, "is that we are all *one*. But do not trouble your heads with this now, my daughters. Soon you will see, and you will learn all that is required of you."

Wednesday, April 13

Do it big, or stay in bed.

Larry Kelly

TWENTY-SIX

Wednesday morning on Mora Utu dawned, unperturbed by the petty machinations of the men and women who currently inhabited the island. The sun rose, the birds chirped and twittered, the insect population began its noisy morning symphony as the men gathered agitatedly near the pool in preparation for their parlay with the women.

"We're to meet them in an hour," Thoros said to Alex, his voice tense. "Emilio has set the place. And, Jack," he added, turning to Doherty, "they've insisted that you come along."

Jack nodded. He was sure Tiffany was behind that request, but he was happy to have a reason to participate. They couldn't afford any more blunders.

Alex, Thoros, and Jack drank a quick cup of coffee and set off.

"Thoros," Alex began coaching quietly as they walked. "No matter how upset you are about what's been done, you must promise me you'll keep your temper. This is a very volatile situation—just the kind of powder keg that can be set off by a single spark. If we do this correctly, we may be off the island by this afternoon."

Thoros nodded acknowledgment, but made no reply for a long moment. Then he spoke. "I have no intention of escalating this damned foolishness, Alex, you may be sure of that. I fully intend to end it at this meeting."

The two men followed their host into the jungle. From the terrace, Tony watched them go, an unreadable expression on his hard face.

Liz, Christie, Justine, and Tiffany waited nervously, at the place where Nelida had told them the men would appear.

"How the hell do you think Nelida and Emilio set this parlay up?" Liz asked.

Justine shrugged noncommittally. "Perhaps they made the plan before she left the compound. We still can't be certain she isn't a double agent of some sort, you know. It makes me uneasy having her here—her livelihood depends on Gagarian."

"I love Nelida!" Tiffany piped up. "She's no spy! How about those spectacular things she says at the drop of a palm leaf? And that woman-Power stuff, I really dig that. She's been telling Chesi and me about finding our wild natures, and how women are part of the animal family, so we're at home in the woods. . . . Anyway, she's a real kick. And you have to admit the food's better since she got here."

Liz nodded so affirmatively that her long ponytail bounced like the real thing. "Are you ever right about the food! The idea of eating our cooking for a week was enough to make me want to capitulate. Now that we Robinson Crusoes have a Friday on staff, we can hold out till doomsday."

"There they are," Tiffany called out, spotting the men coming toward them through the trees. "Thanks for letting me tag along, guys—I'd really like to help get things settled."

"Yeah, yeah," Liz replied with a knowing smirk. "We know

you're dying to see Jack, even across a clearing. Besides, I think having Jack in on this parlay was a great idea—he has a level head, and he seems like a pretty nice guy."

Justine stood up, managing, somehow, to look regal in shorts and a halter. She looked great with only lip gloss and mascara, Liz thought, assessing her own status at the same time—hair slicked back, a little blush, a little strategic eye shadow and lipstick, maybe even in the right places. She knew she looked terrific in the tank top and short shorts, so that part was okay. Wonder if Henry Kissinger checks his wardrobe before chatting with Arafat? she thought irreverently.

They were all standing face-to-face now. The sexual tension in the air between Jack and Tiffany was so palpable it almost made Liz laugh out loud.

"For Christ's sake, would you go ahead and kiss the woman, Jack," Alex stage-whispered, "so we can get on with it."

Tiffany looked at Jack and blushed; he seemed as embarrassed as she. She smiled reassuringly at him, then shook her head no for both of them. "Let's just get on with it," she said primly. Jack winked at her and smiled, but said nothing.

Thoros took the lead. "We would like to end this insane . . ." he began, then remembering Alex's instruction, changed his tack. "Ladies," he started again, his voice hoarse from restrained emotion. "This has been a most unfortunate experience that's caused us all a good deal of . . . aggravation." He'd be damned if he'd acknowledge how much havoc they'd wrought at the compound.

"We want you to know we fully understand your anger. It was high-handed and downright stupid of us to disable the G-IV. It's just that we thought we could salvage something of our holiday if we kept you here . . . perhaps make you understand that the week could still be a wonderful vacation." He shook his head at the absurdity of that; he seemed sincere.

"We were fools to do what we did, of course. I see that

now. . . . But you must understand that we meant you no harm, whatsoever. We simply thought we could persuade you to reconsider, if we had a bit more time to talk things through . . . and then it all got out of hand, when you started destroying things."

A sound in the nearby brush broke Thoros's concentration. Jack could see in the tensed, throbbing veins on the side of Gagarian's neck, how much keeping his temper in check was costing him, and admired his restraint. Tony emerged from the undergrowth, crushing back the heavy foliage as he came. "Goddamned vines are like rubber bands, you can't get through them without a machete," he said as he neared the assemblage.

Thoros's brows nearly met in the scowl that blackened his face. "Tony!" he said sharply. "What are you doing here? I told you to let *us* handle them." *Damnation!* Why hadn't he said handle *this,* as he'd intended—now, the word *them* was out and he couldn't retrieve it. Damn Tony for his asinine bullheadedness. It was like he had a death wish where these women were concerned. . . .

"I handle my own problems, Thoros," Tony spat back, confrontation in voice and aspect. "This is all my fault, right? Everybody's blaming old Tony, so get out of my way and let Tony fix it." He pulled out his checkbook and pen in an exaggerated gesture.

"Okay, girls, what'll it take to end this? What exactly is the price you want to get everybody back in everybody else's beddy-bye?"

"Really, Thoros!" Justine snapped, disdainfully. "This is *too* absurd. We were under the impression you had decided to behave in a civilized manner."

Tony moved forward, closer to Justine. "You don't think I'm civilized, you arrogant cunt? How civilized would *you* be without your father's money? That's all civilized is, anyway—just another name for rich, right? And I'm richer than you could believe."

Justine turned her back on him, a studied gesture of dismissal, a look of utter revulsion on her autocratic face.

"Don't you turn your back on me, bitch!" he growled, grabbing her shoulders. He'd spun Justine halfway around when she smashed her fist into the side of his face with stunning force.

Everything happened so fast after that, it was a blur. People were shouting, Jack grabbed Tony at the same time the other three women came to Justine's defense, fists and feet flying. Liz landed a stunning right cross to Thoros's jaw before he thought to defend himself. Tiffany's long arms and legs seemed to be everywhere at once. Christie fought like a Fury. The men were cursing, the women shouting. And then it was over and the women were racing back toward the cover of jungle.

Tiffany got as far as the edge of the clearing, then half turned back toward the men to call out, "Good-bye, Jack!" over her shoulder, before she ran to catch up with the others. He could hear the tears behind her words.

The four men stood transfixed, stunned by the events of the previous three minutes.

"God damn you, Tony!" Thoros thundered, rubbing his injured jaw. "I told you to stay away from these women! Now see what you've done!"

"Asshole!" Alex shouted, unwilling to contain his anger any longer. "We could have had them eating out of our hand in another thirty seconds, if you hadn't blown it all sky-high."

"What the hell is it with you, Tony?" Jack demanded, angrily. Tiffany had been within arms' distance. "Are you *trying* to screw things up for everybody else, or are you just too dumb to know what you're doing?"

"Back off, both of you!" Thoros roared. "I have something to say to Tony and I need to say it *alone*."

Jack and Alex exchanged looks; this was unexpected, but understandable. Thoros stood to lose the most in this fuck-up.

"Right you are," Alex said shortly, answering for both of

them. "We'll see you back at the compound, then." The two men turned abruptly and were swallowed up by the jungle before they'd gone twenty steps.

Tony and Thoros faced each other radiating anger. Like two old bulls squaring off, neither intended to give an inch.

"I don't know what your game is, Tony," Thoros spat, "but by God, it's going to stop right here. When whatever happened with Marika happened, I was angry at your blunder *and* at the fact that you were disrespectful enough of me to let it happen under my roof." He paused for breath and control. "But I remembered that you were my friend and I took your side against these women. But today . . . this incalculably arrogant stupidity . . . this is very hard for me to disregard. I want the gun, Tony," Thoros said, his voice harsh and deadly. "And I want you to stay away from these women until I can get them off my island."

"I told you, I haven't got your gun, Thoros," Tony shouted back at him. "As to the women, I don't give a flying fuck what you want."

Thoros's mouth was a grim line of fury. "Every instinct tells me you have the gun, Tony. Every instinct. You have been my friend for thirty years. We've seen each other through poverty and opportunity and dangerous times. I was mad as hell at you for being such a fool with Marika—but I've been a fool myself often enough to know that when it happens, you must hope the Gods will relent enough so it doesn't bring the house down."

He paused, and the vein at his temple throbbed ominously. "Nothing irreparable has yet happened here—our holiday is ruined, no more, no less. But so help me God, Tony . . . if anyone *dies* here because of a temper you can't control, or some stupid-ass vendetta you think you have with this Marika . . . you are on your own, and our friendship is at an end."

Tony's eyes were hard, his jaw set like granite. "You would threaten *me*, Thoros, my friend?" His voice dripped acid. "When you got to Vegas and you needed introductions to keep your casino doors open, who vouched for you with the boys? When that second wife of yours thought she had you by the balls and threatened to take every dime you'd ever earned, who sent Uncle Vinny around to help her see the light? When that slant-eyed geek from Makashimayo tried to keep your boys out of Tokyo, who put in the fix for you with the Yakuza? And *you* would threaten *me?*" He looked genuinely aggrieved.

Explosive emotion was everywhere in Thoros's aspect, but it was hard to read exactly what kind of emotion it was; guilt, fury, sorrow, all jumbled into one. "You have been my friend, Tony, and I have been no less yours," he said, his deep voice hoarse with tension. "But murder on my island does not come within the bounds of friendship. You have the gun. See that it doesn't help your anger to destroy you."

Thoros didn't wait for a reply, but turned on his heel and headed for the compound. This madness had to come to an end. It'd be a damned shame if his friendship with Tony ended, too, but if it couldn't be helped, so be it. One thing was for certain, those women had to be gotten off the island, and fast.

Thirty minutes later, Thoros struggled to open the large window in his study that faced the sun, then realized that it was sealed in some way he couldn't fathom, and resisted the urge to throw something through it. He cursed audibly at the window and by extension at Rand, who was supposed to be on top of things like this, and at Tony, who had caused it all. He heard Jase enter the room behind him.

"You can forget the windows, Thoros," Shindler said quietly. "We'll be better off meeting on the terrace, anyway. There's a breeze out there, and tempers are hot enough as it is. Everybody's waiting to hear what comes next."

Thoros turned and nodded. He'd formed a definite plan on the way back from the aborted parlay, which had made him feel better; there was nothing worse than being out of control. He followed Jase to the terrace knowing, finally, what had to be done.

The men sat on the terrace looking grim. An undefined anger permeated the group, as it only awaited Thoros's arrival out of strained politeness, not because they thought he'd present a solution.

"Up to now, gentlemen," Thoros said with authority, "due to the extraordinary turn of events that has marred our holiday, we've been playing a defensive game with our adversaries—part out of guilt, I expect, part out of gentlemanly decorum. I believe this has been a serious mistake."

Several men started to speak at once but Thoros silenced them with an upraised hand and a scowl.

"I have no intention of backtracking to place blame . . . pinpointing who hit Nelly in the belly with a flounder is not going to solve this problem. Direct action might.

"But first let's clear up a few of the questions that have been raised. Several of you have asked about off-island communication. I, as well as the rest of you, left strict do-not-disturb orders with my people, so I don't expect any of my employees or yours to get concerned about our safety until Sunday night, if we fail to return on schedule. And, as some of you know, we have very limited radio-range potential in the G-IV, while it's on the ground.

"The long and short of it is, we need the fuel controllers the women have stolen. Once we've recovered them, the plane is operational and all obstacles to our departure are removed." He paused to let that sink in.

"To that end, I'm afraid we must take a new tack with these recalcitrant women. No more gentlemanly parlays, no more pussyfooting. It's time we started acting like men."

"What do you mean, exactly, Thoros?" Jack voiced the question on every man's lips.

Thoros let his eyes rest for a moment on each of the men as

if assessing them. "We cut off their access to the interior of the compound. We guard our flanks. We post watch. We do serious reconnaissance on their camp. We find out where they're hiding the fuel controllers . . . and we retake possession."

"Steal them back, you mean?" Jase asked pointedly.

"Exactly."

"What if they're guarding their flanks, too?" Alex asked, dismayed. "How far are we prepared to go to get what we want?"

Thoros kept his gaze steady as he replied judiciously. "Once we find where the fuel controllers are hidden, I don't imagine much physical force will be necessary to achieve our end. They are women and we are men, let us not forget that."

"From the look of Tony's jaw," Jack put in with a short laugh, "I'd say they're women with a wallop. I'm considering signing Justine to a contract."

The others laughed, but Thoros had no intention of losing control of the meeting. He called for order, but Jase broke in. "Look," he said seriously. "We all want out of here. Let's *find* the damned fuel controllers first, then we can decide how best to get them. Meantime, I, for one, will feel like a real horse's ass if these women steal anything else, or screw up one more part of our life. And with all due respect to our esteemed architect friend, I'd say Rand gets *A* for brilliant choice of personnel, and *F* for ability to fix anything his personnel demolishes."

"That's totally uncalled for," Rand said hotly. "If our crack negotiating team hadn't fucked up royally, the women wouldn't have blown the generator in the first place."

"Our crack negotiating team was doing fine," Alex snapped acidly, "until Tony tried to bludgeon another one of the women. If you men had kept him under wraps for half an hour, as we'd asked . . ."

"Enough!" Thoros shouted, pounding his fist on the table so hard that the glass cracked. "Squabbling like children is *not* the answer. We are all hot, frustrated, and angry. It will do no good whatsoever for us to step all over each other's egos. Now dammit!—we will *not* be a house divided against itself. We have five days to solve this riddle before we call in outside assistance and look like consummate horses' asses to the world. Is there any man here who thinks we can't do that? If so, now's the time to speak your mind." Thoros glowered over the assembled faces, waiting for a response. Finally, Jack spoke up.

"I'll take first watch, if you'd like, Thoros . . . after that we can draw lots for hours. We all know each other pretty well—that should help in divvying up responsibilities."

Tony spoke up. "Look, guys, I know I'm on everybody's shit list at the moment, but I want you to hear me out, for a moment; you owe me that. Thoros is right-on with what he's saying, but we gotta pull together to make it work. Rand's an architect, but he knows squat about construction—maybe I can help him out. Construction is my line of work, and demolition is what I did in the Marines. We should booby-trap the areas we don't want the women messing with . . . maybe dig some trap trenches to make sure they don't screw up anything else."

"That's crazy!" Jase snarled. "We don't want anybody getting seriously injured here. We don't have access to medical attention."

"So, forget the traps for now," Tony countered. "We still need to get the plane parts back. You were in the service, Jase, and you're wily as hell. So let's put you in charge of reconnaissance, to see if you can find the fuel controllers. At least then we're mobile again." He paused for breath. "Give Rand a shot at fixing what he can, Alex and Thoros strategy and negotiation, Jack and Jase, security, and me construction and demolition . . . or however the hell you want to divide it up. But let every man do what he's good at. Let's get off our keesters and get moving.

"Look," he pressed, earnestly. "I've got something I've been wanting to say to you guys, and I guess this is as good a time as any to say it. I'm sorry as hell about all that's happened here. The last thing I wanted was to screw up everybody's vacation, and yeah, I got a big problem with my temper. But I'll do anything I can to make amends. Maybe we can still pull this thing off. I don't know about you men, but I hate like hell to have to call for backup like we're a bunch of old ladies. If we can't clean up our own shit here, we're not the men I think we are.

"I mean, I've been hearing a lot of bellyaching for the last couple of days about how we ain't got air-conditioning, or cold beer or gourmet meals . . . and, that really makes me laugh, you know?

"I grew up in a shack—Thoros, you grew up in a tenement; Jack, too. Who the hell knows about the rest of you. So, we got smart and we worked our asses off to make a better life for ourselves. You mean to tell me we can't do it again for a few fucking days, for Christ's sake? We all got so frigging many people on our payrolls now, maybe we forgot how to roll up our sleeves? Hell, if we pull together here, and pull this one out of the toilet, it might even make us feel young again."

Tony sat down and looks were exchanged all around. They'd remembered why he was one of them, why he was their friend. He was a hothead, but he was a good man, and what he'd said made a hell of a lot of sense.

Heartened by their new plan, the men began to divide up duties.

While the men sat on the terrace animatedly planning their next moves, Chesi, Christie, and Tiffany lay hidden in the dense foliage at the edge of the Mora Utu compound, awaiting their opportunity. It hadn't taken them long after the disastrous parlay to decide to play their trump card in retaliation. Finishing off the sabotage they'd started would at least vent some of the fury they felt, and make them feel less impotent. And, it would make the men's lives nearly as precarious as their own. Chesi only hoped that Rand hadn't set a guard on the water cistern yet; there was no doubt in her mind that he would, if they didn't get in there first.

It was frightening to be this close to the enemy, but the men on the terrace seemed intent on their conversation. It was a piece of luck that all of them were together, instead of wandering around the compound separately. Maybe it would give the demolition team the chance to get in and out of the house without detection.

Chesi pointed silently to the stone stairway that was nearly hidden by overhanging bushes and shrubs. The others nodded acknowledgment, and made their way stealthily across the short distance of clearing, to the cover of the foundation plantings.

"What if it's locked?" Tiffany whispered, staring at the heavy door looming in front of them.

"It won't be," Chesi replied, "unless Rand has figured out our schedule." She pushed open the door to the water-collection cistern, and motioned for the others to follow her inside the vast cellarlike structure under the compound, which housed the water tanks for Mora Utu.

"After you screw up the desalinization system, won't you have to drain off all those humongous holding tanks?" Christie asked, awestruck by the size of the giant vats that supplied the main house and its satellites.

Chesi shook her head emphatically. "The water in these tanks is filthy, Christie—salty and full of bacteria. Without going through the cleansing cycle, all this water will be absolutely useless to them, unless they want dysentery."

" 'Hell hath no fury . . .' " Christie intoned with a smirk. "What do we do while you're at your dirty work?"

Chesi pointed up to a catwalk that occupied the cavity between the tanks and the floor above. "That catwalk will give you access to the whole main floor of the Great House. Most of the floor vents are twenty-four by eighteen inches, plenty big enough for you and Tiffany to get through. Just stay quiet as church mice when you hit a vent, and you'll be able to see what they're up to inside the house. When you find an empty room, make your hit and get out fast with your booty."

"How are those grilles attached?" Tiffany asked.

"Just set into the floor. You can pry them out with a screwdriver."

Tiffany smiled and patted the tools sticking out of the back pocket of her cutoffs. She gave Chesi a thumbs-up, then she and Christie started toward the steel ladder that led to the catwalk.

"Watch out for Emilio," Chesi called after them in a whisper. "Nelida says he's got more senses than a Star Trek empath." The two women nodded, and continued on their mission; while Chesi disabled the water system, they would loot the house.

"We'll cover more ground if we go in two directions," Tiffany whispered when they'd reached the top of the ladder. "This trick is only going to work once, so we'd better get out everything we need, as quickly as we can." Christie nodded and headed toward the west side of the house.

It's eerie in this dark, dank place, Tiffany thought as she moved stealthily into a darkness that was pierced periodically by grids of light shining through from the room above. *This must be what it feels like to be in prison,* she thought with a shudder—*seeing the outside world in tiny patches, desperate for light and warmth and human touch. . . .* She shook her head to clear it of such morbid thoughts and concentrated on what she was about to do.

The first grille came off without a hitch. Tiffany hoisted herself into the room off the kitchen, thankful as ever for her agile body that always did exactly as she asked of it. The house was stifling, and she nearly recoiled at the stench of spoiled food and stagnant air that hit her in the face. The pantry was empty and she could hear voices on the terrace, far away, so she made short work of the kitchen shelves, then deposited the two sacks she'd filled up back on the catwalk and replaced the grille. The second grate gave her considerably more trouble than the first, but within a minute or two, she'd freed it from the floor and was standing in the small gallery off the empty dining room.

She could see through the window that Thoros and the others were still in a meeting, outside. . . . *Probably planning strategy,* she thought with a grim smile, *just like we did.* She held her breath, trying to assess if she could make it to the second floor without being caught or having a heart attack. The whole experience at the parlay, an hour ago, had been terribly unnerving; her pulse still hammered wildly, and not from exertion. Tiffany took a deep breath, said a small prayer, and ran for the staircase. She scampered up as fast as she could, wincing at the small creaks her footfalls engendered.

Thank God! She made it to the landing, then glancing right and left to orient herself to the diagram Chesi had provided, pulled the list of needed supplies from her pocket. Medical supplies were in a closet off Thoros's dressing room, Nelida had said—bandages, gauze, antiseptic, even snakebite stuff and morphine, that was her first priority. Tiffany made it to the bedroom door, and sighed with relief at being safe; she looked left and right again, then darted into the master bedroom. She nearly collided with Jack, as he came around the dressing-room corner. He looked as stunned to see her as she was to see him.

"What are you . . ." they said in unison. Jack started to speak, but Tiffany put her finger to her lips urgently.

"Please . . ." she whispered, stricken at having been caught. He saw in her eyes the entreaty not to betray her.

Jack's eyes widened, taking in everything about her—the beauty, the fear, the disappointment at having been discovered, the love, or something very like it, on seeing him. He put his finger to his own lips conspiratorially and then, on impulse, opened his arms to her encouragingly. She walked hesitantly into his embrace and he marveled at how right it felt to be holding her, despite the mess they were all in; how extraordinary that she should trust him, despite the disaster of only an hour ago. He bent his head to kiss her, and she responded, wanting him every bit as much as he wanted her. He felt the bittersweet yearning as she pulled herself away and tried valiantly to regain her equilibrium.

"Oh, Jack, what are you doing in Thoros's room?" she whispered. "I thought everyone was out on the terrace."

"Band-Aid," he said, pointing to his hand, where a freshly applied Band-Aid was soaked with blood. "Things got a little intense out there . . . there was this broken glass . . . Thoros said he had Band-Aids . . ."

"That's what I'm after, too," she whispered, smiling a little at the irony. "Medical supplies for the troops, in case we need them. They're up here, somewhere."

"I suppose after what happened earlier, I can't just talk you into coming back to me?" he said, with a rueful chuckle. "I'm sorrier than I can say about all this, Tiff."

"I wish I could, Jack," she answered, wistfully. "But I can't let everybody down—it's like we're a team, now. We have to decide what's best together. All we really want to do is put the plane back together again and get out of here, but it's all screwed up after what happened with Tony out there." She took a breath. "I don't suppose you could talk Thoros into just making peace? This is all pretty scary, and . . . I really miss you."

His eyes softened and he reached out gently to brush some stray hair from her cheek. "I'll work on it, babe," he said genuinely, "but he's pretty pissed off at the moment because of all the damage to the compound. And everybody's worried about this whole story coming out. . . . I mean, a lot of these guys have wives."

Tiffany looked up sharply. "Do you have a wife, Jack?" she asked. "I guess I should have asked you that a lot earlier . . . anyway, I didn't—but I would like to know."

Jack's eyes crinkled a little, reading her, wanting to comfort her, an emotion he hadn't felt toward anyone in ages. His voice was gentle when he answered, "I don't have a wife, Tiff. I would have told you if I did."

She let out her breath, relieved, then bobbed her head, as if to say, *I knew that*. She reached up suddenly and kissed him again. "I sure hope this mess doesn't last much longer," she breathed when they pulled apart. "I really miss you, Jack, and I don't want this to spoil things for us."

He nodded acknowledgment and almost smiled, but he looked so serious, like a solemn child. "I won't let it spoil things," he said, meaning it. "And I'll show you where the Band-Aids are."

He led her to the medicine cabinet, and waited until she'd hurriedly filled her sack with first-aid necessities. "I'd better get out of here," she said nervously, as she emptied the last shelf.

"Let me check the stairs first for you, babe," he said conspiratorially. "If the coast is clear, I'll start to whistle Dixie on my way out. Okay?"

She laughed, and he thought it was the sweetest sound he'd heard in a long, long while.

TWENTY-SEVEN

"Hand me that hammer and chisel, will you?" Tony called down from the ladder to Jase. He felt a helluva lot better since getting everything off his chest at the meeting. The sealed windows would have to be opened; the louvers on the other side allowed air to circulate, and once this side was free, the house would seem less hostile. There was a lot of work to do, and getting to it was making them all feel better.

Jase handed the tools up to Tony, and continued the digging he'd started an hour before. The idea of setting traps for women didn't sit all that well with him, but neither did the guerrilla raid they'd made so successfully. He doubted they'd venture so close in again, but just in case, they'd dig the trenches on the outskirts of the house and a few farther out. It irked him that they hadn't been able to plan a strategy that would turn the tables enough to get the girls to capitulate. The whole thing was like a lousy sitcom.

But it felt damned good to be doing *something*, not just sitting around anymore, complaining and sweltering. As far as

Jase was concerned, Sunday couldn't come soon enough. If the plane was still inoperable by then, Thoros's air force would know there was trouble and send in assistance; embarrassing as their story would be to tell, it would be preferable to staying in the middle of this farce.

Inside the house, Jack and Alex nailed the last grate into place in the dining room and prepared to move on to the living-room foyer; after two more rooms, all ducts from the catwalk below would be sealed off. Jack looked ruefully at the blocked access and thought about Tiffany; now there would be no more surprise visits.

Thoros and Rand completed the plane check and locked the doors to the aircraft.

"No point in letting them steal anything else," Thoros said as he pocketed the keys. The two men walked down the steps to the runway and stood briefly, looking around them. Everything was still and hot. The usually incessant island breeze had subsided for the moment, and heat waves radiated from the runway and plane, distorting the air around them.

Thoros turned toward his friend, a troubled far-off look in his eyes. "I would never have believed this week could turn into such a fucking disaster, Rand," he said musingly. "Mora Utu is so right for me, so much as we'd planned it." He hesitated, then said quietly, "You don't think there could be anything to that curse business the sailors who evacuated the natives spoke of, do you? I remember there was some talk about an old medicine man's making some unexpected ritual gesture."

Rand's eyes came up, sharp and clear. "Absolute rubbish," he said emphatically. "I doubt it ever even happened. I mean, one old man, and a bunch of superstitious natives . . . Nobody ever really said it was a *curse* per se—only some odd hand motion the old bugger made that the others interpreted as meaningful—he was probably just scratching his arse. . . . You know how these stupid rumors get going, Thoros. Absolute nonsense. All of it." That damned idiot story should never have gotten back to Gagarian. Who the hell had even mentioned it to him? Whoever it was had drawn his last paycheck.

Thoros looked out to sea again, the same disconcerting expression on his face. "You're probably right," he said, finally, sounding unconvinced. "But, there *are* such things, you know, Rand." His voice was oddly ruminative. "Curses, I mean. In the old country, strange things happened, everyone respected those who had occult knowledge. I remember as a boy, I once saw a man killed by a curse . . . at least my grandmother said that's what killed him. Somehow in America you feel removed from all that primitive peasant knowledge . . . you feel out of reach of it, so you forget the power that can be called forth by those who know how. Not that the Kennedys were out of reach, of course—some sort of family curse working there, I'd wager." He stopped for a moment.

"My grandmother had the gift," he said quite seriously. "Everyone in our village knew she could make things happen . . . cure things, cast spells, remove curses. . . ."

"Pity she's not around now, Thoros," Rand said with obvious disdain. "Perhaps she could whip this place into shape for you." It was apparent from his tone that he was contemptuous, not just skeptical.

Thoros laughed shortly. "I can see you have no experience of such things, Rand, so we'll just leave it at that. I'm probably just feeling morbid about all that's happened . . . but you never know."

They turned back toward the compound and spoke no more about it on the return trip, Thoros lost in his own depressive thoughts. He was shocked by the magnitude of disappointment that had welled up in him at the weird turn of events. He felt a deep and troubling sadness over the decimation of his week, his plans, his island, his Paradise. He had meant only good to come of it for everyone, and now . . . He shook his head to clear it of unwanted emotions and strove to force himself to clarity, but the sadness kept welling up from some hidden reserve. And behind it was a terrible, unspoken loneliness.

TWENTY-EIGHT

Tiffany finished her self-defense class and everyone collapsed to the ground for a breather. In only a couple of days they'd learned an enormous amount and had started to feel confident. The incident with Tony earlier in the day had made it clear to everyone how important this training was.

Tiffany stood surveying the group like a proud mother hen; this was really working. She dried the sweat from her arms and shoulders with a scrap of towel. "Great work, women," she said, meaning it. "Let me tell you, Liz and Christie and Justine were absolutely fantastic in that fight today. Let's hear it for our heroes!" All the women clapped and hooted their approbation of one another.

Tiffany raised her hands for quiet. "Before we split up, there's another part to your class for today."

Everybody groaned at the thought of more exercise, and Tiffany giggled. "Relax, sisters. You can sit right where you are for the rest of this lesson. Christie and Liz are going to tell us how to pull our little army together."

Christie stood up on cue. "We need to organize ourselves like a military unit would for max efficiency. Liz and I have made a list of what we need to do and to talk about, so we can divvy up jobs and make a duty roster. Here's how we see it: We need more secure shelter and bug-proof beds—Chesi and Nelida seem to be the best choices for that job.

"We need four-hour watches, an early warning system, and weapons training as a deterrent to the guys. After the incident with the men earlier today, we know they're coming after us, we just don't know when or with what, so we have to be prepared. Justine and Marika, our mighty hunters, know weapons best—we'd like to suggest they train the rest of us just like Tiffany's doing, but with spears, knives, and bows, so whoever is on watch can protect herself and us.

"We need better sanitary facilities, latrine trenches that carry waste *away* from the water supply . . . that sounds like a Chesi task to plan and an all-hands-on-deck task to accomplish. Nelida and Chesi are the best cooks, by far . . . they already seem to be divvying that up, but they need some sous-chefs to help with the scut work, so I think we should all just take turns on KP, odious as that is. Same with cleanup. We've worked up a schedule."

She paused to wait for dissenters, then proceeded, when no one protested. "As to negotiation, I still think *I'd* do it best, but Liz and Justine are adamant about participating, *so* . . . I suggest we all battle out possibilities in as parliamentary a way as we can, without scratching each other's eyes out, then put our strategy to a vote about who delivers the news to the other side. Everybody okay with that?"

Assents were sounded around the circle. Christie's crisp efficiency was comforting in a way, and her former irritability seemed to have been mitigated by her military skill. Or maybe she just liked giving orders.

"All right," she said, seeing no disapproval on the faces

around the circle. "That leaves us with the question of dangers—other than the men—we have to avoid as long as we're here. Jungle pitfalls, poisonous whatever, and general tropic safety. Nelida will address these concerns next, and then we'll work out a duty roster and hear from each woman about questions and suggestions." She sat down as if she'd just called a board meeting to order. Liz made a gesture that said she had nothing to add at the moment. All eyes turned toward Nelida.

"I have observed the snakes and insects who dwell here and have consulted certain sources in Nature for advice," the Mexican woman began; no longer did they question her about such curious statements. "You must walk with considerable care in heavy jungle or rain forest like this one. We have not the proper boots for safety, so sneakers must be worn at all times, instead of sandals."

"*You* wear sandals, Nelida," Liz pointed out, and the older woman smiled.

"The women of my lineage have an agreement with the serpent kingdom—it is a matter of respect between allies," she continued. "*You* do not have this protection.

"Insects, too, can be dangerous. There are nasty scorpions, and the mosquitoes carry fevers here, including malaria and a mild form of sleeping sickness. There are many kinds of ants, which may appear less frightening, but they, too, can be quite lethal. Fire ants can tear flesh from bone and pick a whole carcass clean in one day, as can beetles. Watch where you walk and sit and lie. Ant and beetle stings can cause infection and ulcer. Even a tiny scratch can become a wound that is gangrenous."

"What do we do if *that* happens?" Chesi asked.

"Maggots," Liz and Christie answered in unison, and Nelida smiled at her precocious students.

"My little generals are correct. Maggots eat only dead flesh—in dire circumstances, a wound can be cleaned of all dead meat and pus by a swarm of maggots."

"Soldiers in war zones use that technique," Christie added. "Then they clean the wound with their own urine."

A chorus of "Oh, yuk!" and groans greeted this information; Justine muttered something in French that needed no translation.

"Certain plants like papaw can cause blindness and extreme pain," Nelida went on. "It is green with a milky sap that is delicious, and most deadly to the eyes if rubbed there.

"In the sea, of course, there are urchins, sharks, barracuda, sting rays, and a number of predatory clams and coral. The experienced scuba divers among you can take you to the beach and point out some of these to any who are unfamiliar." She stopped her soliloquy for a moment.

"In this place, you must never let down your guard. There is quicksand in the swamps, and Nature that has been disrupted and disrespected."

"What do you mean by this?" Marika asked.

"This island is *un sitio sagrado,* a sacred place, a place of Power."

"What does *that* mean, exactly?" Christie asked, the reporter again.

"The earth is alive," the Mexican woman replied. "She lives, breathes, moves, thinks, chooses . . . but on a scale we humans can barely imagine.

"Just as there are energy centers on the human body, so are there centers of special energy on the Earth Mother's body that vibrate at a different frequency from the rest. In your culture, there are many such places . . . you build cathedrals there, or shrines or monasteries, and call them hallowed ground. People sense the Power, but do not understand its source. They know only that it is far larger than they can comprehend and it cannot be harnessed or changed—these places you call sacred. Mora Utu is one of these."

She paused to see if they were following. "There are great

spirits who guard all sacred places—in some countries they are called Shining Ones or Devas—you might think of them as Mother Nature's warriors and protectors. On Mora Utu, much was done foolishly, heedlessly, arrogantly, in the clearing of the land. The old natives who served these forces of Nature were removed . . . the sacred land was violated, cut down by those who did not seek to preserve the balance or make offerings to the offended spirits. Emilio conversed with the old ones before they were evacuated and was deeply troubled by what he heard."

"Are you saying that what's going on with us here on Mora Utu is some kind of curse?" Chesi pressed.

"What has happened here thus far is petty annoyance, child—*retribution* has not yet been exacted. *That* is what we must fear."

"Like a volcano erupting, or a tidal-wave wipeout?" Christie urged.

Nelida shrugged.

"But, assuming you are correct," Justine said skeptically, "it seems as if there is little we can do about Thoros's transgressions, Nelida. So we cannot guard against their repercussions."

"We must be alert," Nelida replied. "The warnings will be given to us; we will know if we are part of the plan of payment."

"Why should we have anything to do with it at all, Nelida?" she pursued. "Thoros is the one who made the choices here, not we. And, perhaps, after him, Rand and Chesi could be held accountable, if such a thing were possible. But the rest of us are innocent bystanders."

Nelida threw back her head and laughed.

"There is little innocence in this universe, Justine," she replied. "*Everyone* gathered here has some karma to play out. With the island, with Nature, with the others in the group. And remember, you are able to see only *this* one lifetime of yours. . . . What of all the others?"

"One's enough for me," Liz said, standing up, wanting to

end the disturbing conversation. "I think maybe we'd better get the duties parceled out before we lose the whole day, here, Nelida. If any kind of natural disaster is coming, we'd better have our act together about food, shelter, and sanitation."

"She's right," Christie added. "There's plenty of work to do." She pulled a list from the pocket of her shorts, and the other women, sobered by what Nelida had just told them, listened as she read their duty schedules.

"Just a moment," Justine said, as the women prepared to go to their chores. "I believe we must discuss strategy. Combat, if there is to be any, demands very specific disciplines and mindset. Negotiation is an art form. All of what has been discussed here is defensive, but it doesn't get us a damned bit closer to the solution."

"Clausewitz said, 'Defense is the stronger form of combat,' " Liz offered. "Antietam, Petersburg . . ."

"The Alamo," Christie added, dryly. "A defender with a small force can hold back an army—but only for a little while. Then it's wipeout time. Justine's right, Liz—we don't want to go down in the military history books, we just want to get the hell off Mora Utu. So let's hear what the woman has to say."

Justine moved forward, encouraged. "What has happened here seems to me classic. I hit you, you hit me back. I hit you harder, you drop a bomb on my head. That's how conflict works . . . *emotionally*. Negotiation deals on a level of rational thought, not emotion, not fear. I believe we must reopen talks with the men in an effort to come to an agreement about sharing the plane parts."

"*There* you're wrong!" Christie put in quickly. "Our only leverage is those fuel controllers. If you let them talk us out of those, we're dead meat."

"We don't *know* they mean us harm."

"Yes we do. They're holding us prisoner."

"We're holding *them* prisoner, too."

Liz stepped forward. "Look. You've both made your points—let's live with them for today. Maybe talk more tonight."

"Right now we have very specific needs and time's being wasted by arguing. Justine and Marika need to hunt, the rest of us need to build a better shelter. Let's table this until after supper. Okay?"

Inasmuch as no one had a solution, they did as Liz suggested.

"Look, Nelida!" Chesi called out, pointing across the camp where they were working. "It's happening again. I told you Tiffany has this weird attraction for butterflies." Everyone looked up to see what had occasioned such an outburst from Chesi, who was usually so controlled.

"My God! That's a Queen Alexandra's bird-wing!" Liz said excitedly. "They're incredibly rare."

A huge crimson butterfly, nearly a hand's breadth across, had landed on Tiffany's shoulder, and two smaller yellow ones hovered around her head like landing craft looking for a place to dock. Tiffany laughed acknowledgment of their arrival, and reaching up, offered her arm to them, providing a perch. She was as puzzled by her attraction for the butterflies on this island as anyone else; having grown up in the city, her experience of the delicate flying beauties was extremely limited.

Nelida smiled and waved to her. "You are *Mariposa Woman,* Tiffany!" she called out cheerily. "This is very sacred, this gift of the butterflies."

Tiffany smiled and walked in Nelida's direction, as the brilliantly colored winged creature took off from her shoulder, fluttered above her for a moment, then disappeared into the jungle in a magical dance of giant wings that left everyone awestruck by its extraordinary beauty.

"What is it with these butterflies, Nelida?" the dark-skinned girl laughed, as she drew near. "I have no idea why they're always all over me like that. They must like my perfume. Some people attract mosquitoes, I attract butterflies." She laughed her infectious, giggly laugh—it was a pleasant sound, especially now, when everyone felt so depressed about their prospects.

"No!" Nelida answered emphatically. "Do not demean this gift, Tiffany. You are *Mariposa Woman* . . . a chosen one. The butterfly is the pollinating spirit, all over the world it is the same. She is the fertile one who spreads life—she takes a little from *this* place, and puts it in *that* place, and life occurs." Nelida thought for a moment, as if deciding how much to impart. "Mariposa Woman teaches transformation as she is herself transformed . . . from the lowly crawling caterpillar to the glorious winged *criatura* . . . and she does this by her own Power."

"That's beautiful!" Tiffany said wonderingly, and everyone in earshot murmured agreement. "But it doesn't explain why they always find *me*."

Nelida put her hands on her full hips and reared back. "Because you are a *chosen* one!" she said merrily. "You are close to the nature of things—there is purity in your spirit, and they applaud you! There is a sacred dance of Mariposa Woman that my people do. It is very sexy because she is very potent. I will dance her for you when the time comes, and you will recognize yourself in her wild freedom."

"When *what* time comes?" Liz prompted. Listening to Nelida always made her want to take notes, like an anthropologist capturing an ancient culture before it fades to dust.

The laughter left Nelida's eyes and she answered seriously. "The time when each of you must come into your own Power."

The women looked at one another with curiosity.

"You say that as if you know what's going to happen to us," Christie said, anxiously.

"Can't you just tell us what to do, so it all turns out right?" Liz prompted.

"And rob you of the journey?" Nelida spat contemptuously.

"The journey is all there is! The destination is *una illusión,* an illusion . . . only the path is real."

Try as they would to get more out of her, Nelida kept her own counsel for the remainder of the day, but she did promise to tell them a story after supper.

Emilio stood on the beach watching the surf carefully; two of the men had come here to swim and he had followed them. There was a restlessness to the sea today, a disgruntled anger amid the creatures populating its depths—the surface looked calm and benevolent enough, but underneath, something seethed. He would let the others know, as was his duty, despite their obstinacy.

Only Alex and Jase were on the beach now. The other men were back at the compound fulfilling the various tasks they'd assigned one another in their little army. They were all feeling macho since they'd found a purpose; Emilio smiled to himself at the game's progress, and at how little they understood what they were in the grip of. The Gods were inexorable in their demands for respect, and they had not been respected on Mora Utu. It would not pay to be careless here.

He looked over at the two on the beach, assessing them. Despite his fair coloring, Alex liked the sun and the sea; Emilio had seen him often on the beach or in the water. Jase swam like a dolphin; he had obviously grown up near water and felt at ease in its proximity. Emilio turned his steps in the direction of the two sunbathing men.

"It would not be correct to enter the water today, señores," he said respectfully, as he drew near. "The ocean has a treacherous heart today."

Jase looked amused. Emilio was a cocky little son of a bitch, but colorful, and would make a good character in a novel.

"More so than every other day, Emilio?" he asked skeptically.

The Mexican nodded sagely. "Oh, sí, señor. She is in a willful mood. Today she will treat intruders with insolence."

"And how exactly do you know this, Emilio?" Alex asked with a somewhat supercilious smile that in a less well-bred face would have been a smirk.

"It is a fullness of the moon, señor," he answered. "*Como una mujer*. Like a woman, there is capriciousness when the moon is full. And something else I cannot name, troubles her."

Alex laughed. "And this capriciousness makes her dangerous, eh? Well, to be honest, I'm tired of capricious females and have no intention of letting another one spoil my afternoon. I worked hard today, at manual labor that appalls me even to contemplate, and I need a swim." He got up and stretched.

"Do not swim, señor," Emilio said sharply, with no banter in his tone this time. "Today she looks for a sacrifice."

Alex squinted at the small peasant, annoyed by his pretenses at sagacity. "You know something, Emilio," he said, "ever since this all happened, you have grown to be a chronic pain in the arse. You're so busy giving advice, you don't have time to do your job, which is, as I understand it, that of a Mr. Fixit. There's a good deal in this compound that needs fixing at the moment, so while I'm sure you are well intentioned, I don't think I need your advice."

Emilio watched the arrogant gringo with interest; he no longer had any obligation to teach this one, and would leave that effort now to the sea. He shook his head in disgust, as he turned to go, but then he saw Jase Shindler watching him with curiosity and a less closed mind, so he relented a trifle in his resolve to do no more.

"Across the tide, señor," he said cryptically. "Diagonal to the shore, in opposition to the current." Then he was on his way back up the beach.

"What did he say?" Alex asked.

Jase looked after the retreating figure on the sand, wondering what his words could have meant. "Something about the current. I didn't quite catch it."

Alex looked unimpressed. "The water looks inviting, despite our sepulchral friend. I'm going for a dip." He laid his sunglasses and crumpled white hat on the sand chaise and headed toward the sea.

The tide was coming in; rolling breakers inched their way forward on the beach, each new one creeping slightly farther up the sand. Alex breasted the shallows, half turning to meet each new onslaught of wave. The water was rougher than it had looked from the beach, but annoyance at Emilio pushed him toward recklessness rather than admitting that the little man might have been right. Besides, he felt restrained and aggravated by all that was happening, and swimming tended to free him from such feelings. His breaststroke was strong and confident as he left the frustration onshore behind him.

The bottom fell off sharply, twenty yards out; there must have been a sandbar beneath him up to that point, Alex realized, as he recovered himself in the sudden buffeting of powerful waves, and began to swim in earnest, long breaststrokes seaward in an effort to clear the rough water nearer the shore.

That was when it caught him. Sucked him down so fast he had no time to think or breathe or escape. Wildly spiraling water in a funnel shape was sucking him in and under, tearing at his body like a giant drain, thwarting every effort to break free. Alex managed to get his head above water long enough to gulp a mouthful of air before he was under again and spiraling down.

Jase had intended to doze on the beach. Maybe it was the Mexican's warning, maybe just dumb luck, but before closing his eyes, he raised his head and searched the sea for Alex. What was he doing out there? Flailing and—*disappearing! Oh my God . . . riptide.*

Jase was on his feet and running; he shouted as he ran, in case anyone was in earshot. There was no time to go for help.

Alex would be long gone before he'd ever reach the house and return. *Stupid son of a bitch,* he thought as he splashed into the surf, *he should have listened to Emilio.* Jase was not a hero by nature, nor the least unselfish, but he was a strong swimmer and he trusted himself in the water; he dove beneath an incoming wave and headed instinctively toward his friend. *It could kill both of us,* he thought as he swam. *How the hell do you get someone out of riptide?* It had been thirty years since he'd been a lifeguard, and who the fuck knew if he still had the physical strength for a rescue in a rough sea?

"Across the tide, señor." The Mexican's words filtered back to him against the pounding of the water. *"Diagonal to the shore, in opposition to the current."* That little wetback had known exactly what would happen! *Shit!* Long, powerful strokes brought Jase abreast of the vortex as Alex went down for the final time. Hesitating only long enough to pull in as much air as his lungs could hold, Jase plunged into the swirling caldron after him. He was no longer sure he could make it; he wished he knew how to pray.

"Across the tide." The words beat over and over in his head like hailstones blotting out all else as he dove for Alex's body, now completely in the water's control. If he let the fear flood him, they were both dead men. Jase grabbed wildly for the red swim trunks that made the man visible, and the body they encased. *Got him!* he thought triumphantly. Now the challenge was to hold on to him and fight his way out for both of them against the relentless undertow.

"Across the tide." He silently repeated the instructions to blot out the fear. *"Across the tide."* Easier said than done. *"Diagonal to the shore, in opposition to the current." Christ! I hope I've got it right.* Gripping the near-dead body under the armpit and around the chest, Jase fought desperately to do as the Mexican had commanded. He felt the full force of the current beat at their two rag-doll forms that were caught inexorably in its tow. Jase felt his

strength ebbing fast but refused to let that thought in, as he fought the tearing water for release. Alex had saved his life; he couldn't, *wouldn't* fail him now. Inch by agonizing inch he drew closer to the edge of the water funnel, praying that his stamina would hold out long enough to keep them alive. Finally, with absolute exhaustion draining his last meager reserves, he broke free. The normal current caught them on a cresting wave and lifted the two men, speeding them shoreward as if on a giant surfboard.

Other men were in the water now. Shouting voices pierced the terminal frenzied exhaustion of Jase's semi-consciousness. Other hands pulled Alex's body from the death grip Jase had on it, fingers prying at his own to let go. Voices. Shallow water now. Waves slapping at the shouting men who were carrying them onto the sand.

Someone was working over Alex. Voices were coming clearer. *CPR. Breathe, damn you! One thousand and one. One thousand and two.* Someone breathing. Gasping. Coughing. Sputtering.

Jase opened his eyes and struggled to sit up, but someone pushed him back down onto the sand. It was Emilio, his eyes deadly serious. Jase tried to murmur thank you, but the words wouldn't come clear. The small Mexican man inclined his head minimally in acknowledgment of the gift he had bestowed, and Jase felt himself slipping gratefully back into unconsciousness, as unseen hands lifted him up and carried him back to the compound.

TWENTY-NINE

The firelight flickered and danced in the starlit dark over the women's camp. The night sky was dotted with brilliant pinpricks of light and a clear full moon that glowed vivid as a painting on black velvet. The sky was an important fact of life for the women now, like the jungle and the sea; it was impossible not to feel a oneness with the Power of Nature here, so different from the sky and earth and water of home.

Nelida had agreed to regale them with a story tonight, and they felt eager as children at the prospect; entertainment was in short supply on Mora Utu at the moment. Supper was finished, and they'd hurried to complete their chores in anticipation of what was to come, for Nelida intrigued each of the women according to her own needs.

Nelida surveyed the group as she began, marking each face in its anticipation; they were changed, already, from whom they had been. She smiled as she decided which tale to weave—there was much to teach and little time for the teaching.

"I am *Cantadora,*" she began. "A storyteller. A keeper of the old tales of my people." She stood in the firelight, hands on hips, proud and womanly with her large breasts straining their peasant-blouse covering, a concho belt that had to be worth a king's ransom wound tight around her waist, then wrapped a second time and slung low around ample hips.

"Stories are instructions for life's complexities," Nelida began. "They summon from the depths of us our inner knowings."

Her eyes took in the group mesmerically, her voice was conspiratorial, as if she was about to share some important secret. "I bid you listen with the ears of your souls, for some things cannot be comprehended by the merely human parts of us, for these parts are limited, and the knowing we require is infinite." She paused to let that sink in, then continued.

"Once upon a time, a million years ago or yesterday, I forget which—but in a time that is gone forever or will be back soon, it's hard to know . . . there was a man of the great North Water who was a fisherman, and very lonely.

"All day, and sometimes through the night, he would fish in the icy straits to the deep music of whalesong.

"One night, as chance would have it, he came upon a great rock in the sea and on this rock there were dancing the most graceful women he had ever seen. Their skin was luminous in the moonlight and their hair was of silver and glittered like the stars. They were the sealwomen who had doffed their sealskins for one night of naked revelry. As they danced, he crept close enough to steal one of the skins.

"When the dawn had begun to cast rose across the northern skies, the sealwomen put on their skins and dove back into the great sea, but one, the youngest and most beautiful, could not find her skin. The fisherman stepped from behind his hiding rock and showed himself and his hostage sealskin.

" 'Come with me and be my wife,' he cried out. 'And in seven years I will give you back your skin.'

" 'But I am not your kind,' she sobbed in alarm. 'Surely, I shall die without my skin.'

"But he was lonely and desperate so he made himself believe that what he would give her would be worth the price she paid.

"The sealwoman looked long and deep into the fisherman's eyes and was captured by the need and the longing she read there, for seals are a kind lot, and she forgot her own need and agreed to his plan. She did this in the way of women of every species who are ensnared by being loved.

"Soon a child was born to them, a little girl who was neither human nor seal, but half the nature of each. She could breathe air or water, could fly through the icy sea like a seal child or wander the earth, but wherever she went she felt a longing for the other place.

"The fisherman loved his seal wife, for she had healed the loneliness of his solitary world, and he loved the wild child she had spawned, although both had a fierceness within them that frightened him and a wistfulness that he could not understand.

"As time passed by, the sealwoman began to die a little. Her skin lost its sleekness and began to shrivel and crack. Her hair began to shed on her pillow and her eyes became blinded by gazing always toward the sea that was her home. On the evening of the first day of the eighth year, she stood before her husband, weakened and withered and frail. She drew herself up as best she was able, and she begged the return of her skin as had been promised.

" 'Never!' he thundered, frightened into meanness that wasn't his true nature. 'If I give it you will leave me and I will be alone.'

" 'You made a bargain and I fulfilled my part,' she cried. 'To live, I must be myself once more.'

" 'If I give it back you will leave me and our child. I cannot allow you to be so selfish.' And with that he ran out the door and left her dying and bereft.

"It was then that the girl-child rose from her bed and embarked on a great sea journey to entreat the King of the Seals to save her mother, for the old seal was wise and knew the whereabouts of every sealskin in the world. When the child had completed her journey of redemption, her mother's fate was carried in her hands.

"The mother gasped her thanks as she donned the blessed skin, and grabbing the child under her arm she scrambled wildly toward the sea.

" 'No, Mother, no!' the girl-child screamed, realizing that the mother's wild nature had taken hold and she would leave now forever.

"The mother clasped the half-human child to her heart and breathed three magical breaths into her lungs and the child was filled with songs and stories that had grown from the wind that flows forever in the sea.

" 'I have hurt your human father, my child, although I love him dearly,' the mother said, a silver tear running down her sleek brown cheek. 'But I am a wild thing and must return to the wild. Come and rejoice with me, for I have found my true nature once again.'

"The child was made immortal for her courage and she became the greatest singer of songs and teller of stories the world had ever known, for she carried the breath of two worlds within her.

"This tale was told to me by one who has seen her many, many times and knows it to be true as God is true."

Nelida's voice was soft as a whisper as she ended her soliloquy. The listeners around the fire hated to hear it end.

"What a gorgeous story!" Liz said. "And so brilliantly told. Where did you ever hear it, Nelida?"

The older woman smiled. "I am *La Narradora,* I capture stories in my web and give them voice as they are needed."

"Needed? You mean for entertainment?" Chesi asked.

"No, child, for the acquisition of knowledge. What you *hear* goes to your brain by a special path . . . the soul listens, and receives guidance and knowledge."

"What learning are we to take from the seal story, Nelida?" Christie asked, feeling as if she should write down the reply.

Liz leaned forward eagerly, like a child in grade school who knows the answer. "It's about understanding our true natures, isn't it?" she asked. "About not letting anything keep us from our truth."

"It's about soul loss, isn't it, Nelida?" Chesi added. "About how we allow the theft of our souls."

"It's about love," Justine added, musingly. "That's how we get undone, literally and figuratively, isn't it? Women give themselves over to some man, body and soul, then the man grows bored and moves on and the woman shrivels and dies from the hurt. I know you all think I'm cynical, but truly the only way to keep a man interested is to give him very little of yourself. Anything they know they can have, they don't want. Men hate a done deal."

"That may be true, but it's horribly unfair!" Christie said.

"All Nature is unfair to women," Nelida replied with equanimity. "I will tell you something very important now, that you will not believe," Nelida said with great seriousness. "It is, in fact, a secret known only to certain women of my lineage, but I have chosen to share it with you for particular reasons. Every time a woman has sex with a man he leaves within her a host of energy fibers, like little worms electric with his energy. . . ."

"What!" Exclamations and protests rose all around the fire.

"That's disgusting!" Liz responded indignantly. "To say nothing of unfair."

"Hear me out!" Nelida said sternly. "All Nature is *injusto* to women. Only a fool thinks otherwise. These luminous fibers that a man leaves inside a woman form a subtle bond of energy through which the man can collect and steal energy from each woman he has slept with."

"Forever?"

"For seven years these links live within us, then they extinguish and they die. But only seven years of celibacy can break our servitude, for each new sexual encounter refreshes the energy fibers."

"How could you possibly know such a thing?"

"I have been trained to *see* this energy. I see it in each of you, here. And in myself. I see the means by which your energy is drained by the men on this island and by all you have ever slept with."

"But nobody's going to go without sex for seven years!" Tiffany said, incredulous at the idea.

"I have done so," Nelida answered relentlessly. "I chose to break the cycle to restore my own Power. Now, only Emilio leaves his energy within me. For you, it would be best to choose partners wisely—to choose those who will use their Power over you less ruthlessly than others. I tell you now so that *you* may know your own vulnerability. Which, of course, brings us back to our story of the sealwoman."

"How?"

"Because another way women lose their skins is by unselfishly taking care of everybody in sight—right, Nelida?" Liz said, realization dawning.

"Bingo!" Nelida laughed with gusto. "Very good! The world longs for the comfort of woman's soul gifts as well as for her body's pleasures. A hundred voices call to us in need. Help me! Help me! Give to me! Let me suck! It will only take a minute. Listen to me. I need. I *want*. It is womanly to listen and strive to help—but if we give to all indiscriminately, there is none left for us. Our Power dissipates."

"God, that sounds grim!" Liz pronounced.

"And accurate," Chesi added emphatically.

"So, how do we save ourselves, Nelida?" Justine asked for everyone.

"First, you must be *aware!* Wifehood, motherhood—if these are your first choices, they will make great demands upon you, which you must fulfill to the best of your ability. But they may not be your *only* choices, and they may not be *forever.*"

She waited for that potent thought to sink in before speaking again.

"You must be confident of your own worth, always. Say over and over to yourself: *My* work is important. *My* destiny, *my* painting, *my* book, *my* soul is worthy of my time. *Now!* Not later. Now! Your work cannot be done after you've spent all your energy on everyone around you. You are worth more than that. Dance! Sing! Think! Create! Live! Establish boundaries. Take back your sealskin. Let *no one* steal your Power!"

"Holy shit, Nelida!" Christie blurted. "You should have been in sales."

"Or evangelism!" Tiffany added. "If you don't mind my asking this, Nelida, what the hell are you doing as somebody's housekeeper?"

"Even the wise must eat," she answered with a small laugh. "It is a means to an end. It is not my true work."

"What is your work, then?"

"You are not yet ready to know this," Nelida said with great seriousness. "Perhaps, later. We shall see. For now, I am a teller of tales."

THIRTY

Emilio watched the men gathered around the poker table. They'd moved it outdoors to the terrace because of the oppressive heat, and it sat now, near the pool, looking foolish and out of place, but the six around it were feeling good again. Young. Full of purpose. They had a common enemy, a reason to exist; their anger and purpose had made them feel like men again, not dilettantes. They were fending off fatigue tonight with alcohol, fatigue from real work, not from boredom. Just as they were fending off the fear of death that had touched them on the beach and in the jungle.

"Hey, Emilio!" Tony called out suddenly, just drunk enough to be expansive. "Do you and your compadres play poker in Mexico?" It had never occurred to him to engage the man in conversation before, but what the hell.

"No, señor," Emilio answered with a sly smile. "This is a game for gringos." This was not entirely true, but it served Emilio's purpose to say so.

"Gringos, eh?" Tony replied. "You don't like gringos much, Emilio, am I right?"

Emilio smiled again; this fool would bait him now, a show of manhood for his friends.

"It is a thing of individuality, señor," he said gravely. "In Mexico we judge a man by his *cojones*. Gringo or no gringo, this is the measure."

Tony laughed heartily. "And just how do you do this measurement, my friend?" he pressed. He waved his hand around the table. "How would you measure the *cojones* at this table, for instance?"

Emilio pursed his mouth judiciously. "This measurement cannot be done at the poker table, señor. There, it is the wallet and the cunning that can be judged. But for the *cojones*, señor . . ." He shrugged, as if the subject was too big for discussion.

"Come now, Emilio," Thoros prompted; this was an intriguing line of inquiry. "I've heard you be far more eloquent than that. Surely you can tell us how a man's balls are measured in Mexico."

The sophisticated assemblage laughed with condescension and looks were exchanged; they were being generous sharing intimacies with a servant, and they had all been drinking freely.

Emilio pursed his lips. "There is the question of the *corazón*, the heart, to examine," he said finally.

"Heart?" Tony exploded with laughter. "I thought we were talking about balls here."

"Sí, señor," Emilio agreed, amiably in control. "But in battle do you wish a comrade at your back, who has balls, but no heart? No! Courage is a thing of the heart *and* the *cojones*." He paused and looked from face to face.

"There is then the question of *fuerza*, strength, to be taken into account." His unblinking gaze embraced each man at the table, in turn, as if examining them for the virtues he was describing, and finding them wanting.

"What kind of strength is that, Emilio?" Alex ventured. "Physical, mental . . . ?"

"All of these, señor. But for the measurement you spoke of . . . we must consider other qualities."

"Like?"

"Endurance. Cunning. Perseverance. Intelligence to use the world sparingly."

"What does that mean?"

Emilio's eye glittered oddly in the firelight. "It means that a man with *cojones* does not squeeze the life from people and shrivel them, señor. It means that he does not destroy the forest to build a shopping center. It means he does not kill four deer when one would feed him."

"That's bullshit, Emilio," Jase said. "A man takes what he can hold—that's what power is all about."

Emilio smiled a wolf's smile when he has his prey in sight. "Power, too, is to be considered," he said noncommittally.

"We know plenty about that part," Tony said with a short laugh.

"Do you, señor? This is good. For it takes Power even to recognize what Power is and to seek it correctly. A man with substantial *cojones* must know this, so that he may be a warrior." He stopped for a moment. "It is a thing of decision, as well. A man of *cojones* must make decisions with great care, so that nothing can happen to surprise him and drain his Power." He paused again, and looked from face to face.

"And finally," he said carefully, "it is a thing of humility."

"Why humility?" Thoros asked.

"Because every day is a good day to die, señor. When you are prepared to die, you cannot be undone by unwelcome surprises. But in the face of death we must be humble, must we not?"

"This business of *cojones* is a complicated one in Mexico, it seems, Emilio?" Jase said, intrigued.

"Oh sí, señor. There is much to determine."

"Emilio," Alex said, suddenly, fascinated by the man's explanation and confidence, "do you believe that we are equals?"

Emilio smiled. "You tell me first, señor. Do *you* believe that we are equals?"

Alex looked nonplussed. "Well, yes, I suppose in some ways," he said, obviously feeling quite the opposite.

"Then you would be wrong, señor," the Mexican said with equanimity. "We are not equals. I am a warrior and a hunter. And you are not my equal."

"Well, I'll be goddamned!" Thoros said, genuinely taken by surprise. "You forget yourself, Emilio. These are my guests."

Emilio was unperturbed by the rebuke. "They will need to know these things, Señor Thoros. They ask, I must tell them. It is a matter of respect."

"Leave him alone, Thoros," Jase said amiably. "There's a lot to what he's said. He's pretty subtle when you get down to it. I doubt any of us could come up with a better description."

"Is anyone planning to play poker in this lifetime?" Rand asked, picking up the deck, and starting to shuffle them dexterously. "I had some seven-card stud in mind for tonight."

"Anybody ever tell you that you shuffle a deck like a riverboat gambler, Rand?" Jase said with an admiring laugh, taking advantage of the distraction to change the subject. He loved the game of poker, but he was a wild card. He could bluff with the best of them, but he admired the true nuts players like Rand and Gagarian, who could go for the jugular with genuine relish.

"I had a great teacher, when I was a boy," Rand replied easily, as he dealt out the first three streets. "An old stableman named Mick who was a friend of my father . . ." The conversation ambled on in a new direction and the betting began.

Seven-card stud could produce a really big pot, so the players turned their attention to the cards. Emilio melted back into insignificance and left the men to the pursuit of their gringo games.

Thursday, April 14

In love there are two great evils:
war and peace.

HORACE

THIRTY-ONE

Justine pulled in the fishing line disgustedly and packed away her tackle; she'd have to move on. The lagoon was usually a reservoir of eager fish, but today for some reason nothing was biting. Instinctively, she looked to the sky for signs of heavy weather that might be moving in, but the blue canopy was brilliant and cloudless, despite the choppiness of the water. She shook her head in annoyance and prepared to move to another spot. Maybe Marika was having more luck on the hunt than she was at fishing.

Because of Nelida's storytelling last night, the women had forgone their promised discussion of reopening negotiation; it troubled Justine that no further contact had been made between the warring factions. And that wasn't the only thing that niggled at her.

All morning long, waiting for the fish to bite, she'd brooded on Thoros; there was no doubt in her mind that he was the key to an early escape, but there was more to her musing than strategy. She missed him, and she *wanted* him, much as it disturbed her to admit this, even to herself. She couldn't dismiss him from her mind as she had so many men before him, and it disconcerted her that he had gotten beneath her guard so completely.

Justine's mental wanderings had eaten up the morning; she chided herself for wasting so much time, and packed her gear to leave. She cast an appraising look at the sea; it seemed so exquisitely jewel-like and benevolent. If the fish continued to elude her, it might be necessary to dive for food. Under different circumstances she would have welcomed the idea, but here, in this strangely hostile place, far from medical attention or even competent diving companionship, it might be foolhardy to risk it. She had firsthand experience of the creatures of the deep that stung, bit, or poisoned—she'd been snorkeling and diving since she was ten—so she never treated the sea with anything but respect.

And, where the devil was Marika, anyway? She'd proven herself so well at hunting and fishing that they'd decided to split up today to cover more ground. Maybe it hadn't been such a good idea.

Suddenly uneasy, Justine picked up the tackle box, rod and reel, and instead of moving to another spot on the water, turned toward the heavy jungle foliage Marika had disappeared into hours earlier. She tried to intuit the most likely trail for Marika to have traveled, but after ten fruitless minutes it was apparent that she was wasting her time. There were a million side trails the Swedish woman could have taken, and if she was following spoor, she could be anywhere by now.

Justine glanced at her watch and was shocked to see it was already two o'clock. Maybe Marika had doubled back to camp with her catch. No. That didn't make sense. Even if she'd bagged something large, she would have stopped back to let Justine know. There was no point in wandering any farther; the best bet was to return to camp and get help, so Justine turned her steps in that direction.

When she reached camp, she found that no one had seen Marika all day. Nelida listened to Justine's concerns, asked one or two questions, then closed her eyes and rocked back on her heels, as if communing with someone Justine could not see. She remained like this for several minutes. Seeing Nelida's trancelike state, Liz walked over to find out what was happening. Justine retold her story as they waited for the Mexican woman to snap out of whatever she was doing.

"I've never tracked anybody," Liz said, wanting to help, "but I remember quite a lot of *The Foxfire* books, so I think I basically know what to look for, if you'd like some help searching for her."

"I'm probably just being foolish," Justine replied, "but I feel very uneasy about her. It may turn out to be a wild goose . . ."

Nelida came back to consciousness with a small cry. "Marika is northwest of us," she said sharply. "We will have to carry her."

"What?" Christie broke in, joining the group. "Carry who? Why? What's wrong, Nelida?"

"Marika has been injured," Nelida answered, not explaining how she knew. "She cannot walk. We must hurry—she is in trouble."

Liz, Justine, and Christie exchanged glances; it sounded like Nelida knew what she was talking about. "What should we take with us?" Christie asked. "Will we need a litter?"

"Bring my herb bag—it is by my blanket roll. Bring Marika's blanket and enough else to pass the night—we may not get her back here before dark."

Wonderingly, the women did as they'd been directed and were ready to leave ten minutes later; all six set out in a northwesterly direction.

* * *

Marika lay a few feet from where she'd fallen; painfully, she'd managed to pull herself to an almost upright position against a large, rocky embankment before passing out. She didn't know what it was that had felled her.

She'd been stalking a beaverlike creature she'd never seen before, following it closer and closer toward the riverbank when the injury had happened. The animal looked plump, edible, and easy to kill, so she'd followed its track beyond the territory she'd originally staked out as her hunting ground. She'd been crouched low in the undergrowth when whatever it was had struck; fast, sharp, fiery pain had shot up her leg with near paralyzing shock waves.

Marika had instinctively tried to step away, but her leg had gone out from under her, landing her flat out on the dense prickly foliage of the jungle floor. Stunned and nauseated, she'd looked down at her leg in wonder, and found it rapidly turning black. Then shocked and frightened, she'd tried to take stock of her options, but the poison seeping into her central nervous system had made clear thinking nearly impossible.

With sheer animal survival instinct, Marika had pulled herself laboriously toward the embankment. She'd be more visible there sitting up than lying flat in the dense green camouflage. She tried to fight the feeling of despair that threatened to engulf her along with the pain. No one would ever find her here, where she wasn't supposed to be.

Nelida sniffed the air like a bloodhound. Watching, Christie rolled her eyes to heaven and Liz nearly laughed out loud; the feeling that she was living in a Fellini film was growing daily.

"We'll have cocktail party stories to tell for life," she said to Justine, who, she had to admit, was no longer acting so much like a spoiled brat.

"Provided we ever *see* a cocktail party again," Justine replied ruefully. "Or Marika, for that matter."

Nelida stopped sniffing and pointed in a new direction.

"This one's better than Triple A," Christie smirked, as she picked up the bundle she'd dropped on the ground and slung it back over her shoulder. The sound of running water had become audible on their far right—Nelida seemed to be heading them in that direction.

Marika's platinum hair caught her eye first; it was spread out against the rock that propped her body semiupright. "Over there!" Christie yelled. "I can see her!"

The women scrambled down the embankment to the comatose girl's side. Liz pushed away the hair that obscured Marika's face, and gasped—it was bug bitten and swollen to twice its normal size. Ants were crawling everywhere, even in her ears and nose, but the unconscious woman was oblivious. With intense revulsion, Liz brushed away the swarming marauders as best she could, and looked to Nelida for what to do next, but the older woman was already deep in concentration over Marika's leg. It was swollen, black, and grotesque.

"Scorpion," Nelida said sharply, as she lowered Marika's body to a horizontal position and began giving orders. "Bring me my herb bag," she snapped in a head-nurse voice they hadn't heard before. "She has been unattended too long."

Liz fetched the bag and Nelida extracted a long braid of some grasslike substance with dried blue flowers still attached. She handed this to Chesi with the order, "Boil this! Quickly. Three cups of water, no more. Christie—make a bed with the blankets we have brought. Justine—help her hammer in four stakes at the corners; we will have to tie Marika when she becomes delirious."

Everyone moved quickly to do Nelida's bidding, all question marks about the validity of the woman's knowledge forgotten. The leg looked like an overripe eggplant, mottled and oddly dimpled in patches; without someone who knew what to do, Marika was in serious trouble.

"Shouldn't we suck the poison out or something?" Christie asked worriedly as she spread out the blankets.

"That only works in the movies," Liz said definitively. "We need some kind of antivenom. Scorpion bites hit the central nervous system, I think I remember—sort of like cobra venom, but not so deadly. Right, Nelida?"

Nelida's eyes were closed and her hands were wrapped like a vise around the swollen leg; she seemed to be in her trance state once again. Her body swayed a little as she knelt there, and a soft sound emanated from her lips. She appeared to be communicating with the leg. Finally, she opened her eyes and barked more orders.

"Move her to the blanket. Get cold water from the river for compresses. We will have to tie her hands and feet to the stakes to keep her from thrashing when the crisis comes. Remove any tight clothing."

She took an evil-smelling black ointment from her bag and made a poultice, which she applied directly to the leg wound, then she forced the liquid from a small vial between Marika's clenched teeth, as she waited for the herbal concoction to boil.

Nelida soothed and crooned and sponged and spooned medicine into the sick girl for the better part of an hour, before she relented, and gave over the task to Liz. Just as Nelida had predicted, Marika began to thrash wildly; she groaned and clawed the air, talking to people who weren't there; they had to tie her arms and legs to keep her from hurting herself or those who were nursing her. Nelida said they would take turns on duty until the crisis was past, and it would be morning before they could move her back to camp. She also assured them that Marika wouldn't die.

"Funny, isn't it," Christie murmured to Justine, watching

Nelida's tireless concentration. "Up to now, I never really thought we could get hurt here."

There was none of Justine's usual bravado in her retort. "We could get hurt here," she said solemnly. "Perhaps, we could even get dead."

THIRTY-TWO

The combined incidents of the snake and the near drowning in two days had begun to prey on the men; war games were amusing, death was not. The oppressive sense of disaster that hovered over Mora Utu had drawn closer; they'd spent most of the day trying to push it back again by whatever means they could. By nightfall, they'd decided to cheer themselves up with one of Tony's famous spaghetti dinners and a poker game, on the beach where the stifling heat in the house couldn't depress them further.

"I'm sure I don't have to give you guys pointers on this subject," Tony said, standing on the sand, near the fire pit they'd constructed late in the afternoon. "But it's been a while since most of us were in the military, so what the hell, a little recap couldn't hurt any of us." The night was dark and clear enough to make the danger recede from consciousness for a while, and the prospect of a good dinner had the potential to improve everyone's mood substantially.

Two pots hung on the spit over the fire, one containing

water, the other the version of Tony's famous pasta sauce he was able to make with what was unspoiled from the pantry and the salad garden.

"You look just like my old CO in that apron, Capuletti," Jack called out, grinning. "Real military."

Tony laughed. "An army moves on its stomach, Doherty," he shot back. "Anybody tells you different don't know shit from Shinola." Tony was never in a better mood than when he was cooking.

The men had hauled the table and chairs out to the beach for Tony's impromptu feast. Some of the best times they'd ever had together over the years had been at Tony's pasta nights, an event that took place only after days of preparation on his part. Tony prided himself on his sauce, which he called gravy, the thick rich product of fresh tomatoes picked from his own vines, olive oil of an extraordinary specificity that he imported from some tiny village in the old country, and a secret blend of herbs and spices, many of which he'd grown himself.

Something about cooking brought out the best in Tony; the expansive and joyous, the parts of his nature that wanted his friends to be well fed and warm and cared for. It was an extension of his willingness to help out a buddy no matter what the cost to himself, and a legacy of his Uncle Vito, who had owned a restaurant near the docks, and who had kept Tony going in some of the toughest times of childhood with his big heart and his warm kitchen.

Tony took a spoonful of thick red sauce from the caldron, held it up to his mouth, and blew on it. As he tasted, he pursed his lips in a judgmental frown, then nodded. "Not so bad, considering," he said finally, adding a sprinkle of some chopped-up condiment from a pile on the tablecloth that was spread out beside him, on which his ingredients and cutlery were all neatly laid out according to some design of his own making. He nodded again, satisfied, and turned back to the men who'd gathered around the table, drinking beers. They'd set up nets in the water to submerge the beer and wine; it wasn't a perfect way to keep it cold, but it was the best they'd devised since the refrigeration went down.

"Now remember, men, there are six points for a successful patrol: *One*. Always vary your route out and back. *Two*. Don't fatigue your men, if you can avoid it. That's when mistakes happen. *Three*. Call a halt now and then to listen for every sound of activity. *Four*. Know your territory. Sights, sounds, smells of the area. *Five*. Make sure your equipment is packed right so it doesn't squeak or rattle."

"Hey, Tony!" Jase called out, feeling himself again. "We haven't got any equipment." The men laughed. After a couple of beers, and with the gravy smells and the cool breeze on the beach, life looked better than it had for a few days. Alex was on the mend from his bout with near death, and Sunday was nearing.

Tony waved away the comment and continued. "*Six*. Always look through, not at, thick bushes and vegetation. There are things the recce patrol commander needs to know. Gather all information about the positions of friendly and enemy forces."

"That's easy," Thoros said with a deep laugh. "We're here, they're there." Everyone chuckled.

"We're going out tomorrow to find out for sure where *there* is," Tony countered, taking the jibes good-naturedly. "We need to know anything affecting the route. . . ."

"At least we don't have to worry about minefields in this war," Jack interjected. "I hated those little suckers."

"Time in and time out is important," Tony continued.

" 'And a decision about what action to take on meeting the enemy,' " Jase added, quoting the command manual verbatim.

"Yeah," Tony said. "Let's talk about that. Do we want to take prisoners.?"

"Holy shit!" Jack said. "What would we do with prisoners?"

"I hope to hell we get to rape them," Alex said, his voice heavy with sarcasm. "It's the only thing makes war really worthwhile, in my book."

"Let's consider that question, gentlemen," Rand said more seriously, speaking from a beach chair near the fire. "Not rape, of course, attractive as that thought might seem at this celibate moment. But some form of persuasion . . . If we had one or two of them alone, maybe we could convince them to deal."

"Yeah, good idea," Jack said wryly, "you pull out a woman's fingernails, it really fucks up her manicure."

"We don't want prisoners," Thoros said, with authority that brooked no argument. "We want the fuel controllers. If we send out the right recce patrol, we'll find what we need. They've got those engine parts stashed somewhere in or near their camp and they're probably guarding them conspicuously. These girls have no military know-how, so they'll reveal themselves. I've never known a woman who could keep a secret, have you?"

"Don't be so sure of that," Jase laughed. "My first wife kept all her lovers secret. Also her Swiss account."

Thoros smiled crookedly. "I stand corrected on this fine point," he said graciously. "Nonetheless, I don't anticipate problems if we do our jobs correctly. And, all joking aside, I believe Tony is right that it makes sense to observe basic military procedures in all that we do. That should cut down on the possibility of anything unforeseen happening."

"Does anybody remember their basic hand signals?" Tony asked.

Jack's hand shot up, fingers extended, thumb down. "Cease fire!" he said. "That was my favorite."

Jase raised both hands above his head, palms out. "Disregard previous command, was mine."

Laughter exploded around the table. For most of them there were good memories from wartime, along with the bad. It was a time of camaraderie, something like now. When the chips were down, it was good to have friends like these.

"Five minute warning for food," Tony said, watching the bubbling pot full of spaghetti with a practiced eye. "Somebody swim out to the wine, will you? We got some serious poker to play after we eat and I'd like you guys to be as drunk as possible."

Mucho ruido y pocas nueces, Emilio thought, watching from the edge of the beach. *Much noise but few nuts.* Tony had said they'd have no need of his services tonight, and he intended to take full advantage of that curt dismissal. He had urgent business with Nelida.

He glanced at the position of the moon and scanned the pattern of the water in its silvery light. Emilio frowned. Then he turned toward the jungle and began to walk.

Marika lay quietly now; the swelling of her leg had gone down considerably, and the ominous blackness had eased to a dusky bruised hue.

Justine, Christie, and Liz had made camp while Nelida worked on the injured woman; they were proud of their newly learned survival skills and managed to gather wood, build a fire, and prepare a meal with vastly less difficulty than would have been the case just a few days before. In some ways, it seemed as if they'd been out of the compound a very long while.

After they'd eaten, the women gathered close around the fire. They were tired, but not sleepy; the events of the day had keyed them up and made them garrulous.

"You know, Nelida," Liz said, sitting with her knees drawn up and her arms wrapped loosely around them. "I've been thinking a lot about all you've told us about Power. . . . I think we all have." Everyone murmured assent.

"What I don't really have a handle on is why it's so hard for us women to gather Power or hold on to it. Do men really steal it from us, or do we hand it over to them without thinking? Or do we just not know how to go about getting it until it's too late?"

Nelida's eyes sparkled as she answered. She showed no hint of the fatigue that marked the younger women. "All of these things are true in different measure," she answered.

"The theft of Power is a very tricky deception, my daughters, and one at which men are adept. But in this robbery we women tend to help them. There are leg traps in the woods of love that ensnare us, leg traps that we find curiously seductive.

"The deception is that we will be *la reina,* the queen . . . the forever beloved, the forever protected. In truth, the likelihood is that we will be quickly unwanted, hand over our Power, live life as everyone else's lackey, and learn to survive with a soul craving that can flay us alive, if we are not, in fact, murdered in spirit, entirely."

"Come on, Nelida, that's pretty extreme," Liz complained. "Men don't have that kind of power over us."

Nelida laughed. "Not without our consent, they don't, but they do if we give it to them, as we so often do in loving." All the women started to talk at once and she put up a hand for silence. "Men do not deceive us out of malice, any more than we deceive *ourselves* out of desire for pain. It is a simple story: the species wishes to continue, so it has built into us certain psychic programming to ensure that woman, the carrier of the species, will be fertilized. We, and they, most often operate as we were programmed.

"If to fulfill that biological destiny is enough for you, as it is for some, there is no need to be wary. If, however, you seek a broader destiny—if you seek to be a Woman of Power—you must expand beyond your biology. Does this make sense to you? That you can be doomed to too small a life and die of the disappointment?"

Liz nodded, suddenly understanding viscerally. "My mother died of that," she said softly.

"But you women *allow* these things to happen to you," Justine said somewhat archly. "If you demanded more for yourselves from men and life, you'd get more."

"You can just stuff that superior horseshit, Justine," Christie said, annoyed. "Face it. You're just as programmed as the rest of us, only at a higher price point. You've done all the things rich girls do . . . you'll marry someone of your class, and produce 2.3 children, who go to Choate. And, who knows, maybe when you're old and gray and your husband has a mistress young enough for pablum, you'll have lost dreams to regret, just like the rest of us mere mortals."

Justine was momentarily speechless, but it was apparent that Christie had hit a nerve. Finally, she answered. "You know, Christie, you often have something important to say, but you say it with such venom, no one wants to listen."

This time, Christie was caught unguarded. "Thank you for sharing that armchair analysis with me," she said acidly, but everyone could see that the truth had found its mark.

"*Basta!*" Nelida broke in with authority. "When we return to camp, we will speak more of Power. And many things now hidden from you will become clear."

"Why not tell us now?" Christie asked.

"Because we have a woman to care for, so that she may be well tomorrow. And because the time is coming soon when you must learn to live as an arrow, not a target." With that tantalizing thought, she moved out of the circle and returned to Marika's side to prepare her for the night.

An hour later, Nelida nudged Liz, who was nearly asleep. "I must leave you for a time," she said solemnly, and that startled Liz into full wakefulness. She sat up.

"Leave us? Where are you going? What about Marika?"

"Marika will sleep peacefully until morning. The danger is past and the night is yet young. I have business to attend to. You will all be safe enough here for the night. I return at first light to lead you back to camp."

Liz was still arguing about why she should stay when Nelida had already left the encampment behind.

THIRTY-THREE

Emilio moved through the jungle night with the liquid stealth of a cobra. The darkness enveloped him, shielding him from prying eyes—the fools at the compound didn't even know he was gone. He had been weaning them from their dependency on his servitude; servant was no longer the role Fate demanded of him.

He was a man of Power. The gringos, of course, did not know this yet, for they were blind to all but their own self-centered needs and wants. He had begun to insinuate his wisdom into their closed minds, but as yet they were slow to absorb. *Into the full cup, it is difficult to pour tequila,* his own Naqual, Don Javier, would have said with his nearly toothless grin. These hombres were full of themselves, full of gringo self-importance, full of machismo, full of memories of themselves when they were young warriors, street fighters with balls of iron.

But those days were long gone from these old bulls. Once, they had possessed the *cojones* to conquer worlds, but it had been years since any had *worked* with his hands or guts. Their work was of the brain, now, and they had been spoiled by underlings, softened by too much *having*. It would be of interest to see which among them could meet the challenge that would be soon set before them. The sea accident had been Nature's opening volley. The pace would accelerate now; the dangers would escalate rapidly and the spiral would swirl them down.

He hummed softly to himself as he strode through the malignant undergrowth. Occasionally, a bird or small animal would call to him, or he to it. Once, he bent to converse with a gnarled and leafy plant; it was a cousin to the peyote, which was his ally, so he stayed awhile to show his respect. There was plenty of time before sunup, and Nelida would understand the necessity that had delayed him.

Nelida built a small fire in the clearing she had chosen for their rendezvous, and sprinkled into it an herb that had the capacity to keep little flying insects at bay. She stood watching the fire crackle and flicker, reaching out with her perception to sense why her husband had been delayed. *Bien*. She sensed no danger. He had merely stopped for conversation. He had always been one to dawdle when the opportunity for camaraderie presented itself.

They had been married long and fruitfully. There was *respecto mutuo*. Long, long ago they had been apprentices to neighboring Naquals, and had met in the course of their magical studies. The work was different for each, of course. Women's sorcery was vastly different from men's, their Powers coming from different sources. But their knowledge of the unseen world was similar enough for compatibility, and because of their special skills and knowledge of the old ways, sex had always been excellent and had bound them with many cords, as is the way of the universe.

Nelida sang softly as she undid her long lustrous hair and fanned it out over her shoulders. She loosed her dirndl skirt and dropped it in a colorful puddle at her feet, stepping lightly away from its entanglement. Next, she pulled the white batiste blouse over her head, exposing her large breasts to the warming fire-glow. She stood naked and unmoving for a long moment, absorbing the fragrant firelight into her being, feeling the tightening of her nipples as the evening cool caressed them in counterpoint to the fire. She ran her hands down her body from throat to ankles, once, reveling in her womanhood. It was good to be naked, good to be free of the constraints of other people's needs. Good to be awakening her body in anticipation of her mate. There was danger all around now, drawing stealthily nearer. Tonight could be their last chance at solitude for some time.

Nelida had a sorcerer's body, lithe and fulsome, sleek as a seal despite her age. It was one of the pleasanter side effects of sorcery, this control of Nature that permitted the suspension of time—not forever, of course, but for a substantial number of years as they were counted in this dimension.

She was full breasted and full hipped, in the manner of the Earth Goddess she served. She had been fecund in her time and had brought forth life in her youth, but her body showed less ravagement from that service than did most. Not that such would have mattered to Emilio, who could see the luminous part of her that others called the soul.

Nelida spread the soft blanket she had brought beside the fire, and wrapped a red and yellow pareu around her loins before she lay down to wait for Emilio. These were the colors that empowered the first and second energy centers that were needed for the sexual act. She had no compunction about pleasure. She was woman, he was man; the interwoven energies of their mating would carry on the fertility dance that kept the universe in motion.

Moments later Emilio entered the small clearing. He smiled at Nelida's blatant readiness and went to her eagerly. When he kissed her, he greedily cupped her breasts with his hands, and teased her large dark nipples in playful greeting.

"I have hungered for you, my little eagle," he said tenderly, as she helped him free himself from his encumbering clothes. "It is all very well to do the work we have been called to do, but it has left me empty, thus far. These gringos are thickheaded."

"I, too, am longing to be filled, *mi amor,*" she murmured, pulling him down on top of her willing body, and guiding his ready cock into the warm, wet center. Emilio was smaller in stature than Nelida, but he was powerfully built, stocky muscles hardened and defined, and they were old lovers who knew each other's needs and intimate desires without prompting.

Emilio was feeling randy tonight, and generous. He would tease his wife's comings out of her in ways that she was not expecting, and he would relish her surprise and delight at his cleverness. It was hard to surprise a witch of her stature, of course, he thought with a small chuckle, but he had a few cards up his sleeve that had not yet been played. The challenge had much merit, as the hardness of his member attested. Emilio bent his head to Nelida's breast and caught the unresisting nipple in his teeth, as he pulled himself free of her velvet wetness, just for a little while.

Nelida laughed now, softly, for she knew in her instinct where he would take her—high, higher now over the moon and rainbow stars, far out in the galaxy of love known only to men and women of Power, men and women who had paid a great price for the ability to transcend the small ecstasies that other mortals felt. She lay back, laughter bubbling low in her throat where primal sounds began, as she let the world slip away beneath his hands and mouth and life-affirming cock.

It was an interesting game of the Gods they had been called to participate in, and each would do the part expected—they were equipped by the universe to deal with far more than a bunch of fools who thought that mere money made them powerful. But for tonight, none of that mattered at all. Tonight they were man and woman, and even the Gods respected the Power they would share in this clearing in the heat of the jungle, in a playground that they alone, of all on the island, had paid their dues to enter.

Friday, April 15

Men are born with two eyes, but with a single tongue,
in order that they should see
twice as much as they say.

CHARLES CALEB COLTON

THIRTY-FOUR

I feel like I've been on a chain gang for a month," Jack said, plopping down on the ground with a groan. "There isn't a muscle in my body that hasn't screamed uncle." Minutes before, they'd finished constructing a new fire pit near the house, as Emilio had announced that the kitchen was permanently inoperable now, and their first pit was too small for their needs. The effort of digging and of collecting the wood had taken hours.

Jase nodded in response. "You're telling me? My little swim fest with Alex was not only sobering, it damn near killed me. My arms and legs still feel like anguished cement. I have pains in muscles I didn't know I owned."

"I hate to say it, but there's a possibility we're too old for jungle warfare," Jack said wryly. "Digging ditches and setting snares wasn't all that much fun even when I was young, and I gotta tell you, fighting with women is a real pain in the ass. I mean, you don't want to hurt them, you don't want to get hurt . . . everybody loses. . . ."

Jase laughed without much mirth. "If we do our reconnaissance right today, I think we'll just get the hell out of here before Sunday. But to tell you the truth, Jack, I kind of get a kick out of all these shenanigans . . . there's an adrenaline rush of some kind to it. Scratch the surface and we're all primitives."

"Yeah? Well, this primitive hopes that recce turns up those fuel controllers before nightfall, so we can all just get the fuck out of Paradise in one piece."

"Okay, Jack, you're on the first patrol with Alex, and I hope like hell you guys find the women's camp."

As Jack and Alex made their way out of the compound, they spotted Tony and Rand dragging jungle foliage and tree branches to cover over a freshly dug trench. The two men, both naked to the waist, stood sweating beside their handiwork.

"I can't believe you've actually dug those pits," Jack said, drawing near enough to see what was happening. "You think you're dealing with the VC here? You guys are nuts. What'll you do if you catch one of them? Hook her up to a car battery?" He shook his head with disgust.

"They've got to know we mean business here," Tony replied briskly. "And they've got to stay out of our pants while we search for the fuel controllers."

"Personally," Alex said with a small laugh, "I'd rather have them *in* my pants, but I suppose it's a matter of personal preference."

"What if somebody gets hurt in one of these trenches?" Jack pressed. "A broken bone could be serious this far from help. You guys are really asking for trouble."

"Nah. They're shallow trenches," Tony answered. "If somebody falls in, she's more likely to get shaken up than hurt. Although, maybe if somebody did get hurt, it would bring those damn fool women to their senses faster."

Jack just shook his head and made a hand gesture that said "enough." He and Alex left the diggers behind and headed out toward the perimeter of the jungle on their reconnaissance patrol.

The men's camp had divided up daily labors as equitably as possible; having real work to do helped with the boredom and passed the time. Jase and Tony were the best fishermen, and Thoros, Jase, and Alex were experienced hunters, as was Emilio, so there was no real hardship where food was concerned. But there were a million petty annoyances, and there was a helluva lot of hard physical labor to maintain any semblance of decent life inside the compound.

Water had to be boiled for drinking and cooking, that was an obvious priority. What hadn't been obvious, until Rand warned them, was that bathing, too, could be dangerous. Bacteria could be ingested while showering, and eye and ear infections were common in places where unboiled water was used for bathing. Nobody needed dysentery.

All the water in the holding tanks was salty as well as contaminated, and without the desalinization system it was useless, so every morning and evening a team of men with containers set out for the nearest water source. As long as the jitneys had gasoline, it hadn't been too much of a hardship, although the four-wheel-drive vehicles could only take them within a half mile of the river and they had to complete the journey on foot. There was a second route into the mountains that afforded other water sources, but it was better than an hour's drive in each direction, so, for the most part they opted for the river.

"Those guys are liking their war games a little too much for my taste," Jack said to Alex as they walked rapidly past Nelida's farm.

"Most men do," Alex replied, thoughtfully; in his estimation, men and war were really a subspecialty of economics. "Testosterone and ego combined in just the right proportions make war a very popular pastime, historically."

Jack laughed shortly. "They must have left something out of me. I wasn't all that crazy about it even when I had to do it."

"You were in Vietnam, as I recall, Jack?"

"Yeah. I was there. Rifle Squad Leader, Twenty-fifth Infantry. I was just a kid, but I had a gift for shooting—some kind of natural aptitude—that got me through it. But I sure didn't see much I thought was good there. I've known guys who reupped two or three times . . . thought it was the high point of their lives. Not me. The high point for me was getting the hell out of Saigon."

Alex nodded, understanding entirely. "Queer things happen to us men in war, Jack. Some primal need for domination. I've seen it often around the conference table, too. Men who are educated, cultured, brilliant, really, hear some clarion call within themselves to warriorhood and respond like Pavlov's dog."

"Well, Tony, Rand, and Jase seem to be hearing the call, at the moment. Even Thoros, although he's basically too smart and rational to do anything stupid."

"Trouble is," Alex replied, "if the blood is up, so to speak, judgment falters . . . irrational acts begin to seem rational, even justified. To tell you the truth, Jack, I'll count us damned lucky if we get out of here without anybody getting seriously hurt."

Jack followed Alex through the tangled undergrowth, the damp green tendrils reminding him of the jungle of long ago. Jungle meant danger in Jack's visceral memory, the unexpected and the unendurable. Even this jungle.

"You're moving like you know where you're going," he said, suddenly realizing that was true. Recce was a slow, careful process, paths were noted and marked, charts were made for future reference, but Alex was moving swiftly.

The tall Englishman slowed. "I remembered a place that took Liz's fancy when we were out hiking," he said. "I didn't mention it back there for several reasons. I'm not certain I can find it again, for one. I'm not bad on sense of direction in forested country, mind you, but jungle is another matter. And then, I suppose if it does turn out to be the women's camp, some part of me is reluctant to let everyone know just yet for all the reasons we've just been recounting. I'd rather be able to monitor the girls, maybe find those damned fuel controllers ourselves. With tempers running this high, I don't want the location of their camp to be tinder for some crazy conflagration."

Jack nodded; he'd had the same thought. He was about to reply when the trees fell away suddenly, giving sight to a more rocky terrain and the sound of rushing water.

"There's a rope bridge somewhere close around here," Alex said, scanning the path ahead. "I think they're on the other side of it. I'd like you to take a look at the span, too, Jack, if you will. It appeared none too safe to me when we went over it on our trek. You have more jungle experience than I, but the vines or ropes or whatever they suspend those contraptions with are rotting in places." He stopped suddenly and pointed. "There she is! Ahead on the right, through those trees."

They walked on rapidly; the terrain seemed to end abruptly in front of them, as if some ancient cataclysm had simply slit the earth and pulled the edges apart about fifty feet. Jack and Alex crossed the last few yards to the edge of the gorge and looked down. A steep, rocky slope dropped abruptly to the bottom of the fissure; a thunderous stream rushed below, breaking into small white-water fragments at every place where it hit the rocks that were strewn in its path, like a giant's causeway.

"I hope the bridge is sturdier than you say, Alex," Jack said. "Getting across here would be damned near impossible without it, and I don't see a fording place in either direction for miles. You're sure the girls are on the other side?"

Alex nodded. "I'd bet money on it. There's a place maybe a mile further on that was rather idyllic, and somewhat clear and habitable—with a waterfall and pool by the side of one of the smaller tributaries of that river down there. I remember Liz said something about it being a charming place for a picnic—so sylvan and benevolent. We stopped there to rest a bit, and Liz scouted around a little. There really weren't any other spots we passed that would have made as good a campsite."

The rope bridge was constructed of fibrous vines, woven and rewoven into the thickness of a man's arm. It had obviously withstood the ravages of time, but had taken a few hits as well from nature. Slats of some bamboolike wood had been woven together to form a kind of flooring for the suspension span that hung swaybacked and graceful, high above the brown and white turbulent water below.

Jack examined the sturdy pilings that supported the structure, attaching it to the rocky face of the cliff, and tentatively checking as he proceeded, he moved out stealthily onto the bridge itself. The undulating motion beneath his feet made each step queasily uncertain.

"It feels okay to me," he called out to Alex from near the middle of the span. "They're never great, but this one seems sturdy enough. Not that I'd like to trust it in a storm, though—there's a fair amount of erosion around the place where it attaches to the shoulder."

Alex nodded. He, too, accomplished the precarious walk across the bridge to the far side of the gorge.

Jack looked in every direction for an alternative to the bridge; finding none apparent, he spoke again. "So where are we headed?"

"The spot I'm after is not more than a mile and a half to the northeast," Alex said, squinting into the distance. "We'd best tread carefully from this point on—they may have booby-trapped the trail, you know."

Jack frowned, thinking the idea ridiculous. Then he remembered the traps set back at the compound, and began to watch his footing. At least in this jungle you didn't have to wonder about being blown to buzzard bait.

Something metallic whipped past Jack's ear. Instinct propelled him to the ground. "Incoming!" he screamed. "Get down! For Christ's sake, get down!"

"Don't come any closer," an accented female voice shouted from somewhere ahead of them to the right.

"Are you fucking out of your mind?" Jack shouted back, furious and feeling like an ass. "You could have killed somebody!" A steel arrow was embedded in the ground not two feet from him.

"I wasn't aiming *at* you," Marika called out. "Otherwise you would be dead now. I was *warning* you. This is private territory. You must go back."

Alex lifted himself up on his elbows. "We've only come to talk. We're trying to make sense of this bloody mess. Can't we . . ."

"We know why you're here," Liz called out from the same direction. "If you want to parlay, set it up through Emilio and Nelida. Until then, we can't be sure you speak for everyone, and it's not safe for you to come nosing around here uninvited. Our sentries won't let you get any closer."

" 'No military training,' I think Tony said," Alex whispered with a disgruntled laugh. "Liz probably remembers Patton's war diaries word for word."

"Somebody sure as hell's got crossbow training," Jack responded. "Let's get our asses out of here. At least we've found their camp."

"We're going!" Alex shouted toward the disembodied voices, moving backward as he called out, "Hold your fire!"

Crablike, the men scuttled into taller grass, then rose to a crouch and ran toward the cover of the trees. No more arrows pursued them. When they'd reached safety, they stopped to catch their breath and reconnoiter.

"Son of a bitch!" Jack exploded. "They're as fucking nuts as we are. We're digging trenches, they're shooting crossbows.

Somebody's going to get killed. There must be something we can do to end this, Alex. Isn't that what you do for a living?"

"Look, Jack, in my experience, the best thing a negotiator can do is observe all participating factions studiously—try to get an accurate feel for the spirit of the conflict. Not what's said, so much as what's not said. This whole mess has to do with respect—most wars, by the way, do, in some fashion. But this one, most assuredly. There's generally a moment or two, somewhere in the conflict when everyone has pounded his breast, made his statement, told the other side to bugger off, and neither side really has a clue what to do next. *That's* the moment when negotiation works best. If you can slip in with a logical face-saving suggestion at precisely *that* moment, very often sanity can be made to prevail."

"And you think now's the time?"

Alex nodded. "I think it's worth a shot, before another incendiary incident escalates the action."

"Then let's get back to camp and talk the others into parlaying while there's time," Jack said grimly.

The two men headed back, each with a sense of foreboding. Each side had weapons now, and each side seemed unconscionably willing to use them.

THIRTY-FIVE

Christie skirted the perimeter of the compound on her run. Usually, she ran her three- or four-mile exercise stint on the beach, but today she'd decided to change her route. The hour was later than she would have liked, because of the heat, but her work had taken up most of the morning. Chesi and Nelida had been talking about the ancestral caves of the volcanic beaches on the west coast of the island, and the stories had caught her imagination, so she decided to wander off her usual route. She didn't like the notion of passing so close to enemy territory, but so far there'd been no sign of the men and she ran easily and well on the path she'd taken.

The air was muggy, and hot; she hated running in the island heat, but after five years of doing this four times a week, and five years of track in high school and college, she knew how fast a girl could get out of training. One week with the flu or finals could set you back a month; one week of late nights could make you lazy enough to skip a day or two of training, and it was god-awful hard to get back into rhythm, once you let yourself take a break. Besides, running was an easy way to keep her weight down, and weight was the nemesis of all TV reporters. The camera put twenty pounds on you, and Christie tended to be baby-faced and round to begin with.

She skirted the last bend that hid the compound from view and saw the vast crablike structure of the Great House lying straight ahead, shimmering in the late afternoon sunlight. The route ahead looked relatively clear, compared with the tangle of growth she'd already left behind. Christie was feeling good now; the adrenaline of the run had kicked in and her body was acclimating to the humidity as her steady strides carried her on toward the sea.

The ground gave way under Christie so unexpectedly that she was already suspended in midair on her way to the bottom of the pit, before her brain fully registered what was happening. Leaves and twigs and debris cascaded all around her wildly, as she plummeted down, down. Then the ground came up to meet her hard as granite and full of painful stones and branches that tore her body, lacerating her skin. Christie screamed as she fell, but the force of her landing knocked the wind out of her completely; dazed and disoriented, she wondered if she might have blacked out briefly. One minute she was running and the next she was in a painful heap at the bottom of a hole, her leg folded hurtfully under, her wrists bent backward in a fruitless effort to save herself. Her head ached and her back throbbed, and she was having trouble breathing, but that felt as much from shock as injury.

On autopilot, Christie attempted to move her leg; a sharp pain in her pelvis made her move gingerly, unfolding her leg carefully with the help of both hands. Straightening it as best she could, Christie felt for broken bones. It was hard to tell for sure, but she thought her leg was more likely sprained than broken, so she pulled herself upright and tried to stand, but the dizzying pain set her down again fast.

"Damn!" she spat. "*Now* what do I do?"

Christie, frowning, looked around at her surroundings for the first time. "Son of a bitch!" she said into the dampness. "Those fuckers *dug* this thing!" The side showed shovel marks, and it was too symmetrical for nature to have engineered it.

With that weird realization, panic flooded Christie; if this was dug as a trap, the men would be back soon to check it for prey. She had to get out of here. *Fast.*

Christie forced herself to stand again, painfully; this time she used one of the fallen branches as a support. Cursing the pain, she hobbled close to the side wall and looked up. Nine or ten feet, maybe. Not bad at all, if her leg were normal, but under these circumstances . . .

Full of rage at the men's audacity, she took a deep breath, grabbed a sharp rock from the debris beneath her feet, and tried to scrape out a handhold in the resistant earth. A profusion of vines and roots were matted beneath the surface; it made digging hard, but finding footholds easy. Worms and hairy beetles crawled out of the handhold but she steeled herself to ignore them.

Inch by hurtful inch, Christie made her way to the top of the hole, cursing every step of the way. Tears streamed down her cheeks and her nose ran; she slipped several times, and had to regain her ground, but anger and fear goaded her steadily toward the top.

Just below ground level Christie paused to catch her breath; she waited, heart pounding, to listen for the footfalls of her captors, but she heard no one, so she pulled herself up and over the edge of the pit, with her fingers filthy, scraped, and bleeding from the climb. Grateful that no one was near to see her graceless clamber over the edge to safety, Christie lay a long moment prostrate on the edge of the hole, straining to catch her breath and equilibrium.

And vow her revenge on the bastards who'd dug the pit.

Then she began the long and arduous trek back to camp.

* * *

The women sat in a glum knot around the fire pit, fear and fury rampant. It was all well and good to make a brave statement about being taken seriously, and to play at warfare from a distance, but this was escalating into something really dangerous.

"A pit trap?" Chesi exploded, as Christie finished her story. The women were circled around her as Christie talked and Nelida examined her injuries, making judicious, clucking sounds as she did so.

"There are no broken bones," the Mexican woman announced. "Many cuts and scratches . . . a badly strained ligament in this leg. Nothing that will not heal in a few days. Fortune goes with you."

"Scorched earth," Liz said angrily. "We need to retaliate bigtime. Suntze says you need to demoralize your enemy as well as rout him. Your opponent has to believe you have the capacity to beat him into the dust and make his life hell on wheels while you're doing it."

"Haven't we been doing that?" Chesi asked, annoyed.

"*Now,* do you still think they won't resort to violence?" Christie spat, disgustedly turning to Justine.

"I think their egos have been injured," Justine replied quietly. "And obviously, we have hit them where it hurts, so they are vindictive and dangerous. But, remember, we are not blameless here—we have escalated the war by sabotaging their compound. I still believe we should attempt to negotiate."

"Negotiate?" Christie said harshly. "How do you negotiate with guys who set animal traps for people? Liz is right. We have to retaliate."

"And do what?" Marika interrupted. "Escalate this into a real disaster? Why not just wait for the rescue plane to come for us on Sunday?"

"First of all, nobody's coming Sunday," Christie snapped. "It'll be Monday or Tuesday before they figure out we didn't leave on Sunday, and what if they don't *intend* to let us live until rescuers come? *They* have a gun. We don't. *They've* dug traps. We haven't. Now we know they're capable of violence and they don't give a damn if we get badly hurt. And who the hell knows what they would have done to me if I hadn't gotten out of that hole. I say our lives are in danger."

"I think our lives are more in danger from our living conditions than from the men," Tiffany said, trying to calm things down. It was awfully easy for a mob mentality to take over and get people acting crazy, especially if they were genuinely afraid.

"I'm going to get a message to Thoros," Justine said suddenly. "He is a rational man, even if he is pigheaded, dammit! And we must end this lunacy."

"Don't be an ass!" Chesi snapped hotly. "He's a rational man whose hundred-million-dollar toy we've just trashed. Do you have any idea how much it's going to cost him to fix this place, Justine? Maybe a million dollars—these guys run on money. They're elitist, male chauvinists, and we've fucked them over where it hurts—in the ego and the wallet."

"Face it, Justine," Christie snarled, "you just have the hots for the guy and all the rest is rationalized horseshit."

"So, what are you all saying?" Justine answered, angry and wounded. "That we apologize like good little American girls, and ask sweetly to be forgiven? That's absurd. We need to negotiate a détente and that's what I intend to do."

"How?" Liz asked. "By giving up the fuel controllers and all our leverage? And I resent that crack about American women. We all know the French wrote the book on capitulation to the enemy, but nobody's throwing stones about that."

Justine's eyes narrowed at the insult, and she seemed about to speak. Instead she turned abruptly and headed out of the circle.

Nelida stepped forward. *"Basta ya!"* she commanded. "This cannot be a divided house. You women have much to learn about the exercise of Power. Tonight, I will tell you a story so that you may understand that you, not they, are connected to the great source itself, the Earth Mother."

"Face it, Nelida, men rule the world. Not us," Chesi countered hotly.

"This is true, Chesi. So we are forced to fight our way back to our own truth, eh? Who has told you this would be easy? We come here to earth to learn this lesson . . . to win back our Power in the face of adversity. Men have a different lesson to learn which has to do with ego and nurturance. This is as hard for them as our task is for us. So, for now, you will stop shouting at each other, and tonight I will tell you a story from between the legs."

"That sounds perfectly obscene," Liz said, still angry.

Nelida smirked. "This is the great beauty of it. *Habla por entre las piernas*. There is no greater compliment for a woman than to say she speaks from between her legs, for that is where we keep our truth."

Before anyone had a chance to question that pronouncement, Nelida, too, rose and left them.

"Listen, guys," Tiffany said after Nelida had gone. "We were pretty rough on Her Majesty just now, don't you think?"

"You mean Justine?" Christie responded. "She needed a swift kick in the ass. She's always so fucking superior."

"Face it, Christie," Liz said thoughtfully. "She *is* superior. She's gorgeous, rich as Croesus, educated, perfectly bred, and smart as a whip. How much more *superior* could you get?"

"You know what's really bugging us about her?" Tiffany asked, obviously troubled. "We're just jealous. She takes for granted everything the rest of us have to work our asses off to achieve, and that galls the shit out of us. But to tell you the truth, it's not fair of us to treat her like we just did. She's working just as hard as we are to figure this out and fix it and we just kicked her in the stomach because we're jealous and bitchy. I think I'm ashamed of us."

Deflated and bothered by all that had been said, the women dispersed.

Justine stormed through the jungle, crashing roots and tangled vegetation deliberately as she went. She was furious at being attacked verbally by the other women, furious at her own impotence in this mad situation. And she was more hurt than she wanted to admit. The others were stupid sheep. Lemmings. *Idiots.* Democracy be damned—she'd never understood the notion that ignorant masses should be left to make their own decisions about anything of real magnitude. *Merde!* This was the worst disaster of an irretrievable fuck-up. It would serve them all right if she simply handed over the fuel controllers to Thoros, and helped him get off the island. Everyone would benefit. She never intended to see any of these women again, except perhaps Liz, anyway, so who cared if they felt betrayed by her action.

Justine needed to find a place of solitude to think. Being in the constant company of these stupid lemmings was enough to drive her mad.

THIRTY-SIX

You look like hell, Rand," Jase said, studying him carefully. The men stood on the pool patio near the house at sundown. "Are you okay?"

Rand's face had an unhealthy gray tinge to it, and beads of sweat dripped down his face and neck, at odds with his usual pristine grooming.

"I must be coming down with the flu," Rand replied, sounding uncertain. "Queasy stomach, chills. I feel quite rotten, actually."

Jase nodded; he'd seen symptoms like this in the service, and it wasn't the flu. "Why don't you talk to Emilio, Rand. He's got a lot of folk knowledge. Maybe he's got a cure for whatever ails you. It could be a fever of some kind, you know. We are in the tropics here—you could have malaria for all we know. To say nothing of parasites from the water."

Rand acknowledged the possibilities with an inclination of his head. "I'll be all right if I just lie down for a while." He moved shakily toward a lounge chair; he didn't want to say so, but he didn't think he could make it to Emilio. "It's too hot inside to sleep—I think I'll just stay out here for a bit."

Jase watched the man who was usually so controlled, curl up on the pool chaise, his legs drawn into a fetal position. He decided to find Emilio or Thoros; whatever Rand had, it needed attention.

H. Douglas Rand lay shivering on the bed to which Thoros, Jase, and Emilio had carried him with considerable difficulty. His symptoms had worsened and his teeth chattered audibly. His gray-tinged reddish brown hair lay plastered against his forehead in sweat-soaked tendrils. Emilio had told them to strip off his clothes, which were soaked with acrid-smelling sweat. Rand had submitted to the men's awkward ministrations only because he was too sick to protest effectively.

"You must sponge his face and body with cool water," Emilio instructed the two men, as he looked up from his diagnosing.

"What the hell do I look like to you, Emilio," Jase snapped irritably, "Nurse Nice?" He hated illness; hated being anywhere near it.

"I must search for fever herbs," Emilio replied, ignoring the tone. "It is dangerous to the brain if the fever rises too high."

"I'll take care of him," Thoros said from a corner of the room. "I used to watch my grandmother nurse people when I was a boy. I believe I can handle it." He moved toward the bed. "Is this contagious, Emilio?" he asked, reaching for the sponge in the bucket of water the Mexican had provided. If it were only he himself who was in danger, he wouldn't be deterred, but perhaps certain precautions should be taken for the others' safety.

"No, señor," Emilio replied, standing up, and preparing to leave on his quest. "An insect, perhaps, has bitten him. We must cool his fever to guard his brain. There are certain barks that I must find to ease the fever before it does damage we cannot repair."

"Is there something we can take to protect the rest of us?" Jase asked anxiously.

"Perhaps, señor. The cure is always provided by Nature in the same place as the illness. We must hope the ones who destroyed the jungle to build here did not destroy that which we now need."

"That would be a boot in the ass, wouldn't it?" Jase replied shortly. He wanted to leave the room, but it would be unseemly; Thoros might need help.

Emilio left the men, in his soundless, stealthy way.

"Tell the others what's happened," Thoros said to Jase, as he sponged the sweat from Rand's shivering chest, then pulled the blankets up to the man's chin to cover him. The vulnerability of his naked friend troubled Thoros in some deep way he couldn't name. "We don't know how long Emilio will be gone—I'll need someone to spell me in caring for Rand."

"Let me give you a hand, Thoros," Tony said from the doorway. "I just passed Emilio in the kitchen, and he told me what's up." Tony moved into the room confidently, obviously unworried about contagion.

"I got a lot of experience with jungle fever in the service. Nursed a lot of buddies through bad times—they used to say I was half medic and half old lady. I got no problems with shit and gore, I've seen piles of it."

"Better you than me," Jase answered, relieved that now he wouldn't have to help. "What do you men need in here? I'll get it for you."

Tony had one hand on Rand's forehead, the other rolling up an eyelid to assess his condition, his manner professional. "We'll need plenty of cold water, not the crap from the cisterns—send somebody out to the ocean or river. Get a pile of blankets, too, while you're out there. He's hot as hell, now, so he's gonna be cold as ice, next. Get Thoros and me some clean clothes to change into, and a pile of towels. Maybe a bucket, in case Rand gets the heaves. See if there's any quinine left in one of the guest pod medicine chests. You might grab some rope or belts and ties, too, in case he goes delirious on us, and we have to tie him down. Oh, and if you can get somebody to make coffee and sandwiches or something, that'd be good, Jase. This could be a long night and we had no dinner."

Thoros watched the confident competence with which Tony had taken charge. He was a man of damnable contradictions, but at moments like this it was easy to remember why Tony was one of them. The one most likely to roll up his sleeves and pitch in . . . the one most likely to find a way to help. The one least likely to bitch and moan about being asked.

Jase glanced at the clock on the dresser. Half past ten. Unbelievable . . . they'd been here for hours. He was amazed at himself that he'd stayed, but he'd been listening with an editor's ear; he felt he should be taking notes on the conversation, as the five healthy men sat around the bedside of the sixth. They'd gathered one by one; he wondered why every man felt he had to be here. Thoros and Tony were taking care of Rand—beyond the two times the sick man had become wildly delirious and they'd had to wrestle him back onto the bed, there was really no need for anyone else to be in that room, yet, one by one they'd stopped by and stayed.

Endless coffee had been consumed. "This is like a fucking AA meeting," Tony had quipped, making the rest wonder if he knew from personal experience. Endless sandwiches had been eaten. And, Tony wouldn't let anybody smoke in the room, despite the fact he was probably the one most likely to be craving a cigar about now. The tableau was a throwback, Jase knew instinctively, to the rare times when men were permitted to be close, to talk, to connect, to bond. Maybe that's what war was really all about—not just rampant hormones and the need for power. Maybe war gave men a chance to share intimacies that would have been unthinkable in different circumstances. Maybe there was a book in that, somewhere. He made a note on his pocket pad and tuned back in to the conversation.

"Khe Sanh was a real motherfucker," Jack was saying. "I was still a street kid, so I thought I had it figured. The best way to stay alive was never to volunteer, never do a goddamned thing more than you had to. But, you couldn't do that over there—you know? You had to help your buddies no matter what it took.

"I remember this one ambush patrol we were on that got into deep shit because the VC was somehow on to our route. We were stuck in this fucking bomb crater, and those gooks were up our asses every which way you looked. And the jets were bombing in the woods all around us, *ba-wham!* I mean the ground would rumble and shake and this was going on from midnight to dawn, and we were running low on ammo, and scared out of our minds, and our RTO looks up at us and says, like he was a general out of West Point, all dignified and dead-serious, 'Somebody's got to get us some ammo or we're done for.' Well, my buddy Jackson stands up and says, 'I'll do it.' Holy shit! I think. He'll have to run straight across no-man's-land to get ammo for the .50s. And all of a sudden I hear myself saying, 'I'll go with him.' I couldn't believe I'd said it, you know. I fucking well couldn't believe my own ears."

The other men laughed in empathy. In some way or other, they'd all been in the same kind of situation. "So, did you get the ammo?" Tony prompted.

Jack nodded his head affirmatively, and his eyes grew sad. "We made five trips across before they got Jackson. He just kept telling me, *'You can do it, kid,'* and laughing at the VC and giving them the finger. I can just see those big white teeth flashing in that black face, in the light of the mortar fire. 'Why the hell'd you volunteer back there, Jackson?' I asked him, my teeth chattering I was so damned scared. 'No ammo, you ain't got no fightin' chance, Jack,' he said. 'Always gotta give a man a fightin' chance.' "

Jack paused to clear his throat, emotion momentarily getting the best of him. "Christ! They gave me a fucking medal for that night, but truth is I wouldn't even have been there at all except for Jackson. There were a helluva lot of heroes in Nam nobody ever heard of."

"That's for damned sure," Tony agreed. "Bravest guy I ever knew was a medic. We called him Bandaid. Never fired a shot, but I swear to God he would've walked into Hell itself and thumbed his nose at old Satan to get a wounded guy out."

Thoros spoke from the other side of the bed, his deep voice charged with reminiscence. "I spent some time in Koje-do—a place called Compound 76—as a guest of the North Korean military." Eyes came up around the room—Thoros had never once spoken of being a POW in Korea.

"It's a barren brown country and cold as a witch's tit, so one of the ways they used to demoralize a man was to take your clothes away and stand you outside staring at those cold brown mountains for hours, with the freezing wind whistling through you . . . Jesus, they have wind there that makes Chicago look like Kenya." He shook his head forcefully as if to banish the anguish of the cold, and took an audible breath. "Then you'd be thrown inside a damp stone cell with ice water dripping on the floor, your nose running and your teeth chattering and your feet and hands turned blue and lifeless. It took the heart right out of you. It wasn't something you could fight, just endure or die. But there was this one officer who kept us all alive through the winter. Maybe there's one in every prison camp.

"He devised a tap code we all learned and he'd tap out messages to the guys who were freezing in these icebox cells. He would tap out prayers and poems and Bible verses . . . he had the goddamnedest repertoire you ever heard of. But he had the capacity to keep you alive by what he tapped—I don't know what it was exactly that he gave you . . . hope, maybe? A memory of some better time . . . just the knowledge that you weren't alone in your suffering and that somebody cared about you." He paused, remembering.

"Did the gooks figure it out?" Tony asked.

Thoros nodded, grimly. "Jim never made it out of Koje-do. But there are a lot of men who did, who bless his name."

Rand began to groan again and thrash at the blankets that covered him. Tony was on his feet in an instant, as was Thoros. "It's an intermittent fever," he said. "Probably malaria. Where the fuck is that little Mexican?"

"I am here, señor," a voice said from behind him. No one had seen or heard the man enter the room.

"I have found the proper bark with which to treat Señor Rand. It will be boiled and ready soon." Moving to the bed, he checked Rand's vital signs and grunted satisfaction.

"You have dealt with such things before, señor?" he asked Tony. "You have done well for your friend. Do not be concerned."

"Are we all in danger of dying from this fever?" Jase asked as he headed toward the door; he'd be happy to get out of the sickroom.

"Every man who is born is in danger of dying, señor," Emilio answered. "From this thing or that."

Jase, caught off guard by the reply, laughed out loud. "You know, Emilio," he said, "I'm getting to like you. I hate to admit it, but I am really getting to like you."

THIRTY-SEVEN

Nelida looked around the circle, every face anticipatory. These women were changing, she thought with satisfaction; growing, deepening. They looked forward to her stories now. She sat herself down with her knees apart, her skirt puddled into a colorful lap, as she began.

"I have promised to tell you dirty stories tonight," she said with a sensual chuckle. "Tonight, there are to be no ladies here. Only *women* with brass *ovarios* are permitted at our fire."

She put her hands on her knees and arched her back luxuriantly. "Tonight we loosen what is tight . . . we let out what is in the closet . . . we cut the chains and uncork the bottle. We laugh ourselves silly, eh? We unleash the Belly Goddess and speak of the obscene."

"Sounds like my old sorority," Liz said with a giggle.

"In my culture, we preserve the Belly Goddesses, the ones who create the belly laugh that comes up from the genitals like truth rising. Up from the loins and the gut to bring laughter and lifeforce to where it is needed. These Goddesses have no heads, but they have vulvas that are their mouths to speak through, and nipples, through which to see. Their stories cure depression and illness, restore life, replenish lust—they do this with sacred laughter over all that is obscene in this foolish world. To speak from between the legs is to speak the truth.

"So, let us begin. I want each of you to tell us something obscene—something that you would never tell a man, but that will make us women laugh."

"You want us to tell dirty jokes?" Christie asked, incredulously.

"It could be a joke, or a story, true or otherwise . . . it could be an observation. But it must be of sex and it must give us laughter."

"Okay, what the hell! I've got one for you," Liz said. "Anybody know the difference between sexy and kinky?"

The women were all looking at one another, not knowing whether to laugh or feel uncomfortable.

"Sexy is when you tickle a man's balls with a feather," Liz blurted, "kinky is when you use a whole chicken."

Justine exploded with unexpected laughter; this was a side of Liz she hadn't seen. "I once slept with one of the British royals," she chimed in, "who couldn't get it up unless his wolfhound licked his balls. If I'd known about the chicken, I would have tried it. The dog took up an enormous amount of space in the bed." She wasn't over her anger at the others, but she thought participating in Nelida's ribald games might lighten her mood; and besides, there was nowhere else to go.

Christie leaned forward. "I don't know if *this* is exactly what we're after here, girls, but I've got this little theory that I never told anybody." She hesitated.

"Go on, go on," Nelida prompted. "Make us laugh from between the legs."

Christie smirked. "Well, you know how everybody says,

you can tell the size of a guy's dick by the size of his hands?" All heads nodded.

"Well, I know how to tell the size of a woman's cunt."

A chorus of "How?" responded.

"By the size of her pocketbook!" Christie said triumphantly.

Howls of laughter greeted the statement. "Oh my God!" Chesi gasped between peals. "What does that say about women with backpacks?"

"Hey, wait a minute, girls," Christie called out, laughing so hard she could hardly get the words out. "I just thought of a joke.

"There was this young man who wanted to impress his girlfriend so much he bought her four dozen roses. When he arrived with the huge bouquet, she tore off her clothes, ran to the bed, and spread her legs wide open. '*This,*' she said, exuberantly, 'is for the roses.' And he said, 'Does that mean you don't have a vase?' "

The laughter had escalated now, with everybody in on the act.

"Wait, I've got another one," Christie interjected merrily. "This old Jewish guy named Abie falls in love with a pair of hundred-dollar red alligator shoes that he thinks will make him the sexiest guy alive. So for two months, he saves his pennies and finally he buys the shoes. He goes home to his wife Becky and says, 'Vat do you notice dat's different?' and Becky says, 'Nuttink.' So he goes to his bedroom and rips off his coat and shirt and comes back out to see her, still in the shoes. '*Now,* vat do you notice dat's different?' he says, and she says, 'Nuttink!' So he runs back to the bedroom, rips off his pants and shorts and comes back wearing *only* the red shoes. 'Now,' he says, 'vat do you see?' And Becky says, 'Only the same old putz.' And Abie says, 'But the same old putz is pointing at a pair of hundred-dollar alligator shoes!' And Becky says, 'Better you should have bought a hundred-dollar hat.' "

The whole gathering was laughing uncontrollably now, tears rolling down their faces, everyone clamoring to tell another story. Nelida smiled benevolently at her pupils, and Liz spoke through her own laughter.

"This really does remind me of my sorority sisters. We used to stay up all night and tell dirty jokes and laugh ourselves sick."

"I see what you're up to, Nelida," Chesi said with a conspiratorial chuckle. "This is some kind of female bonding ritual. Right?"

Nelida beamed approval. "Sexuality is your birthright as women," she said. "Raunchy, earthy, dirty sexuality to share with others of your kind—to loosen the bonds that civilization imposes. Sexuality, my children, is the lifeforce that perpetuates the species. What could be more powerful than that? Everybody strives to regulate women's sexuality . . . churches, men, dress designers. Anyone who tells you what your body must look like or what it is allowed to do.

"We must share who and what we are with each other. In truth. In laughter. This is how we honor the Belly Goddess. And we honor each other's souls."

Nelida stood up and stretched. "As a reward for your fine storytelling, I will teach you a female secret from the women of my lineage. It is called the Breath of Power."

"I'm too weak from laughter to learn anything else," Liz said, falling backward onto the ground.

"Fortunately," Nelida replied with a sly smile, "for this lesson, you can lie down."

She moved to the center of the circle.

"Lie with your heads toward the fire, now," she commanded, and exchanging looks with one another, wondering what she intended this time, they all did as she'd told them. "I will teach you a trick for increasing your Power, sexual and otherwise."

The Mexican woman stood near the fire and surveyed the

six supine women; they were stronger now than when they'd come into her care. And they had more open minds and hearts.

"To find your Power you must be one with the universe," she began. "The Earth Mother will feed you, as will the great universe of stars and moon and planets, if you learn how to receive energy from these sources.

"For now, you must wiggle your arms and legs . . . pound them and wiggle and jiggle them as hard as you can on the earth to get the kinks unknotted and the blockages moving." Nelida watched as everyone did as she asked, the silly process making them giggly again.

"Stop!" she said. "And now, raise your knees, so your feet are flat on the ground and your pelvis is loose enough so you can feel your breath through it, as if it is capable of breathing. Do not be modest, or you will stand in your own way. You must open yourselves to the energies, as you would to a man. Try to imagine a clear channel that runs from your crown to your vagina . . . a clear cylinder through which energy can flow freely.

"That's it!" she said, watching carefully as each woman in turn began to relax her legs and let her knees fall open. "This is the way. Take in the air deeply, and feel it traveling all the way to your private parts, filling your bellies like balloons, as it goes. We are not here to look fashionable and skinny, but to imitate Baubo, the Belly Goddess, who speaks through her vulva and sees with her nipples."

Titters ran around the circle as everyone tried to do what Nelida instructed. "Give me a break, Nelida," Liz gasped, finally. "I can't laugh and breathe at the same time!"

Nelida made a circuit around the circle, going to each woman in turn and instructing her, before returning to the center, satisfied with what she observed.

She let them practice all she'd said, for a time, walking from one to the next, helping, observing, advising. Finally, she told them to return to normal breathing.

"Whenever you need it, breathe again this Breath of Power, and it will strengthen you," she said. "Over time, it will be as second nature."

The women were beginning to sit up and compare notes over what they'd experienced.

"I felt like a cool, clear river of energy was running through me, then fountaining up and out over me," Liz said enthusiastically.

"What'd you see, Justine?" she asked gaily. She felt slightly giddy, as if she'd downed a fifth of champagne.

"I believe I saw what really happens between men and women in sex," Justine answered thoughtfully; she was obviously quite moved by whatever she'd experienced. "Perhaps when we make love, we share more than we realize."

"Very good," Nelida said approvingly. "You begin to understand the complex exchange program the universe has devised for us. Can you see now what extraordinary gifts men and women can share with each other? And what Power is available to each of us?"

"Perhaps, I do," Justine replied, thoughtfully, remembering Thoros making love to her with a sudden visceral ache of desire. "But if it's really so profound and awe inspiring, what does it all mean?"

"Ah, but that question is for another night," Nelida replied easily. "Tonight it is enough to meditate on what you have felt and seen. And, of course, to remember what you dream when you close your eyes. Important information may have been pried loose. We shall see."

Nelida left them to their individual conversations and prepared to sleep. She had grown fond of her charges; there was so much to teach, and so little time now left for the teaching.

Part II

TURBULENCE

Nature never breaks her own rules.

Leonardo Da Vinci

In nature there are neither rewards nor punishments;
there are consequences.

Ingersoll

Friday, April 15, New York Saturday, April 16, Mora Utu

He who hesitates is a damned fool.

Mae West

THIRTY-EIGHT

Friday, New York

Marcos Gagarian was shaving when he heard the Friday morning weather report. He stopped what he was doing, razor poised in midstroke. It was something about a hurricane . . . but where? He'd only been listening with one ear, as the Aston-Harwich deal he was working on occupied most of his brain this morning.

He wasn't concerned about not having heard from his father; not that it wasn't odd—usually the old man stayed in close touch, no matter where he was in the world. But this week was different. This was Thoros's private time in his private Eden, and up till now Marcos had taken pride in the fact that nothing had gone awry in his father's empire that only Thoros's own touch could rectify. Thoros's shoes were large to fill, even if only for ten days, and Marcos had been priding himself mentally on having done it without a single phone call from Mora Utu.

Now, he wasn't so certain.

There was an AWOS station on the island, and the plane radios could provide communication, of course. If Thoros was concerned for the party's safety, surely they'd have heard from him by now.

Unless they weren't paying attention.

No. That wouldn't be his father's way. Thoros was thorough and could sense danger a mile away. Besides, they'd probably beat the storm out of there on Sunday, which would be Monday on Marcos's side of the international dateline.

Marcos finished shaving hurriedly and made a mental note to call the aviation department at the office. Maybe they'd know if the storm posed any real threat.

Marcos stopped by Margaret's desk on the way to his own office.

"Have you heard from my dad?" he asked, dropping a stack of mail he'd picked up at reception into her In box.

Margaret shook her head and removed the half-glasses she used for typing. "Nary a word," she said, frowning. "At first it was restful, now it's odd, don't you think?"

Marcos smiled. "Probably just having too much fun to check in with us, Marge," he said more convivially than he felt. "But you never know. Why don't you get me Harry Schenck in the flight department and put it through to my office."

"You're concerned about that storm, north of Hawaii, too, eh?" she said with a knowing smirk. Margaret didn't miss much, Marcos thought as he continued into his office. Probably a little in love with Thoros, or why would she have worked twelve-hour days all these years? She didn't make *that* much money.

A moment later Margaret buzzed to say that Schenck was on the line, and Marcos picked up.

"Harry?" he said. "Thought I'd touch base with you about that storm they mentioned on the news this morning. Any chance it'll land in the neighborhood of Mora Utu?"

Harry Schenck was a huge man, mostly bald, mostly good-natured despite his toughness; he'd been Thoros's chief pilot for more years than Marcos could remember. Now, he ran Thoros's corporate air force from a desk in the flight department.

"I was gonna call you on that, kid," he responded, his deep voice serious, but not overly worried. "Don't know the status yet. Not enough data from the weather service. They're outta there Sunday noon, anyway. But I'm on it. You'll know soon as I do."

"Harry?"

"Yeah, kid?" Marcos had been "kid" to Harry since he was born; the younger Gagarian knew the name signified affection that went back a long way, not a slight to Marcos's official status.

"What do we do if it's headed their way?"

"Thoros will be on that AWOS station like white on rice. If it looks too dicey, he'll most likely beat the storm out of there. He's got a limited range of transmission on the ground from the G-IV, so there's no reason he'd check in with us to tell us his plans. Besides, remember the first rule of Schenck? Never worry in advance, there's plenty of time for that once your ass is in a sling."

Marcos wanted to respond with the expected chuckle but it stuck in his throat. He had a sudden uneasy feeling about his father's silence. So did Harry Schenck, but he decided to keep it to himself until he knew more about the path of the storm.

THIRTY-NINE

Thoros stood at the window looking toward the sea, just before dawn on Saturday morning. He'd slept little after leaving Rand's sickroom, and had thought much about the men's conversation there. He'd never needed much sleep, and less now that he was older, so he wasn't as tired as he was keyed up this morning. Anxious, restless, and ill at ease. Justine was on his mind and somewhere in his gut as well. He missed her; the thought was unnerving and unexpected, but he wished that she were near enough to talk to.

Anger had been his primary emotion since all this business with the women had escalated into madness; anger and frustration were all he'd felt at not being able to bring them into line, at looking the fool in front of his friends, at not being in control of his world. . . . But tonight, which was rapidly becoming morning, something else had surfaced from God knew where. Something vulnerable and lonely.

He liked Justine. *No.* More than that . . . he had begun to care for her, an alien feeling. She had appetites as gargantuan as his own—and she had infinite expectations. Expectations of the world, of herself, of him. She'd been a grand surprise—the scope of her had not disappointed him even when she made him furious. And she didn't fear him, didn't toady or wheedle or scheme. She would dare to live as he did. The thought was heady, sexy, seductive. *Dammit!* he thought suddenly. *I'll bet I can still make her see reason.*

A swarm of small multicolored butterflies hovered above Tiffany's head and shoulders, very early Saturday morning, making her look like a character out of Disney. She no longer puzzled over the strange phenomenon of the butterflies; she called them her little air force and enjoyed their frequent unexpected appearances. She laughed now as they circled around her, and she swung her hair from side to side to clear the flying rainbow away from her field of vision. The others nearby stopped to watch the odd happenstance.

Nelida too was watching. "My people say that migrations of butterflies are ancient spirits searching for the Power sites of once great cultures that have vanished. They honor us with their presence."

"Why do your people hold the butterfly so sacred, Nelida?" Justine asked with genuine curiosity. She was beginning to like Nelida more than she cared to admit to the others.

"It is said that the Great Spirit gave the world a butterfly tree so that we could learn the colors of life," Nelida answered, gaily. "It is said that the butterflies formed the rainbows and from these rainbows were hung the stars and the moon and the sun, and all the planets of our galaxy.

"All ancients know of the existence of a sacred tree which is our destiny; different people call it by different names, but the stories are the same. Just as we are all leaves, but we are not merely leaves, we are the tree itself, so everything alive shares lifeforce with the butterfly. Many believe that the Great Spirit made the butterfly so beautiful to teach us how to live with joy in the process of *becoming*. All life is in transition . . . worm to chrysalis to winged *criatura* . . . we are all becoming something more than we were. The butterfly performs this process with infinite grace."

"That's very poetic," Justine answered, pondering the metaphor.

The Mexican woman searched the faces around her as if deciding how much to say.

"I believe we and the butterfly are one," she replied. "And that one, is one with God." She smiled graciously upon the gathering. "Tonight, I will dance for you, La Mariposa, and perhaps, many things will be seen in a new way."

Justine didn't enter any further into the early morning banter; she still felt deeply troubled and full of undifferentiated agitation. She'd tried to stay clear of everyone since yesterday; now she fled their silly discussion of butterflies and headed out of camp in the direction of the Mora Utu compound. She'd been brooding all night about what to do next, tossing fitfully, never quite asleep or awake, the aggravation of the previous day still roiling inside her. Nelida's story . . . her fight with Liz . . . her conviction that they were going about this all the wrong way . . . *everything* made her want to make contact with Thoros.

He was on her mind now in deeply felt and unexpected ways. The memory of his touch, his laughter, his body holding her close after lovemaking was inside her somewhere, lingering where she couldn't reach or change it. And he didn't fit her preconceptions as other men had; he was larger than her imagined parameters, and admirable on so many counts. Formidable, in fact. He made her reach, as no man ever had. Because she couldn't manipulate him, she wasn't in control; that disoriented her, disturbed her. Made her feel vulnerable, young, uncertain. But it also made her joyous in ways she'd never before felt joy. Made her feel giddy and girlish. Made her feel *hope*. That it wouldn't always be for her as it had been. That just perhaps, the kind of love the poets wrote of, the kind she'd abandoned with her lost dreams, could really exist in this sordid world.

Justine wasn't certain what she would do if she actually got to Thoros, but she'd decided she would head in the direction of the compound, and maybe Fate would take a hand so she would meet him not quite by chance.

Dawn was already up and tinting the world with its red-gold light as she cleared the bridge. When she was fifty yards beyond the vine-covered span, on the men's side of the river, she saw Thoros coming toward her in the opposite direction. They stood staring at each other for a long moment before either one spoke; he appeared haggard, she thought, and very much more human than a week ago.

"You look different, Justine," he said, mirroring her thought; his voice carried an emotional residue of some kind she couldn't readily identify.

"Perhaps we've all been changed by this, Thoros," she said, hearing the wistfulness in her own voice. She resisted the urge to touch him that rippled through her suddenly, and tried to get her emotions back in check. How had he become so important to her?

"I was coming to find you, Justine," he said simply. No recriminations, she noticed. No hostility. "I've missed you."

She smiled, genuinely touched. "I was coming to find you, too."

He looked startled by that admission. "Why?" he asked.

She tilted her head to the side a little, and looked at him intently before answering. "I don't know, exactly. I thought if we talked, perhaps we could find a way to untie the Gordian knot before the outsiders get here . . . I wouldn't like us to part enemies."

He watched her, taking in details. She no longer looked perfect or pampered; her hair was tousled, she wore no makeup, her nails were clipped short and polish-free, and there were scratches on her face and arms. She was obviously braless under her T-shirt, and her shorts needed laundering. He thought she looked marvelous; suntanned, young, real—needing no further enhancement to take a man's breath away. The stirring he felt within himself was more than simple lust.

"I've missed you, Justine," he said again, reaching out for her hand. "Will you come talk with me awhile?" She nodded, reaching back. His hand felt warm and comfortably strong in hers; she let herself be pulled off the path into the deeper cover of foliage that could hide them from passersby. Pulled, too, into an embrace that said many things about longing and loneliness, emotions she hadn't known she was feeling so substantially, until this moment. She sensed the intensity of emotion in Thoros, as well, in the clasp of his hard body against hers; and she was shocked at her own response, immediate, urgent, overwhelming intended control, as if no time or any of the events of the past week had separated them. Justine lifted her head for his inevitable kiss, and let it resonate throughout her body, the energy of their connection tingling up her center, opening her senses to pleasure; moistening, swelling, anticipatory and alive.

The roughness of his imperfectly shaved skin scratched her cheek, his hands, too, were rougher now, hands used to *doing* things, creating things from nothing. Now they were leading her where she hadn't really intended to go. *Or had she?* The warm, moist air on her nipples tightened them as he eased the T-shirt up over her head, and brushed her breasts, lightly, with the backs of his roughened hands.

I wouldn't be doing this except for having had that fight back at camp, she thought, suddenly, wary and self-protective. *Be careful, Justine.* But it was too late for caution, she had cast the die when she took his hand, and they had both known they would touch in some deeper, more intimate way, or they would never have sought each other out.

"I didn't intend this . . ." she said with more honest vulnerability than he'd ever sensed in her, and he forced himself to slowness, carefulness, for her sake, removing his own clothes less hurriedly, watching her make a bed of their combined scant wardrobe beneath them on the ground.

Thoros rifled his past for what to do next, in this strangely out-of-context encounter. *No mistakes here,* he thought. *Tread carefully*. He had been a student of sexuality for a very long time, yet he felt oddly like a neophyte.

In his youth he had rutted endlessly, thoughtlessly, to feed a prodigious appetite, but that excess had eventually paled. He despised mediocrity in anything, and had realized that his plebeian encounters, while pleasurable and constant, were only the beginning of a lifelong study. After that, he had sought out whores of every inclination, *professional-caliber training,* he characterized it for himself . . . a chance to learn women of every fascinating category. Not that there weren't plenty of gifted amateurs along the way, but it delighted Thoros to recall that he had honed his skills with some of the more inventive sexual aficionados on the planet.

Despite all this, he felt nothing but uncertainty now, because this encounter mustn't go awry. He rifled the sexual index in his mind, and suddenly knew he must abandon everything studied and let nature take what it demanded and give what it could in return. He smiled a little at his own foolishness and turned his attention to this woman who had touched him deeply. *Think of her,* his instinct told him. *Think only of her.*

Thoros leaned his mouth in close to Justine's ear and whispered, "The Koran says, 'You will be called upon to account for all the permitted pleasures in life you did not enjoy while on earth.' " She smiled at the implication of the words and as he spoke he touched her throat beneath her ear tenderly, gently, tracing a slow, languid line down the front of her body toward her nipple, which hardened beneath his fingers. He pinched the pink-brown bud between his thumb and forefinger, testing it, learning it once again, then substituted his mouth for his hand, as he let his fingers travel down toward their destination.

Justine moaned a little, or sighed, he couldn't tell precisely what the soft purring sound was that escaped her, but as he ran his hand lightly over the soft inner skin of her thigh, she opened her legs to him, all challenge left behind in her wanting. And she was all willingness, open and yearning, as he cradled her in his arms and kissed her belly to the edge of the dark silken hair that veiled her secret self.

"No games," he whispered, as he reached her center.

"No games," she answered breathlessly.

He stroked her nether lips and spread them with deliberate care, pulling back the protective hood from her clit, and then he bent his warm wet mouth to the rarest nerve endings of her being, licking gently but relentlessly with his tongue, its slick underside like warm glass, making thinking impossible. He pulled the throbbing button of flesh into his mouth and sucked so softly it was a whisper of pleasure on the brink of pain.

Justine sobbed, "Please . . ." in a soft, vulnerable way, "Oh yes, please, *please* . . ." and he realized he had never heard her ask for anything, and this least of all. He licked at her swollen wanting for a long time, ignoring her wriggles that tried to break free of too much pleasure, holding her hips firmly in his large hands, judging her need and her desperation for release. Then he pressed her legs apart, stretching her far enough to ease himself inside her aching lips, sliding inward on the wet satin of her, deeper and longer and thicker and more urgent than he had been with her before. And she was crying out for more as the sky exploded and he burst with a spurting intensity that sent sharp waves of pleasure everywhere in both of them, drowning and crashing as they melted and melded and finally came to earth again in each other's arms.

Afterward, Justine lay contentedly on Thoros's shoulder for

a long wordless while, nestled long and lean against his far larger frame. Finally she spoke, dreamily, her voice husky from love and reverie. "How beautiful to lie here in this Eden with you, Thoros," she said softly, as if talking to herself. "And how far removed from all the anger and foolishness of the past week. How could we ever have allowed it to go so far?" She knew now for certain that it would be wrong to betray the other women by giving up the plane parts to Thoros, but perhaps there was a way for their minds to meet as gracefully as their bodies had.

"We need the fuel controllers, Justine," Thoros answered, without thinking through how it would sound to her. "That's the way to make it all right again." The statement jolted her back from the pleasant reverie she'd drifted into. Justine sat up and reached for her T-shirt.

"It would have been more gentlemanly, Thoros," she said, annoyed at herself for having been taken in so easily, "to wait until our pulse rates were back to normal before beginning to negotiate."

"But don't you see, Justine," he plunged ahead, "I want to end all this precisely so we *can* be together. This damned foolishness is not merely costing me money—it's keeping me away from you. Something happened last night that made it clear to me I don't want that." He turned beside her and propped himself on his elbow.

Justine frowned and searched his face, trying to sort the wheat from the chaff. Was he merely covering his faux pas, or was there something genuine and vulnerable in what he was saying? Why the hell was her usual radar so off kilter where this man was concerned? She started to pull away, but Thoros reached out to stop her. When she hesitated, he moved his hand from her thigh to her naked crotch, insinuating it between her legs in a proprietary way, as he spoke, urgently.

"There's something far more than the ordinary between us,

Justine," he said, touching her to remind her of their recent intimacy. "You know that as well as I do."

"I'd like to find out if there could be more for us, too, Thoros," she answered, annoyed at the manipulation, yet turned on by the pleasure of his touch. She tightened her thighs, making it harder for him to reach her private places. "But we really do need to sort this out first, don't we," she said huskily, surprised by the strain in her voice; surprised that she hadn't just gotten up and walked away.

"Justine, surely you know where the fuel controllers are," he whispered, moving toward her again, covering her body with his own. He edged her legs apart with his strong thigh between them, and pressed his mouth close to her ear. "We can solve this for everyone by helping each other. After what's just happened between us, Justine, can't we finally be civilized?"

"After what's just happened between us, Thoros," she said, sadly, loath to push him away but angry now. "You shouldn't be asking me to betray my friends."

"Friends!" he said contemptuously. "They're not your friends. . . . I am."

"Really?" she answered, pushing at him to disengage the tangle of their bodies. "Friends don't *use* each other—not like this. The fact that we've made love isn't likely to change my mind any more than threats did. I would have thought you'd know that."

"You're being obstinate," he said, exasperated, as much with himself for having made the wrong move, as with her.

Justine laughed shortly. "No more than you, Thoros. It was foolish of me to think we could agree on this. I shouldn't have come."

"That's where you're wrong, my dear," he said with a sly smile that reminded her of the Thoros of *before*. "You should come and come and *come*." He squeezed her mons in a proprietary way, then pulled his warm hand away abruptly. She felt simultaneously relieved and bereft.

Justine reached for her clothes, furious with herself for the way things had gone. "There's always Sunday to look forward to, Thoros," she said coldly. "I'm sure when they haven't heard from us on schedule, somebody will show up to retrieve us."

Thoros nodded, but said nothing. He, too, felt foolish and unsatisfied by the way things had worked out. It was damned frustrating that all could be lost by the slip of a tongue, or a single inept move, but that was the way life was. This one was a rare bird and he wasn't going to let her slip away just yet, but neither could he pursue her in a common fashion. He dressed without speaking further, as did she, the sudden awkwardness between them palpable and dampening.

"Are you headed in my direction?" he asked, finally.

"No. Back to camp."

"I'll walk with you as far as the bridge, then. I'm not of a mind to go back to the compound just yet."

Something in his voice touched her, again—it was wistful, not about her, but about something deeper.

"I'd like that," she said, suddenly wondering if in all wars there are moments when generals and soldiers long to walk each other home and talk of random, human things.

FORTY

It was three o'clock on Friday afternoon when Harry Schenck's massive frame filled the door of Marcos's office. *Bear,* Marcos thought, looking up as the man lumbered in. *He's like a great, bald bear.*

"Listen, kid," Harry began. Marcos motioned him to the leather sofa; no chair would hold Schenck comfortably. "We gotta talk."

Marcos moved to the sofa, too.

"I've had the weather guys tracking this mother all day. It didn't look too bad earlier, but it's gaining power as it moves, and it's heading in their direction. We could be talking class III, here. Maybe even a IV, although that's pretty remote."

Marcos's eyes sharpened. "Class-IV hurricane? Like *Andrew?*"

Harry's big head bobbed up and down. "Yeah. Only in the South Pacific they call them typhoons and they move counter-clockwise. But you know all that, I keep forgetting."

The creases in Marcos's forehead deepened with the frown this news evoked. "They're on the other side of the dateline,

Harry. It's already Saturday there—they were planning to leave Sunday. Any chance they'll get out ahead of it?"

Harry shook his head. "We've been trying to raise them on the G-IV radio via satellite relay but so far no dice. Now, that's not unusual—they got no phones on Mora Utu, remember. And there's no reason for them to be sittin' around inside the aircraft unless they're already on the move. Anyway, my bet is Thoros is on this one and packing, but I can't be sure because they got limited weather data on the island and they might not even know it's coming till it's too late to duck."

Marcos sat back for a moment, digesting what Harry had said. "Plan on spending the weekend here, Harry," he answered, finally, sounding very much like his father; this was not a request. "I have a hunch about this one—it's not going to go down the way we want. What do we need to get them out of there if there's real trouble?"

Harry Schenck leaned forward, his knees apart and feet planted, big hands clasped loosely between his knees, elbows resting on his huge thighs. It was the way he sat to puzzle things out; Marcos had seen this posture before.

"Depends how big this gets and how fast." When things got tough, Harry began speaking shorthand. *"No grace and no bullshit,"* Thoros had said once. "If we're talking rescue, we'll need mercs."

"Mercenaries?" Marcos answered, surprised. "Why not our own men?"

"Too risky. Our guys ain't got the training for this kind of op. Need the guts-and-glory boys. And their equipment."

"So where do we get these guys? Call the Pentagon?"

Harry looked thoughtful. "Could be. We got connections. But they got red tape up the yin-yang."

Marcos had that look again. "What about the mob? Tony's on the island, too."

"It's a cash-on-the-barrel deal whichever way you go, kid. We're talking big bucks."

"We're talking my father, Harry."

The large head nodded a few times, and Marcos could see in the older man's eyes that he had no need to be reminded. He wondered what memories Harry Schenck and Thoros shared. Schenck was ten years older than Thoros, but he was the one man in the operation who could sass the Chairman and get away with it.

Margaret appeared in the doorway, an overnight case in her hand. Marcos did a double take; he had never seen her in anything but prim suits and blouses. Now she wore black stretch leggings with boots and a lightweight cashmere sweater, another with its arms tied loosely around her neck. Her glasses were pushed up on her head, not perched on her nose as usual. She glanced at Harry. "Good to see you, Hank," she said in the voice of an old friend. "Just wanted you to know I'm back for the long haul. We haven't done one of these lately, have we? I'll assume we're in code blue unless I hear otherwise."

He smiled back warmly at the woman.

"Don't worry, Mags," he said. "We'll get him out." She gave him a thumbs-up and left.

" 'Hank?' " Marcos mimicked with a smart-ass smirk. " 'Mags'? What the hell was that all about? 'Code blue.' You two sound like an old movie."

"Let me tell you, kid, they don't make 'em like Margaret here, anymore," Harry answered, shortly. "She'd fly into that typhoon herself to get Thoros out. Did you know she's a damned good pilot?"

Marcos shook his head, annoyed with himself that he'd missed things he should have known.

"Is there something between you two?" he asked.

"Yeah. She's my friend. Yours, too."

Marcos nodded, wondering if he should probe more; deciding there were other, more pressing things to do. But there were a hell of a lot of question marks in their surprising camaraderie that he made a mental note to pursue at another time.

"Tell me all you know about the storm, Harry—or is it Hank?"

Harry looked up, his expression serious. "Nobody calls me Hank but Maggie."

Marcos took that in, nodded acceptance, and turned his attention to the weather map on the table between them.

FORTY-ONE

H. Douglas Rand got up shakily and tried his legs. His feet on the floor felt unfamiliar, as if made of an unrecognizable substance. He sat for a minute to regain his equilibrium, then feeling he could make it, got out of the bed and headed for the bathroom. He wondered how long he'd been sick and was surprised to find he could navigate pretty well, if slowly.

He looked into the large mirrored wall over the sink and was shocked by his appearance. Gaunt and with graying stubble on his chin, he looked an older, scruffier version of himself. But he was steadier on his feet now, as if recovery from a long debilitating illness was already under way; brushing his teeth would give him a new lease on life. He wished momentarily for a newspaper to check the date, feeling like Rip Van Winkle who might be surprised by the time lapse since this had begun.

Rand stripped off his wrinkled, sweat-stained pajamas and turned on the hot and cold taps in the shower. Just the sound of the water was inviting, until he remembered there was no hot water. And the cold water was contaminated.

"Damn!" he said aloud, suddenly angry at himself for having been bested by Chesi's sabotage. He turned off the shower.

Maybe there was still a way to turn things around and redeem himself in everyone's eyes, he thought suddenly. He couldn't afford to lose Thoros as a client, and maybe it had been part of his delirium, but somewhere in the night he'd had an idea about jerry-rigging at least some of the electrical. All he really needed was some small success to redeem himself with Thoros.

Tony was in the kitchen when Rand made his way there.

"Hey! Rand," Tony called out when he saw him. "You're out of bed." He stood up and walked toward his patient, eyeing him with the wary observation of a doctor. "You okay on your feet, buddy?"

Rand nodded and headed toward a chair; Tony noted the uneasy movements and the extreme pallor of the man.

"What in hell happened to me?" Rand asked as he sat. He seemed gratified to have gotten as far as the chair.

"Malaria, I'd guess. Or something a lot like it. Real high fever, shakes, delirium, dysentery . . . the works. Better get it checked out as soon as you get Stateside. These jungle fevers have a nasty habit of reoccurring."

"I feel like I died."

Tony laughed. "Yeah. Well, you had us all going for a while last night, but all things considered, you look pretty good to me at the moment. Emilio found some kind of bark he boiled up that did the trick. Probably the quinine family. Want something to eat?"

Rand nodded absently. "I could eat something for strength, I think. Then I'd like to take a crack at putting the electrical system back on line."

Tony laughed again, good-naturedly. "Whoa, boy! Slow down there. You gotta take it real easy today. Tomorrow maybe you can do some work, not today."

Rand shook his head; the color was coming back to his

face, Tony noted. This bout of whatever fever it was, was definitely passing.

"I had an idea while I was lying in bed about how I might be able to rewire at least one of those panels, but I need to see the damage again to be certain."

"So do it tomorrow. We lived this long without electricity, another day ain't gonna make a difference. Eat something, get your sea legs back under you, rest a lot. Then tomorrow you can rule the world. Meantime, I'll fix you some grub."

Rand waited until Tony had left for his own quarters, then he headed toward the nearest work trailer to look for tools and schematics.

The fire started about an hour after he began his work on the wiring. Smoke began to seep from behind the panels, a trickle at first, but within minutes, a black torrent. Rand looked around frantically for the fire extinguisher but the place it should have been was empty. He didn't know what had gone wrong; it didn't matter. A sizzle of flames was now creeping along the edge of the panel and the smoke was blackening. He'd have to get help.

Rand left the small building at a run, shouting, "Fire! Bring fire extinguishers!" But it was a long way back to the house in his condition. His heart was pounding so loudly he thought his chest might explode, and he had to slow to a walk to keep from falling.

Men were running toward him, shouting, too. Smoke and flames were rising now, visible from the Great House. Thank God the jungle was moist; unlike forest, it was hard to set a jungle on fire, he thought just before he passed out.

"Water!" Thoros shouted to the men behind him. "A bucket brigade to the cisterns. Grab anything that can hold water!"

"It's an electrical fire, Thoros," Tony shouted back. "Water'll make it worse. Where are the fire extinguishers?"

"Those damned women have them. The holders are empty."

Thoros shouted to the other men to get the bucket brigade going. Emilio appeared in a golf cart; he motioned for the men to get in, and turned the pokey vehicle back toward the house.

"There are empty cans and buckets near the cisterns, señor," he said urgently. "We will load them on the cart. And there is sand in bags at the work trailers. This also may be useful."

The men did as Emilio instructed them.

The small outbuilding that had housed the systems of Mora Utu was a gutted, smoldering ruin. Steam rose from the wreckage and added to the insufferable jungle heat, but the fire itself was out.

Six exhausted men and one sick one surveyed the remains of what, an hour before, had been a building.

"This is the final straw," Thoros said evenly. "Those women could have killed someone by stealing the fire extinguishers."

"I've had it, Thoros," Jase said, breathing heavily. "I say we get those fuel controllers, *now,* whatever it takes."

"I'm with you," Tony agreed. "We tried to reason with them. Now we need action."

"It isn't the women's fault this happened," Alex put in sensibly. "Rand started the fire tinkering with the panels. You can't blame the women for that."

"I was trying to *fix* those panels," Rand shot back. "If the women hadn't fucked things up so badly, none of this would have happened."

"That's a lot of crap, Rand," Jack said hotly. "What the fuck did you think you were doing out here? You're not an electrician. You're not even much of anything architectural from what I've seen—Chesi's been ahead of you every step of the way."

"You're way out of line, Jack," Jase said angrily. "Rand was trying to help."

"Rand's an incompetent asshole, and we all know it," Jack shot back. "And who the hell are you to tell me I'm out of line?"

Tony stepped forward, his jaw like granite. "We're all assholes if we don't go after those broads and get the fuel controllers. What are you men going to do? Wait till one of us gets killed before you listen? I say we go after them *now.*"

"Hear, hear!" Jase shouted. "Get the fuel controllers and sort it all out back in the U.S."

Thoros stepped forward. "These women are out of control. They've gone beyond inconveniencing us this time. They've endangered us. We can't let that happen again."

"*Rand* endangered us, not the women," Jack argued hotly.

"You've been on their side since the beginning," Thoros shot back. "This is *my* island and it's my G-IV and I want them out of my life before they destroy any more of it, and by God I'm going to make that happen."

"Give me a couple of hours, Thoros, that's all I ask," Jack insisted. "Let me talk to Tiffany and see if I can make her see common sense, here."

Thoros took a deep breath. "You have two hours," he snapped, as he turned abruptly and headed off. Jack, fuming and frustrated, stood for a moment, then made up his mind and left, too.

Fuck the war, Jack thought angrily—*fuck Thoros's vendetta, and Tony's stupidity, and the whole frigging lot of them.* He was going to see Tiffany. Maybe he could talk her into giving up the plane parts, maybe not, but at least she'd know that he wasn't part of this escalating lunacy.

A surge of energy flooded Jack with the decision made. He headed back to his guest quarters and raced up the stairs to the second floor two at a time, despite the stifling heat. He was going to see Tiffany. Maybe hold her in his arms, kiss her mouth, hear her voice. He felt the tingle of anticipation run through him, and marveled at himself that he hadn't come to this sensible conclusion sooner.

Tony was an asshole, and maybe more than that. Some weird psychotic need drove the man, where the women were concerned. He might be a helluva nice guy otherwise, but not about this. Even Thoros, who was as stable as they came, was trapped somewhere in his ego and his intense, irrational connection to this blighted piece of real estate. In fact, everybody seemed to have developed some weird agenda—so much so that Emilio was beginning to look like the most rational one of the whole damned bunch, and nobody would give *him* the time of day. It was just like in Nam. Extraordinary circumstances changed people, made them the best or worst they could be. Everything was upside down and screwed up . . . but he was going to see Tiffany and somehow that would help. He didn't know how or why, but he knew at least then *something* would make sense.

Jack kicked off the sneakers he'd been living in, and laced up his hiking boots. He grabbed bug spray from the bureau and slapped it on all over; then, wrinkling his nose at the citronella smell, took a bottle of Equipage aftershave from the bathroom counter and slapped that on, too.

Sunglasses. Penknife with compass, a souvenir of the war he'd kept with his wallet ever since. He took mental inventory as he stuffed things into pockets; any jungle could hold surprises, he learned that long ago. He left the compound swiftly and headed for the line of distant trees that marked the edge of the dense tropical growth.

The icy water in the pool beneath the waterfall felt wonderful on sunburned, mosquito-bitten skin. Tiffany, Chesi, Liz, and Christie splashed or swam, grateful for the small respite from work and the heat. There didn't seem to be a minute when Nelida couldn't think of some damned thing for them to do, and as much as they liked Tiffany's aerobic self-defense workouts and their weapons training with Justine and Marika, both were exhausting in this murderous unrelenting climate. As was everything else that comprised their life here.

Justine lay topless on the riverbank. The first time she'd appeared with only a bikini bottom, she'd provoked annoyed or envious responses in everyone. "Why the hell is she showing off her wares out here?" Christie had said, disgruntled at the sight of the near-perfect breasts. "Do you think she swings both ways?"

"Probably," Chesi answered pragmatically. "With boobs like that, why keep them to yourself?"

Now, the general consensus was that in Justine's European perception, being topless was quite an ordinary act, and no big deal.

Chesi was doing laps, of sorts, and Tiffany and Liz were sitting on stones near the falls, trying to talk above the sound of rushing water. Christie was watching warily for snakes or other waterborne killers, as she waded near shore, certain that lurking in those depths, were slithering creatures waiting to strike her down. The icy water felt soothing to her still painful leg; the swelling had gone down with Nelida's treatment, but the leg still hurt like hell if she moved without thinking, and the muscle had nowhere near its normal strength.

Jack watched the tableau of women from the heavy cover of trees, not knowing exactly what to do. He had proceeded warily from the bridge, expecting another sentry attack, but none had greeted him, and now he knew why. He felt like a peeping Tom; the women looked happy as water sprites in the pool, and he pushed down a sense of regret at the lost opportunity for what this week could have provided them all.

He waited impatiently, trying to dope out a way to get Tiffany's attention without alerting the others; he felt certain she would see reason if he couched it the right way, then maybe they could get the other women on their side. He saw that it would be impossible to separate Tiffany out from the gathering until the women tired of their sport and began to straggle out of the water.

Jack settled in to wait for an opportunity.

FORTY-TWO

Thoros paced back and forth beside the pool at the Great House, the other men stood or sat around the terrace. Everyone's mood was grim.

"Look, Thoros," Tony said, glancing at his watch. "You told Jack two hours and it's almost up. I don't want to tell you your business but I say we go get those fuel controllers *now.* The women can't possibly defend themselves if we just *take* the damned things and end this once and for all."

Thoros knew Tony was right; the engine parts were the answer to everything—get them, and the nightmare was over. But he hated to resort to force.

"Where's Jack? Any sign of him?" he asked with agitation.

"Jack's not back. But if he has talked them into giving up the fuel controllers, we'll find that out when we get to their camp."

"Tony's right, Thoros," Jase said. "We should end this now. I'm sick to death of it."

"I'm with Jase," Rand chimed in. "Let's get the job done. Are you in, Alex?"

Alex, frowning, stood up; hands in pockets, he faced his host. "I'll come with you, Thoros, but certainly not as an advocate of force. If you insist on going, somebody with a level head should be there. Assuming, by the way, we can get past their bowman."

"We'll get past," Tony said. "Don't worry about it."

Thoros looked Tony squarely in the eye; he felt so ambivalent about the man, it was hard to make decisions that involved him. "You come along only on one condition, Tony. That you keep your temper under strict control at all times. I don't want any of them seriously hurt—just neutralized. Understand?"

"Yeah. I understand. I'll keep it under control."

"Good man. Let's get moving then."

Tiffany swam to shore and stood poised on the riverbank, feeling refreshed and rested. She shook her dark head like a small dog, sending water splatters in all directions, then picked up a towel to dry the rest. She looked so pretty, standing there, Jack thought with a pang, watching from his hiding place. So young and robust and free. He waited several minutes until she finally glanced in his direction, then inching closer, he called out her name, very softly. Tiffany's eyes came up, puzzled by what she thought she'd heard, but she didn't see anyone, so she turned to go. He called again, more urgently this time, and waved to her; somehow she spotted him half hidden amid the dense jungle camouflage. Jack put his finger to his lips and gestured for secrecy, motioning toward the others.

Tiffany's brow furrowed again; she was startled by his presence, uncertain what to do. How had he found her? Was he alone? He beckoned silently for her to come to him; she hesitated a moment more, looking indecisive, then wrapped the towel around her hips pareu style, and turned back toward the other women. "I'm heading in . . ." she called out to no one in particular, trying to sound nonchalant. "I'll see you all back at camp."

"I'll come with you," Justine offered, sitting up suddenly, her breasts bobbing at the effort. "I don't really need any more sun."

"No!" Tiffany said hastily. "I mean, I need a little solitude, if you don't mind, Justine. I'd like to do some meditating on the way back."

Justine shrugged. The rebuff, if it was one, was not offensive to her. She really had no urgent desire to return to camp now anyway, so she waved casually to say "no matter," and lay back down on the blanket to relax a little longer.

Relieved, but anxious, Tiffany made her way through the tangled undergrowth toward Jack, hoping he was alone. He took her hand when she came up close enough, and led her farther from the group before he found a place that seemed relatively safe from prying eyes. He stopped, finally, then turned toward her, arms open, and Tiffany entered his embrace, breathing him in, feeling the good, hard strength of him, gratefully. The two clung to each other for a very long moment, then his mouth sought hers and they were lost in the taste of each other, the longing welling up in an urgency that made everything else unimportant. When he released her, he whispered, "Is there a more private place, Tiff?" She nodded, and taking him by the hand, led him to a small clearing farther down the river from the waterfall.

It was a secluded, peaceful spot where the rushing water only hummed and gurgled as it traversed the river rocks, but didn't overwhelm the listener with its insistent crash, as it did closer to the falls. Tiffany had searched it out when she'd needed to find solitude and a place to do her katas and chi kung, far from eyes and questions. She loved teaching the others self-defense, but sometimes, she just needed to practice martial arts in solitude—to center herself, and gather in replenishment from the universe to refill her depleted energy system. Sometimes, she needed a space in which to get away from the other women and simply think things through.

Jack looked the area over with a skillful eye; it was a good choice, private and as safe as jungle ever gets.

"I need to talk to you, Tiff," he said urgently.

"I need a lot of things . . ." she responded. He searched her eyes quickly, but she lowered them, and said no more.

"Things have happened back there," he said, wondering how to say what he must. "Nerves are raw and we've taken a few hits . . . What I'm trying to say, Tiff, is that we have to end this thing or somebody's liable to get really hurt. Some of the guys have pretty big tempers and this thing seems to be escalating out of control."

She watched and listened, her brow furrowed in concentration, listening for whatever was beneath the words. "I can't give you the fuel controllers without the group agreeing, Jack, if that's what you came for," she said steadily. "I wish I could help you fix this, really I do, but we've had casualties, too. Christie fell into one of those pits you guys dug."

"Shit!" he said, meaning it. "I knew somebody'd get hurt with those damned traps."

"Isn't that what you dug them for?"

"*I* didn't dig them, Tiff. And the ones who did were playing macho games, they just didn't think it through." He seemed very agitated, as if he found it hard to stand still.

"I'll be *damned* if I know how this thing could have gotten so nuts, so fast. It's like this fucking place is cursed—we should never have come."

Her eyes came up sharply to meet his. "Don't say that! If we'd never come here, I'd never have met you. And no matter what happens, I'll always be glad I knew you . . . even if it's only for a little while." It was so honest a statement, no subterfuge, no manipulation, just the truth.

Jack reached out to touch her cheek, but once he touched her, it wasn't nearly enough. He pulled her into his arms again, and held her tight against him. Then he kissed her, tenderly at first, then more urgently, as she responded in kind.

"I've missed you so . . ."

"Missed you . . ."

"Want you so damned much . . ." He kissed her lips and face and throat, wanting to touch every part of her. Wanting to say so much, and do so much, and be so much of what she wanted him to be. And words were of no use anymore.

Jack and Tiffany sank down to the warm ground, their bodies still locked together, and he was slipping her wet swimsuit straps down over her bare shoulders, his hands seeking her breasts, but more than that, seeking *her.* Tiffany. The truth of her and the openness, the kind and generous spirit that called to him. His lips slid down from mouth to throat to breast naturally, inevitably, and Tiffany was pulling at his clothes, unbuttoning, pushing, pulling them away from his willing, hard body that she'd longed for and dreamed about and hoped to touch again. And then he was inside her, in the tight wet well of her, moving in her, burrowing, thrusting, hard in the depths of her, and she was arching to meet him with her own need paramount, tightening, drawing in, absorbing him into her. And there was nothing else on earth and no one, and never could be again, as the tremors started and circled outward and inward, and outward again. As her heart pounded and her nipples tightened, the rhythmic thrusting and retreating faster and harder and deeper until she nova'd, the impossible perfect fulfillment flooding, zinging, reverberating through her, and they both lay spent and happy in each other's arms.

"You are impossibly wonderful, Tiff," he whispered into her ear, reveling in the feel of her body tucked in beside him, and the sense of completion she always seemed to provide him.

"We can be safe for a while, Jack . . ." she answered, her

voice heavy with love, and he wondered if she meant now, here in this place, or later in the real world.

They stretched out side by side, needing to touch again, each needing simply to know the other one was within reach.

"I've been trying to figure out how to make this whole mess better, Tiff," he began. "It's all gotten so outrageous, it's really hard to put the pieces back in order, but I know the bottom line is we need to fix the plane and get off this island before anything worse happens."

She propped herself on her elbow and nodded affirmatively. "I know we do, Jack," she agreed quietly. "All we women want is to be treated as equals, and to know we'll be safe once we hand over these engine parts. They're our only leverage—we really don't have anything else to protect ourselves with."

Genuinely startled by her fear, he raised himself on an elbow to look at her closer. "Protect yourselves?" he echoed. "You mean you think we'd harm you in some way after you've given the parts back?" That thought had never occurred to him. *Damn.* You could never know what went on in *anybody's* mind, least of all a woman's.

Tiffany pulled herself to a sitting position, so she could talk better. She reached for the shirt he'd discarded and slipped it on over her bare shoulders. "Look, Jack," she said earnestly. "You're one kind of man. I know *you* wouldn't hurt us. But, these other guys . . . I don't know *who* they are, and from what I saw at that last get-together, Tony's got a real hate-on for us, and Thoros isn't far behind him. We want out of here, too—we just want out of here alive."

"That much I can guarantee, sweetheart," he said with conviction. "If fear is all that's screwing up the works, I can make sure everybody calms down enough so we all get out of here safely, and fast."

Tiffany looked unconvinced. He'd never called her *sweetheart* before, but maybe that was just a figure of speech he used with lots of girls. "I could tell everybody what you've said, Jack," she answered uncertainly. "Maybe we could work out a deal . . . you know, a way for everybody to save face."

He smiled at her earnestness. Maybe the rape and the subsequent happenings had genuinely scared the women—it made a helluva lot more sense that they'd done what they had out of terror, than out of bitchiness. What a stupid-ass mess this had turned into. Jack reached out to touch her skin with his hand, it was warm and smooth and inviting.

"I'd like to make love to you, Tiff," he said, tentatively touching the bare skin of her abdomen, marveling at its perfection, as he felt a quiver of response. He moved his hand a little lower and said softly, "Slow this time, so we have time to find things out."

Without saying anything more, Tiffany wiggled back out of the shirt she'd just put on, and let him ease her down onto the moss that covered everything like a warm green carpet. As she raised a knee to shift her balance, Jack glimpsed the dark and light that awaited him, still wet from before, still swollen with pleasure and anticipation, the place he longed to be, his erection straining to propel him there, determining the destination and the pace. But, remembering his promise, he resisted his own urgency, and forced his eyes back to Tiffany's. He saw the love in them and the desire. How could he hurry her, or be selfish with her? She trusted him to know, to do, to care, and he could be no less than what she thought him.

Jack moved his exploring fingers into the slippery wetness of Tiffany, and played there lovingly until he knew from her responsive movements that only his lips and tongue would do now, and then his penis, finally, to bring the world in close and safe around them. He was sure now that he loved her, a fact that filled him with wonder and concern and several other emotions far less easy to name. He didn't hurry this time, and he loved her with his eyes as well as his other parts. She let him lead, never struggling for control; let him play and give and love without restraint. Afterward, she lay with her head on his shoulder and one leg overlapping both of his.

Jack watched Tiffany's sleeping face and tried to sort through the why of it. She was so very special, so full of life and fun and sweetness, even her lust seemed sweeter to him than others'. So different from the endless stream of self-interested gold diggers who had made him feel jaded and bored. What would she be to him when they left this star-crossed, but still enchanted place? In Chicago or New York the fact that she was black would be an issue, maybe not insurmountable, but an issue just the same. Certainly one the press would exploit, to say nothing of his friends. And there was the age difference to think through. Not that anyone would balk at that, middle-aged men and very young women were an ordinary fact of life. But in the world of reality, his own world, what would that mean? How long could he keep up with her, sexually or otherwise? How much of a strain would the fact of his being twice her age bring to bear on both of them as time went on?

Her even breathing was tranquil, a soft rising and falling, gentle and undisturbed by circumstance. He leaned in close and kissed her hair, soft as a baby's, damp from lovemaking. As he did so a butterfly landed on Tiffany's outstretched sleeping hand, its delicate yellow and black wings fluttering gracefully in the sun. How odd that it seemed content to stay there, like a tiny protector or a magical living ring for her finger.

Like a marriage ring, he thought—an omen of some kind. He lay back beside her, feeling the sweet comfort of her body, and the warmth of the earth beneath them. Even if they could be happy like this for just a little while, perhaps it would be worth everything. Forever never happened anyway, so why worry about what no one could control? Jack drifted off to sleep feeling contented and replete. Decisions lay back in New York, but not here. Here, there was only Tiffany and the chance to love and be loved back.

Marika, Liz, and Chesi had just come out of the water to dry themselves; Christie and Justine were dressed and sitting on the riverbank about ten feet away when the phalanx of men came tramping out of the heavy foliage. Justine saw them first and screamed a warning, as all the startled women attempted to run for cover.

The men intercepted them or tried to; each one attempting to catch hold of the woman closest to him. The terrified women fought like Furies, kicking and punching in a wild attempt to escape. Thoros was shouting, "Wait! We just want to talk!" but over the screams, he went unheard.

Jase grabbed Liz, who responded with an unexpected right uppercut that, catching him unguarded, knocked him over backward. Rand lunged at Chesi with all the pent-up rage that the trouble she'd caused him had engendered, but Chesi used the power of her legs to drive his none-too-steady body backward into a tree; Thoros grabbed Justine and attempted to keep her at arm's length to avoid injury. He was bellowing, "Stop! You *must* stop! We just want to talk!" as she kicked him full in the stomach. Cursing, he let go of her arms and she flew at him, clawing at his face and the arms he'd raised to protect himself.

Tiffany and Jack, roused from their reverie by screams, crashed through the undergrowth and, horrified, took in the incredible tableau just as Tony grabbed Marika and tumbled with her to the ground. Jase bellowed in pain, as Christie managed to stab him in the shoulder with the small knife she'd had in her pocket.

"No way!" Tiffany shouted, as she sailed into the fray. The two newcomers thrashed their way into the center of the struggle shouting, "Stop! You've got to stop!" Miraculously, Alex and

Thoros were shouting the same thing, and struggling to disengage those still grappling on the ground.

The winded, injured, and spent men and women dragged themselves to their feet and stood panting in a ragtag circle.

"Holy shit!" Tiffany said, staring wide-eyed at her student self-defenders. "Way to go, girls!"

Thoros stood panting, surveying the scene around him, his fury near the explosion point.

"It has never been my intention to hurt you, but we seem doomed," he said, a fierceness in his voice that didn't invite comment. "We will meet at eight tomorrow morning, and we will end this lunacy before someone dies."

The women watched the men storm off, wondering if that had been a premonition or a threat. They, too, retreated to their camp.

Tension in the women's camp was epic, but surprisingly orderly; they'd protected themselves, and now they needed a strategy. Liz and Christie called the meeting to order, but Justine spoke first.

"What happened today really shocked me," she began. "It's easy to see how lynch mobs happen, even wars. So I want to apologize to all of you. I've thought you exaggerated our danger and made stupid decisions based on your own ridiculous fears. Now I know you were closer to the truth than I. Even among rational people, insane acts can happen." She paused for breath and clarity.

"So, I propose that when they come tomorrow morning, we do *not* give them the fuel controllers, because that would put us entirely in their power—a power which I no longer think it prudent to trust. We must trust only each other until we are safely off this island.

"Tomorrow is Sunday. If we do not return to Oahu, there will be inquiries. I believe within forty-eight hours, others will come to Mora Utu to investigate our silence. We have only to protect ourselves for another two days, which I think we showed we can do successfully." She hesitated, as if there were more to say but she wasn't certain how to say it. Then she sat down.

Christie stood up. "I agree with Justine," she said simply. "For *once*. We're too close to the finish line to shift the leverage now. Unless anybody wants to argue the other side, let's take a vote."

There were no dissenters.

Liz cleared her throat and stood up. "This may be overkill on my part," she said, with a glance at Nelida, "but I have a really bad feeling about tonight. I know they said tomorrow morning for the parlay, but it wouldn't be the first time an enemy attacked while their opponents slept. I'd like to propose that we send a spy to their camp, just as added insurance."

There was murmured assent all around. They drew straws for the task and Marika landed spy duty. Nelida watched the beautiful young woman move off in the direction of the compound; the look on her face held nothing but compassion.

Night fell quietly and the mood around the supper circle was somber.

"Tonight there will be no story," Nelida said, as she began to fill the plates from the large pot in which she'd made stew with the last of their meat. She held up her hands to stay the immediate flood of requests to reconsider. "I have promised you the Butterfly. Tonight La Mariposa will show you the Soul of the World."

When all had been cleared away and everyone sat watchful and anxious around the fire, Nelida disappeared for a time and then reemerged from the jungle in a costume she obviously had constructed for this moment.

She wore a blouse that exposed both shoulders; it was apparent she wore no bra beneath it. Her hair was thick and loose, fanned out in a silver and black cascade nearly to her waist. She carried two large, multicolored feather fans, and her body clinked with silver and turquoise beads. Two hide-covered drums were also in her arms; she gave one to Liz and one to Chesi, instructing them each in the rhythm of the drumbeat they were to pound out in counterpoint to each other. Her demeanor was solemn and electric at the same time, as if a current ran through her veins, awaiting only the flicking of a switch to set it free.

"I always wanted to play the drums," Chesi said with a delighted smile, picking up the sticks, "but my brother got to do it."

Liz smiled, too, as she picked up the large leather-headed sticks and tested them on the big flat drum nestled between her legs; this might be a good diversion. They were all so edgy tonight that the odds were no one would sleep anyway, so a little entertainment was probably just the right medicine.

Nelida suddenly hopped and flitted to the center of their circle; she was no longer quite human, but had taken on the aura of the *criatura* she would dance. She wafted her large feather fans in every direction, as if testing the air for something unseen and then swooping it into her energy field; the fans were wings and the wings were magical. Her shell and silver bracelets rattled, and little bells worn somewhere hidden, tinkled musically with every movement. Without warning, she leaped high into the air, then landed with a resounding thud onto the earth. She moved with mighty pounding footsteps, making the ground reverberate with her force; this was not like any butterfly the watchers had ever imagined; this was La Mariposa, the Mother of Butterflies, the great fertilizer of all life on the planet.

Nelida was lost now in the dance, for she had opened herself to the Spirit of Mariposa. She felt the earth rise up inside her, seeping first into her soles, then pushing its way upward through that doorway into her legs, her hips, her spine. Brightness expanding. Vibrancy and power rising into every artery; whole body vibrating. Fire raging to the heart center, spiraling outward to the circle of women watchers.

Nelida's body whirled and turned and fanned and twisted in an ever increasing rhythm that was mesmeric to the watchers. Suddenly, Tiffany was on her feet and moving, too. Primitive, magnificent, dancing like her ancestors; the jungle her métier, the firelight flickering on her dark skin, making her look like freshly polished teak as she pounded and spun and leaped to some primal rhythm that she, too, heard calling in her soul. And then Justine was on her feet, too, beating out a wildly escalating pattern of intricate movement she'd never before imagined. Almost reluctantly, Christie entered the vibrant circle; like the children called against their will by the Pied Piper, it was impossible to remain passive, to resist. A fluid medium of some kind engulfed them, and they all felt sucked into the energy of the dance. It filled the space beyond the body, lifting it, palpitating, swirling it far out into the unknown, where time had no meaning and forever could be felt in a moment of epiphany.

Tiffany circled to where Chesi beat her drum, and dropping to her knees beside her friend, rasped, "Go! Dance, girl!" as she swooped the drumsticks from Chesi's hand and freed her to join the monumental movement. There was no time to think or be afraid, no reticence could be in this primal place of women. They were a tribe now, a sisterhood. Chesi felt sad for Liz, who was left behind, but then as she whirled past her, she saw that Justine had taken Liz's place and Liz was dancing, dancing, now, twirling, swooping close to the flame, a moth or a butterfly caught in the eternal rhythm that beats in the blood and calls to all who have the ears to hear.

How long the dancing lasted, they never knew; it felt like hours, minutes, days. Entranced in some manner, time had no meaning, for they were one with the heartbeat of the world that pounded in them as surely as their own heartbeats. Finally, one by one, they felt themselves return to the bodies they had inhabited before, the ones with limitations they had momentarily left behind. One at a time, they dropped exhausted from the dance and lay on the ground, emptied, yet replenished in ways they had never dreamed.

Each felt Nelida's feathered fan pass over her body, sweeping energy before it, balancing, grounding them back into themselves.

"You are a tribe now," she said softly, as she moved among them. "Whatever comes, there will remain in you the knowledge that once you had been sisters on the Great Journey. La Mariposa's blessing goes with you, now . . . yours forever."

One by one, they drifted off to dreams more vivid and strange than any they had ever experienced before.

Gently, Nelida covered each woman with her blanket, before she left the clearing, and her sleeping pupils far behind.

She had a rendezvous with her husband tonight, that she must not fail.

FORTY-THREE

Emilio reached the appointed meeting place; Nelida had her back to him, staring into the fire she had built when she'd arrived.

"Welcome, my husband," she said, without turning, although he had made no sound to betray his presence. She turned unhurriedly, and acknowledged him with her eyes, as he drew nearer. This time there was no hint of sexuality in their connection, rather an attitude of colleagues coming together for a conference.

"Death is very near," she said quietly, turning and speaking first.

"Sí," he replied gravely. "He is never far, my little falcon."

"Did you speak with the dolphins about what is to come?" she asked with concern.

"They were unwilling to give me what I asked."

"Ask again!" she snapped, her voice relentless. "They always know first of the severity."

He shrugged as if to say, *It does not matter.*

"Have you prepared the women?" he asked.

Nelida shrugged. "Those who could hear have heard. There are warriors among them. But they do not know how cold and abstract and impersonal Nature is—this will be a shock to them. And you? How do the men fare?"

Emilio smiled, the weary smile of a teacher who has seen too much for illusion. "The men were warriors, once. Some will be again. Their arrogance will be more useful to them than your women's naïveté."

"Perhaps. Perhaps not. Arrogance can make you underestimate your opponent—as you, dear husband, now underestimate me, in attempting to lull me into providing too much information about my little army. *No hagas el ridiculo!* Do not be an idiot, Emilio. I must reprimand you for your foolishness."

Emilio laughed heartily. "It is always a pleasure to deal with an equal, is it not, my hawk?"

"I will be your *vulture,* if you forget yourself with me again, my husband!" Nelida answered more snappishly than usual, and Emilio looked carefully at her energy field, which was full to the bursting point.

"Enough, *enough!*" he said with a genuine smile this time. "I am sick to death of teaching them *de verdad.* Sick of their hard heads and their gringo ignorance. I must be growing old to tire of the game so easily."

Nelida's expression softened. "We too could die here, Emilio. What Nature intends, we are not immune to, eh? The smell of death increases on this island. We, too, are stalked."

"This is true, wife. But we, at least, will engage Death in a fine struggle, should he have us on his collection list. And if annihilation is to come, or it is not, let us love tenderly this night, for we will have no time beyond now. And if this is the final time, let it be magnificent, and worthy of our talents."

Nelida smiled, aroused by his words. "You would fornicate

with Death at your shoulder, Emilio, or perhaps even in the grave. This is a quality in you I have always admired."

She reached out and touched his face caressingly with her hand. As she did, she knew psychically that he had already spoken with the dolphins and had chosen not to divulge their entire message. No matter. Tomorrow all would be however Nature intended it. Tonight another of its aspects could be served that was, although far more delicate, no less powerful.

Emilio stood at the edge of the sea and called the dolphins. He had left Nelida sleeping; there was no reason to spoil their rendezvous with the kind of news the dolphins had to tell. That was why he had not pressed them for details earlier; there would be no good news from that quarter.

Death was everywhere tonight. In the trees, in the wind, in the sea; he pushed back the fear that natural human responses demanded in the face of such danger and sent his message to the creatures of the deep.

According to the lore of his lineage, the dolphins had been placed on this planet eons ago by the space people who monitored our progress as a species. To what end, he was not certain, but he accepted that they were the messengers and the communicators of the deep. And, for whatever reason, they were fond of humans, and willing to give them information.

A silver missile broke the dark surface of the water in his line of sight, then another and another. Emilio cleared his consciousness of the debris of lovemaking and reverie, to make his contact. Dolphins were polite by nature and orderly. It was important to inquire first about their well-being, and to thank them for their assistance. He did all this as protocol demanded. Then he asked his question. The storm. Would it be a typhoon? If so, of what magnitude? When would it be upon them? Was there likelihood of survival?

Patiently, he awaited their reception of his message, their polite rejoinder to his pleasantries. And their answer.

Emilio stood for a moment digesting the complex information he had been given. It was always important for telepaths to sift the input for perceptual anomalies or translation errors.

Then he sighed, and stood a moment longer in making his decision. Such information would have to be given in its entirety to Nelida. But he hated to wake her up with such dire news. Even though she already perceived the danger, this news would force her to action, as it would him.

Turning toward where he had just left her sleeping, he was startled to find her standing just behind him, her arms folded across her chest, as if protecting herself from a strong wind.

"You have heard their answer, my little owl?" he asked, knowing the answer.

Nelida nodded and walked forward into his arms. A single tear shone silver in the moonlight, as it ran down her otherwise unreadable face.

FORTY-FOUR

Harry, Margaret, and Marcos sat tensely in front of the TV watching CNN. The storm was worsening and moving fast. Margaret got up unasked and turned down the sound as the anchorwoman moved on to less important news.

"I don't like the fact we haven't heard they're in the air," Harry said gravely. "Who've we got in our pocket in Washington, Mags?"

"I've been making a list, Hank," she answered, tearing a sheet from the legal pad in her hand, passing it to Harry.

"We need somebody high enough up in the Pentagon to know the straight poop, not so high he'll only want to cover his own ass."

"I got two generals in procurement, plus the head of the armed services committee we've got pull with. And that navy guy Dad likes . . . Admiral Johnson."

Margaret leaned forward. "Don't forget Alex Barclay-Fontaine's on the island—we may be able to play that card all the way up to the White House."

"We don't have time for bureaucracy," Marcos said evenly. "Where do we stand on finding mercenaries?"

Harry took out a paper of his own. "There's a guy who works for me in Flight gave me a couple of names. Says the one we need to get to is somebody named Darkman. He's a pal of that Marcinko guy, who headed Seal Team Six and got canned by the brass. Gordon Liddy's still tied in, too—we could use him in a pinch, but my guy says Darkman's the one to find."

"I got a phone number," Harry answered. "And a list of what we'll need to do the job. A C-130 for starters, *that* we haven't got, but they will. And they'll need a piss pot full of cash to work this fast. You got a price tag in mind, kid?"

"Whatever it takes," Marcos replied evenly. "I can access a million eight-fifty tonight; the rest may have to wait till Monday when the banks open."

Margaret and Harry locked eyes, a decision made. "We got access to more," Harry said. "Thoros leaves nothing to chance."

Marcos fought down his disappointment that they were privy to something he knew nothing about. He scribbled something on his yellow pad to cover his chagrin.

"He called it the Kidnap Fund, Marcos," Margaret said, seeing the young man's discomfort. "When you were a boy, he worried that you might be kidnapped. Later, as the world changed, he figured it could be himself or a key executive who got snatched. Thoros would never have trusted outsiders to negotiate, so Harry and I got the job."

Marcos nodded, trying to quell his injured pride. "How much do you have, and how do you access it?" he asked, all business.

Again the two older sets of eyes met across the space.

"Ten million," Harry answered. "It's half in the building and half ten minutes away. Mags and I have the codes."

Marcos digested that, then handed Margaret the paper in his hand.

"Get me these men on the phone, in this order, Margaret. And send out for food for us all."

He turned to Harry. "Brief me on exactly what we're asking them for, and stay with me while I make these calls. Washington won't move fast enough for us, but it can't hurt to get some clout going there in case we need to break some rules.

"I assume you've set up a command post in the flight department to monitor weather and move whatever mountains need moving?"

"I got eight guys in the building, all ground and aircraft personnel on beeper call, and another shift backing up this one," Harry replied with equanimity. He liked this kid.

Marcos nodded acknowledgment.

"Then let's make some calls."

Margaret was already on her feet and moving.

FORTY-FIVE

An hour later, Marcos and Harry slid into the red vinyl seats in a nearly empty waterfront diner and looked around. A dark, bearded man, about five foot eleven and built like a John Deere tractor, slid off a stool at the counter and moved in close to Harry.

"We're not staying here," he said, his voice a low fuzzy growl. Then he turned, and dropping some money at the cash register, headed out the door.

Harry's eyes met Marcos's; he read the annoyance there, but saw that the younger man intended to contain it. They rose and followed the stranger to a long, dilapidated nearby pier; at the end of the pier, the man stopped and turned his eyes toward the other men, taking in everything around them, and behind them, before he spoke.

"I hear you got a job to do," he said evenly.

Marcos studied the swarthy face and body. A gray-black ponytail reached well below the man's shoulders, and the black beard covering the lower half of his face was like Brillo. The face was hard, the eyes harder; there was a coiled-spring resonance about him, as if the wrong word would release some ill-contained force of nature.

"You come highly recommended," Marcos said, uncertain where to begin.

"Yeah, sure, kid."

Marcos straightened visibly. "No one calls me 'kid' but the man on my right," he said steadily, and Harry smiled a notch. "I'm the man who'll be paying you to do a job that can't have any fuck-ups. Do you want to talk to me, or trade attitude?"

"What *do* I call you?"

"Marcos. This is Harry."

The man nodded. "Okay, Marcos. Here's how it goes down. You tell me specifics. I listen. If it can be done, I'll tell you. I'll also tell you if I've got the men and equipment. We get paid half in advance. Cash. I don't negotiate, but the price will be fair."

"Okay, so far," Marcos replied. "We've already got your bona fides and we haven't much time, so listen good. My father and eleven of his friends, some of them very prominent, plus two servants, are on his private island in the South Pacific, about midway between New Guinea and Pitcairn. They were due to fly out on my dad's G-IV Sunday noon. We haven't been able to raise them by radio and they haven't got any sophisticated weather equipment on the island."

"Let me guess," the dark man said. "They're in the path of that typhoon that's heading for Hawaii?"

"Right. I want them off the island, safely and fast."

"Who are you?" the mercenary asked, inclining his head toward Harry.

"I run the corporate air force."

"Air force? Sounds fancy. You got a C-130 for the job?"

"No. I was told you'd supply one."

"Yeah. It'll cost you, though."

Marcos and Harry nodded in acquiescence.

"What *can* you give me that's useful?" the mercenary asked.

Harry had his mental inventory ready. "Specifics. Sophisticated weather tracking. High-level aeronautic clearance. Cash."

"Does that mean you'll do it?" Marcos pressed.

"It means I'll set up a team to try. Don't know yet if it can be done. We ain't got a helluva lot of time here; from what I know of that storm it could be class III or more. Those suckers make tracks. And we're twenty hours out of the South Seas. That means maybe I need a team and equipment out of Oahu or Asia. But that's my headache. Give me an hour and I'll tell you what's possible. The Murphy Probability here is real high and I don't do FUBAR."

" 'FUBAR'?" Marcos echoed.

"Fucked Up Beyond Repair," Harry translated quietly, and the dark man looked up at him, a hint of amusement in the veiled, sad eyes.

"You look like a guy who's been around," he said simply.

"You can make your calls from my office," Harry answered.

"No way. Too many people with big ears in my line of work. You'll hear from me in an hour."

"This is my father we're talking about," Marcos reiterated, as Darkman turned to go.

"I hear you, k—" He'd almost said *kid.* "Marcos. There ain't too many guys who stand to inherit three billion, who'd like to save their father's ass. I'll be in touch."

The two men watched him melt into the shadow of an abandoned warehouse and disappear.

"What do you think, Harry?"

"I think he asked the right questions. Let's go. We gotta have our ducks in line in an hour."

FORTY-SIX

Alex was pacing, something he never did and didn't approve of. But his frustration was at the eruption point. It was his modus operandi to wait, watch, strategize, then act rationally. And now was certainly the moment for all his skills.

Tony was agitating relentlessly for a surprise attack tonight, instead of waiting for morning. The hour was late and everyone's temper was at the boiling point as they'd gathered outside the house, seeking a place to escape the increasingly oppressive heat.

"There's something weird with this weather," Tony was saying. It was true; there was an eerie, humid stillness that had folded in on them, but with everything else going on, no one had paid much attention, although Thoros had checked the AWOS system two or three times since sundown.

"If we wait till morning they'll be ready for us and we'll be back to square one," Tony continued. "I say we surprise them during the night, grab the fuel controllers, and get the fuck out of here in case there's a storm coming. If we save their butts, we can worry about calming them down in New York."

"There's a lot to be said for that," Rand put in. "We've seen how recalcitrant they are. I vote with Tony." Rand looked awful since his illness, yellow and watery eyed.

"We've fucked up every negotiation so far," Jack said. "I think they'll play ball if we just do as we've said we would. Wait till morning, act like grown-ups, and use the storm possibility for leverage. Morning's only a few hours away."

"Just what *is* going on with this weather, Thoros?" Jase asked. "You're obviously worried about something."

Thoros shook his head from side to side judiciously as he spoke. "I can't really be certain yet what's going on. It's more instinct than anything that's got me worried. Could just be an extreme low-pressure cycle we're in, but this calm heat feels like prestorm to me. I've been monitoring the AWOS station every hour, but a good part of the equipment isn't on line yet—we don't have a satellite relay or weather fax, so I don't have full data. Of course, just because there's a storm somewhere close by, doesn't mean it has to hit us . . . but I don't want to let it slide, either."

"Can't we just fix the goddamned radio and hook in to some weather transmission?" Jase pushed, agitatedly.

Thoros frowned as he spoke. "It's not that easy. There's very limited range of transmission when the G-IV's on the ground. Only if someone were flying directly overhead would he hear us, and we're way off the usual sea and air routes." He paused, rubbed his jaw absently. "We have an ELT, of course. That's a portable transceiver that sends out a steady signal that's monitored via satellite by an air force base in Illinois—in case somebody needed to find us, they could. But we can't transmit voice on it."

"So what's the bottom line here, Thoros?" Jase pushed his point. "There could be a *storm* coming in here? If we don't know how serious a threat that is, shouldn't we just get the hell out before it hits us? To do that we need the fuel controllers, right? I gotta tell you, I'm with Rand and Tony on this. Maybe we can't afford to wait till morning."

"No!" Thoros shouted, a sharp edge to his voice. "We can reason with Justine. She's a pilot, she'll understand the danger, if the indications worsen. We do this according to Hoyle, not by force. And we do it tomorrow morning unless the AWOS readings alter drastically."

Tony stepped forward.

"With all due respect, Thoros, this is my life you're fucking with here. A lot of these men agree with me, tonight is better than tomorrow, and getting tough is the only way to get those engine parts back. I say we go after them now!"

Thoros took a step closer, too. "And *I* say we abide by our word." The tension between the two men was a forcefield.

"Who the hell died and made you king?" Tony said contemptuously.

"This is *my* island, and *here,* my word is law. You *will* abide by it." Thoros's voice was dangerous.

"Fuck that!" Tony spat. "I'm not waiting around to get creamed by a hurricane to massage your ego. I'm going after them tonight." He turned to go.

Thoros reached out with his large hand and grasped Tony's shoulder to stop him. To the astonishment of every man in the group, Tony turned violently and lobbed a vicious right cross at Thoros's jaw. Thoros, stunned for an instant, retaliated with a swift left jab and a right uppercut that pushed Tony backward, nearly knocking him off his feet. Tony, head in and down, rushed Thoros with a bull-like roar that sent the two men tumbling to the ground, all the explosive emotions of the past week finally erupting for both of them.

Neither was a stranger to street fighting, both had fought to protect their lives, long ago. Jack and Alex moved toward the fighting pair, but Emilio called out sharply, "No, señores. This is an honorable quarrel. Do not interfere." Then softly, for only Jack to hear, he added, "Time will defeat them."

Jack nodded; he'd seen it a thousand times in the fight game. The old bulls' aggression level was just the same as it had been at twenty, but their physical strength was not. Thoros and Tony would be lucky if nobody had a heart attack from this kind of hostile exertion. But Emilio was right, their stamina would be short lived.

Winded, the two wily, aging men were on their feet again and circling, crouched in fighting position, breath coming hard now.

"You've got the gun, Tony," Thoros rasped hoarsely. "Don't go after them."

"I haven't got the fucking gun," Tony panted back, then he lunged again, but Thoros sidestepped the worst of it, and landed a blow to Tony's midsection. The tiring men grappled and fell again; Thoros's reach was longer than Tony's, but in fighting skill they were evenly matched. Tony's right seemed to be in Thoros's face on some kind of automatic, but Tony was taking a lot of punishment in ill-defended body blows at the same time.

Thoros seemed willing to take the head shots to protect the rest of his large body. He was bleeding under his right eye now, and a small trickle ran from the left eyebrow. But for every head blow Tony landed, he took one to the ribs. Thoros's hands and arms were lethal; if Tony raised his right to punch, Thoros was in and under with a body blow or uppercut.

They were working hard now, panting, exhausted, aware that only a mistake or nature would tip the scales in one direction or the other. The rest of the men were crowded in close around them. They could see the fury in Thoros's eyes, the hatred in Tony's, that was blocking the pain of physical punishment from the combatants' minds.

Jack caught Emilio's eye over the fray—the look said, *Now* is the moment to save them both from the humiliation of being defeated by their own bodies. "They've made their point," he whispered, moving close to the Mexican, "no one needs to win this."

"Next time they go down, señor," Emilio whispered back. The Mexican was no stranger to bullfights either.

Tony's strength was going fast; he knew now that he couldn't beat Thoros fairly; he had maybe one more attack in him, then it would be over. His breath was coming in rapid bursts, his heart beat wildly, a trip-hammer out of control.

Thoros sensed the fatigue level in his opponent, could almost smell it, with that sixth sense that fighters have that shows them the weak defense, or the injured rib, or the infinitesimal window of opportunity for the one punch that will end the contest. The knowledge gave him a second wind. He sailed in swinging, showering Tony's head and shoulders with blows. He drew his right elbow back for an attack to the jaw, but never got to deliver the punch.

A powerful blow hit his right kidney, stunning him, as Tony's knee connected with his groin. Excruciating electricity seared up Thoros's spine, and he went down on one knee, fighting for equilibrium. The men were all shouting, "Foul!" around him. Alex, Jack, and Jase rushed forward, grabbing each of the men from behind, and yanking them backward.

The pain mist cleared, and Thoros stared at Tony's still-raging face across the space, both men struggling for wind and dignity. The others loosened their grip on them, and moved back to give them air. People were speaking, shouting, but neither Thoros nor Tony could hear, their eyes still locked across the intervening space.

Tony turned and crashed his way toward the jungle.

Marika, perched uncomfortably in the crook of a tree branch near the men's battleground, was finally shocked into movement. She had heard and seen it all. Her heart pounded in her chest so hard it was making her ears ring; fear of some epic dimension had risen in her at the men's shouted words, at the violence that lay in them so close to the eruption point. Thank God Liz had thought of sending her to spy on the men to hear their strategy. No! This was not strategy, it was betrayal. Carefully, she slid down the tree to the ground and stretched her long legs to get the cramps out. If Tony and his followers reached the women's camp while everyone was sleeping, the women would be doubly vulnerable, weaponless and perfect targets for rape. Marika didn't wait to see what would happen next among the men—she made her way as fast as she could toward the bridge and the women's camp.

Tony shook himself free of the bloodlust that had suffused him in the fight, as he left the compound far behind. This was the end for him and Thoros, thirty years of friendship down the toilet because of these bitches. He stopped only long enough to grab the .45 from its hiding place; it was good that he'd had the presence of mind to hide it away from the compound, away from prying eyes or searching hands. Closer to where he'd need it. On autopilot, Tony snapped the loaded magazine into the butt, pulled back the heavy slide, and let it drop. The most satisfying sound in the world; *Good old Colt A-frame,* he thought, as he checked to see that the safety was on, then slid it into the waistband of his chinos and headed toward his goal.

Tony was fast in this kind of country, fast and sure. He felt a surge of adrenaline energize him as he made for the bridge.

FORTY-SEVEN

The C-130 Hercules is the sturdiest warhorse in the business, kid," Harry said as he and Marcos entered the huge hangar and looked at the bustling activity around the large camouflage-painted aircraft in its center. "It's one of the great success stories in military aviation history—they launched it in fifty-four, and now it's in the military inventories of fifty or sixty countries and a million other legal and illegal ops. It's used as a transport, an operating theater, a flying mercy mission, you name it.

"That belly can drop tanks, cars, men, and supplies into terrain other aircraft couldn't touch, by penetrating at real low level. And they got more specialties than a Singapore whore. Like rescue and recovery equipment for retrieving parachute loads in midair, terrain-following radar, and every conceivable gizmo for precision airdrops . . . they even use these birds as a survivable airborne link between command authorities and ballistic submarines. And they fly into hurricanes and typhoons better than almost anything in the air. If any aircraft can get in there and out, it's this one—especially equipped like this baby."

Marcos knew that Harry had inspected the C-130 from nose to taillights as soon as it arrived; he'd pronounced it, and its crew, acceptable for the critical mission.

Darkman and eleven other men in camouflage and backpacks stood talking and checking equipment beneath the belly of the C-130. The men looked tough and purposeful; there was a contained excitement in their outwardly controlled manner, as if they couldn't wait to get airborne.

"This one was used for resupply, among other things," Harry continued to Marcos as they drew near the assemblage. "It's configured to make drops."

There were pallets, cargo chutes, a jeep, and medical supplies being loaded in.

"Where do they refuel?" Marcos asked. The one area of the family business that he didn't know, other than the financial aspects of it, was aviation. Thoros handled the aeronautics division himself.

"Maximum range on these Hercules is usually thirty-two hundred miles," Harry answered. "But this one's got additional tanks. They'll still have to fuel up in L.A. and Oahu. We're talking twenty-two hours easy."

Spotting them, Darkman headed in their direction.

"We expect to be in conversation range with Greywing at 0200 hours Sunday," he said. "If we can still get in by then, we'll pull them out of there. If not, we'll divert to the Solomon Islands and pluck them out after the storm passes over."

"I told you I want them out *before* the storm hits," Marcos said.

"Yeah. Well, I want to look like Redford, but it might not happen in this lifetime. I'll do my best for you, Marcos. If anybody can get in and out, we will. I got the best pilot and naviguesser in the business, and nine iron men in that bird. This is *my team*—not some unknown mercs out of Taipei. You don't buy balls this size in Podunk."

Marcos nodded; every instinct told him that Darkman would keep his word, if possible. The men shook hands, then Marcos and Harry stood silently watching, as the mercenaries finished loading and disappeared into the belly of the plane.

Harry folded the piece of paper Darkman had given him and put it into the pocket of his windbreaker, an unreadable expression on his face.

"What's on the paper?" Marcos asked, as they turned to go.

"Where we send the money, if they don't make it back," the older man said. The hoarseness in his voice made it clear that Harry thought this a real possibility.

Fear was all Marika could think about, all she could feel in her viscera, as she tried to remember her way back to camp. The dark was disorienting, or maybe it was this unexpected wellspring of fear, but something was confusing her. She made a wrong turn, corrected her course, forced herself to slow down—an agonizing thing to do when she needed so badly to get home.

It was easy to get lost in the jungle, especially at night, she reprimanded herself. *Pay attention.* With her mind in such a turmoil, she could get in serious trouble. Marika forced herself to think clearly. She would get back to camp. She would warn the others. Prepare for attack. She made a final choice of turn, and saw the clearing that marked the bridge. Elation and relief flooded her as she sped out into the clearing, knowing she'd made it.

Tony hit her from behind and sent her sprawling to the ground, with a grunt of triumph. He'd spotted her a hundred yards back, and tracked her, knowing she had to cross the bridge to get to safety. She was alone, and she was finally his.

"You caused me a helluva lot of trouble, bitch," he breathed into her hair, as he pinned her struggling body facedown beneath his own.

The panic that surged in Marika was larger than anything

she'd ever experienced. The weight of him, the smell of his hot breath, the malice in his voice brought back the horror she'd relived in her nightmares. She was alone and he meant to kill her. Some primal part of Marika's brain knew unequivocally that this had gone far beyond sex, this was a fight for her life. She felt the hard steel of Tony's gun pressing into the base of her spine and tried desperately to think what to do next. He would not know that she understood firearms . . . maybe that would give her an edge.

"Don't do anything crazy, Tony," she begged, barely able to speak or breathe; she felt the hardness of his erection, too, pressing into her, but she couldn't let her mind focus on that.

"I'm gonna finish what I started," he said, breathing hard, too. He reached one hand down to her buttocks and squeezed to reinforce his intent. *If he wants to rape me, he'll have to change position,* she thought, survival instinct bringing clarity.

He shifted his weight fractionally to get a better hold on her, and she took the opportunity. With all the strength of her terror, Marika twisted herself under him and out, arching him backward as she scrambled up. His rough hand closed on her leg like a vise as she tried to crawl away. She attempted to kick herself free, but he was up now and punching. A shocking pain hit her ribs, and she was thrown sideways. Marika lurched up again and tried to remember what Tiffany had told them about defending themselves. *Legs.* She had to use her long, strong legs. He was coming at her again with a vengeance. Marika shot out a kick that caught him in the solar plexus with stunning force. She started to run, but he was right behind her. She felt his hard hands close on her shoulder. Fear, terrible, all-consuming fear, surged through her. She was trapped now. She could never make it over the bridge. She screamed as he turned her forcibly to face him. And, he was laughing, leering, victory in his eyes as he tore at her shirt.

"No!" she shrieked, as he pulled her hard against him. His

hand clutched her arm like a tourniquet; he twisted her flesh to force her to her knees in front of him.

"Unzip my pants, bitch," he said, his voice low and lethal. "You're gonna have some fun before you die."

Marika looked up with the expression of a wounded animal and her eye caught the semiautomatic shoved into his belt. Tony followed her glance and put his hand on the pistol.

Marika's mind was in overdrive, whatever she had to do to get the gun. . . . She forced herself to think. *The safety is probably on for carrying. Think, Marika. Think!*

"I'll do whatever you want, Tony," she whispered. "Just don't kill me!"

"You'll do what I want, all right, but not here. They'll be looking for us." He took the gun from his belt and clicked off the safety.

"Get moving . . . over to that heavy foliage." He motioned toward the left of the bridge and she began to move, her legs like jelly under her. The jungle was dense there and provided considerable cover; when he brought them to a halt they could no longer see the bridge.

"Now, get back on your knees," he ordered, unzipping his pants with one hand, the gun still in the other. "This reminds me of the army, you know," he said with a short laugh as she slowly sank to her knees in front of him. He freed his swollen penis from its cover. "We used to say, '*This is my penis, this is my gun. This one's for shooting, this one's for fun.*' Now we're gonna have some fun."

Tears ran down Marika's face, her large eyes filled with stark animal terror. She knew he would kill her; he was crazy and there was no way he would rape her again and then let her live. She would have one chance. Maybe . . .

Marika let her shoulders sag forward in as subservient a posture as she could muster. "Don't hurt me, Tony," she begged, as she reached for his penis with her mouth; encircling the head with her full lips, she tasted the salt of her tears.

One chance . . . *one chance.*

Marika slammed her teeth shut on the object in her mouth as hard as she could, then shoved him backward with the strength of absolute terror. She knocked the gun sideways as she came up, and felt the bullet zing by her as he discharged it. And she was on top of him this time, using all her strength to grapple for the gun as they rolled over and over on the damp jungle floor.

And then she felt the cold metal hard against her belly and her hand was on it as well as his. His hands were bigger, stronger, but she was fighting for her life. Both their fingers were struggling to get inside the trigger guard and there was a terrible explosion, and the sound of flesh and bone rending, and blood spurting everywhere.

Marika didn't know until he crumpled motionless on top of her which one of them had been shot. She pushed the loathsome weight off her, blood all over her hands and body. She staggered to her feet and stood galvanized over Tony's prostrate form, utterly unable to move or think. She should do *something,* touch him, move, run, hide the body, *something,* but she couldn't think what. The .45 was still gripped in her hand, sticky with gore.

She stared at the gaping wound in Tony's chest, at the puddle of blood, at his dead, staring, startled eyes, and she had to get out of there. Had to run, had to get as far from this as she could go.

Unthinking. Blind with panic. Marika headed for the bridge and help.

The weather was worsening. The wind was blowing now, swaying the palm trees uneasily, and rain had begun to fall. Thoros and Jack were talking over the possibilities, when they heard the crack of gunfire through the drone of the wind.

Jack's head went up sharply at the sound.

"That was a gunshot!" Thoros said for them all. Every man was on his feet and moving toward the sound.

"We've got to find Tony," Thoros shouted as he ran. His bruises and all the unused muscles around them that had been called into play in the fight were already stiffening up, so movement was painful.

"Wait!" Rand called after the others. "We don't know who's shooting at whom. We can't just go blundering in there!"

No one stopped or answered him, so he stood for an undecided moment, then reluctantly followed where the others led.

Ten minutes later they reached the clearing at the bridge; it took just minutes more to find the body. Tony lay illuminated by moonlight amid a swarm of tiny, crawling and flying insects, despite the rain. Jack and Emilio reached him first.

"Shit!" Jack said, as his hand groped for Tony's carotid artery; he knew by the scope of the wound that the man was long dead, but had to make sure. "He's gone." Instinctively, he reached down to pull up Tony's pants and cover his nakedness.

"The women had the gun all along," Thoros said with disgust.

"No, señor," Emilio corrected him hastily. "Look to the ground. This was not an ambush. This was a fight to the death."

Thoros nodded acceptance of the fact, and moved in close beside Tony's body; he bent over to close the lids of his friend's staring eyes, so much grief and guilt welling up in him that he had to fight back tears.

"He didn't deserve this," he said hoarsely.

"We don't know what he deserved," Alex amended, in a steadier voice. "I don't see the gun anywhere around, do you? Inasmuch as we don't know if this was provoked or not, I'd say we'd best proceed with caution."

"The first thing we need to proceed on is some kind of protection for Tony's body," Jack said with finality. "If we don't bury him or cover him, the animals will get him before morning. You can see the fire ants are already on the case."

"Quite right," Thoros replied. "We'd best take him back to the compound."

"Thoros," Jack said quietly, compassion in his voice. "That house is an oven—if we put him there he'll start to decompose overnight. It might be smarter to get something to wrap him in and bury him under a cairn outdoors, until help comes."

Thoros searched his friend's face and saw both knowledge and common sense.

"That sounds right," he answered, his voice thick with the emotions of the last hour. "And the sooner the better."

The grim phalanx of men headed back to Mora Utu. Thoros felt violent, as he walked; he wanted to strike back somehow. At the women, at Fate, at whatever had cursed this island. At himself for having fought with Tony, a grim memory that would be his to carry forever. At himself for not having figured out how to change this incredible downward spiral that kept sucking them in deeper and deeper.

He'd *felt* death around them for days; that's why he had quarreled so violently over the gun. It was in the air here, hovering, waiting to strike. Why had he not sensed it before? Why had it all seemed so perfect until this week? As if the evil had been veiled, until something, some sinister spark, had freed it.

FORTY-EIGHT

Justine faced the others in the women's camp, more agitation in her body language than they had seen there before; she and Chesi were both soaking wet. "There is a major storm moving in around us," she said seriously. "Chesi and I have been to the weather station—the barometer's dropping fast. Despite what we decided earlier tonight, I think we must reconsider our options. It might be safest to make truce immediately and repair the aircraft."

"After what those sons of bitches did at the river this afternoon? I thought you were on our side earlier, Justine," Christie said, her voice hot with anger. "I should have known you'd recant. They'll kill us after they've got the fuel controllers."

"Bullshit!" Liz said. "We don't *know* that—we're just trying to make the best decision we can, given the givens. Tony's the only real nutcase they've got. Let Justine finish." She motioned to Justine to continue.

"Who the hell made you dictator, Liz?" Christie snapped. "Did Justine abdicate?"

"Shut up!" Chesi and Liz said in unison. "We need to hear her out," Chesi added.

Justine took the floor again. "Look, I'm really worried about this weather. Hurricanes happen in this part of the world. They're called typhoons. The air moves in an opposite spiral to the ones above the equator, but the result is identical. Even though Chesi says there hasn't been a really devastating typhoon here for a hundred years, maybe we simply can't rely on that fact now, because we are far more vulnerable than the men are. We have *no* shelter . . . *no* storm cellar to go to. Our best hope is to repair the plane and get out of here ahead of the storm, or to hole up in the compound cellar for the duration. Either way, we have to make peace with the men, and quickly."

"Is there really time for us to get out?" Tiffany asked sensibly. "If it is a typhoon, how fast do these things travel?"

"Quite fast, I'm afraid. There's just no way to know how bad this will turn out to be. I'm really operating on instinct about this—the weather station isn't fully on line yet, there's no weather fax, no satellite hookup, no tracking. These storms are quixotic. They move in erratic paths. It could veer away from us, or hit us head-on. . . ." She shrugged in frustration.

"We have to tell the men," Tiffany said suddenly, thinking of Jack. "We'll just have to help each other."

"Bullshit!" Christie said. "What if we help them fix the plane, and then they leave us behind? This is exactly the kind of accident they need to be rid of us. Don't you see? The storm wipes us out, it's nobody's fault. Nobody ever knows the truth."

"What you say is certainly a possibility, Christie," Justine said, considering. "But I think it's remote, don't you? Whereas the storm appears to be *real* and immediate. Whatever we decide, I think it must be *now.* There's a typhoon coming! You can feel it all around us now, instruments or no instruments."

"Nelida," Chesi said suddenly. "You know everything. How bad will this be?"

"For Christ's sake, Chesi!" Christie interrupted contemptuously. "She's not the Oracle at Delphi."

Nelida chose her words with care. "This storm is of great magnitude, my daughters. No one can know for certain the whims of the Gods in these matters, but there will be much devastation. A time of grave testing."

"So, we should try to leave?"

"This I cannot tell you, child. Only that grave tests are at hand. Each of you must make choices now and live with the consequences. Each must find her own Power."

A crashing sound moved all eyes toward the edge of camp. Marika, soaking wet and covered with blood, eyes red and wild-looking, stumbled through the undergrowth and into the open.

"Tony's dead!" she shrieked, as if she'd been waiting forever to blurt the news. "I killed him!" She dropped to her knees at the periphery of the huddled group and threw the gun to the ground, wiping her hands on her clothes like Lady Macbeth.

"Christ almighty!" Christie yelled, leaping forward. "You can't throw guns around like that. That thing could go off!" She scrambled to the weapon and grabbed it; then lifting it toward her nose, she sniffed. "It's been fired," she announced, "recently."

"What happened to you, honey?" Tiffany prompted, putting her arms around the sobbing woman. "Where is Tony?"

Marika was semihysterical, her speech disjointed.

"They're coming!" she cried. "The men. They're coming here. After us. I heard them."

"In the morning, for the parlay?"

"No!" she shrieked wildly. "*Now.* They were fighting. They decided not to wait. I was running back to tell you when he grabbed me."

"Who? Tony?"

"Yes! *Tony.* He grabbed me by the bridge. He was tearing at me." Marika was sobbing as she spoke. Her voice was full of revulsion and her hands were pulling at her clothes, mimicking

Tony's. "Oh, *God!* He was on top of me. And he said he would finish what he started, and I was so scared. And I couldn't get away. And then there was the gun, and I tried to get it but he was so strong and then it went off and at first I didn't know who got shot, but then he was dead. *Dead!*" She stopped for breath, looking at the blood on her hands and body, her eyes frenzied, her breath coming in gasps. "I killed him!"

"Oh my God!" Tiffany breathed the exclamation on everybody's lips. She turned toward the others.

"This has to stop!" she cried out emphatically. "Don't you see? We have to give back the fuel controllers. Now!"

"No!" Christie said sharply. "You can't do that. We have to figure out what to do—now there's been a murder. We're all implicated."

"Fuck that!" Chesi spat. "That's not murder. It's self-defense."

"It's her word against theirs," Christie shot back. "They could say she stalked him."

"I can't listen to this anymore," Tiffany shouted, her agitation extreme. "We're all getting crazy. The *only* sensible thing to do now is to call a truce, fix the plane, and save everybody's life. Oh, *God!* . . . Don't you see where this has taken us?"

The wind was an escalating moan, now; trees were whistling and swaying and the warm rain was turning colder.

"Let's put it to a vote," Liz said, trying to stay calm.

"Forget the vote," Chesi snapped, as the shelter above them creaked and moaned. "Listen to that wind. Let's get practical and figure out how to protect ourselves right here in camp."

"There's *no way* to be safe outdoors in a typhoon!" Tiffany said, incredulous that anyone could be so naive. "We have to warn the men and ask their help. This isn't *just* a storm, I feel it in my bones—this is something big and dangerous. Don't you see? If we warn them, then we'll all be able to help each other!"

"There's no need to warn them," Justine countered, sensibly.

"Thoros already knows. He's a pilot. He knows exactly how dangerous this is—that's probably why they decided not to wait until morning."

"Then let's stop talking, and start cooperating with them," Tiffany pleaded urgently. "It's the only way to end this mess."

"And what if they don't *help* us, just use us?" Christie persisted.

"She could be right," Chesi said, frowning worriedly. "They haven't shown much goodwill so far, and the fuel controllers are our only trump card."

Christie, Liz, and Justine started to talk at once.

Tiffany got up soundlessly and moved out of the circle of arguing women. There was no time to waste on arguments and selfish agendas. This was a moment for personal decision making. She wished she could talk to Justine about it, but she couldn't risk a veto. Jack was in danger. *Everyone* was in danger and she simply had to make up her own mind to do what seemed most right in a sea of awful possibilities. She hoped and prayed it wasn't a wrong decision. Tiffany stopped by her belongings only long enough to grab a backpack, then headed for the hollowed-out log where the plane parts that had caused so much dissention were hidden.

Five minutes later, Justine looked around the circle and realized that Tiffany was missing. "Damn!" she murmured under her breath. "She should have known I would agree with her." She left the others still arguing and went after her at a run; there was no question at all where Tiffany had gone.

By the time Justine reached the hiding cache it was empty. The wind was rising precariously, and rain had started to fall in earnest. There simply wasn't any choice now but to repair the G-IV and get out; Tiffany, with her kind, uncomplicated heart, had made the only sensible decision. Justine looked up at the ominous sky worriedly and wondered how long the option to leave would exist.

The wind tore at Tiffany's face and body as she ran, and rain was splattering down in large relentless drops. *The bridge will be a bitch in this weather,* she thought, worriedly, even before she saw it dead ahead. The ropes and vines were swaying ominously in the wind, and the tree-limb floor clattered like an old man's teeth.

Gusts were escalating, as Tiffany stood uncertainly at the edge of the rungs that led down onto the oscillating span. "Shit!" she said aloud into the wind. "I *hate* this thing!"

Justine cleared the jungle just as Tiffany started forward on the bridge. She screamed out her name, uncertain if she could be heard against the rising wind. Tiffany's head came up, and she hesitated, then turned toward the sound and spotted Justine far behind her.

"Don't try to stop me!" she shouted back. "We've all got to get out of here."

Justine was running toward her shouting something—Tiffany took a step closer, trying to hear. As she stepped back onto the cliff edge, a tree branch blown from nowhere sailed directly at her. Justine shrieked a warning, but too late. Tiffany threw up her hands instinctively to protect herself, but the large branch glanced off the side of her head pushing her backward, off balance and stunned. She felt the ground beneath her feet give way and began to slide downward. Desperately, she clawed at empty air; her hand grasped a hanging vine but it gave way in her grip and she was falling, falling. Her terrified shriek as she disappeared from sight was scrambled into nothingness by the wind and the rushing water below.

"Mother of God!" Justine breathed as she watched Tiffany disappear over the side of the gorge. She raced forward to crouch at the edge of the precipice; peering over, afraid to think what she might see, she spotted Tiffany fifty feet below, sprawled on a small rocky ledge, one arm and one leg hanging uselessly over the abyss. How a ledge so small could ever have caught her was unimaginable. Justine grasped the bridge rope with one arm to steady herself and fought down nausea; this was unthinkable, unbearable. If Tiffany moved even five inches she would fall to the bottom of the ravine. If she wasn't already dead.

Justine screamed Tiffany's name a half-dozen times, but there was no response from the inert figure on the ledge. Then she got unsteadily to her feet, and glancing up at the sky, trying to divine both the weather and the right thing to do, she ran back to find the others with the deadly bulletin.

Tony's body was wrapped securely in plastic garbage bags. Jack, Alex, and Jase placed it in the shallow grave to protect it from animals and the worsening storm. Once the rescuers came, they would retrieve him for a proper burial. The rocks they'd collected to cover him stood beside the gash in the volcanic earth, and the wind whipped at their faces and clothes as they hurried to finish their work. Jack picked up the first rock and placed it on Tony's dead body, now cold as if no one had ever lived there. The other men hurriedly followed suit.

Thoros stood resolute at the head of the rocky cairn, looking stern as a general signing a treaty of defeat. He waited until the last rock was in place before speaking, and then his voice was hard and thick with emotion, and difficult to hear against the background noise of the storm.

"We do not know for certain how Tony died, or at whose hands. We do know how he lived. He was my friend for a lifetime. Always there to help, no matter what the cost. Always fair-minded. Always keeping the bargains he made. He never reneged on a bet, and he played a damned good hand of poker.

"So, here's to you, Tony—wherever you are. May you find a

good game over there and keep it hot till we join you at the table. You will be sorely missed by us, I promise you that!"

"Hear, hear!" Jase and Alex echoed. Both Jack and Rand said, "Amen."

Thoros lowered his head to his chest for a moment, then looked up, the sadness gone, replaced by fire. "I'm going to the AWOS to check on the storm," he said, "then we're going to get those damned engine parts."

"Neither act will be necessary," a clear female voice cut through the noise behind them. They turned to see Justine and Liz, wet and bedraggled, standing a few feet away. "We've got a casualty at the rope bridge," Justine called out urgently. "If you help us get Tiffany out of there, we'll fix your plane."

Jack grabbed Justine's arm. "Did you say Tiffany?" he shouted. "What happened to her?"

"She decided to take matters into her own hands," Justine replied, her voice charged with emotion. "She was coming here with the fuel controllers to give them to you."

Jase's head came up. "The fuel controllers? You mean she's got them with her?"

Jack turned on him ferociously. "Fuck the engine, Shindler! And fuck *you!* Tiffany's hurt."

"Where is she?" Rand pressed. "How do you know she's not dead?"

Liz answered. "She's on a small rocky ledge forty or fifty feet down the ravine. She seems unconscious and her leg looks broken. Maybe other things, too. She got hit by flying debris before she fell. Marika says the climb's impossible in this wind. She said to tell Thoros it's a mantelshelf and there are overhangs to contend with. Also vegetation. She said you'll have to rappel."

Thoros took that in, his mind in high gear; he started shouting orders. "Emilio, we'll need equipment. Biners, chocks, wires, slings. I need my rack, a drill. And plenty of rope, three-quarter-inch static lines . . . Jase, Alex, go with him. There'll be a lot to carry. Rand, get me any information on the kind of rock we're dealing with. I assume it's porous volcanic, but you must know more from the excavating you did. And get me any medical equipment you can find. We'll have to fashion a backboard. Tear up sheets for bandages, get sticks for splints. You'll have to construct a litter or travois. Jack," he said, looking with compassion at the easily read emotions on his friend's face, "you come with me to the site."

No one even mentioned Tony.

FORTY-NINE

Marika, blond hair soaked and flying, stood at the edge of the ravine trying to stay upright in the worsening wind. Thoros was on his knees looking down, attempting to assess the possibilities. Jack, too, was on his knees. They looked as if they were praying.

"We could get her out, if it weren't for this bloody storm!" Thoros shouted, as much to himself as to the others.

"You would be a fool to try in this wind," Marika said definitively. "It would be suicide."

Thoros spoke, looking up at her. "Not necessarily, Marika. During the war, I rappelled in some pretty lousy weather. It can be made to work."

"Sure! If you have the whole U.S. Army to help you," she said hotly.

Thoros's mouth was a grim line. "Look, Marika, if you're scared, I'll do this alone. No one will blame you."

"I'll go with you," Jack said quickly.

Thoros shook his head emphatically. "Jack, this is one for experienced climbers, not willing amateurs."

"Fuck that, Thoros," Jack yelled into the wind. "I'm in love with her."

"All the more reason I don't want you on the climb," Thoros said determinedly. "There's no margin for emotion on this one."

Thoros stood up and began to check the equipment that lay piled at his feet. He picked up the kernmantle rope and began to stack it carefully. A tangle on a climb like this could cost you your life. Suddenly, Marika picked up another rope vengefully, and began to stack it, too. Thoros looked at her hard.

"I have a full-body harness," he said evenly.

Marika bit her bottom lip; the last thing on earth she wanted to do was risk her life for Tiffany, and she was still badly shaken over what had happened with Tony, but it galled her to seem a coward in front of Thoros. And she was a good and experienced climber; there was a code among climbers that she, too, adhered to.

"Full body is best," she replied noncommittally.

"Does that mean you *want* it?" he said with measured exasperation.

She reached over and yanked the harness from the pile.

"I don't need any reluctant heroes around here, Marika," he said low and even. "You're either in or out. There's no halfway here. I have to know if I can count on you, and I can't baby-sit."

"I'm in," she said fiercely, as she began to fasten herself into the safety equipment, in her agitation, neglecting to triple back the buckle on her harness. "And you won't have to baby-sit. I'm quite competent and I have rescued before."

He studied her for a moment, assessing the wisdom of taking her at her word. If she could be trusted, having a partner would be a real asset.

"One or two rappel lines and a litter line, with an equalized redundant anchor for each will do it here, Thoros," she said, all business now. "Do we have belay plates? And figure-eight descenders?"

"We have what we need," he replied, heartened by her words—they were the right ones. He began to snap necessary items on to his harness; as climb leader he would carry much of the equipment. Chocks of varying shapes and weights, camming devices, that could be hooked into outcrops. Down climbs were tricky even in good weather.

"Tell me what I can do, Thoros," Jack asked, desperate to help. He was obviously in great distress. Tiffany hadn't moved at all on the narrow ledge; she could be dead or nearly so. "How can you get her up here, once you're down?"

"I won't lie to you, Jack. If her spine's injured we may kill her or cripple her by moving her. We'll have to assess that when we get there. You'll just have to trust whatever decision I make. Getting her up may be her only chance to stay alive. Emilio is a very competent doctor, as you have seen, and he'll construct a travois—we'll strap her in and hoist."

"I will lower the medical equipment to you, señor, when you are on the ledge," Emilio said. Thoros nodded, and having secured the descenders and the safety ropes, walked to the edge of the cliff.

"I give you my word, Jack, we'll give it our best shot," he said with great seriousness.

Jack, too worried to reply, simply nodded acknowledgment. Thoros hoisted himself over the edge. He hoped the trees to which he'd anchored his lines would hold their combined weight in the storm.

Marika, cursing herself internally for being in this position, checked her safety harness. The locking carabiners were all secured, the rope was in perfect condition, threaded in a figure-eight knot, and a prusik to back it up. Obviously, Thoros had no rescue eights available, but they could make do with the equipment they had.

Grabbing the descender securely, she gave Emilio a thumbs-up sign and followed Thoros over the side. The rain-soaked wind hit her like a wet wall and she had to fight to breathe, but, that accomplished, she began her descent. The rain and wind made footholds precarious on the wet rock, but the leather gloves held her with relative safety. She had good hands for this; strong, able hands that she prided herself on. She'd done little climbing in the past few years, since she'd become a model and needed beautiful hands, not competent ones, but before that, she and her friends had scaled up to class 5.12 on the U.S. system, with only one small mishap.

But not in weather like this, she thought acidly as another gust swung her out far from the slickened rock face. Thoros's extra weight was helping him descend. She saw that he had already reached the ledge on which Tiffany lay.

Thoros stopped his descent at their destination and got a foothold on Tiffany's ledge. He let the prusik tighten and tied off the descenders. It was a frigging miracle the ledge had caught her body—the outcropping was barely big enough to hold her supine form and his standing one. He bent to touch her throat and felt the pulse, faint beneath his fingers. He reran in his mind what Justine had said of the accident; it always helped in rescue work to re-create the accident mentally to determine the nature of possible injuries.

"She's alive!" he shouted up to the watchers, hand signaling as well, in case they couldn't hear. Then he moved in as close as possible and crouched carefully beside Tiffany's inert form. Keeping steady on the precarious perch of rock was no easy task in the high wind and pelting rain. Thoros bent to examine her injuries as Marika landed on the far side of the tiny ledge. He saw her find a foothold and turned his attention back to Tiffany's wounds.

The right leg was still sprawled over the edge of the rock at a grotesque angle, the femur obviously fractured; the right arm was similarly askew. He checked her breathing, the airway seemed clear. Next he looked for telltale blood; lacerations would have to be dressed and bandaged before moving her, if they were severe. Finding none that demanded immediate work, he turned his attention to her neck and back, trying hard not to jostle her; there was no way to know the extent of internal injury, but there was no bleeding from the mouth. A small trickle came from the nose, which could have happened on impact, or could be a red flag for serious head trauma.

Marika, too, was on her knees now beside the body, touching tentatively.

"She's cold as ice," she said. "And her pulse is weak and thready. She is in shock and bottoming out."

Tiffany groaned as Thoros pressed her upper body, looking for more broken bones; he thought there was most probably a humerus fracture and shoulder dislocation. She moved and her eyelids fluttered open briefly, then shut again.

The world around Tiffany swirled in and out of focus in a tidal way. At first, she seemed to be swimming in some amorphous sea of pain. She thought she'd tried to move her head, to lift it, but her head was no longer attached to her body the way it used to be and it wouldn't move at her command. So she had drifted back into the sea again.

She thought she heard Jack shouting her name but that couldn't be or he would come to save her. Fire raged in her hips and legs; she didn't know how that could be true at sea. And her right arm was a bright ring of agony that radiated out and up to her shoulder. She was wet all over, but that was from the ocean. Water ran in rivulets down her face, she let it run into her mouth and she drank it gratefully. Funny, but it wasn't salty, except a little from her tears. She drifted back into unconsciousness, completely unaware of the scene she had engendered all around her.

Thoros thought hard for a moment, then looked upward. "Emilio!" he shouted, hand signaling simultaneously. "Lower the backboard!"

Moments later the homemade travois was suspended at the edge of the shelf on which they perched. Behind it came a basket filled with torn strips of Porthault sheets and adhesive tape. Five-foot-long wooden poles were suspended above the bag.

"Have you ever made a splint?" he asked Marika urgently as he hurriedly cut one strap of Tiffany's backpack to free it, so she could lie flat. "And we'll need to fashion a C-spine collar before we move her."

"Ya. For animals. I could do it."

Carefully, they attempted to straighten the crooked limbs enough to immobilize them. The work was awkward because of their perch, and nearly impossible because of the high winds and rain.

Tiffany groaned pitiably as they worked on her, and she tried to beat them away with her one good arm, but Thoros held her hand in his strong grip as Marika worked to straighten the broken limbs enough to immobilize them for the ascent, using in-line traction to reduce the fracture. Tiffany screamed once when Marika pulled her leg in agonizingly from the edge and then sobbed and gasped incoherently when she couldn't struggle anymore against the hurt they were inflicting.

Finally, after what seemed eternity, the limbs were both splinted enough to move her.

"We'll have to turn her over to get her onto the backboard," Marika shouted, doubtful that there was room on the ledge to do all they must.

"She's dead weight," he shouted back. "I'll have to hold her up while we get the sling in under her. Mind the edge behind you."

Marika nodded, looking down. The stream, another seventy-five feet below, was swollen and raging. White water swirled and bubbled like a vast caldron and the water level was rising crazily.

Marika reached for the suspended litter and pulled it in, trying to keep from losing her balance as she did so; she looked worriedly at the volcanic rock above them. The kind of friction they'd already generated could cut through a static line on rock as sharp as this.

Shifting Tiffany's body was nearly impossible in the constrained space. Marika carefully moved herself into place to hold Tiffany's head, as Thoros positioned himself at the injured girl's side. He moved the arm closest to him above her head and steadied the fractured one, as best he could against her abdomen. He grabbed hold of her pants waist and shirt on her far side as firmly as possible, and looked at Marika.

"You have her head. You do the count."

She nodded and began. *"One! Two!"* Thoros rolled Tiffany's body toward him and rested her against his own body briefly. He had to hold one hand on Tiffany's back and use the other to slide the bodyboard behind her.

"Okay!" he called to Marika. "On *three* we roll her back."

Thoros cursed in English and Armenian, Marika in Swedish, Tiffany cried out, sobbed, and begged, but somehow they managed to position the injured woman onto the board and tie her in. Thoros signaled the men above to hoist her up the steep rock wall, using the three-to-one pulleys they'd constructed, not an easy task even in good weather conditions.

"Bravely done," Thoros said to Marika when the litter was finally on its way.

"Ya," she acknowledged with a weary smile. "You too."

He laughed shortly. "Now all we have to do is ascend to the top."

"Piece of cake, ya?" she said, with a small defiant laugh, and Thoros laughed loudly at the unexpected reply, thinking fleetingly what fools they'd all been. There was substance to all of them in this crowd, if only they'd looked for it. He stood and clipped the ascenders onto the rope, in preparation for the ascent, his legs cramped and painful from the long crouch; then he stepped back to look upward, ready to climb up the cliff.

The ledge, undermined by water and erosion, suddenly gave way beneath Thoros's weight and with no warning whatsoever, flung him far out into empty space. In stunned horror, Marika watched his slackened rap line snap taut, entangling Thoros's arm, as he cast it out to save himself. In seconds he was trussed on one side, unable to use his right arm at all, crippled and helpless for climbing, and dangling far out over the gorge below.

"Hold on, Thoros!" she screamed. "I'll bring you in."

Thoros pendulumed in the rising wind, the buffeting blasts swinging him far out over the chasm. Marika assessed the possibilities rapidly, understanding fully the danger of what she must now attempt to do. She must pendulum out to reach his dangling body, but the task would be hard at her size and weight, and in this wildly erratic wind it would be nearly impossible to gauge the momentum needed to reach him.

Marika took a deep breath, willing her heartbeat down to a bearable rhythm. She had to face her fear, it was there to protect her, she just couldn't let it make her decisions. "*There are always two climbs going on, Marika,*" her climbing mentor's voice was suddenly in her head. "*One on the mountain, and one in your mind.*"

She pushed herself off the ledge and swung pendulumlike in Thoros's direction, but she didn't have the momentum to reach him, and swung back in fast and hard, barely catching another foothold on the crumbling ledge. Marika eyed the ledge warily as she pushed off a second time, harder; what was left of the sodden rock wouldn't take much more punishment.

Marika's second pendulum almost made it to where Thoros hung suspended, but the opposing wind caught her just short of him, and pushed her back. *Damn!* she thought, as she was flung back in toward the cliff wall at increasing speed. *I've got to get him next time!* The escalating wind made judging the force needed to swing the pendulum an almost impossible task. Marika closed her eyes for a moment, and breathed deeply, centering herself for the next attempt. Everything depended on her now. "I am up to this task," she said aloud. "I have to try." *"Never concede to the mountain, Marika,"* her teacher's voice was saying now, *"unless you have done your best. If you die, at least die trying."* She opened her eyes, gauged the distance to Thoros, and launched herself out over the intervening space like an eagle in well-controlled flight.

His arm was flung out to meet her; both he and she grabbed hard at the other's outstretched hand as she neared him; this time they connected with a fierce thunk of bodies. *"Jesus!"* he grunted as they clasped each other, twisting in the wind. "That was beautiful!"

As hurriedly as numbed fingers would allow, the two struggled to disentangle Thoros's arm so he could again climb. Marika clipped onto Thoros's harness with a sling, slipped it through another biner, and stepped into it. At her belay point the strength of her legs pulled Thoros to her, taking the weight of both their bodies on her line, as she gave him enough time to disentangle himself, an arduous maneuver.

Relieved, and anxious to move on quickly, Marika unclipped and started to ascend. She had gone only three feet, when her static line, frayed by the three massive pendulum swings it had endured and the weight of their two bodies, snapped clean through.

Marika's body lurched backward, violently; flailing desperately for a grip on anything, a look of astonishment on her terrified face, she started to fall. Thoros, shocked and unready, grabbed for her wildly, catching her flailing hand in his own, but barely. He held on with all the strength of desperation, but the entire weight of her nearly six-foot-tall body wrenched cruelly at his grip. The wind was swinging her now, and the drenched leather glove she wore slid inexorably from his fingers.

"No!" they shrieked in unison as she slipped from his hand. Clutching helplessly at thin air, her body splayed on the turbulent empty space, Marika plummeted down, down, to the raging water and deadly rock below, her screams ricocheting off the walls of the gorge, distorted by the droning rain.

"No!" he bellowed after her as if to call her back to him, his rage and anguish echoing through the canyon louder than the wind. "No! No! *No!*"

The others, on top of the cliff, watched riveted and aghast, as Marika's body hit the maddened river more than a hundred feet below, and bobbing crazily a few times, disappeared under the raging current.

Thoros hung on the rope that had saved him for a time, his body motionless, mind in a frenzied replay. *She must not have triple-backed the harness buckle . . . anyone could forget that under pressure . . . but it might have given her a fighting chance. . . .* The rain beat back the tears that ran down his face, and the unbearable sense of failure that he felt in his gut made movement out of the question. Marika had died to save him. She, who he had thought a mindless bimbo, had died to save his life. The thought played over and over, flashing neon in his mind, blotting out all but guilt, and the crushing knowledge of his failure.

Someone was calling his name. Somewhere far away. The sound filtered slowly through Thoros's numbness and the drone of the storm, snapping his brain back to attention. He looked up toward the sound and was shocked to remember the truth: he still had to ascend the gorge.

Forcing his mind and will back under his control, with all

the strength he had left to muster, Thoros assessed the possibilities. His belay was tied off and backed up with a prusik; he could use the prusik to ascend the rope. Such a climb in these conditions would be strenuous, difficult, but doable.

Pushing his grief and defeat back down into insignificance, Thoros began his laborious ascent up the face of the cliff.

FIFTY

Forty minutes after Marika's death, Thoros Gagarian stood resolutely at the top of the gorge, the shock of all that had just transpired etched in every line of his face. Justine had hugged him silently, the others saying words that barely registered. He couldn't let himself think of Marika now; if he did, he'd never function. Later, there would be time to remember, and to mourn. Now, there was only time to try to save as many others as possible.

"We've got to get Tiffany back to the compound," he said, his voice hoarse from intense emotion and the grim effort of the climb. "She's in a very bad way. Jack, you, Rand, and Emilio see what you can do to make her comfortable. I've got to get the G-IV operational, and try to get us out of here, while there's still time."

"I'll come with you, Thoros," Justine volunteered, stepping closer. She felt so shaken by what she'd only *witnessed,* she couldn't imagine how he was still standing. "It's not going to be easy working on her in this storm."

"Right you are," he replied shortly. "Alex, you and Jase better come along with us to hold the engine scaffolding. The way that wind is kicking up, it may be next to impossible to access the engines."

"I might be able to help," Liz volunteered.

"Do you know anything about aircraft?"

"Not a jot," she shouted back earnestly. "But Justine once made me read the manual, so I remember every word and diagram. Maybe that will help, somehow."

Thoros shook his head, as if to say nothing now would surprise him. He watched as Jack, Rand, and the remaining women picked up the improvised litter and carried the injured woman away, her moans blending eerily with the relentless wind. Justine, looking at the unreadable expression on his strong and determined face, wondered what, in the name of God, he must be thinking and feeling now.

The sky was dark slate and the rain pelted down like stinging needles, as they reached the Mora Utu airstrip. The sleek, silver G-IV looked abandoned and forlorn on the parking apron where they'd left her.

"We've got to tie her down to the runway anchors," Thoros shouted as they neared the plane. "There's heavy-gauge rope in the building near the fuel farm." He searched the runway avidly, then knelt down and reached into a depression in the concrete for the tie-downs.

"Here's what the anchor bolts look like," he shouted, hoping his voice would hold out. His arm and shoulder hurt like hell but he willed himself not to feel them, or to think about Marika and the tragedy at the gorge. "Alex, Jase, see if you can get her tied down while Justine and I find the equipment we need to repair her. Liz, you check the AWOS and let us know what the readings are, will you?" Everyone dispersed in different directions.

"Thoros!" Justine called out as they started to move. "Do you really think we'll fly her out in front of this storm? It's pretty dicey."

"The odds are against it, but I think we have to try. Tiffany's in a very bad way—if she has internal bleeding I don't know how long she'll last without serious medical attention. I say we do our damnedest to get out and let the Gods decide."

Justine had to run to keep up with his long strides toward the small building that housed the equipment. They'd need the engine scaffolding, and a few rudimentary tools to repair the damage. With a pang, she saw that Thoros still had Tiffany's backpack slung across his shoulder, as they pushed the ladder out the door of the shed, into the wind and rain.

Rain slalomed down their faces, arms, and bodies, and debris was rolling like tumbleweeds across their path as they fought their way toward the G-IV. Jase and Alex were already on the ramp, busy securing the aircraft to the tie-downs wherever they found them.

Thoros shouted orders, in urgent command. There was no hesitation in him, Justine noted, confidence in his decision-making skill apparent in every word and gesture, despite the horror of the last hours. He stood stalwartly against the battering of the wind, the rain pelting his large form, slicking down his dark gray hair and clothes. *God, he looks glorious standing there giving orders,* she thought briefly; *like a king on the battlefield, born to command, defiant in the face of overwhelming odds.* She shook her head to clear it; this was no time for romantic nonsense.

The aircraft swayed as they grappled with her, the rain making frustrated fingers slide and lose their grip on the ropes, time after time. Finally, after many failed attempts and much cursing, they managed to secure the plane to the tie-downs.

The engine scaffolding slipped and slid, the level platform catching the high winds like a sail. Jase, Alex, Thoros, and Justine pushed and pulled it into position under the G-IV's engine, which stood twelve feet above the runway.

Gripping the wet metal ladder tightly, Thoros climbed toward the access panel on the underside of the right engine with grim persistence. Even raising the aluminum panel was made difficult by the storm, and once it was up, the sturdy flap groaned and shuddered in the battering wind. Once the internal engine was exposed, he struggled to maneuver in the cramped, wet space. The socket wrenches and open-end wrenches slipped and slid off the wet bolts maddeningly. The overused flashlight provided only a trickle of light, inadequate to its task, and his cold, wet, slippery fingers were too big for the confined space. Cursing, Thoros twice dropped the wrench he was juggling, and Justine, watching from below, retrieved the wrench, and climbed resolutely up the ladder behind him. In order to cling to the ladder perch in the high wind, she had to press her body in close to his; she could feel not only the heat of his body but the electrical high tension that propelled the man.

"My hands are smaller than yours, Thoros," she shouted up toward his face, now hidden from her view. "That might make it easier for me to work in that confined space."

She felt him tense further at the intrusion, assessing, then he shifted his body on the ladder to give her better access to the interior display under the upraised panel.

"Try it!" he agreed hoarsely, moving back down the ladder a step, to give her room to operate. "Smaller hands might help—the rain has everything slippery as an oil tanker."

Justine struggled to move the igniter box into place with infinite care, her smaller hands making the tricky task possible. She mumbled a string of expletives in several languages, only a few of which he understood, but finally got the wires connected and snapped it snugly into place. She craned her neck to look back at Thoros, now two rungs below her on the ladder.

"The igniter's in. . . . Do you want to handle the fuel controller or shall I?" She saw no acrimony on his face.

"You're doing fine," he replied with a grim smile. "Handle it. But hurry, this wind is a son of a bitch."

She nodded and returned her attention to the engine. Thirty-five minutes after they'd begun, they were able to deal with the second engine.

On impulse, Justine put a hand on his shoulder as they descended to the runway. "I'm so sorry about all this, Thoros," she said, great emotion in her voice. "We're all fools."

"And we may pay for it with our lives," he answered ominously. "We're not out of here yet, Justine. Let's get everybody loaded into her as fast as possible and see if we can get out of here in this crosswind."

He shouted to the others and Alex took off in the direction of the compound with Jase not far behind him.

"We're in the grip of something, here, Justine," Thoros said, shielding his eyes with his hand, so he could look up at the blackening sky.

"This storm, you mean?" she asked, but he shook his head.

"No. Beyond that," he said. "Something inexplicable."

He reached for her suddenly, unexpectedly, and pulled her close for the briefest moment of embrace. He did not kiss her and she did not expect him to, but clung as hard as she could to him, understanding the need for human comfort, however small, in the face of rampaging nature.

It was a terrible struggle to carry Tiffany's stretcher to the plane. Rand was ill, Jase injured, Jack and Alex in little better shape. Tony and Marika were gone. The bedraggled remains of the group, drenched and somber, found places in the passenger compartment of the G-IV while Thoros and Justine occupied the cockpit. No one had seen Nelida all day; she must have been stranded somewhere by the escalating storm. Now Emilio, too, had vanished.

Justine headed automatically for the pilot's chair, but Thoros grabbed her arm to stay her. "*I'll* fly her out of here," he said with authority.

"Like hell you will!" she retorted. "This is *my* life you're dealing with, Thoros. You asked me to fly this aircraft to Mora Utu and back, and by God, I intend to do so."

Thoros towered over her. "There's no time for ego here, Justine. You're a damned fine pilot, but she's mine, and I intend to get us out of here. I have five hundred hours in this aircraft and I know her backwards and forwards."

"So what!" she shouted back, the strain of the past few hours fueling her anger. "I have six hundred and fifty hours!"

Thoros was genuinely startled by that fact, but it really didn't matter. "I don't give a shit how many hours you've got in G-IVs, Justine," he shouted, the frustration of everything that had happened coming to a head. "I was flying *thirty years* before you were *born,* for Christ's sake! This is *my damn plane* and I'm flying her out of here."

"It's *your* plane, but it's *my* life, you arrogant son of a bitch," she shouted back, the words tumbling rapidly. "Listen to me, *damn you!* There are a number of things in this life you can do better than I, Thoros, much as I hate to admit it, but flying this bird is not one of them. Now, for God's sake, get out of my way! We don't have time for this shit."

Thoros stared at the woman, trying to keep from simply picking her up and *lifting* her out of his way. He hadn't anticipated a fight, now, of all times. Fierce determination radiated from her every muscle; this wasn't just bravado and a rampant ego, she genuinely believed she was the better pilot. If he forced his will on her she'd never forgive him; if he backed down she'd never respect him. If he made the wrong choice, they'd never make it out alive. Exasperated beyond words, Thoros pulled his lucky golden eagle from his pocket.

"Heads," he said, holding it out to her. Caught off guard by the gesture, Justine answered, "Tails," and watched wordlessly as Thoros flipped the coin into the air and caught it. The eagle lay heads up on the back of his hand.

Justine flashed her eyes to his; there was no look of triumph in the man's face, only extreme agitation and concern. "Fair enough," she said clearly, and turning, slipped into the large copilot's seat and fixed her attention on the immense instrument console in front of her. Thoros, relieved, but no less worried, seated himself, and let go of the breath he seemed to have been holding for quite some time.

Thoros flipped the Annunciator Panel switch, the DC metering selector, and the APU PWR fuel switch, as he commenced the start sequence and the long-silent aircraft hummed, once more, to life.

Sunday, April 17

Nature is a hanging judge.

Anonymous

FIFTY-ONE

The mercenary known as Darkman hovered over the shoulder of the pilot and peered through the blackened rain-dense windshield of the C-130. The tension in the cockpit was palpable.

"This one's a real motherfucker," the pilot said, with an edge to his voice that was seldom there. Darkman saw the concentration with which the man worked, every move spare, every word minimal. The co-pilot said nothing, but that wasn't unusual; his taciturn manner had earned him the nickname Quiet Man.

"Winds are eighty knots, rain like a son of a bitch, pressure dropping like crazy," the pilot said, tersely. "Radio says it's gonna roll right over those poor bastards."

"Those poor bastards are paying us to retrieve them first."

"No shit, Sherlock. I thought we were here for R and R." Darkman marked the intensity beneath the wisecracks, and glanced sideways at the silent co-pilot, whose face was set in a grim knot of concentration.

"How far are we from our target, Sure Thing?"

The pilot let out a snort of near laughter with his reply. "Could be about as far as you can get, Darkman. From where I sit, odds are we ain't landing until this sucker blows over."

"Doom on you! and that kind of crap, Sure Thing. We said we'd try, we gotta try. We close enough to raise 'em on the G-IV's radio yet?"

"If they're stupid enough to be sitting in it, maybe."

"Or smart enough to be trying to get out."

"Read my lips, Darkman. With these winds, eight-thousand-foot mountains, and no visibility, they ain't gettin' out and we ain't gettin' in. Man proposes, God disposes."

"I didn't bring you along to be a fucking candy-ass philosopher, Sure Thing. I hired you to get us *in* there."

"And, I'm telling you it ain't gonna happen."

"You read *my* lips, skipper. I gave a man my word. We took his money. We ain't going home without giving it our best shot. Now, dammit to hell, cut this shit and get me onto that fucking island!"

Sure Thing took a deep breath and counted to ten, by twos; he and Darkman went back a long way. His eyes met those of his co-pilot, who smiled crookedly in empathy.

"Aye, aye, Cap'n Queeg," he said finally. "I'll see what I can do for you, short of dying."

Darkman slapped him on the shoulder, relieved. "Listen, asshole, cut that *short of* crap. We don't talk limits in this man's navy."

"Yeah, right, I forgot," Sure Thing said with a smirk. "Piece of fuckin' cake, sir. Here's the deal: We got enough fuel for one approach. All he's got is an NDB on that island, so we may not even be able to find his damned runway with no visibility and limited instrumentation."

"But you've got the latitude and longitude coordinates for his runway from Schenck, you're using the Global Positioning

System, and you got your RMI pointing right at their beacon. What the fuck are you complaining about?"

"Yeah," the pilot responded with a tight laugh, "but we're bucking and shaking out rivets now, and I gotta hold one helluva correction angle in these friggin' winds. . . . If I can't see that runway at six hundred feet, we abort. End of story."

"Six hundred, my ass. You can get down to three hundred, easy. I've *seen* you do it a thousand times."

"We're about twenty miles west of them, Darkman," the pilot said, ignoring the last comment completely by changing the subject. "We might be able to raise them on the radio. Want to give 'em a thrill knowing we're in the neighborhood?"

Darkman laughed, too, and clapped the pilot on the shoulder again with gusto. Sure Thing was solid as they made them; a damned good pilot and a damned good man.

Justine breathed a sigh of relief as the electrical system came on line, both the console and the plane alive again. She and Thoros turned in unison; he held up a large palm and she slapped her own against it gleefully. She watched the INS align itself, the temperature gauges, the TIT, and the Horizontal Situation Indicator all exactly as they should be.

The wind hurled some large unidentified object into the port side of the aircraft with a heavy *thunk*. Again, their eyes met. There were two hulls on the aircraft, the outer aluminum one and the inner pressure vessel; damage to either one would ground them. They had to move quickly, not easy to do in this weather.

The storm was worsening, and Armageddon-like darkness shrouded the world of Mora Utu utterly; the wind raged so violently now that trees were being uprooted, and sailed across their path. The roof of the sixty-by-eighty-foot shed behind them was flapping like a toupee in a gale. Work trailers were rolling around like Tonka toys, and the rain was now a relentless, droning tattoo all around the G-IV.

But they were moving. The seventy-thousand-pound aircraft started to taxi from the parking apron toward the runway, inching forward, unable to move any faster because of the dangerous conditions. Despite its weight, the G-IV was being buffeted and battered by the wind, sometimes sliding sideways in the immense puddles that hydroplaned the wheels. Feet on the brakes and rudder, giving it just enough throttle to move at a snail's pace, Thoros watched the instruments worriedly and tried to see, through the beleaguered windshield, the yellow center line, to help him taxi onto the runway. But visibility was nonexistent. They'd have to take off with the least possible crosswind, but the wind was harrying them brutally, now, and none of the variables were working in their favor.

The plane began to back taxi down the runway, Justine concentrating on the takeoff checklist. A part of her was relieved that she'd lost the toss, so many lives hung here in the balance; another part desperately wanted to fight this battle herself. Thoros's face was grim from the strain of what he was attempting, to say nothing of the tragedy at the ravine. He wasn't young anymore; Tiffany's rescue and Marika's death would have put men half his age out of commission. Justine realized with a pang how very much she admired him. He was remarkable in so many ways; she wondered if she would ever have the chance to be in love with him.

She forced her eyes back to the instruments.

"Thoros," she said, on instant alert, watching the needle begin to climb. "The engines are ingesting too much water and the TIT's dropped. We may have to abort."

"I can get us out!" he said determinedly, ignoring the urgency in her voice. She felt the aircraft slew sideways.

"You've got an eighty-degree crosswind, Thoros. When we

untied, the wind was only twenty degrees off the center line. It's shifted to the west. I don't think we can make it."

"I'll make it!" he barked, his jaw like granite. He started to apply more power and she felt another lurch, as the G-IV slewed again, wildly.

"You are a pigheaded son of a bitch, and this aircraft is going to weathervane into the wind if you don't chop the power. . . ."

Almost like the fulfillment of prophecy, the wind picked up the right wing and pushed the enormous aircraft sideways, with a violent shove.

"She's sliding!" he shouted. "Dammit to hell, the crosswind's too great." He fought for control, but knew even as he did so, that the struggle was futile.

Justine took a deep breath, forced her voice to steady itself, and spoke urgently. "We would never have gotten airborne with that much water in the engines, Thoros. There's *nothing* you could do—nothing *anyone* could have done." He did not reply, but she felt his frustration of defeat all the way across the cabin. She reached over and grasped his arm.

"Listen to me, Thoros!" she said, forcefully. "We did *everything* in our power. Don't blame yourself. You are fighting a fucking act of God, here! You've got to know when to stop—we must get everyone out of this aircraft and back to whatever safety we can find at the house."

He was about to answer her, when a burst of cacophonous sound emanated from the radio. The sound repeated itself twice before they could decipher it.

"Greywing, do you read me?" a static-filled deep male voice rasped out. "This is Saga One." Thoros turned up the volume on the radio. Whoever it was must be very close to get a transmission through the interference of the storm. He spoke quickly into the microphone.

"This is Greywing. We read you, Saga One. Identify yourself. Over."

"We're here to bring home the bacon, Greywing. Marcos and Harry send their best. But it's tough getting in. This is a class-IV typhoon, in case you didn't know. Over."

"Saga One. We're on the ground with casualties. We have two dead and one dying. We had to abort takeoff. How close are we to the typhoon? Over."

"You're in it, son. Up to your elegant ass. The eye should pass here in less than three hours. Hang in there, we're thirty miles west of you. We're in a C-130 with medical personnel. Over."

"We copy, Saga One. Say intentions. Over." Static made it increasingly hard to hear.

"Greywing, we're gonna try the NDB approach. No promises. But we're coming your way. If you're on the runway, get the hell off. Over."

"Roger that, Saga One," Thoros shouted into the mike. "We are taxiing back to the ramp now. Extremely dangerous conditions. Debris on the runway and it's blowing like stink. Over."

Thoros caught Justine's eye with his own, and she saw that there was hope in it again. "A C-130 just might be able to get in here. Let's do what the man said."

Ten minutes later they were off the runway and back on the apron west of the airstrip.

The C-130 bucked and shuddered in the turbulence; the tension in the cockpit was electric and silent as Sure Thing turned the aircraft inbound to the NDB and slowed it down. After crossing the Mora Utu beacon, he dropped the gear and put down fifteen-degree flaps, and watched the needle swing ominously on the RMI dial.

"Gotta hold a thirty-degree correction angle to come in on this heading," he snapped, his first words in some time, as he fought to keep control of the bucking and pitching aircraft. "This is a real bitch."

Darkman could feel the tension rising in the pilot and co-pilot as Sure Thing battled to keep the aircraft upright. He watched the two needles on the RMI dial and the Course Deviation Indicator on the GPS. The turbulence outside the aircraft was worse than anything he'd ever experienced; he was strapped in to the navigator's seat, but even that didn't feel secure.

He watched Sure Thing and Quiet Man go through the prelanding checklist and bring the nose of the aircraft around to track inbound to the beacon, a big crab angle set up because of the crosswinds. The C-130 crossed the electronic homing device, and turned outbound, then made its procedure turn and started back in toward the airstrip.

"I'm fightin' this one every inch, Darkman," Sure Thing said once, his voice grim and determined.

"The runway's fifty feet above sea level," Darkman answered, peering out into nothing but storm. "Where the hell are we?"

"We're nearly at three hundred feet, and we're getting beat all to hell here," the pilot answered tersely. "I don't see a runway down there." A tense silence was followed by a single expletive.

"Shi-it!" he spat. "We just passed over their beacon and I still can't see a fucking thing! That's it, Darkman, this approach is history. We'll have to abort. I'm damned sorry, man."

Darkman opened his mouth to protest, then changed his mind. If any pilot could get them in there, Sure Thing would be the one. If he'd had to abort the approach, nobody short of the angel Gabriel was flying into Mora Utu.

"Let's give those poor sons of bitches the bad news," Sure Thing said, activating the Push-to-Talk switch on the wheel; Darkman saw by the grim look on the pilot's face that he, too, hated like hell to give up.

"Greywing," Sure Thing said into the headset microphone. "This is Saga One. We have had to abort. Repeat. We have missed the approach. Do you copy that?"

"Saga One. This is Greywing. We copy you. Dammit to hell. Say intentions. Over."

"Greywing, advise you get the hell out of that aircraft and seek shelter! Over."

A blast of static covered the end of the transmission.

"Saga One. We repeat. Serious casualties. Dead and dying. Need medevac ASAP. Over."

"Roger that, Greywing. We're on the case. We are diverting to our alternate at Honiara until this typhoon clears. Whatever it takes, we'll be back. Good luck down there. Over and out."

Thoros's eyes locked with Justine's. There was no way out, and no one coming in. This was a class-IV typhoon and the only possibility for survival now was at the Mora Utu compound.

"Our only chance is the cellar," Thoros said.

"*If* we can get there," she replied as they scrambled to their feet, and headed back into the passenger cabin.

Tiffany's stretcher occupied the center aisle, with Jack and Chesi on the floor beside her.

"Her breathing is getting worse," Chesi said, brushing back a rain-flattened strand of hair from Tiffany's pallid face. Jack's eyes looked so stricken already, she could have bitten her own tongue for having said it. He held one of Tiffany's hands in both of his; he was about to answer her when Justine and Thoros entered the cabin.

"We've learned this is a class-IV typhoon," Thoros said gravely, "the eye of which will pass over us in less than three hours. We have to abandon this aircraft as quickly as we can, and head back to cover at the compound."

"It'll be a helluva trip back," Rand said, the weariness of illness in his voice. "We almost didn't make it in."

"There is absolutely no choice," Thoros replied, relentlessly. "During *Andrew,* aircraft considerably larger than G-IVs were tossed about like corks."

"And we're damned close to the water," Jase reminded.

"No point in bellyaching," Liz said with a determined effort at keeping her voice steady. "Let's hit the road, ladies and gentlemen." They waited only long enough to wrap whatever they could find around Tiffany to protect her from the rain.

"Thoros," Justine said, grabbing his arm. "Do you have a portable radio we could take with us?"

"I have it right here," he answered, patting the canvas bag in his hand. "The battery will only last a few hours and our friends on that C-130 won't be back for a long while, but what the hell."

When the G-IV door folded down and the stairs dropped into place, a wall of wind and water engulfed them. To get Tiffany's litter down the steps they had to form a relay of hands, each man and woman holding tight to the next, or to the metal railing for balance, as they hoisted the litter awkwardly down the aircraft's steps. Once on the ground, they all grabbed what they could of the heavy burden, and took off in the direction of the compound.

"I feel like a pallbearer," Christie said.

"Shut up!" Chesi snapped back. "She's not dead yet."

People slid or fell repeatedly on the slippery, mossy mud, as they battled the gusting seventy-mile-per-hour winds on their laborious way to the compound. Finally, exhausted, cold, and wet beyond their wildest nightmares, all ten men and women reached the haven of the devastated Great House. Windows everywhere were broken shards, what shingles were left flapped mournfully, and large parts of the roof had been shorn away.

"Looks like the bomb dropped," Liz said, awestruck by the inconceivable power of nature.

"The cellar," Chesi and Rand said almost in unison. "It's the only safe place."

One by one they filed into the enormous pitch-dark cellar, the huge water vats like immense specters all around them. The women went in search of candles or flashlights, while the men cleared space for Tiffany's litter. Then they all stripped off what they could of their ravaged clothing and huddled, exhausted, in the darkness.

"Maybe we could salvage some dry clothes from the house through the grates?" Chesi suggested.

"We nailed them shut," Jase said.

The irony of it seemed the perfect metaphor for all that had happened so far on Mora Utu.

"Greywing. This is Saga One. Do you read me?" Sure Thing repeated the message twice just to be certain.

"They hit the road, Darkman," he said to the man in the navigator's chair. "We should, too, while we still can. Honiara in the Solomons is our best bet. We don't have a helluva lot of fuel left." As if to reinforce his statement, the aircraft lurched violently in the turbulence.

"They're in big trouble down there, Sure Thing—they got somebody dying," Darkman said by way of reply.

"We may only be picking up pieces when this blows over, Darkman," Sure Thing responded. "This here's one shitload of weather they got crashing in on that island. I sure hope they know how to tread water."

Darkman nodded, frustrated and angry that he couldn't keep his word. "I kinda liked the kid," he said in non sequitur.

"Yeah," Sure Thing answered. "Well, I kinda liked the big old guy. He really knew his aircraft. Asked the goddamnedest questions when he checked us out. Turned out he flew a Thunderbolt in Hubert Zemke's Wolfpack. Those guys made flying history, man."

"No shit?" Darkman said, impressed by the fact that Sure Thing was impressed. "Wouldn't like to let a guy like that down, then, would we? How many hours is it back to Honiara?" Darkman asked, his face a black scowl.

"Three to get there, three to get back, three for refueling and bureaucratic fuck-ups with our general declarations . . . maybe nine, till we're back on Mora Utu."

"Shit! That's not gonna do it if they've got heavy casualties. Come on, Sure Thing! Give me an alternative somebody like Harry Schenck would like."

Sure Thing took a deep breath and checked the radar and the fuel gauge, doing calculations rapidly in the head.

"We got maybe enough fuel to hold at the edge of the storm, Darkman, instead of diverting. Then we could get back in there when the eye hits them . . . but it's real dicey whether we'd have enough fuel to get back out."

"They gotta have a fuel farm on that fancy island of theirs," Darkman answered, getting excited again. "Maybe they got enough Jet A for guests. You game to go for it?"

The pilot smiled just a little as he changed his Honiara heading and moved the C-130 in the direction of the edge of the typhoon.

"Sure thing," he answered.

FIFTY-TWO

The wind ripped at Nelida and Emilio as they fought their way toward the sea caves at the ocean's edge. The sky was dark as night and enormous waves battered the shore; flying beach sand bit and stung their faces as it fled before the wind.

"There has to be a way into the place of the dead that is not covered by the sea, husband," Nelida shouted as she struggled to remain upright in the gale.

"Sí, I was shown the way by the old ones, but it will be treacherous. Once we are inside, we will be safe from the storm, but not from the ancestors whose spirits reside there."

"It is the only way, Emilio. This island knows only blood sacrifice."

"Sí," he agreed, morosely. "And we may be the sacrifice."

The two figures, beleaguered by the storm, fought their way inch by inch along the rocky ocean cliff. The gray-black waters raged around them, threatening every step, and Nelida prayed incessantly for guidance and for surefootedness.

Finally, exhausted by the struggle and the fear that dogged

their steps, cut by the sharp rocks and wet to the skin, the two Mexicans found the funnel-shaped rock chimney that Emilio said was the entrance they had sought.

"Are you afraid, my little seagull?" he asked as the two started down into the black cleft in the mighty volcanic rockface.

"Sí, *tengo miedo.* I am afraid," she replied, looking up at him. "What does that matter to our course of action?"

Emilio laughed, soundless in the wind. "This is what courage means, does it not? To fear greatly, but not to let it change your plans."

She nodded, caught his eyes once with her own, then began the dangerous descent to the ancestral burial place.

The eerie cave was as still as the death it enshrouded, in sharp counterpoint to the thunderous storm raging far above them. The air was thick with energy fields not their own. Nelida and Emilio each made a swift protective sign against evil, and Emilio drew a large flashlight from his pack, as well as two extra batteries, hoarded for just such a moment of grave emergency. Nelida nodded, grateful for the sudden beam of light, despite the fact that it illuminated the staring, gaping eyes and mouths of the dead.

All around them were the skeletal remains of generations of Mora Utuans, standing for the most part, or sitting in fragmentary heaps where the ages had finally collapsed them from their sentinel posture.

"Many uneasy spirits dwell here," she said needlessly, for Emilio already saw this to be the case, but he knew she needed the sound of living voices in this place of the timeless dead.

"Come, we must find the place we seek quickly," he answered, moving out into the flashlight's beam.

They passed through a hanging veil of feathers, shells and bones that rattled with their movement. The air was warmer as they moved, and not as lifeless as it had seemed at first; there had to be another hidden opening through which air circulated to the crypts below.

"We follow the footsteps of the priests," Emilio said, pointing to the walls, where hefty torches with heads of pitch were placed at intervals along the passageway.

Grotesque drawings of demonic faces adorned the rough-hewn sides of the cave, and the floor was worn smooth by the passage of millennia of feet. Everywhere were human remains, stacked in niches cut into the rock, hanging from baskets suspended above, lining the walls like dead soldiers still attentive to their eternal posts.

The two intruders were aware that their path was gradually spiraling downward; on impulse Nelida reached out to touch the wall and was startled to find that it was warm and vibrant; could it be from the force of the storm above? The passage narrowed and steepened; only a rope railing anchored securely to the walls allowed them to navigate the steep slope to the interior.

"We go to the Underworld," Nelida whispered, and Emilio squeezed her hand for comfort. Many times, in spirit journeys had they both explored the world of the dead, in their times of training and beyond, but never before while in the body. Nelida instinctively called her Power animals to her side, and heartened by their psychic presence, she stepped up the pace.

At the end of the rope passage a large corridor opened into a vaulted cave. Emilio shone the flashlight around the walls and ceiling, shocked to see that every inch of the vast space was covered by human skulls.

"We have reached the dreadful place we sought, husband," Nelida said, tugging on his arm. "Let us light the torches. The dead will not mind, I think."

The torches flared into life at the touch of Emilio's match; whatever the chemical composition of the tarlike substance they'd been dipped in, it had withstood the test of time. Four immense statues carved from volcanic rock glowered down on them and on a smooth stone table with slots cut lengthwise in its surface; the slots emptied into substantial troughs beneath.

"Not all were dead when they arrived here," Emilio observed hoarsely, and Nelida felt a chill run through her nervous system at the depth of anguish that still resonated in this place of pain and torture.

"*Sacrificio de sangre,*" she said. "Many perished here in agony. We should hurry, Emilio. These Gods will not tolerate our living presence long."

He nodded. "We must plead the ignorance of those who trespassed on this island," he said. "And beg for mercy."

"Sí," she replied, uneasily. "But these forces require death to appease them, Emilio. I can feel their hunger."

He considered that for a moment. "Then we must ask them the number required to appease the transgression, must we not?"

Nelida nodded and opened the sack she carried tied to her body; she began to unpack her tools for ritual. She disliked the spirits of this place; they were dark and full of bloodlust. Perhaps the friendlier Nature Spirits could be called in to help them; then at least there would be a possibility of bargaining. She racked her brain for the correct ceremony with which to summon them. A misstep in this place of death could have only one conclusion.

FIFTY-THREE

Tiffany lay in a corner of the wine cellar, covered with the dry rags that had been found. The women, shivering in the vestiges of their own damp clothes, took turns nursing their injured friend as she alternately tossed feverishly and lay motionless as if already dead. Jack sat next to Tiffany on the floor, holding her icy hand to his lips; he talked to her constantly, softly, words no one else could hear. Between the two-day stubble of beard, the dark circles that ringed his face, and the blood on his shirt, he looked little better than she did. The light of a few salvaged candles barely illuminated the huge space enough to stave off total darkness.

The storm raged above them in an endless, raucous cacophony. The shattering of glass, the clatter of flying furniture, the wrench of wood and metal being torn from their moorings, had punctuated the rain and wind sounds ever since they'd made it back to the house. Now, the sounds seemed to have settled into the relentless rat-a-tat-tat of rain, and the mournful cry of wind that howled like a banshee convention. They'd surmised that everything that could be wrenched free by the wind had already been shorn away.

Liz let her eyes roam the ravaged group of survivors, shrunk now considerably in size from their arrival, she thought with a tightening of the stomach. Tony and Marika were dead, Tiffany might be dying, Jase's shoulder was badly cut and possibly infected, Thoros's hands and face were a mass of bloodied scratches, cuts, and bruises, Alex looked gaunt and exhausted, and Rand was obviously starting another bout of malaria. Each had been tested, she thought grimly; and each had shown himself.

Both the Mexicans were gone now. Most likely, they, too, were dead.

"Some vacation!" she said aloud, to no one in particular.

"Yeah," Christie answered, moving gingerly to find a more comfortable spot to sit. "Club Dead."

Chesi moved in closer, too. "I've been thinking about Nelida," she said. "I have a feeling she'd be saying, 'You've learned a lot on this island.' "

"Trial by holiday, eh?" Justine said with a small, rueful smile. "A novel concept. But, I think I would have to agree with her. We have all been changed profoundly."

Tiffany groaned and tried to move onto her side, restless and in great pain; a garbled cry escaped her, and she settled back, crumpled as a fractured bird. Her face was ashen now, no longer honey colored, and her skin was clammy. Dark circles ringed her eyes, and her lips, bitten in pain as she'd lain on the ledge, had dried blood laced across their cracked surface. Jack stood up suddenly, and turned away from the bed, as if he couldn't bear to watch any longer without being able to help the woman who lay there . . . he swiped at his eyes hastily and pulled a handkerchief from his shorts to blow his nose.

"You've done all you can for her, Jack," Justine said, moving in close beside him. "She knows you love her." It was easy to see by the way he moved, that he, too, was more injured than he'd let on. He had borne the brunt of getting the stretcher back to the house, falling badly twice in the slippery mud, badgering the others mercilessly to keep them moving, dragging the litter himself when the rest had faltered. His shoulder and arm hung awkwardly, as if he could barely move them, and there were bloodstains on his shirt, both front and back.

The sound of an immense wrenching crash above them riveted everyone's attention upward. The cellar shuddered and vibrated violently; some significant part of the house above them must have been ripped from its foundation.

"If the house goes to Kansas," Christie asked for everyone, in nervous response to the sound, "where do *we* go?"

"The structure is safe enough," Rand answered definitively. "That's not what's threatening us at the moment."

"What are you talking about?"

Chesi stood up in agitation. "He means the water," she answered for him. "We're only a thousand feet from the ocean. If we miscalculated the mean high-water line, or if this just happens to be the one-in-a-hundred-year storm that changes the record books, we could drown in here like rats in a cage. Even if we don't drown, those water tanks could be compromised and we could all be awash in contaminated crud. Everybody's wounded, and we don't have much fight left in us."

Everyone started to talk at once, all pretense at politeness lost in fear.

An earsplitting whistle shocked them into silence. Liz stood, legs apart and planted, fingers in her mouth. She lowered her hand and yelled, "Shut up, everybody!" like a drill sergeant. "We're all scared shitless—that's just sensible. But the only thing that counts right now is whether or not we can *do* anything about the flood possibility." She looked from Rand to Chesi.

Both shook their heads. "We haven't any equipment to protect ourselves," Rand answered.

"Then let's play poker," she said.

"What?" Thoros boomed, looking up at her as if she'd lost her mind.

"Poker," she said, pulling a salvaged deck of cards from her pocket. "We may all be dead by morning. We've already been through Purgatory. If we sit here waiting for the water to swallow us like Jonah in the whale's belly, we'll all go nuts."

"She's got a point," Jase said with an admiring laugh.

"No!" Jack called out from the far side of the enclosure. "Not with Tiffany like this. Count me out."

"I have no stomach for cards now either," Thoros said. "And we don't have enough light to play."

"If Nelida were here," Justine said wistfully, "she would tell us a story. I could use one just now."

The ten tired, hungry, wet, frightened men and women sat huddled in the gloom, for a time, in silence.

"Is it Sunday yet?" Christie asked suddenly.

"Yeah, it's Sunday," Jase answered. "Why?"

"I was just thinking Sunday is when we were supposed to leave Mora Utu. We almost made it."

"Some of us, anyway," Liz amended.

Christie suddenly laughed; the unexpected sound brought all eyes her way.

"Seriously, folks," she said, "would anybody believe this vacation? I mean, short of nuclear war, what'd we miss?"

" 'Aside from that small interruption, Mrs. Lincoln, how'd you like the play?' " Liz sniffed.

"Yeah. Wouldn't it be a real kick in the ass if we all could've had a swell time and liked each other. I mean, I don't know about you guys, but I thought Marika was pretty spectacular saving Thoros, and Thoros was unbelievable saving Tiffany, and Tiffany was brave as hell deciding on her own to go get the plane fixed. And Justine and Thoros looked pretty damned good out there fixing the engine with all that rain and wind and debris flying around, and Jack damned near beating us with sticks to get that stretcher back. . . . It was like a fucking movie full of heroes. I mean, this is one incredible story, if we could ever tell it." She stopped, thinking of whom she'd left out.

"And Chesi did one helluva first-rate job on my compound," Thoros added, with a short wry laugh. "Don't forget that part."

"My Sicilian blood was up, I guess," Chesi answered with a smirk. "You're lucky you don't sleep with the fishes." They were long past deference or differences; it was all starting to seem weirdly funny, now, or at least absurd.

"Do you think anyone ever had a worse vacation?" Christie asked, needing to keep the talk alive.

"Napoleon on Elba?" Liz offered.

"The Donner party?" Jase suggested.

"How about Czar Nicholas and his family at Ekaterinburg?" Alex said, warming to the gallows humor.

"I know what we should do if we survive," Liz said. "We should stage a reunion every five years, like the survivors of the *Titanic*. . . ."

"Say, *that's* another great vacation we could add to our list," Jase mused.

"At our reunions we could see how we've all been changed by this," Liz finished.

"What makes you think we're changed?" Jase asked, curiously.

"Well, for starters, some of us are dead!" Liz replied in her wry way. "And if the rest of us aren't changed by what's happened, we damned well should be."

"We're changed, all right," Thoros said. "When your life's on the line, your ego bruises tend to fade."

The sound of clanging on metal startled them all into momentary silence; Nelida and Emilio, soaked and tattered, were making their way down the catwalk ladder. Chesi and Liz got to their feet in a hurry and ran toward the Mexican couple, excitedly calling their names.

"Nelida! Emilio! Where have you been?" Chesi asked, throwing her arms around Nelida and hugging her despite her soaking clothes. "We were sure you were dead!"

Nelida hugged the girl soundly, then stood back, peeled off her soaking poncho, and dropped it in a puddled heap on the floor, beside her mud-blackened feet. "We went to the ancestral caves, child, to bargain for our lives with the Spirits." Emilio nodded agreement, as he, too, stripped off his wet and tattered clothing.

"So what did these spirits of yours have to say to you?" Rand asked, contemptuously.

"The lives that have been sacrificed may be enough to propitiate the Angry Ones," Nelida answered. "This island is a place of blood sacrifice, and sacrifices have been made."

"The Spirit of the Ancestral Cave gave us this information, señor," Emilio added. "She has no fondness for the Spirit of the Land which you abused, so she was willing to communicate."

A week ago, Thoros would have thought them mad, but now he simply listened. "Does this mean we will be spared, then?" he pressed Emilio, feeling only half a fool in asking the question.

"We do not know this, señor," Emilio answered, gravely. "We know only that the sacrifices have been accepted."

"We know, too, that we were spared to return here," Nelida added wearily. "The allies of our lineage pleaded for us, and we were permitted safe passage. Beyond this, we know nothing, but I believe it is a sign of benevolence." She straightened her drenched garments as best she could and turned to Chesi.

"Now, we must see if we can wrest Tiffany from their grip, or if she, too, will be taken from us."

"You know of her accident?"

"Sí, child, I know of this sad occurrence."

"Three sacrifices would be better than two," Emilio said pragmatically. "It could be best for all the rest, to let her go."

Shocked by the matter-of-fact discussion of Tiffany's life or death fate, Thoros and Jack began to protest, but Nelida cut them off, speaking rapidly and sternly.

"I am not of a mind to let them have her so easily, my husband. Two lives are sufficient for what was done here in ignorance. There are limits even for Gods . . . rules must be observed! She is on the borderline; we may yet be permitted to pull her back."

"They will not be mocked, woman! You may pull her back, crippled and destroyed."

"I do *not* mock them, husband. I *bargain,* as is permitted. The skill of my lineage against their thirst for blood." She sounded angry but sure.

"You, too, could die, my little hawk."

"Any day of my life, this could be said."

The others were listening in fascination; no one could doubt either the tension or the sincerity of the exchange.

"What can we do to help you, Nelida?" Justine asked, stepping forward. The women's eyes all fastened on her; never before had she openly admitted Nelida's worth.

"Come with me," the Mexican woman replied with seriousness. "You have great strength of mind—this may be useful to us." Then she turned, and, moving toward the makeshift bed where Tiffany lay, she set about examining the girl's injuries.

The rest of the survivors returned to their circle, but this time many of them sat in pairs, as if some unspoken decision had been made. Liz and Alex huddled together, talking quietly and trying to keep each other warm; Jase and Christie sat together, his arm around her shoulder. Jack, Chesi, Justine, and Nelida remained steadfast at Tiffany's side. Rand, too weak to sit up any longer, lay listening to the incessant sounds of the storm.

He felt the tremors and the fever toxically flooding his system, and he wasn't certain he could survive another bout of fever.

Nelida worked on Tiffany's body for some time, but without her herbs and remedies she was handicapped in what she could accomplish. After what seemed hours but was not, she rose wearily to her feet, and motioned the three at the bedside to follow her back to the group sitting huddled and waiting. She stood for a moment to gather appropriate words and then spoke softly, but with great emotion.

"This beautiful child's body is badly broken," she began. "Her leg and her arm are shattered, her shoulder badly torn. Her spleen is swollen and seeps blood, and her kidneys are in decline. Her skull is fractured and her brain is swelling. If she were in a hospital it is possible she could be made to live . . . but here in this cellar, her chances and her lifeforce ebb with every hour."

"How can you be so certain of her internal injuries?" Thoros asked, his voice thick with emotion. "You are not a doctor."

"In our village, señor," Emilio interrupted, "my wife's lineage is respected for its knowledge of healing."

"I, too, love this child of Nature," Nelida replied gently. "I speak the truth, señor."

"What are you saying, Nelida?" Chesi asked, tears running unabashedly down her cheeks. "What can we do for her?"

"There is a possibility that we can keep her alive by sharing our own energy with her, but this will tax us all to the brink of our endurance. If we can keep her spirit in the body long enough for help to come, we may yet win her back. But Death hovers near her side and we cannot hold her from his embrace for long."

She turned to Thoros. "How many hours, señor, until the rescue plane returns?"

Thoros shook his head in consternation. "They've gone to the Solomons, that's three hours out and three back. Plus whatever bureaucratic nightmare they encounter landing a quasi-military aircraft in some half-assed airfield. . . . Eight hours, at least. Maybe more."

"Do not attempt this, wife," Emilio reprimanded Nelida, sternly. "We will need all our energy for our own survival; do not drain the batteries to save this girl who is beyond our help. She is on Death's schedule."

Nelida turned on her husband, eyes full of fire. "She is on Death's schedule, but she has not yet been collected! We can save her if we share our strength!"

"He will collect us all if you defy him," he said ominously.

"For this brave child, I will make him pay a great price, husband. Will you not fight at my side?"

"*We'll* fight for her!" Justine broke in unexpectedly. "Tell us what to do—there are still ten of us on our feet, maybe that's enough."

Nelida turned to Justine, studying her carefully, as she spoke. "We must battle for her courageously and unselfishly . . . and the rescue plane must be made to return in *three* hours, not eight," she said.

"But that's simply not possible, Nelida," Thoros argued. "They've diverted to the Solomons."

"Pray, señor! *Demand* this of your God. To God, nothing is impossible! Demand a fair fight, and demand it very loudly."

She turned to the rest. "Form a circle around this woman," she said. "We must put Death on notice that we draw the line of battle, eh?"

The women did as Nelida had asked, then one by one all the men, except Rand, who was too sick to move, joined the circle, too.

"I don't believe in any of this crap," Jase said, as he took his place with the rest.

"Who cares?" Christie shot back, taking his hand in her own firmly. "Just do it."

"I need one man at her feet and one woman at her head at

all times," Nelida instructed. Emilio stepped into the circle and put his hands on Tiffany's feet, thumbs beneath the sole, fingers on her instep.

"So, you are with us, my husband?" Nelida said, pleased with his decision. "Then you must use your talents as a telepath to send a message to the rescuers that they must return within three hours."

"If the radio can't get through, how the hell do you expect a telepathic message to reach them?" Jase asked with heavy skepticism.

"Emilio's lineage is known for its telepathic skills, señor. He is a sender."

"It's no crazier than the rest of what we're doing," Alex said with a laugh. "I rather like the notion of the commander of a C-130 responding to a telepathic message from a Yaqui Indian, don't you, Thoros? It's marvelously ecumenical."

"Don't laugh at them, damn you!" Justine shouted. "I can vouch for Nelida. I've seen what she can do that's *far* beyond our understanding. If she vouches for Emilio, that's good enough for me. And, one way or the other, by God, after all they've done for us, they deserve your respect!"

Alex looked at her sharply, then nodded.

"Quite right," he said, contritely. "You have my sincere apology, Emilio, Nelida."

"Mine, too," Thoros echoed, startled by Justine's passionate defense of the Mexicans. "Just tell us what to do and we'll give it a try. It's a damned sight better to do something than nothing."

Nelida placed her hands on Tiffany's head. "Ask for the blessing of your deity and share from your soul place . . . the cords of love are very strong and binding. Not even Death can sever them completely. We will take turns sharing our energy in this way until the rescuers arrive."

"We can't do this for eight hours, Nelida," Thoros said worriedly.

"Then you must pray harder that it will only be three," she answered, a trace of a smile on her weary face. "They like to bargain, señor—perhaps, you should consider carefully your own conscience. You stole their playground. Maybe they'd like to have it back, eh?"

"Are you suggesting Thoros hand over a hundred-million-dollar investment to a bunch of displaced natives?" Jase asked, incredulously.

"I do not know, señor, what is the price he would put upon your lives. I know only that we must pray now. And share with one another."

Justine, standing next to Thoros, squeezed his hand tightly with her own. "She is very wise, Thoros," she whispered. "It took me too long to know this, but she is very wise."

"She may be wise," he replied wearily, "but we don't need a philosopher right now. We need a miracle."

The group kept their exhausting vigil for an hour and fifty-seven minutes before a blast of static from the portable radio snapped them back from the fatigued reverie into which they'd drifted. Intent on their vigil, no one had noticed that the sounds of the storm had diminished as the eye approached them.

Justine and Thoros dropped out of the circle and hovered around the handheld radio, struggling to hear; the battery was badly drained and the voices nearly indecipherable.

"Greywing. This is Saga One. Do you read me?" Static.

Excitedly, Thoros flipped the switch to the Send position.

"Saga One. This is Greywing. Where are you?"

The reply was too garbled by static to be understood.

"Saga One. Repeat message. We do not copy. Where the hell are you? Say intentions."

Static blasted their ears once again.

"Greywing. This is Saga One. We are thirty miles to your west. We've been holding at the edge. You'll feel relief from the storm in twenty minutes. We're inbound and making our approach and we're real low on fuel. Over."

"Saga One. This is Greywing. We have all the Jet A fuel in the world down here. Come and get it. Over."

"Greywing. We copy that. Can you evacuate your wounded to the airfield for pickup?" Thoros looked around the room, making a quick assessment.

"Saga One. We have wounded and dying. Need assistance to move them. Over."

"Greywing. State location of casualties. Over."

"Saga One. Cellar of main house. Half mile northeast of airfield. Do you copy? Over."

"Greywing. We copy you. We're coming in."

FIFTY-FOUR

The eye of the typhoon was just settling in over the devastated island, as the C-130 flew out of the edge of the storm to begin its approach. Sure Thing was cutting the time as close as he could because of his critical fuel shortage; he had watched the storm's progress on radar, waiting for the precise moment the eye would hit Mora Utu to make his move.

Sure Thing locked onto the NDB beacon and took a 275-degree heading for two minutes, then turned 230 degrees for his procedure turn. The rain and wind were stopping and with them the turbulence. When he hit the 095 heading, he turned inbound to the runway, holding his wind-correction angle easily, to start his rapid descent.

"I don't know how in the hell they still got that NDB operating, down there," he said, relieved, as he locked onto the beacon. "Somebody's guardian angel deserves a raise."

The three men in the cockpit saw the G-IV tethered in the parking area to the left of the field as they passed over; it had taken a severe beating. There was water everywhere and foreign objects littered the runway like a thick blanket of miscellaneous garbage. Even an upended jitney sat near the edge of the concrete, but it didn't look as if anything would block their way sufficiently to make them abort their approach.

"How much time have we got once we're on the ground, Sure Thing?" Darkman asked, assessing the ravaged terrain visible below them; trees were down everywhere, impeding probable evacuation routes.

"Fifty minutes to an hour, tops. After that, we're back in the soup. If the back end of the typhoon hits us, before we're out, we got big troubles again."

"We'll make it," Darkman answered sharply. "I'll leave Quiet Man, Pigpen, and Chip with you to refuel, the rest go with me."

"It's gonna be a job to refuel her," Sure Thing said. "We gotta move that G-IV out of our way with the jeep, and we gotta find hoses in that crap pile out there."

Both men were silent as the huge aircraft made its final approach and landed, this time, without incident.

Darkman and his team poured out of the aircraft minutes after it had come to a halt on the debris-strewn runway. Carrying medevac equipment and enough gear to clear any obstructions encountered, eight determined men took off in the direction of the Great House and its injured occupants, while four others began the refueling chore.

The sound of the C-130 making its approach had sent Thoros and Justine running from their shelter. Scrambling over fallen trees and every other conceivable obstruction, they spotted the rescuers halfway from the airfield. Gesturing wildly, they met the camouflage-clad men with shouts of unfeigned joy.

"I'm Thoros Gagarian," Thoros greeted Darkman when they were face-to-face. "This is Justine Cousteau. And we're damned glad to see you!"

"I'm Darkman," the mercenary replied with an iron handshake. "And we're damned glad we made it in. Marcos and Harry send their regards. What's your status, Mr. Gagarian?"

"We have a girl with massive internal injuries, inside the cellar. A man with malarial fever. A badly infected shoulder wound, and a number of lesser injuries. We also have two dead, but one's buried in a cairn over a mile east of here, and one's at the bottom of a ravine, so we may have to evacuate them later."

"And they say money don't buy happiness," the man named Doc quipped darkly, but his commanding officer flashed him a scowl that said, *Shut up.*

"Big-mouth here is the best medic around," Darkman snapped briskly. "Let's see what he can do for your casualties. We've got less than an hour to get you out of here before the back end of the typhoon whacks us. My men are refueling."

The rescuers started moving in the direction of the compound, Thoros and Justine leading the way.

"Just how low on fuel were you?" Justine asked, as they approached the ruined house.

"We landed on fumes," Darkman answered.

"It took guts to ride the edge of that typhoon," she said, genuine admiration in her voice. "Thanks for not diverting. Most would have."

Darkman nodded his acknowledgment, but made no reply.

"How'd you sustain so many injuries?" he asked.

Justine nearly laughed. "Oh, Darkman," she said, a poignant note sounding in her voice. "That's a very long story, and not necessarily one you'd believe. . . ."

Forty-two minutes later, the twelve survivors of ten days in Paradise were seated in the belly of the C-130; those who still could, were gratefully sipping hot coffee, wearing dry camouflage, and taking inventory of all that had befallen them.

EPILOGUE

Six Months Later

A small, sleek plane glided onto the runway on the island of Mora Utu and came to rest on the overgrown parking ramp.

The day was tranquil; the tropical sky a brilliant, untroubled blue, the air redolent of pineapple and frangipani. The water sparkled as if a million diamonds glistened just beneath its playful surface.

Justine Gagarian exited first; she carried a large bouquet of flowers in her arms. The beautiful young woman stopped at the top of the exit stairs to look around for a moment before descending. Her hair and makeup were serenely perfect, her clothes simple and expensive. Her eyes were filled with quiet tears as she scanned the visible expanse of the island on which they had all learned so much of death and life.

The jungle was inexorably taking back its own; vines crept around the ruins of the runway, shed, and fuel farm. She strained her eyes in the direction of the compound, but could see little in that vicinity but vegetation, so she walked slowly down the steps to the concrete below.

Behind her, Thoros and Jack emerged from the cabin,

Tiffany supported between them. She looked thinner, frailer, but her smile when she caught Justine's eye was just as open and real as ever; despite the suffering she'd endured over the six months since the accident, she was glad to be alive.

Jack squeezed her hand, as he helped her down the steps; he knew how important this trip back was to her, how necessary to lay the demons to rest. *"Gotta get back on the horse, Jack,"* she'd told him, when she'd found out that Thoros and Justine were planning this trip, and had begged to go along. She had guts to spare, he knew that now; having watched her battle for her life, and for every physical competency that had to be painstakingly relearned. Just as now she must battle for the strength and perseverance to walk again, unaided. He'd watched her fight the doctors when they said she'd live a hopeless cripple; watched her fight the pain of rehabilitative therapy, so bad she'd cry and curse as she struggled to bring back her body with her own heart's blood as payment. He loved her more than he'd imagined he could ever love anyone; and he understood her to the bone. He'd managed fighters long enough to recognize courage and heart when he saw it.

"You know, Thoros," he'd said six months ago to his friend, while sitting with him in the hospital, waiting for Tiffany to get out of surgery, "we went to that damned island of yours thinking we were bringing Trophies—but me, I came back with a real prize."

Jack handed Tiffany her crutches at the foot of the stairs and helped her find her balance.

"Kind of like carrying coals to Newcastle, isn't it?" she said, looking out over the profusion of flowers growing wild in every direction. "Bringing flowers to Eden."

"I just needed to bring something with us as a memorial," Justine answered, looking fondly at her friend. "So much happened here. I felt the need of paying tribute, I suppose."

Thoros put his arm around Justine's shoulder, proprietarily.

They'd been married nearly a month, and he felt oddly content with that. The week on Mora Utu with all its excruciating lessons had changed him profoundly, and he counted himself a lucky man.

"Where do you suppose the flowers should be placed?" Justine asked, smiling up at him.

"Give them to the sea," he replied.

They all made their way to the beach, and Justine, taking off her shoes, waded out just far enough to fling the bouquet onto an incoming wave. The multicolored blossoms tumbled in the surf, then spread out and floated dreamily on the shining tropical waters.

"For Marika and Tony," she called out. "Wherever you are!" Then she turned and waded back to the three who waited on the shore.

"Do you think Marika knows we've come to say good-bye?" she asked. "Nelida says even the Gods respect courage."

Thoros didn't answer immediately, but stood staring out to sea, as if concentrating on something she couldn't see.

"I've been trying to decide if I should rebuild this place, Justine," he responded finally. "That awful day in the cellar, I promised I would give it back, if we were saved. But then, when we got back home and were safe again, it seemed a stupid gesture . . . a bargain, made in stress and fear. Now, standing here again, I think it's quite a fitting way to say thank you for all we were given, don't you?"

He saw that moisture hovered on Justine's lashes. "I think they'd respect that, too," she said.

Thoros put his arms around his wife protectively, and on impulse pulled her into an embrace. They stood for a long time in each other's arms without speaking all the complex words in their hearts.

Nearby, Jack and Tiffany sat on the warm sand, their bodies

touching comfortably. "I looked a lot better the last time we played on this beach together," she said wistfully.

"You look so good to me, Tiff," he replied, meaning it, "you couldn't get any better."

She heard the sincerity in Jack's voice, and the love; smiling, she lay back down on the sand to soak it all in; the day, the sun, the love she felt for him. The gratitude that they'd been spared to be together. He'd been with her every step of the way since the accident, never letting her down, never letting her give up.

One lone crimson butterfly fluttered out over the sand, far beyond its natural habitat. It circled once, then came to rest on Tiffany's outstretched hand. Surprised, and delighted, she opened her eyes to watch its elegant grace, memories of other times surfacing kaleidoscopically.

Jack, too, was moved by the sight; he remembered lying beside her once, long ago, it seemed, thinking of a ring. . . .

"Would you marry me, Tiffany?" he blurted, suddenly wondering why he'd taken so long to say these words he'd intended for so many months; maybe he'd had to wait until she could hear them clearly.

Tiffany closed her eyes again, and a tear welled and ran down her cheek before she replied. "I will if I can walk down the aisle without crutches," she said, finally, without looking at him. But she squeezed his hand and he understood her answer.

Jack smiled at her a little, and lay back down onto the sand beside her, satisfied and in love. He knew she would walk again, and if she didn't, who cared, he'd deal with her reticence when he had to. What mattered was that she loved him and she hadn't said no.

"Okay, Tiff," he said contentedly. "Now that we got *that* settled, why was Lou Brock denied the Most Valuable Player award the year he established a base-stealing record?"

"Lou Brock stole a hundred eighteen bases for the 1974 St. Louis Cardinals . . ." she managed to say before he kissed her soundly, with all the love he'd waited a very long time to share with the one person in the world who could truly understand.

Thoros and Justine laughed, watching them.

"Come on," Thoros said, taking Justine's hand in his and holding it tight. "Those two don't need us around. Let's go say good-bye to our island."

Hand in hand, Thoros and Justine Gagarian walked down the long sun-drenched ribbon of sand that had been theirs for a little while. The island paradise of Mora Utu gleamed iridescently in the blazing tropical sun, as if nothing of great importance had ever happened there; lazing upon the South Pacific's surface like a mountainous crescent moon of the sort that usually lives only in pirate books and dreams.

AUTHOR'S NOTE

This book owes both acknowledgment and thanks to Clarissa Pinkola Estes and her brilliant work on women's psyches, as put forth in *Women Who Run with the Wolves.* I am indebted to her for the story of The Sealskin (which she, in turn, attributes to Mary Uukulat) and for many concepts regarding women's empowerment that have enriched my tale.

The concept of the sacredness of butterflies is due in part to the beautiful exposition of this Native American idea by Agnes Whistling Elk in several of Lynn Andrews's books about this Indian Medicine Woman.

The shamanic work of Taisha Abelard in *Sorcerer's Journey* and Carlos Castaneda in his many books about his studies with Don Juan Matus, the Yaqui sorcerer, were extremely helpful to me in fleshing out the magical elements of Nelida and Emilio's experience as Naquals, particularly as they applied to the acquisition of power. The notion of a shaman considering himself superior to an educated man because of his being a warrior and hunter owes its inspiration to a conversation between Don Juan and Carlos Casteneda in *Journey to Ixtlan,* and Nelida's shamanic mantra is from Don Juan's teachings, as well.

I wholeheartedly recommend the work of all these authors to my readers, as they provide both great insight and great pleasure.